CRYSTAL STORM

Battleground

ALEXIA D. MILLER

amiller1009

Copyright

This book is a work of fiction. The names, characters, places, incidents, and the like are the product of the author's imagination and are used fictitiously. Resemblances to any person, place, or events present or past, are unintentional and coincidental in nature.

Published and Printed in the United States of America
Subjects: Young Adult (YA). Fiction. Fantasy.
ISBNs: 978-1-7369965-0-8 (paperback), 978-1-7369965-1-5 (Hardcover)
Crystal Key Book Series. Book 2

Please Be Advised

THE FOLLOWING BOOK IS INTENDED FOR THOSE 15 YEARS OF AGE AND OLDER. SOME READERS MAY FIND SOME SITUATIONS TROUBLING/TRIGGERING. IF YOU ARE HAVING TROUBLE THROUGHOUT THE BOOK, PLEASE TAKE A BREAK OR CEASE READING THE MATERIAL ALTOGETHER. WHILE THE AUTHOR DOES NOT INTEND FOR THE BOOK TO BE TRIGGERING TO ANY OF THEIR READERS, THESE THINGS MAY HAPPEN. PLEASE TAKE CARE OF YOURSELF AND IF YOU ARE FEELING ALONE, HAVING AN EPISODE, OR IN DANGER OF HURTING YOURSELF OR OTHERS, SEEK HELP IMMEDIATELY.

For

For Izzy, who supported me no matter the distance.
For Corliss who applauded every step.
For my loved ones who stood by me and pushed me forward.
For those who purchase this book and support charity .
For all those seeking light in the darkness.
To all those who find their escape through the doors of another world from the comfort of a book.

QR Code

www.admcreations.com
Thank you in advance for reading!

Crystal Storm, Book 2

CKBS

Part 1: Progression...

Bonus Image

One

Victor...

COMFORTABLE.

Victor sat in Homeroom, fighting to finish his homework from the night before. Most of the students were talking indiscreetly amongst themselves or texting away on their cellphones. He couldn't stand to be in the room. He could hardly stand another second of the classes mindless chatter. More than that, the longer he attempted to bury himself in work to drown out his thoughts, the less it worked. Victor pressed his pencil against the edge of his desk until the ends snapped apart.

He'd thought he resigned himself to the notion that he was back at school and thus had to focus on anything but recent events. Clearly, he was wrong. *There's no pretending,* Victor sighed. *I can't just ignore the fact that ridiculous and seemingly impossible things haven't happened.* Opting for a more positive thought, Victor snuck a glance in True's direction.

Today, True was reading another new book, something called Red. Yet another title he didn't recognize. When was the last time he sat down to enjoy a book? Would he even manage to stay awake long enough to read it? Victor wasn't sure. Then again, as things were now, he might manage. Lately his thoughts seemed to scare away his sleep.

He looked quietly down towards her feet, his eyes falling on her blue tennis shoes. Somehow, it displeased him to see her wearing them. Perhaps he had the cold to blame. Snowfall was in full swing. And in little more than that short time, other things changed. More, since the icy night Victor had found himself passing The Death House shoeless and confused. Since the night that True asked him to become her friend.

Like the fact that Victor had taken to picking her up for school every morning, something that seemed much simpler when he'd decided to do it. It wasn't as if he didn't already go that way before—which was exactly what he told himself in an effort to not feel weird about it. He had to get up earlier, as True had some strange habit of being the first to Homeroom, but he didn't complain.

It was an even odder decision considering that True recently became one of the last students back to class every day. When he asked her about it, she'd said she was distracted, so it took longer. Victor didn't care to press her on it. Or rather, he simply decided that he should enjoy those 20 minutes before the school filled with voices and clatters.

Victor told himself, often with a hint of annoyance, that he was becoming too comfortable with True—too *needy*. So much so that he found himself looking forward to the next morning, even when they hardly said a word to each other the entire way to school. He wondered if he had just been overly eager to have someone else around considering Zane had been busy in the mornings. Busier than ever, since The Land of the Dead.

It had been almost a week since they'd been sent back to Snowville, supposedly by Life. Or so, they had no one else to blame. Almost a week since they'd found out the secrets of The Death House and seen Bailey. Victor could almost hear Grace's complaints in the background now. Her displeased voice as she'd said she felt tricked. That Life 'could have sent them home the moment they'd wanted to go.' Somehow, Victor didn't think it was as simple as that, but *if* Life had in fact been the one who sent them back to Snowville, why would she have done it the moment they'd seen Bailey?

Moments after the light flooded in around them, it disappeared and they found themselves back in the cemetery. The bluish hue was nowhere to be seen and they heard Dr. Brand's voice calling them in the distance. According to Dr. Brand, it had been a little over an hour since they'd left him, so he anxiously decided to look for them.

They finished their picnic in a heavy silence, which Dr. Brand made a considerable effort to break. Maybe the doctor thought their hearts were heavy, weighed with the notion of Mrs. Brand. He couldn't have known. What silenced their voices had been their thoughts of The Land of the Dead. None of them attempted to decipher the difference in time since their return nor utter a word about what they'd seen. Time creeped along.

On their way back from the cemetery, Victor couldn't recall who, mentioned quietly that they'd been terrified. And in that moment, everything they'd seen, heard, and felt resurfaced. It had been so acute that he couldn't have been projecting his feelings onto the group. Soon enough, Zane bolted ahead of them all the way home. Victor knew seeing Bailey had unsettled him. He couldn't recall the excuse he'd given to Doctor Brand. And by the time they'd made their way into the front door, Zane rushed past them again, this time with a look of horror on his face.

It wasn't until later that they found out Bailey was hospitalized. Where she had apparently been since days prior. According to Belle, Bailey's older sister that Victor didn't exactly recall knowing in the first place, Bailey had been trying to get ahold of Zane before her incident. Since then, Zane took to spending his mornings and evenings at the hospital. Which left Victor to his daily walk with True alone.

. . .

After school, Victor could just make out True's form darting around the corner and through the parking lot. He looked around, wondering if he could catch a glimpse of anything that would explain how quickly she was moving. When he saw nothing, Victor begrudgingly decided to follow. Only to lose sight of her a couple blocks from school. Victor called out to her as the memory of Grace speeding past him and Zane in FlareWing resurfaced. *Man. Dusted by one and left by the other. Were girls always this fast?*

"Victor...?" True called quietly, her head barely visible behind a nearby tree. What was she doing? Playing hide and seek?

"Yeah. It's me." He nodded. "Where's the fire?"

"Fire?" True asked curiously. "I don't know anything about a fire."

Victor chuckled. *Geez. This girl is so...*

"It's just a phrase. You just seemed like you were in a hurry. I thought you were going to leave me behind today. Everything okay?" He asked. He watched curiously as True tilted to the side and looked past him. She stared off in the distance, as if she was expecting something. Then, as if she'd done nothing strange, she stood upright again. What was she doing? "Umm, True?" Victor called. She turned her attention back to him.

"Yes. Everything is fine." True answered finally.

"Well, since you are around today, mind if I walk with you?" Victor asked. "Have you been leaving school earlier lately?"

"I don't mind. I haven't left school earlier, no." She replied softly. If she hadn't been leaving early then why hadn't he seen her at the end of the day? Was he just being too comfortable with her again? It wasn't as if he *had* to walk her to school and back home. She'd been managing just fine on her own before they'd become friends, Victor told himself.

"Would you like to come inside?" True asked, to his surprise. Part of him wanted to make some excuse to go home although he knew his mother would be working late tonight. If he thought he was too comfortable with her now, couldn't going over her house for dinner make things worse?

What if True's aunts could see his father in him? What if they thought he must have manipulated her into letting him in? Or worse, what if they knew she'd invited him in when they weren't at home that night because she'd given him those fuzzy fox socks, which might have secretly been her favorite, and they knew something was going on because she didn't wear them again?

Oh God. Victor thought, fighting the urge to slap himself. *Secretly her favorite fuzzy fox socks? Aside from being a tongue twister, I'm just making up weird stuff. Get it together, Victor.* He scolded himself. He wondered if it had been difficult to ask him over. "Yeah." Victor nodded, "If, you're sure." Not knowing if he was making the right decision. True nodded her head in his direction as they walked the rest of the way to her house.

When they made it to the gate, Victor found himself questioning what it would feel like walking in the door. Had it been hard for True to be there every day since they made it back? "The ghosts are all gone, I think." True said lowly, opening the gate and making her way to the front door. "The cold is gone inside and I don't feel them like I used to. It feels almost normal, but...*empty*."

Before Victor could respond, the door swung open and True's aunts smiled at them from the doorway. "Good girl, True." Her Aunt Trina laughed, patting the top of her head. "You managed to bring him." Victor took note of the woman's brown eyes silently focused on him and suddenly thought that he'd been right after all. Maybe an interrogation was awaiting him past the threshold. Perhaps torture. He wanted to tell her that they'd just had tea and he fell asleep on the sofa. That he hadn't even seen her face. Would it help?

"Well don't just stand there!" True's Aunt Rose called, waving a hand in the hall, "Come in. You'll let all the cold in."

Inside, Victor could feel that something was different after all. At first, he'd thought that it was just because of the cold. Or because the lights inside the house seemed brighter than he remembered. Eventually he settled on an explanation of the heat circulating around them, but that couldn't be it either. He realized, after a quiet moment standing near the door that even the chill he'd felt wafting down from the staircase that night had disappeared. There were no glimpses of spirits nor feelings of dread. He felt nothing at all, though that did very little to help him forget what he knew. He doubted he'd ever be able to forget the events they'd witnessed.

True's Aunt Trina offered him snacks as Rose recited stories he'd never heard. Including an eerie tale about a group of teenagers she'd known in her youth that disappeared after a night of 'building hopping.'

According to her, they had been searching for a haunted house by visiting the buildings in their hometown with bad histories.

"Surely, they must have found what they were looking for," she said in a hushed tone, "because they never returned. *Gone.*" She snapped. "Without a trace, just like that. Creepy, huh? To think, they even asked us to go with them. Thank the stars for that history homework."

As Victor listened anxiously to her words, he couldn't help but wonder what stories she'd have to tell if she ever visited The Land of the Dead.

Two

Phelia...

FAYTH.

Phelia sat silently on the living room floor, putting together a 2000-piece puzzle to distract herself from her thoughts, which soon proved ineffective. She had spent the last few nights full of worry, confusion, and fear. Zane offered her a lengthy apology for his behavior and aside from visiting Bailey multiple times a day and talking to himself that she'd catch walking past his bedroom, he seemed relatively back to himself.

Still, Phelia didn't quite understand. What changed him in the first place? Why had he fought with Victor? When they went through the door and Victor and Zane struggled with Fredrick Enrich, he seemed nothing less than himself. Phelia was increasingly aware that there were many more variables than she liked to deal with: and she'd thought Mirror was bad. The Land of the Dead or The After Land, as Life had called it, was nothing like she imagined a world after death would be. Although they'd been told that there were more places beyond the one that they saw, Phelia had a hard enough time just trying to wrap her head around that one. How many other places were there, exactly?

What was Bailey doing there? What lay beyond the dark mass those people in chains entered? What would the rest of Snowville have looked like? Why did some people, like the old man with Jewel, and Chester's mother Jess, have colorful eyes? Why did they come into full color without warning? Why did they have to go to The Land of the Dead in the first place?

When Phelia's mind wasn't on her brother or The After Land, her mind flooded with thoughts of the crawlspace in Grace's home. Phelia had the most uncomfortable feeling in her stomach when she thought of it. A feeling so uneasy that the crawlspace crept its way into her dreams, swallowing them whole until they shaped nightmares.

She wanted nothing more than to discuss the horrible feeling with Grace, but things had seemed to happen one after the other. That, and Phelia couldn't forget the sheer horror on Grace's face that day. As if she'd unearthed something *so unspeakable* that it risked their friendship simply by *existing*—a friendship she didn't want to lose, more so when it had just begun.

Hearing keys in the door, Phelia shifted her gaze in its direction, seeing her father. "You're home early, father." Phelia said, going over to greet him. He nodded, smiling widely,

"Phelia, hello dear. Yes, I am early, aren't I? Is your brother in yet?" He asked, calling up the staircase. When he looked back to Phelia she shook her head silently. "Ah, no matter. We have time. I've something to tell you when he's home."

"Good news?" Phelia asked curiously. He was smiling so much today.

"Yes. I'd say so." He beamed again, dropping his bag in his office and coming back to plop down on the sofa with a sigh.

Before Phelia could ask a question, she realized that her father had already fallen asleep. Chuckling to herself, Phelia looked from her father to the puzzle on the floor only a third of the way completed. It wasn't a difficult decision to make. She listened to the doctor's light snoozing and grabbed a throw from the closet. As gently as she could manage, Phelia climbed onto the sofa, laid the cover over him and snuggled in close.

. . .

An hour later Phelia awoke, seeing her father still asleep, his arms wrapped around her. She laid there for a moment looking quietly over his features, noting the dark circles under his eyes. When their mother was alive Phelia didn't think he'd ever had such dark circles. He needed to rest.

Not wanting to wake him, she slowly freed herself from his grasp and slid down to the floor. Opting to take a short walk, Phelia made her way up the stairs and bundled up for the cold. She wrote a note for her father and left it on the living room table before she slowly closed the door behind her and made her way down the snowy porch steps.

Without any destination in mind, Phelia let the swirl of thoughts and recollection of her dreams fly through her head. The brisk air seemed to make them tolerable. What was it about that crawlspace? Why was she having that reoccurring nightmare with the child crying, floating in the dark? She was quite sure there was more to it. Her body felt it, but her mind could not recall what more there was. The moment she opened her eyes, the nightmare floated away to wherever it is that dreams go, leaving her with a sickening feeling and the same few images.

She'd also been plagued with two other reoccurring nightmares. One of which was simply the events of The Death House on a continuous loop. A dream she didn't care to recall, but had too easy of a time re-living, and the other was a translucent dome falling apart above her and voices yelling over each other. She could never hear their words clearly but she could feel their fear and pain. That dream always ended quickly, with the last images she saw filled with blotches of red painting her vision. As far as Phelia knew, she'd never really had nightmares, much less any on repeat.

Lost in her own head, Phelia realized that she'd walked much further than she anticipated. Looking up at the building, she didn't know how to feel. *What an odd thing it is,* Phelia thought, *to find my way here. To look upon the very building, Snowville Temporary Infirmary, that is responsible for the most fascinating and confusing part of my life. Although, I cannot deny that there is some fear to be felt with the unknown.*

She wasn't sure which should exceed the other. All she did know was that there was an odd since of fulfillment as well when they stepped through the doors of another world. Something that fueled her curiosity and diminished the fear too. Something, that continuously reminded her that she wanted answers above all else.

Phelia slowly made her way to the window they'd often used to enter and exit the building. She climbed inside and made her way past the table, the fireplace and over the broken stair. One step at a time, she made her way up to the to the landing closest the open room of boxes. Phelia stood quietly before the empty, blank space on the wall. She knew it was still there, the door. She could feel it.

If the journal had been right, which seemed to be the case so far, there were more out there. More places beyond Mirror, The After Land, and FlareWing. Even Twister had said that Fae worlds could be situated in the confines of another world. The journal had said they each had a room beyond what she could see.

True seemed to believe that she'd been inside her own. No one else had experienced anything of the sort, but Phelia had no reason to believe that she hadn't been telling the truth. If nothing else, she and Zane had entered some other place too. A place no one else had seen. She wanted to see those worlds, she wanted to understand them. She wanted answers.

In a single breath, Phelia felt herself being pulled forward and saw light surround her before dispersing almost as quickly as it had begun. In just the moments it took to blink, she'd found herself *elsewhere.* In her view, there were no landmarks. No hills or buildings, no rocks or stream to follow. There was almost nothing at all.

It was a space filled with clouds as far as the eye could see. Up, down, left, right. She had no real way to tell one direction from the next. It took a calm mind just to keep the dizzy, disorienting feelings at bay. She could feel nothing solid below her feet. Ahead of her in the distance, Phelia's eyes caught a speck of light. Another, then another until she could make out a form taking shape. She watched silently, unsure of what to make of it.

Before long, the light formed the shape of a large animal and as it dimmed, Phelia could make out the contours of a cat. As the immense figure raced in her direction, Phelia realized just how large it was. It would have towered over their house had it been near. She thought for a moment to run, but had no idea where she could run to or if there were any possible way to outrun it in the first place.

"I've finally found you." Phelia heard. It was a voice so thick and heavy that her ears vibrated from the sound of it. Had it not been for the volume, perhaps Phelia would have even thought it calming. Was it possible that the voice she'd heard was coming from that beast?

As it stood in front of her, Phelia could make out the large black cat's shimmering fur and the glowing blue light flowing from its sockets in the place of eyes. The blue gleam swayed like a stream from each eye circling the space around its head. The fur on its cheeks and inside its ears were a striking gold, not unlike the twins' they'd seen in Mirror. Surely, it was large enough to have come from Mirror.

"Found me?" Phelia asked.

"Yes." The beast answered, its mouth parting but not moving to form words. It seemed to Phelia that it did not speak in any natural way she'd known. It was almost as if its words came in the form of vibrations themselves. "I am ashamed to say that it took quite some time to find you." This time, the vibrations still touched her ears but they didn't hurt. "Forgive me. I didn't think to adjust frequencies. I'd utilized that one all this time in order to reach you."

"Reach me?" Phelia questioned. This cat-beast was truly speaking to her? Here, in some space of nothing?

"I am not this 'cat-beast' you think of. I am called Fayth. Surely you can use the name that you gave me. Have you forgotten?"

"Forgotten? Why, I've never *met* you." Phelia said in disbelief.

"The day I was born, the same day as you, you named me so." The beast spoke, closing its eyes with a sigh.

"I suppose that its natural you may have forgotten. You're human and it has been quite some time. Though I am but a child myself, in a sense." As it spoke, Phelia looked on, baffled. What was it talking about? They shared a birthday? She'd named it? As she opened her mouth to speak, the beast lowered its head, "We have time for all of your questions later." It said, slowly pressing its face against her cheek. "We have been apart for so long. I've missed you..."

Its fur was quite possibly the softest thing she'd ever felt. When she breathed in, Phelia could make out a glace, airy aroma encircling her face. What a beautiful scent. For a moment, Phelia was filled with a deep sadness she could not place. "I will explain, but you must take me with you, and you must use my name or I shall not answer you."

"Take you with me? I couldn't possibly do that." Phelia said quickly, shaking her head. "Definitely not."

"Why not? I've just found you; I cannot leave your side again!" It said quickly.

"Well, I don't know you. This could all be a ploy so I'll set you free and you can devour my family or even the town." Phelia said, making no attempt to mask her suspicion. Although this was something she'd recently read in a book of fiction, it seemed much more likely that fiction was reality when it came to the crystals and any world that they'd traveled to.

"I would never harm you. Nor your family if they have meaning to you." The beast huffed. "That would be a horrid thing to do."

"**And?**" Phelia said, raising a brow. "The *town* as well?"

"Does this town hold a special place in your heart?"

"Well, no. Not particularly, but you simply mustn't destroy it." Phelia retorted.

"Then no. I shall not destroy the town." It yawned. If Phelia didn't know any better she'd have thought the cat-beast wanted to stomp the town to dust.

"Well, even if you say so you still can't come with me. You're much too large. You couldn't fit in my door at all. You'd be attacked if I took you home with me like that." Phelia sighed. The beast tilted its head to the side, blinking its large foggy sockets at her before it disappeared. So quickly and without warning that Phelia panicked.

"It's alright." The cat-beast's voice called back as a small silhouette formed near her feet. "I've not left you." As it spoke, its voice became lighter and Phelia could make out Fayth's dark fur. The stream of blue streams from before were replaced with large blue eyes and its golden hairs were nowhere to be seen. "Can you take me this way?" Fayth asked, not waiting for an answer before it jumped into her arms.

Phelia nodded and immediately felt a vibration throughout her entire body. Not unlike the feeling under their feet when the elephant called for The Catcher in Mirror. Before she knew it, Phelia was standing in front of the fireplace in Snowville Temporary Infirmary. "How...?" She began to ask, only to receive the same answer as before: they had time for questions later.

As Phelia made her way out of the window with Fayth in her coat, she placed the board back in its place before starting on her way home. She didn't have permission to have a pet, but besides that, Fayth wasn't a normal animal. There was no doubt about it. So, when she made her way inside a bit later, she asked Fayth to stay as quiet as possible and tip-toed past her sleeping father up the stairs and to her room. Offering him a pillow to lay on under her bed, she asked Fayth to stay there until she returned.

Not long after her return, Zane also made his way through the door. For now, Phelia figured that Fayth would be her secret. Or at least, that's what she'd thought before dinner. Before her father announced that he'd be taking time off of work. With their father spending more time at home, how was Phelia going to keep her secret? How would she manage to keep her father from finding out about Fayth? What if they went through the door and were gone most of the day again? Just what would they tell him...?

Three

Zane...

BAILEY.

Zane made his way down the hall as the florescent lights beamed above him and an orchestra of machines whirred and beeped in an echo of overlapping intervals from other rooms. As he passed the help desk, he nodded politely in the attendant's direction. He didn't have to ask for directions anymore.

Coming to the hospital twice a day, he'd learned more than he would have liked to know about the inner workings of Snowville Medical. It occurred to Zane that he hadn't stepped foot in a hospital since the death of their mother before now, but as his horrible luck would have it, he was there again.

He didn't know how his father managed going to work in the hospital everyday and he'd been honestly relieved to hear that his father was taking a break from work. Zane could hardly recall his father's last consecutive off day. Of course, Zane was aware more than anyone how much his father had been throwing himself into his job since those dark times he didn't exactly like to recall. Although, considering the things that had been happening lately, it felt to Zane like anything 'dark' he had to worry about seemed to lie much less with his father and much more with himself.

The voice in his head hardly made a reappearance since their time at The Death House, but Zane still felt a chill inside of him, some odd spot that ran through his body as if he'd been touched by ice even in the times it seemed to be gone. It was a chill that was much different than Snowfall's winter air—there was just no comparing the two. Zane could hardly gain any perspective when it came to that hatred clouded voice or the things he'd done since he'd began to hear it. He feared, maybe more than anything else, that the events from before would repeat themselves and he'd ruin what was left of his life and his friendships. If those were even still intact.

Rounding the corner to Bailey's room, Zane entered the open door to see Bailey's sister and Grandmother. Even though he'd already come so often, Zane was always a little surprised to see them together. He hardly recalled Bailey mentioning her sister and whenever she'd mentioned her grandmother, Zane never knew she meant *that* grandmother. The woman he'd met soon after their move to Snowville.

. . .

Zane recalled that first week in Snowville when the kids were out and about, they'd always said something about "that grandma" or "that old lady." It wasn't until later that Zane understood everyone was referring to the old dark-skinned woman in town, and even later that he'd understood why they talked about her at all.

The neighborhood children used to invite him to play with them and they'd rush down to a house on the end of an abandoned street. The kids would break the windows and write random words on the fences, scribbling drawings of monsters and who knew what else on their sidewalk. If one of the kids were feeling brave enough, they'd even write on the side of the house. Zane never cared for those types of games, so he'd only watch them, that was until he'd caught a glimpse of the old woman shuffling through the house when a brick smashed through her window.

Zane remembered that feeling of guilt and anger rising from the pit of his stomach. He remembered wondering why he didn't realize that the woman lived there, thus, why all of the children to find such pleasure destroying that house more than any other in the area. When he yelled at the other kids, telling them that the old woman wasn't hurting anyone and what they were doing was wrong, they shrugged him off but continued on as if he'd never said anything at all.

That was the last time that Zane decided to be around those children. Nowadays, he had found a similar sense of disgust with most of the adults and their children in town. He considered himself lucky to have come across people like Bailey and Victor at all. And in some insane sense of irony, Zane thought that perhaps he should have realized back then what that moment meant about the town in the first place. Luckily, to this day, he often found a bit more solace in his actions after his realization about the other children.

One day, after all the neighborhood children had gone home for the evening, Zane made his way over to the fence to look at the new words the others had written. Cow. Darky. Rat. Ape. How could anyone write those things about someone else? How could he have associated himself with people like that and not have noticed? His parents would be ashamed if they'd thought he had anything to do with them.

As Zane continued to walk along the fence, a loud bang caught his attention. The screen door slammed open, so hard that it fell forward and crashed down onto the porch. A tall, muscled man with curly dark hair and thick brows threw his fist in the air angrily. "You get outta here you little monster! To the fire with all of you! Don't make me come down there!" For an instant, he was almost scared off, but Zane shut his eyes and shouted back.

"Why don't you do something about those bad kids, then? I didn't do it!"

The man looked upon him with suspicion as Zane made out the sound of a woman's voice. "Name callin' an' faces don't hurt nobody.

The fence can be painted an' the win'ow fixed." The woman placed a gentle hand on the man's shoulder and shuffled over to a rocking chair to his right.

"Dang it, mama." The man hissed under his breath, heading back inside. "I'll go get the paint. Now I gotta fix the door too." Her son? As the man disappeared inside, Zane looked over the stout old woman. He could make out her dark skin, her silver hair tied in a braid over her shoulder, and her plum dress from the distance.

"Why don't you tell their parents?" Zane asked, looking beyond the fence. "Get them in trouble." He huffed.

The woman laughed. "Oh, child. It ain't jus' their fault they hate the color of my skin. That'd be their parents teachin' 'em to hate. Hatin' on anybody different. Whole town's got that kinda ugly, boy." She said in a thick accent he'd never heard. She shook her head sadly.

"Then why don't you leave?" Zane asked, curiously. If they'd moved to a town where everybody hated them, he'd want to leave as quickly as possible.

"Probably cuz I'm old." She smiled. "An' this here's my home. I been here long before you were born. Servin' the very children an' families of this town. I even raised a few of 'em kids' parents, I reckon. Jus' as my family did before me. Some of 'em turned out right, but ain't no surprise that all of 'em don't. Almost pitiful, really. Wish it'd been different.

"My son, Charlie, wants me to come live with him in some far place he's livin', but I'm his mother. I ain't doin' that. He should be free to live his life without me, and I'm glad he got away from here. But Charlie's a good boy so he makes sure to come see his mama.

"Every time he come here, he's got all this fixin' to do so I'm sure it jus' makes 'em madder at me but I ain't cut out for that life he's livin'. I worked all those years to buy a home in this town an' I done it. Somethin' no colored folk could do back then neither, mind ya. I ain't leavin'. I ain't running away jus' cuz nobody wanna see my face. Yond that, I got two more jobs to do in this town an' I reckon they gonna turn out jus' fine. Better than, I reckon."

Zane didn't completely understand the weight of their conversation that day, but he liked the old woman. This silver haired lady with the strange accent and dark complexion. This woman with a soft smile and surprisingly optimistic attitude. So much so that he'd decided to take Phelia to meet her and her son. For a time, with Phelia sitting on her lap and Zane listening to her stories from what she coined 'times of my ancestors,' their time together seemed to go on forever.

Zane couldn't remember when or why he and Phelia stopped visiting her, but when he made his way to Bailey's hospital room for the first time and saw the old woman offer him one of those smiles and call him by name, he'd started thinking fondly of those memories again. When Zane told her that he was surprised she remembered his name, she chuckled. "Mama Trinity never forgets nobody, boy. An' the day I do, Imma be on my death bed, watch what I tell ya." She'd said, pointing her cane, which she'd called her 'walkin' stick,' in his direction with another smile.

...

"Zane, honey. We're jus' leavin.' Got some business to take care of today." Grandma Trinity said, making her way to her feet. Zane took note of how long her hair had grown, though it still rested in a familiar braid over her shoulder. He looked over the pearl necklace and earrings in her ears, and the silver pin on her chest. Beside her, gently cradling her arm was Bailey's sister, Belle. Like Bailey, Belle also had shoulder length brown hair, but she didn't share her sister's blue-gray eyes. Zane felt her deep brown gaze silently trained on him as he stared at the bright pink highlights in her hair.

"You shouldn't come so often. What about school?" Belle more chided than asked. Zane wondered how much older she was than her sister. She wasn't in high school. College, perhaps?

"I'm not missing any school." Zane said, looking in Bailey's direction, listening to the slow hiss of the ventilator. "But Bailey is. She's got plenty of catching up to do."

"She'll be happy to see ya, Zane." Grandma Trinity said quietly, lightly taking hold of his hand. "Happy for 'em notes, too. If she was up tomorrow that'd be wonderful, but if not...well, we jus' gonna be waitin' till she does." As she reassuringly squeezed his hand, Belle offered a slight nod in his direction and they made their way out of the door, shutting it behind them. Effectively leaving him with Bailey and his own feelings.

Pulling up a chair, Zane sat at Bailey's bedside, looking at the machine and reading the numbers and beats he didn't care to understand. He knew it mean that she was alive, somehow, and that's what mattered. He still didn't understand it. Ever since the moment Zane stepped up for Victor in The Death House, he'd felt more himself.

The voice in his head had appeared less and it didn't take screaming to drown it out anymore. Zane could merely tell it off and it would slowly fade away, sometimes for the rest of the day if he was really lucky. There had been no more watching himself from a distance. He wasn't bothered by True's hidden face as he'd been before. Zane didn't even feel the hot flashes of anger that boiled up in him on his date with Bailey. Something—though Zane couldn't say what—was different.

Gently pushing a few of Bailey's loose strands behind her ear, as he'd often seen her do. Zane couldn't make sense of this either. The fact that Bailey had fallen off of a roof in an attempt to save a bird and ended up in this state? First of all, what *was it* with birds?? Second, even if Belle was right and it was some bird Bailey had been watching—she'd called it Flutter—how did that explain this? It wasn't adding up.

"Bailey, I have so many questions and apologies to make. A million of them probably." Zane sighed, frustrated, running his fingers down his face. "Were you really saving a bird? What happened to you? Why did we see you in The Land of The Dead? Do you hate me for being so horrible to you? Would you want to meet Grace and True? How do I even make this up to you?"

With a heavy sigh, Zane took her hand in his. He realized when he came to visit her in the hospital that he hardly knew her and it was a realization that only amplified since then. After all that time, after all of their interactions and even her coming over to his house those days, she was practically a stranger to him in any sense that mattered. She was someone he mercilessly ridiculed on what was supposed to be their date. Someone he hurt without a thought.

There were other things too, like questions about her family. He couldn't believe that she'd never mentioned Grandma Trinity. Why didn't she talk about her sister? What had her life been like in Snowville? Had she always lived there? What did she do after school? The questions were endless.

"Just hurry up and wake up, okay?" Zane groaned. "Be alright. I've got so much to say to you. Wake up and be your cheery self, like you'd never gotten hurt. At least let me have a second chance at our date. Or, wake up and turn me down in person—hit me for being a jerk if that will make you feel better. I don't care. Anything. Just...get up. Otherwise, I'm coming. I'm serious, Bailey." Of course, Zane didn't know for sure if such a thing was possible, but they'd gone there once. Couldn't they go back again? Couldn't they at least try?

Zane laid his head against the bed and closed his eyes. "I mean it. Somehow, I'll return to The Land of the Dead and drag you back here, back home, myself..."

Four

Eustis...

STUPID.

Eustis sat quietly in his seat, his hands in his pockets, fiddling with erasers. A habit he was hardly aware of. Miss Pine, their teacher, walked through the room and handed out packets of worksheets to finish before the end of the day. Eustis, having finished the assignments right away, soon had very little else to do. So, there he continued to sit, thinking about the most *stupid* thing he could occupy his brain with on a Monday morning: Grace.

Or at least, that's the kind of thing his parents would have said. A girl like Grace, he'd been told, was bound to be dumber than a sack of rocks. Neither were bound to go anywhere in life without someone taking pity on them and chucking them in another direction. That, his mother said, was likely why the Specks adopted her, but even they had managed to be dragged further down the rabbit hole right alongside her. She had a particular way of spewing her opinions and gossip.

"That little girl looks better than most of them, I'm sure. Maybe they were hoping to make her smart. Not that they were ever really worth mentioning before. At least MaryAnne has those baking skills."

His mother had laughed, "Otherwise, even she'd be lacking just about anything of value. The poor woman. I couldn't imagine."

Eustis didn't say so, but he'd found it an ironic statement coming from his mother, who'd almost burned down their kitchen just using the microwave on more than one occasion. In Eustis' opinion, Grace had always been smart. He recalled the first time he'd met her, the first day she'd walked into the classroom and the whispering started.

By the same time the next day, students were bold enough to speak their thoughts aloud right to her face. During recess, he'd seen her crying behind a tree. Until that day, Eustis had never given talking to girls much thought. Most of them tended to do the talking all on their own, but she didn't offer so much as a glance in his direction when he stepped in front of her.

As he stood there, listening to her light sobs and watching the slight rises of her shoulders, Eustis found himself fascinated by her thick, dusty-red hair. Upon closer inspection, he could just make out the bunches of small curls. Wondering what it must have felt like, he reached out a hand to touch it. Immediately, Grace shrunk back against the tree trunk.

"What are you doing?" She asked pointedly, her brown eyes sharp and untrusting. Realizing that he'd done something to offend her, he stopped.

"Nothing." Eustis replied, quickly dropping his hand to his side.

"Don't touch my hair." She warned, before he could open his mouth to say another word.

"Okay." Eustis said, trying to think of what else to say. "Well, when did you move here?" He asked.

"Why?" She retorted. "I'm clearly new." Not knowing what to say, Eustis shrugged. For what seemed like forever, he stood there quietly, the two of them watching each other in awkward silence. "A couple weeks ago." She answered, finally.

"Well, you've started school even more late." Eustis said thoughtfully.

"It's not my fault." She shrugged before another silence set in, only to be broken by more of her sobs. "I hate it here!" She whined.

"Well, you shouldn't hate it." Eustis said, thinking back on when he'd first came to Snowville himself. He also thought he'd hate being there forever. Only when Eustis thought about it now did he realize his hatred never turned to affection for the town, only indifference. "It's not so bad. It's okay." Eustis attempted to console her. "I saw you get your work done fast. Usually, I'm the only one who finishes first. So, you're different than the rest of them."

"The rest of who?" Grace asked, peeking up from her arms.

"You know," Eustis shrugged, kicking his foot through the dirt. "Dark people. Mother says they're feeble-minded but--"

Before Eustis could finish his sentence, his vision tilted backward and he hit the ground. Sitting up, he realized she'd punched him square in the nose. Surprised and confused, Eustis looked up at her as she yelled at him. "Feeble-minded? Dark people?! Don't talk like it's a compliment! You're...horrible!" Before he knew it, Grace had run off, leaving Eustis on the ground with a bloody nose.

A boy from class rushed over, mocking his position in the dirt, laughing loudly. "Did she do that? A girl?! The one with the dirty hair!" He snorted. Eustis hadn't thought her hair was dirty. It smelled clean. But in his embarrassment, he lied—the first of many he would tell.

Later that day, when Eustis attempted to speak to her again, Grace immediately told him to stay away. She'd said he was a racist, a word he'd never been called before. It wasn't a word he thought he'd ever heard anyone use. Baffled and curious, Eustis decided to ask his parents about it that night at dinner. His father asked why he wanted to know. Eustis took note of his father's surprise as he spoke through his napkin.

"The new girl at school said it." Eustis had answered truthfully. "So what does that mean? To be a racist?"

"Oh, goodness. For Christ's sake! The girl's only just gotten here and she's pulling the race card!" His mother snorted. "Eustis, honey, it's just an excuse darkies use to get special treatment. So, people pity them. If anyone around here were racist, we'd all have slaves." She waved her hand dismissively, rolling her eyes. When his father demanded that he stop asking foolish questions and eat his dinner, Eustis wondered if he had asked a question he shouldn't have.

Try as he might, Eustis was no longer hungry. He took enough bites of the meal to excuse himself from the table and made his way to his father's study to find the dictionary. "So, a racist believes that race is the reason for human traits and produces superiority of another race? Another definition is prejudice or discrimination."

From there Eustis continued making his way through unfamiliar words and pieced together what he thought was an understanding. In the end, he ended up more confused. His parents couldn't possibly be wrong, right? Prejudice dealt with an opinion someone has that can damage the reputation of someone else. Race, as he understood it was just the difference between him and her. Or even them and someone else on another part of the planet.

The next day at recess, Eustis again found Grace on the other side of the tree. "You said I was racist, but my mom and dad have always been right. How is the truth racist? Racism is based on opinions that ruin reputation, not fact." This time, Eustis was ready with his hands in the air to cover his face in case she got upset again. Only, surprisingly, she made no effort to hit him or run away. Instead, she sighed.

"Because it ***is** an opinion.* Your parents just think about other people that way. All of you do. No parent is always right, I learned that. You should learn it too. You've never met someone like me but you assumed you knew me. You thought that I had to be stupid because I look the way I look. I've met lots of people that act and think that way."

"But how does that hurt anything? People think stuff about me all the time but I don't think it's racist." Eustis asked seriously.

For an instant he could see the anger shadowing her face, but she didn't move. She sighed again, harder this time. "Because it *does* hurt. How would you like people calling you ugly, stupid, and black? How would you like it if people listened to someone you don't know that lied all of the time? If people just used you to make themselves look better?"

"I wouldn't like that, but I didn't say those things." Eustis frowned. "Besides, you are, aren't you—Black, I mean?"

"You might as well have, believing what your parents said! I'm not anything! And even for a color, I'm not Black! Have you ever looked that word up in the dictionary?! What's wrong with being me? I'm just me—I'm just Grace!" She huffed, and before he could stop her, she was gone again, rushing off to some unknown destination.

Again, that night, Eustis looked up words in the dictionary. Words like 'dirty,' 'soiled,' 'evil,' and 'wicked' brought a lump to his throat. While white was the opposite. White was 'innocent,' 'pure,' and 'lustrous.' That night would not be the last time that Grace sent Eustis home with what he'd eventually call 'word-work.' In fact, it happened all week long.

At some point since then, they'd stopped talking and the word-work ceased. He was ridiculed when he was seen speaking to her, punished by his parents when he repeated the things he'd learned, or even when he defiantly told his parents that Grace seemed nothing like the way they described. Eventually, having learned his lesson, he stopped mentioning it altogether. He learned to say only the things his parents agreed with in their presence—all the things that brought him praise and laughter.

When Eustis decided to try and toughen Grace up by exposing her to the things that angered her, thinking that she would be able to work around it or ignore it as he'd done with his parents so no one would be able to bully her and make her cry, it backfired. His friends and the other kids from school joined in. They lied and laughed at her, tricked her and pulled pranks on her every chance they got. They called her names, and somewhere along the way, his intentions were buried.

Eustis hadn't been able to call her names, or to think of her as anyone other than Grace, after all, that had been exactly what she'd told him one of those days. She was just herself and Eustis was more aware than anyone that when things spiraled out of control, it was his fault. He knew he should have told the truth, that they'd been the ones who did all of those terrible things, even if he wasn't directly involved. But he also knew that it would cause trouble with the others if he did.

So, Eustis stayed silent. Even though he knew Grace didn't have friends and that she was hurting. Sometimes, after the others bothered her, Eustis would separate from the other kids and follow her. He'd sit somewhere at a distance and watch Grace crying alone like she had been the first day he spoke to her. Unable to close the distance between them, Eustis would pretend that he was at her side, patting her back, or giving her a hug and reassuring her that things were going to be okay. Although he knew it was just pretend, he couldn't help but do it anyway.

Eustis sighed, scratching his head. He wanted to be relieved that Grace had stopped fighting because he could pretend to be bored with her. If he was convincing enough, maybe he could stop the things he started. Even if he wasn't sure it would work. The only thing was, Eustis didn't know *why* Grace had been acting so different lately. He could tell that something else had been bothering her, but what? He hardly thought asking would work.

He knew the change had been much more than her deciding not to go back and forth with him and the other students. Whatever it was, it left a sinking feeling in the bottom of his stomach he didn't have the words to explain. Eustis was sure more than anything else, that he had to do something about this mess with Grace once and for all. He had to figure out what to do.

Five

Twister...

NORMAL.

Twister crossed the veil to FlareWing, making his way back home. He was exhausted. He'd spent so much time going back and forth to so many destinations and True's place that even his wings hurt. *If I could just close my eyes for a few hours...* Twister thought. *I'll be good as new. Just a few hours won't hurt.*

Upon entering his home, however, a noise from the bedroom forced him alert. As he made his way towards the room, two figures emerged. "Mother? *Father?*" Twister called in disbelief. "Or, should I address you both as *General?*" He huffed.

"Why do you look so startled? Do you dislike the sight of us that much?" His father asked, his face showing no hint of emotion. Shouldn't he have been at least a little surprised to see him? How long had it been since the three of them were in the same space? Since they could look at each other and speak words in the same room? As for his fear, Twister did suppose that he'd been on edge lately since his travels to the Human World. Since he'd seen what was happening to True and the others.

"I don't dislike the sight of you." Twister sighed. "I suppose I might have thought I was in danger." Was it a coincidence that the very people he thought he might have no choice but to talk to had found their way to his home today? After all, if he was right about The Darkness, who else but the leaders of the Fae Army would he speak to?

"Danger?" His mother asked, raising a brow.

Twister looked upon his parents as if he was searching for something. Perhaps some unknown treasure hidden away in their features. His father's short hair had grown and half of it had been braided down the side, he sported a long beard and moustache where he'd previously had none. But he could make out the curved mark on his forehead and his silver eyes were still the same—serious and stark.

Twister shifted his gaze slightly to the right to focus on his mother. Her hair was still as long as he remembered, her bangs still swooped to the side to cover her face. Or more specifically, the scar over her eye. Her soft green gaze observed him as well, her eyes shifting over his face and his clothes.

In their continued silence, Twister realized they searched for words that didn't seem to exist. Still, they couldn't stay there saying nothing to each other. Besides, every moment that he spent there, wasting time, his companions could be in danger. If he wasn't going to rest, he could at least do what he came to do.

"What are the two of you doing here?" Twister asked, finally. "It's unusual seeing you here."

"Father Wing mentioned that you'd want to speak with us. He said that it was time that we spoke." His father said flatly. Twister didn't try to make sense of Father Wing's apparent knowledge that he'd wanted anything from his parents.

Questioning things like that always managed to be futile, but Father Wing had given him no time. There were no warnings, no days to prepare himself for a conversation with his parents. Was it for the best?

Here goes nothing, Twister sighed. "The Darkness is on the move, I think. If I'm right, I have no idea why, but it can't be anything good. I know everyone thinks we are safe—that you'd probably say there's no danger here, but I've seen things. *Terrifying* things and it went after my friends." He said, as quickly as he could manage, afraid that he'd lose his nerve.

"Your friends?" His father questioned.

Twister nodded, throwing his arms in the air with a frustrated sigh. "Yes. My *friends*! The humans that came here for the ceremony. I've reason to believe The Darkness wants to harm them. They're *special.*" Twister said, taking a deep breath. He didn't know why he was so frazzled. He readied himself to see them shake their heads or make remarks that he was naïve or possibly insane, but neither would come to pass. Instead, they looked at each other in silence.

They didn't look surprised, there was no hint of disbelief. Why? What was going on? Could it be that they knew? "What is it?" Twister asked, impatient. "What does that look mean?"

His parents sighed and they mumbled amongst themselves. Something about Father Wing being right, of course. Before Twister could demand an explanation, his mother shook her head. "Thorne, Twister. Let us sit. We have things to discuss."

Although sitting was the last thing Twister wanted to do, he decided that it would be ridiculous to argue about it. At the very least, there was something important enough to discuss that his parents were willing to sit down in his practically furniture-less hut. When Twister suggested they go to the bedroom, they declined, opting to sit where they stood. He fought the urge to offer them drinks. Why was everything so awkward with his parents?

"You recall the story of the war with The Darkness, yes?" His mother began. Twister nodded silently. "Yes, well, you see...your grandfather led the army after Sir Locus passed. They had been close friends and Sir Locus trusted your grandfather to do well in his absence."

"Right, but grandfather passed right after the war, didn't he?" Twister asked.

"You're not exactly wrong." His mother answered quietly. "Your grandfather became ill slowly after the war. He lived long enough to meet you. To hold you once." Twister could hear the shift in her voice, the trembles of emotion as she recalled the events. He'd forgotten how dear his grandfather had been to his mother.

"I was offered the position after him." Twister's father cut in. "I did not accept it initially because you had been born." Twister felt a wave of sadness drape itself over him and he was instantly reminded of the reason he hadn't seen or spoke to his parents in all this time. It seemed that he was always a burden to carry.

"So, if I hadn't been born, you wouldn't have hesitated. Is that right?" Twister asked before he could think better of it.

His father frowned. "Of course, I would have. I was not your grandfather and I had never saw myself in this position. Until it had been offered to me, I'd never even thought to have anything to do with the Fae Army. I did not think I was ready or would ever be. Aside from that, there was your mother." He said defensively. Twister took note of his mother's gentle gaze as she lightly squeezed his hand. His father nodded slightly in return, clearing his throat.

"If you didn't think you were ready, why did you do it? Why accept the position?" Twister asked.

"There was not much left to lose when I did." His father answered solemnly. Twister felt as though a spear had struck his chest. How could he say something like that? Nothing left to lose? What about their life? What about...? "What about ***me***??" Twister yelled, jumping to his feet. His face flooded with anguish, and he felt the tears falling before he had any chance to stop them. "What was I then, mother, father? Nothing? *Was I **nothing*** to you?!" He shouted, his voice straining with emotion.

His mother covered her mouth and Twister could see her own tears threatening to fall. For the first time since their appearance in his home, his father's expression grew mournful and he closed his eyes. It was a face he'd never seen. "Never." His mother's voice was small, barely a whisper now. "*Never*, Twister. When Father Wing came to us and said that he was sure that our problems with The Darkness were not over, we listened as anyone would have done. He said that he trusted our family, as his own had, to protect the people. And you..." His mother's voice trailed off.

Twister felt a sickening knot of guilt rising inside of him. He'd never meant to make his mother cry. He watched her wipe at her tears. "You'd been so independent all your life, and when you realized you weren't growing...you never seemed happy again. Years and years went by and you never smiled with us. You didn't want to spend time together. Leading the Fae Army meant protecting everyone. That meant you too. *Your life,* if things had ever gone awry.

"The way you were, we didn't know if there was much else to be done to protect you. Once we took the position, within days, you...ran away but we found you doing so well on your own. We didn't know what else to do." His mother sobbed, laying her weight against his father and burying her face in his neck.

"Rune..." Twister's father called to his wife, looking torn. It was almost too much. Twister recalled that his mother had her gentle moments, but he'd never seen such sides of either of his parents. In the past, they'd seemed so cold, and standing at the head of the Fae, distant. As if they were some place far beyond Twister's reach.

"Your mother," his father continued, "was made an advisor who would assume my duties if my life was lost. It seemed that you were more upset after we accepted the positions and you never spoke to us when we came to you. Else, you weren't home."

"Of course, I was upset. I didn't understand any of it. Things had been peaceful since the war ended. Better than before, by all accounts. You'd even said so yourself. And I just—*just*-look at me! I'm not *normal!* It looked bad enough on its own, but for the Commanding General of the Fae Army to have a deformed kid? How would that be alright? I wanted you to forget me. I wanted...you to have more children and be happy! Did you think that I couldn't see how upset I made you? How difficult I made your life?!" Twister shouted. He'd tried to hold it all in and failed miserably.

Twister watched his father's face shift to anger and his frown deepen. "***More*** children? How could you *dare...*? To have ***another*** *child* when we failed to do right by you? Another child to hate us or grow up without parents if we perished on the battlefield? To have another child when our own was perfectly in reach?!" His father, in his fit of emotion, struck his fist into the ground, sending a ripple of magic through the house. Almost enough for the pressure to send Twister flying.

"Of course, we were upset, Twister. Of course, our life was difficult! We are your parents and we could do *nothing to* ***help*** *you!* We could not make you into the "normal" Faerie you so wished to be. But we never once blamed you. We ***never*** made you out to be a mistake!"

"Why?" Twister struggled to ask through his own tears. How could they not understand? If what they were saying was the truth, he wouldn't have hidden away. He wouldn't have thought they'd been as ashamed as *he* had been. He would have come back home. How could they? "If this is the truth...then why? Why didn't you tell me? Why didn't you ask me to come home?!"

"Oh, Twister. We're so sorry!" His mother cried and in a matter of moments he found himself squished between their large frames, practically drowning in their tears. He'd never felt such a mix of emotions. Never seen his father cry. How long had they caused each other's suffering? How long ago had they stopped being a family? Was it possible to find their way forward after a moment like this? Could they be one again?

Twister wasn't sure how they were supposed to mend their heartache, but he felt there, surrounded by a love from his parents he'd never thought he'd had, that he wanted to try. He wasn't a child anymore, but he was still their son. Knowing the truth and all of their misunderstandings shed a light in the darkest portion of his soul.

Maybe he could learn to accept the ways he was different instead of wishing to be like everyone else. The same way his parents had but he'd been too blinded by his own doubts to see it. They'd never tried to change him; he'd known that in his heart. They'd been thinking of him, trying to give him what they thought he wanted. They'd been trying to *protect* him—the very same thing he thought he had been doing for them.

Six

Quill...

AWAKENING.

Quill opened her eyes to the emptiness around her. Well, not exactly empty as far as she was concerned. She'd slept here most of her life. Loved by **HIM**. The moments that she briefly gained consciousness in the past, **HE** told her their story in pieces. All this time **HE** fed her his power to prepare her for what was to come. The power that, in conjunction with her own, would change the world—the outside and FlareWing both.

"YOU'VE AWAKENED." HE spoke. His voice sounded more homely than she remembered. "Yes." Quill answered, feeling a light squeeze around her body. That's right. A hug. How long had it been since she last awoke? Since she'd last gotten a hug from him or focused her eyes on the dark space around her?

"WE'VE BEEN WAITING."

"We?" Quill questioned, unsure.

"YES. OPAL, A FAERIE. SHE WAS BORN HERE AND HAS NEVER LEFT YOUR SIDE. YOUR COMPANION. LIKE YOU, SHE IS DIFFERENT."

If **HE** said so, it must have been true. She'd had a friend all this time? Only then, when she saw her, did Quill realize that she had met the Faerie called Opal before. She had knowledge of the world above that **HE** had given her, Quill recalled him saying in the past. Opal knew many things that would be helpful above the surface.

If memory served correctly, she was born of a Cursed Fae. Even now, Quill could feel her slight fascination rising at the sight of her. She recalled touching the Faerie's hair and wings. Her brown skin and eyes and the vertical scar under the left. Her hair was a midnight blue, which seemed brighter in the dark, shimmering red, green and gold particles cast specks of pale shades around her. Even from the distance Quill could make out her layered black wings—Quill's favorite color.

"You're finally awake." Opal smiled, making her way to Quill's side. "I'm coming with you!" She said cheerily, spinning in a circle. "Wherever you go."

"Yes." Quill nodded. "I understand." Quill turned her attention back to the blackness around them. "May we go to the surface?"

"YES. OF COURSE, YOU MAY. THIS IS WHAT WE HAVE BEEN WAITING FOR. YOU ARE READY. WE SHALL SPEAK EVERY THREE NIGHTS. DO YOU REMEMBER?"

"Yes, father." Quill answered. She remembered *everything.* **HE** cared about her more than anything and sacrificed everything just so they could be together. **HE** taught her about life outside of their world, and of the people who'd betrayed him and her mother. How the Faeries had killed her. Quill, **HE** had said, would be powerful and use everything at her disposal to accomplish their goal.

She knew that the those above the surface often hurt **HIM**. She could hear his cries and feel a tinge of pain herself when it happened. They were undeniably connected after all. Their connection was worth everything. So too, was their plan. Quill was more than resolved. She would do anything it took to free **HIM** from the suffering he endured and their curse. She would let no one get in her way.

Seven

Opal...

WHAT SHE KNEW.

While following Quill to the surface, Opal feeling ITs grasp, pulling her back. **IT**s voice echoed, dancing painfully inside her skull. **"DO NOT INTERFERE WITH HER WORK. YOU ARE MERELY TO GUIDE HER AND ACT WHEN SHE DEEMS NECESSARY. DO NOT TELL HER LIES." IT** threatened.

Lie to her? Opal thought, quick to put up a mental wall between them. Of the two of them, **IT** was most likely to do that. What reason would Opal ever have to lie? To use the same dirty tactics as this...thing? "I'd never." Opal replied through gritted teeth as she enduring the tightening of **IT**s grip, all too aware of the dark slither towards her throat. Was **IT** finally going to get rid of her too?

To both Opal's relief and dismay, **IT** pulled away from her and she wasted no time getting away. As quickly as she could, Opal raced after Quill moments before she broke the surface of the outside world. Immediately, white light enveloped them. Opal found herself completely overjoyed to feel anything other than that cold, desolate place. And as the light achingly gave way to hues of every color, she was less aware of what now sat far beneath them.

Opal couldn't believe her eyes as she rested on Quill's small shoulder, looking off at the blue sky. She was astonished at the beauty of the green blades of grass blowing in the wind around them and the smell of fresh air. They were alone. Finally, she could let her thoughts roam all she liked, now that they were away from **IT**. After all, **IT** knew she did not always believe what she'd heard and Opal had plenty of reason to doubt **IT**. Even more so now that the very things her mother had seen were there before her, close enough to touch.

Opal's mother was a Cursed Faerie. One that was incredibly strong, adaptable and resilient. So versatile, in fact, that she'd been the second in command of the Cursed Fae's Army. Although Opal didn't have a great understanding of what that sort of position meant for her own future, she did know that her mother's position was, at least in part, responsible for her death.

Opal also knew that her mother didn't regret being with her father—a Faerie born in a Fae World that often escaped her. He spent quite a bit of his time in FlareWing, the very place that they would eventually have to go. But Opal was the first of her kind. A Cursed Fae conceiving a child with a Light Faerie—how Fae are naturally born—was bound to be uncharted territory.

It was this taboo, and her mother's position collectively, that ended her life. This pained her. However, her parents had left her with more than just the power of light and dark. They'd left her with memories. They were tucked away inside her even now, half of both her parents' memories swam in calm waves through her mind every moment of every day. Even as she sat on Quill's shoulder watching her take steps through the grass. It seemed almost as if she'd plucked the very memories from her parents' brains in the womb and she'd never forgotten them, though it made it that much more painful to miss them.

But, not forgetting also meant that she never forgot the sound of their voices. She never forgot the times her mother played with her even though **IT** didn't agree to such behavior. Yet, not forgetting also meant that Opal couldn't forget the moment her mother said goodbye. She couldn't forget the way her mother stood there, accepting punishment for her betrayal—accepting death for her daughter's very existence—so that she could live.

Even if it meant that she would be stuck living there with **IT**, her mother had loved her enough to die for her. Regardless of **IT**s lies, that could not be taken from her. No amount of hate could erase that.

Her mother, **IT** had told her as it casted her aside, should have never been capable of breeding with a Light Faerie. Or refusing her orders. The only benefit had been that **IT** now had her: a Faerie not bound by the same regulations as other Fae. One that, like Quill, had the potential to change *everything.*

Opal was never sure if she was all of the things **IT** said, after all, **IT** was a liar and murdered her mother then tossed her aside as if she'd been worthless. As if she'd never risked her life for **IT**s own gain, even if the things she'd done had been against her own will. Still, Opal thought that maybe there was something else different about her. **IT** had never been able to tap into her, control her, or force her into submission like some other Fae. In fact, **IT** couldn't reach into her mind either, because she could force a wall between them. Some odd, white space in the front of her mind that pushed her thoughts to the back in some unorthodoxly undetectable way.

Which was why **IT** worked so hard to keep Opal from knowing about the conversations **IT** had with Quill. Since the day she didn't hold her tongue. After that horrible ordeal, Opal learned never to speak against **IT**, especially if she was ever going to make it to the surface with Quill at her side.

Now that Quill was awake, she'd never have to force herself to sleep endlessly surrounded by nothing. If things went well, perhaps Opal would never have to return to **IT**. She'd never have to sit in a silence so deep she could feel the echo in her bones. If things went well, perhaps **IT** wouldn't be the last thing she would ever see.

...

"Where will we go first?" Opal finally spoke, turning her attention to Quill. With a sigh, she watched her open her mouth to speak. Only, no sound would come from her lips. Instead, a loud growling caught her attention. Upon seeing Quill's eyes widen in surprise, Opal laughed. "I suppose your stomach answered for us. It's no surprise that you're hungry. I'd love to eat something myself."

"Hunger. I don't believe ***HE*** explained that very well." Quill frowned.

"Well, be sure to say that." Opal chuckled.

"I intend to." Quill said sternly.

Opal nodded, but it hadn't surprised her, really. ***IT*** had on occasion dragged food from the surface to feed her when she'd been at her limit and hunger pains woke her from her sleep. By the time the food reached her, however, it was never appetizing. As if by some horrible joke, she could hardly withstand the smell. Let alone actually swallow it. Every piece of fruit was soiled and soft. Every sip of water full of a thick, curdled texture that almost made her sick to her stomach.

Of course, complaining would have never done her any good. Possibly, neither would Quill's displeasure. After all, **IT** could tell her nothing in return. **IT** wouldn't be able to tell her about something **IT** didn't feel. Or could **IT** find a way to lie about that, too?

Eight

???...

PAIN.

It hurt—***everything hurt***. For only a moment the pain seemed to disperse giving way to clarity and the illusion of freedom. Thinking was no good as the pain only blindsided every thought until it no longer existed and remembering became a futile effort.

Forever, there'd been nothing but this. This and the feeling of something rushing. Something forcing itself through everywhere. Forcing itself through him. He knew he was male; he knew he bore limbs even though he couldn't feel them—but how did he know that? Who was he? What was he? Where was he?

There was something else too, right there in the back of his mind, eluding him. He willed himself to find it. To grab hold of that something, of whatever important thing he needed to remember more than anything. And just for a moment he knew.

He *knew* it! But...what did he know? He was male. Somehow, he knew that but how did he know? Was that the thing he knew? No. That couldn't be it. Something else was there. Something beyond the echoes of screams filling the space around him. Was there something he knew?

Everything hurt. Everything, everywhere...hurt. As if the very fabric of his existence was being slowly shredded apart and flung to separate ends of the galaxy. All he knew was the pain.

Nine

Grace...

WHY?

Grace sat on the floor of the bathroom stall and cried. She cried loud, ugly tears because she knew there was no one around to hear. Most of the school had gone on a field trip but she'd been excused from attending by her foster parents. Even though Grace wanted nothing more than to leave Snowville in favor of one of the next towns or *any* town. But in the end, it had been her fault.

MaryAnne and Duke had found out, curtesy of a neighbor, that she'd had company while they were away, and Grace never gave them a name. She'd never tell them about Phelia. They were furious. Even though they'd left Grace with no way to contact them. Even though she hadn't been allowed to use the phone. It was back to **That** room for her, of course, after her punishment. Still, Grace never expected them to keep her at school with no students around. She wasn't even allowed to stay home.

Maybe if it had been that alone, she would have dealt with it better. Being the only one in the classroom might even have been peaceful. But she never could catch a break. Not even from Elephant Spit's goons.

One of them—or all of them—decided to put super glue into her bag. Everything had to be thrown away. Even the walkie-talkie that Phelia had given her. Which was horrible enough on its own. Only, they hadn't stopped there. They'd super-glued her seat. Grace had to have her bottoms cut from the chair and she sat there in the classroom pants less. Again, she'd been taken to the lost and found. And again, it was empty.

Everything happening right as the entire class was leaving for the trip was a double-edged sword. Her parents never picked up the phone and almost every teacher went as chaperones. The only teacher left in the building seemed much more invested in the movie playing loudly on their cellphone than in her comfort, although she offered her two pillows from the reading corner to cover up with. It hadn't felt legal. She didn't offer her help. Instead, every so often the woman would sigh or look up from her phone in annoyance.

Grace couldn't completely blame her since she was the reason the woman couldn't go home early. So, she lied. She'd told her that they finally got in touch with her foster mom, and she'd wait in the office until she picked her up from school. She'd never seen someone pack up their things in such a hurry. She didn't ask a single question and she didn't look back before she left.

In the bathroom stall, sitting on pillows in her underwear, Grace wished she could call Phelia on the walkie-talkie again. If she could, she wouldn't tell a single lie. Even so, Grace wasn't sure what she would say to Phelia either. She wished she could forget when she came over to her house. She wished today had never happened. More than anything, Grace wished she had *pants*.

If she could simply disappear, she would have. Grace rubbed her crystal in her shirt pocket. At times like this she wished the crystal could make her invisible so she could at least get home. She knew she had to get out of there before the entire school returned from the field trip. Otherwise, she'd never be able to forget today no matter how hard she tried. Probably not for the rest of her life. Maybe the entire school would join in her torment. Grace had enough of Elephant Spit and his goonies. Enough to last her the rest of her life and more.

Not knowing what else to do, Grace wiped at her tears and forced herself to stand. She'd stopped fighting and the bullying wasn't stopping. Still, she was being good so things would get better, wouldn't they? If she never invited Phelia over things wouldn't have been awkward and she'd never have found **That** place. It was her own fault.

When everyone first started to make fun of her, she'd always gotten angry. She always acted out. Maybe, if she never said anything, never started fighting in the first place, things would have been different. She knew she couldn't do anything about the way she was before, but she could keep doing what she said, right? She could choose not to fight anyone. She could be nice and quiet.

She could stop telling the teacher who never believed her in the first place. Miss Pine told her she shouldn't have stolen the super glue from the cabinet. Even though she didn't do it. Even though she'd never known there was glue in the cabinet to begin with. Not that it mattered to Miss Pine—it *never* mattered to Miss Pine. It never mattered to *anyone.*

Grace took a deep breath and walked out of the stall; the pillows pressed to either side of her. She took a few steps forward and walked to the doorway. She smacked into something on her way, crashing to the floor. Looking up, Grace's heart sank. *Eustis?? Why isn't he on the school trip?!*

Suddenly aware of the scattered pillows and her dark pink underwear making an appearance, Grace shrieked. She rushed to the side of the doorway, peeking out. Her heart raced a marathon, and her stomach was in knots. *No, no, no! Of every person in the entire school, why Eustis??!* "Go away!" Grace yelled, feeling her tears threatening to fall against her will.

She watched in horror as he took a step her way, moving his arms erratically, his face flushed. "No! Don't come *in!* This is the girls!" Grace shouted, immediately bolting back into the stall. She watched nervously through the crack of the door, holding her breath as Eustis made his way closer. Grace could just make out his eyes as they shut and he covered his face with one hand.

She cried out in fear as he flung something over the stall and it dropped over her face, blocking her view. "S-Sorry! Don't tell!" Eustis whispered. As Grace pulled the dark fabric from her face, she could just make out his blonde hair disappearing out of view. She didn't dare move until she heard his quick steps fade down the hallway.

Looking down, Grace realized it was a jacket. A jacket that looked oddly similar to the one she'd worn the last time she was left in her underwear during school hours. Was this some kind of trick? She didn't understand why Eustis wasn't at the field trip or why he'd given her a jacket, but she cried in relief. She didn't hesitate to slip the jacket around her, zip up the front over her legs, and tie the arms in a tight knot on her waist.

All Grace knew was that she was glad to have the jacket, to be able to leave the building without those stupid pillows. She could get home before everyone returned to school. Even if it was a trick or she'd come to regret it later, she would deal with it then.

Ten

True...

WINDOW GLASS.

True sped around the corner, nearly dropping her bag. She could hear the thumping of footsteps rushing after her. She hadn't imagined that things would get this bad. She looked down at her feet and tried to ignore the throbbing of her ankle and fumbled up the stairs as her thermos fell behind her. Stopping, True watched the cylinder clack against the staircase. Just when she'd thought to retrieve it, she heard the girls drawing near. Now wasn't the time to worry about her tea. Even if it was her favorite.

"You dropped something, *Freak*!" One girl called out. True turned on her heels and continued on. "I guess that makes *three* things in our possession!" Someone called at her back, followed by a slew of laughter. Not knowing where else to go, True ducked into Mr. Van-Dayton's classroom.

"True?" Victor called curiously. She turned around, peeking outside of the door, just catching a glimpse of the girls entering the hallway before she shut it behind her. Turning around, she saw Zane and Victor sitting near her desk. True wondered why she was surprised to see them. It was lunch after all. They'd long ago made it a habit to eat in homeroom.

"Hello, Victor." True said with a nod. Somehow, she felt calmer being in a room with the two of them. Anything beat going back into the hall. And Victor was her friend, at least. "Hello, Zane." She greeted, doing her best to straighten.

"Are you gonna try out for track or something? Bolting in here like that. You nearly gave me a heart attack!" Zane sighed, laying a hand over his chest.

"No. I have no plans like that." True replied, slowly making her way to her seat. "I'm sorry for scaring you."

"Just ignore him." Victor yawned, striking Zane with his elbow. "He's being dramatic." True watched Zane shove Victor roughly in return, almost spilling his tray. Had the two of them made up then?

"Actually, I was hoping to talk to you. I gotta talk to Grace too I think, but I guess that will have to wait until we see her again." Zane said, scratching his cheek. "I mean, as long as that's alright with you. I don't want to bother you."

"Yes," True said quietly. "That's alright."

. . .

"I know I don't deserve your forgiveness. Either of you. Any of you really, for everything I've done. I was surprised when Victor was willing to listen to me about Bailey before, but I really *am* sorry. I still don't understand what was going on with me that day. It seemed like the conversation I had with Bailey just made stuff worse. I can't really tell you about that conversation yet though, because I have to ask Bailey first, but..." Zane said, shifting in his seat. "It was...*weird.* There was this voice in my head all of the time."

"A voice?" Victor asked, frowning.

"Yeah." Zane nodded. "A voice. Honestly, it freaked me out. Sorta this weirdly deep...almost **bottomless** sort."

"The voice was *scary*?" True asked, wanting to understand. This was the first she'd ever heard anyone mentioning voices in their head as if it were separate from their own thoughts. She wasn't sure Zane was saying that exactly, but that was the impression she had.

"Yeah. It would say all these horrible things. Like, that I would feel better if I knew what you looked like. I don't think it ever mattered to me before? Or that I should hurry and finish the fight with Victor before he could lie to my dad. Not something I'd ever thought about either. Or, at least, I don't think I ever had that kind of thought." Zane said, his brows creased.

"That doesn't sound a thing like you." Victor said defiantly.

True had tried not to recall that night. She'd tried her best to move on from it and focus on everything else that happened since then. Not because she wanted to pretend that it hadn't happened—that never helped in the past—but because that night had terrified her. The things she felt, and Zane too, had been ***unnatural***.

There was a heavy feeling in the air, so uncomfortable that she almost didn't want to go out. It was as if Zane had become a different person. She vaguely remembered his bright eyes fade. As if the light had been sucked out of them. They'd become so dark she couldn't tell that they'd ever been blue. True thought that even his voice had changed that night.

"Anyway, I didn't think I could ever do something like that. I... can't believe I attacked you." Zane continued, "I can hardly even remember it...what I did. I felt like I was just watching things happen, as odd as that may sound. I don't even know how you could stand to be anywhere near me, but I don't want things to be like that. For all of us to sit around with all that tension. I wanted to apologize properly at least.

"I'd totally understand if you don't want to see me ever again. I guess I kind of thought...that we were friends so I got so upset when it seemed like anyone was calling that into question. Even though I realized I don't really know anything about the people close to me, and that I had no idea if you ever saw me as a friend. I feel like I was taking everything for granted, even with Victor. I hated it. You know? I don't want that.

"And when we went to the cemetery...I don't know. I just didn't want anyone to get hurt. I didn't want that jerk to bother Victor. Or worse. Then, I felt normal again. Almost like nothing ever happened. I wish I could change everything, *honest*. But I know I can't so... If you don't want to see me, I'll do the best that I can. If you want me to lick the floor and risk a number of possible infections, or who knows, even the plague—I mean I have seen how often the janitor *skips* mopping the floors—I'll do that."

"Would you really lick the floor?" Victor asked through another yawn. True watched quietly as he pushed back onto the rear legs of the chair, slightly rocking with his right foot.

"Probably not if *you* told me to." Zane replied hesitantly.

"I thought this apology was for the ***both*** of us." Victor said, raising an eyebrow. "So, that's not the case? Were you just saying empty words?"

"Are you saying you seriously want me to lick it??" Zane asked in disbelief. Did the janitor skip mopping the floors *that* much? Not that putting any body part to the school floor sounded like a good idea in the first place.

"If you were going to be so worried about it then why'd you offer?" Victor chuckled. "I mean, I *was* joking but *now* I kind of want to see you do it."

"You jerk." Zane huffed, looking relieved.

True took a deep breath and quietly made her way to Zane's side. That night, something wasn't right. True understood that much. And while Zane told them about the voice in his head, she felt those unnatural feelings again. She couldn't help but recall what Twister had said. That it seemed like a shadow had been looming over them. That it had been almost as if The Darkness was ***there*** that night. She wasn't sure what to make of the voice. Whatever it was didn't sound good. But she was fairly certain of one thing, if nothing else.

True gently laid a hand on Zane's arm. "I don't know what happened that night, or about the voice you heard, but I don't think you are that kind of person either. If you apologize to Grace too, I think she'd forgive you."

"You think so?" Zane asked, looking uncertain. True nodded, her attention suddenly focused on the tremors in her hand. *Am I shaking?* True wondered in disbelief. *Am I still...**afraid** of Zane?*

"I do." True said, slowly pulling her hand away and tucking it away in her sleeve. Grace seemed like the type of person who could care about anyone, in True's opinion. She'd seemed very worried that night. "I already have a friend, but I'd like to start over with you..."

True wondered if she should worry about extending another olive branch. The thought of causing more trouble hadn't even occurred to her before she'd offered. Wasn't the first one enough? Was she being greedy? Needy, even? Was she so willing to do this because she felt like a hole in her heart filled when Victor agreed to be her friend? Would Zane's friendship fill another?

"I also think, we have to talk to Twister." True sighed.

"Talk to Twister? You mean go back to FlareWing?" Zane asked. "We don't even know how to get back there or anything. W-wait—you *already* have a friend...?"

"Yes, she does." Victor chuckled. "***Jealous?***"

"*Ohh. Of course.* I should have known it was *you*." Zane scoffed.

Victor elbowed him in the ribs. "See? You don't deserve it. Quick True, take it back and make him lick the floor before it's too late." True held in a chuckle as she watched the two of them flailing around in not-so-silent competition.

She wasn't sure what to do. Should she tell Zane that Twister had come to Snowville, again? She'd said so before and there still seemed to be a misunderstanding. Opting to stay silent, True sat down across from them, moving their lunch trays out of harm's way. Since she'd met Victor, Zane, Phelia and Grace, True thought that maybe she'd gotten a little closer to that window glass.

Eleven

Victor...

ALL-NIGHTERS.

Victor unlocked his front door and stepped inside. He could hear his mother shuffling around in the kitchen and registered the smell of something delicious tickling his nose, but he was too exhausted to be hungry. As he slowly made his way near, he watched his mother hum some melody from her head, stirring a bowl on the countertop. “Victor. How was school?” She smiled.

It's getting worse. He could hardly make sense of anything she said. "Luckily, he knew his mother. School was fine.” Victor groaned. “I'm going up.” He attempted to offer his mother a small smile.

“Well, dinner will be ready in a bit, okay? Are you feeling alright? You're looking more sluggish than usual.”

“Mm-hm. Fine.”

Victor climbed the stairs and dropped onto his bed. He wasn't sure what was more exhausting: pretending things were normal or getting no sleep. It seemed like he'd been on a downward spiral since they'd made it back to Snowville after their visit to the cemetery. If he thought he wasn't getting any sleep before, he was getting even less now. If he was completely honest, however, he knew his nights had quickly become a nightmare since the thoughts of his father reoccurred, which was well before that. Only, it hadn't been *this* bad.

It was almost as if his brain wouldn't shut off. He couldn't stop reliving horrible moments in his life. He couldn't stop worrying about the things that happened in Mirror, whatever happened to True when they went through that door in FlareWing—a subject that he still hadn't been able to bring up to her—what they'd seen in The Land of the Dead, and now, this voice making a home in Zane's head. It was something about it that unsettled him to his core.

What Zane described sounded nothing like his best friend. Zane was not some maniac that liked the thought of starting trouble. So why would he have thought things like starting fights? Least of all on the way to his mother's grave? What did any of that have to do with True and her mask? What could have started something like that in one of the most protective people he knew? Had he been cured of his affliction?

He'd also seemed sad since finding out about Bailey. Was her condition worsening? Did it have anything to do with Zane? He didn't want to cast doubt in his best friend's direction, but he'd mentioned that time escaped him many times before their blows in the snow, right? Would any of them have known if he'd seen Bailey and something terrible had happened? *No.* He thought defiantly. *How would he have done that? You're running yourself into walls now. This is Zane you're talking about.*

Still, Victor couldn't forget that moment, hearing voices over the wind in front of True's door. He couldn't forget the terrifying growl akin to a wild animal he'd heard. Nor that raspy, deep voice that seemed to fill the space around them as he made his way towards Zane and True that night. If that was anything like the voice Zane had been hearing in his head, then Victor understood why he would be terrified.

He hated this. Being swarmed by unwelcomed waves of questions and worry. He hated the uncertainty. And right now, there was nothing more uncertain than where the crystals would take them. What was all of this about? Why were they traveling in the first place? Was using the crystals a good idea? Were they *malicious*? After all, every time they found themselves whisked away to some unknown place they were met with trouble of unimaginable proportions.

Victor was so lost in thought that he barely noticed that the night had faded away to a soft daylight casting shadows across the room. He didn't recall his mother ever entering the room with a plate, and yet, there it sat on his nightstand. Cold and untouched.

Stunned, Victor turned his head to look towards his window. He listened to the bird songs and the wind rustling through the leaves before it truly hit him; he'd done it **again**. He hadn't been sleeping much at all lately, but he thought that he'd managed to stop his ridiculous all-nighters. Clearly, he was wrong.

Twelve

Phelia...

TOWER OF GLASS.

"You want to go see Grace?" Phelia asked Zane curiously. *This is a first. Just what brought this on?*

"Well, I figure that I can go to the hospital to see Bailey afterwards. Anyway, we know where Grace lives, right? I want to apologize to her properly too." Zane answered with a frown. "You think she wouldn't want me showing up on her doorstep?"

"Well, that's not it..." Phelia said thoughtfully. Although, she wasn't entirely sure Grace would be happy to see her coming around her house after what happened the last time either. "She hasn't answered on the walkie in days. I can't phone her either so...I'm just not sure we should simply show up *unannounced*."

"I don't see why not. I mean, the two of you are friends, right?" Zane asked. Phelia very much considered Grace to be her friend, but that didn't change the fact that things had been odd between them since her visit. It felt wrong to keep it from her family, but she couldn't bring herself to even mouth the words *crawl space*. And with Grace not even answering the walkie-talkie, she couldn't ask if she'd done something to offend her. Even more, Phelia felt anxious just thinking about going inside Grace's house again.

Sometimes, the best way to get answers is to charge through an uncertain situation, isn't it? Or is it that you're afraid going back there will be the end of your friendship? What? Was that Fayth's voice inside her head...? So before, when they'd met in that room and he'd told her he wasn't a cat-beast, hadn't been a fluke? *You can hear my thoughts?* Phelia directed at Fayth. She knew she'd left him upstairs under her bed. Did this distance from one floor to the next matter?

Our very souls are connected, you and I. You have thoughts separate from my own as I do you, but now that we are together again, we can communicate like this. Over time you may learn to keep thoughts from me, but we've never done so. In any case, if you have so many questions for this Grace, why not simply ask her? What in the world was he talking about now? Didn't he say before that they were born the same day? Why was he mentioning the two of them conversing in past and present tense? *I have many more questions for you than I do Grace.* Phelia thought.

I'm aware.

Phelia sighed. "I suppose we can give it a try, Zane." She answered, trying to focus on the conversation at hand rather than the fact that Fayth could not only communicate via her mind, but that he knew her every thought as well. Should she be worried? Could her mysterious relationship with Fayth get any stranger?

Zane nodded, mentioning that they should go after breakfast. Phelia politely agreed, but she still couldn't shake her nerves. Normally, she could do exactly what Fayth mentioned and 'charge through the uncertainty,' but this felt different. Everything about the situation with Grace felt fragile, like an intricate tower of glass. Almost as if one wrong touch would send shards plummeting down around them and no one would leave unscathed.

. . .

As Phelia and Zane helped their father clear the table, a knock on the door drew their attention. "I'll get it." Phelia called, making her way to the door. Upon opening it, she was surprised to see Grace.

"Grace! Zane and I were just talking about you." Phelia smiled, opening the door wider to let her inside. "We just finished breakfast."

"All good stuff, I hope." Grace said with a small smile.

"We tried to think of a bunch of bad stuff but nothing came to mind." Zane chimed in as Phelia shut the door. "You must be psychic or something."

"Hi Zane." Grace said with a small wave. "Psychic?"

"Yeah. We were thinking about stopping by your place. Actually, we were just about to leave here in a few minutes." Zane said, as he watched their father make his way to his chair. Phelia took note of Grace's eyes widening and the color draining from her face.

"Grace. It's nice to see you." Dr. Brand chimed in with a bright smile. Their father really had been in a good mood lately. He'd even spent his first days off sleeping in. It was nice to see him in such high spirits.

"Hello, Dr. Brand. I'm sorry for coming over unannounced." Grace said, offering a small smile in their father's direction. "I'll just be a minute."

"Stay as long as you'd like, Grace. You're always welcome, I believe I already told you so." Phelia watched her father as he turned around, clicked the button on the remote and flipped through the channels.

"You said you were coming over to my house? Y-you can't do that." Grace stuttered, directing her attention back at them. Had she been right? Phelia wondered. Did Grace not want her to come over ever again?

"Zane...he wanted to apologize to you so we..." Phelia's voice trailed off. It felt awkward just trying to explain their intentions.

"Apologize?" Grace asked quietly, raising a brow at Zane.

"Let's go outside." Phelia suggested. "Father, we'll be just outside if you need us." Phelia called over her shoulder. She watched him raise the tv remote in response.

Outside, Zane shut the door behind them softly and turned to face Grace. "I wanted to see you." Zane said, clearing his throat. "To apologize properly for everything that happened at True's place." Zane shifted on his feet, scratching his cheek. So, he'd really been worried about her being mad at him after all? Not that Phelia could blame him. She was in the same predicament, all things considered.

"Hmm? What do you mean? Didn't you already do that?" Grace asked, looking confused. "I'm pretty sure you apologized."

"What?" Zane asked, looking more uncertain than Grace. "I mean, I started to say something. When we were in the cemetery—in The After Land, but—"

"Yeah. I remember. How could I forget? You had *horrible* timing!" Grace shook her head disapprovingly. "But you meant it, right? That you were sorry?"

"Yeah. Of course. I meant it, but I didn't really even get to explain." Zane said, looking over to Phelia as if she could answer some unvoiced question his eyes were attempting to ask. She couldn't help him even if she wanted to. She had no clue about any conversation she and Zane had in The After Land. Perhaps it was before all of them found each other and were led off by Jewel? If memory served, they'd been walking together when they met up.

"Then...it's okay. Things were bad that night, and honestly...I was *terrified*. I'm even a little worried that something like that could happen again, but I don't think you wanted to hurt anyone. I was scared for everyone. For True, for Victor...for you." Grace looked at Phelia with a nod. "I talked to Phelia about it a little. The entire thing seemed wrong, not just what you did."

Zane's eyes met Phelia's, and she flashed him a reassuring smile. "She did come over. She said that it didn't seem like the two of you would fight like that—it didn't seem like you. That it was *different*." Zane breathed a sigh of relief and thanked them both.

"If it's alright with you, I was hoping to ask if you wanted to be friends. I kind of made the mistake of getting invested in other people without ever asking first." Zane smiled softly, holding out a hand. Phelia couldn't help but smile herself as Grace placed her hand in his.

"I was kind of hoping to add True to the list first, but I suppose you'll do." Grace laughed.

"You too? Man. I tried that. I gotta start from scratch. Though she's technically already made her first friend." Zane sighed. What were they talking about now? Start from scratch with True? Well, at least it seemed like they had one less thing to worry about.

"Can you blame her? I sure don't." Grace huffed. "Wait! She's got her first friend?? Aww beans." She frowned, kicking her foot lightly across the porch wood. "There goes my plan."

"Yep. Victor beat us to it." Zane laughed.

Phelia took a deep breath, not wanting to miss her opportunity. "Sorry to interrupt, but I had been trying to contact you before and there was no answer...? I thought perhaps you were upset with me. By chance, is that why we can't come to your house?" Phelia asked, hardly able to look Grace in the eyes.

"W-what? Wait...**no**! Not at all." Grace stammered quickly. "Actually, I umm...got grounded again. Yeah. MaryAnne and Duke wouldn't let me have company even if you *did* come over...but..." Grace's voice trailed off before she slapped both of her hands onto either side of her face. "Sorry. It's my fault. I took the walkie-talkie to school, and it ended up getting ruined. My teacher threw it in the trash so I couldn't answer you. I'm very sorry for ruining the gift! I was super careless..."

Grounded? *Again*? What was that look on her face a moment ago? Her teacher tossed out the walkie-talkie...? Phelia didn't know whether she should be worried or relieved. Why did it seem that every time she managed to see Grace, she was in trouble? Else, she was nowhere to be found? How did the walkie-talkie get broken at school? Phelia didn't know why, but she felt Grace was the type to take care of her things. Was she making too much of it?

You surprise me. Do you always doubt your instincts like this? Fayth's voice questioned from somewhere in her mind.

"That's a relief." Phelia sighed, trying not to pay any mind to the cat. "I'm glad. It's unfortunate that you can't use the walkie-talkie anymore but it's alright. It was a bit old as is. Perhaps father will help us get another one."

"You're...not *mad* at me?" Grace asked, her voice heavy with surprise. Phelia frowned. Was there some reason to be angry?

"Why would I be?" Phelia nodded. "It's fine, really. Albeit, an unfortunate happenstance."

"Why don't you just call Grace on the home phone?" Zane suggested with a shrug. Phelia, unsure of what to say, looked over to Grace quietly. This was exactly the type of strange thing she'd questioned during her visit. She had no clue why, but she knew she couldn't.

"I'm not allowed to use the phone." Grace frowned, shrugging her shoulders. "MaryAnne and Duke don't like it. House rules."

"Really? That's weird." Zane frowned.

"Why don't we go inside? You never did say if you wanted the leftovers from breakfast." Phelia suggested, attempting to change the subject. *I'd thought it odd too, honestly.* Phelia thought. *There were a lot of strange things about that day at Grace's house. Still, she was so upset back then. I'd rather avoid it for now. Maybe after this weird spell settles, I can try bringing it up to her again.*

"I'd love to, actually. I'm starving!" Grace exclaimed, heading for the door before them.

As they made their way inside, Phelia froze, her eyes fixed on their father. "Look at this cute little guy." Dr. Brand smiled. ***Fayth!*** Phelia called in her mind, nearly rendered speechless. *I told you to stay in my room!* Phelia chided.

"Aww! Such a cute kitty!" Grace shouted, rushing over to pet him.

"Dad, Grace, don't *touch* it! It's probably a stray. You could get sick." Zane warned. "You don't know where that thing's been."

"I think he might've gotten in through the office." Dr. Brand chuckled. "He looks clean for a stray. Even though he doesn't have a collar. Maybe he's lost it."

"What a *horrible* thing to say. I'm perfectly clean."

"W-what?" Zane stammered.

Grace's mouth dropped. "Did that kitty just...**talk**??"

Thirteen

Zane...

PLANTS GALORE.

"Oh Grace," Phelia laughed suddenly. "How silly of you. I sound *nothing* like a kitty!" Zane shifted his gaze toward his sister, attempting to mask his apprehension. "I was just saying that it was a horrible thing to say, Zane. *He's* perfectly clean." Phelia said, clearing her throat. What was Phelia talking about? He'd heard his little sister speak all her life. There's **no way** that voice came from her.

"*Geez*, Phelia!" Grace laughed, with a hand on her chest. "Geeeeez. What a surprise! Don't mess with people like that!"

"Sorry, Grace. I suppose it was bad timing." Phelia smiled awkwardly, meeting Zane's gaze from across the room. Was Grace falling for it? Or was he simply losing his mind? Either way, Zane wasn't sure he wanted to know. He'd had it with strange, unexpected voices.

"I haven't seen many pets in Snowville since we moved here. It's possible someone may be looking for him." Their father smiled, lightly rubbing the cat's ears as it laid on his lap and began to purr. Enjoying the attention.

"Dad, didn't I tell you not to touch it?" Zane frowned.

"Oh, come now, Zane. Don't be a spoilsport. He's adorable. You used to want a pet when you were young." His father chuckled. "Of course, if he's got a home, I suppose we'll just have to say goodbye to the little guy."

"Aww. I hope you guys get to keep him. He looks so young. Maybe he doesn't have a family." Grace chimed in, smiling from ear-to-ear. Phelia, on the other hand looked particularly displeased.

"Kids say stuff like that all the time. I'm older and wiser now." Zane huffed, "Besides, it doesn't seem like Phelia even wants to keep him. Isn't that right?"

"No." Phelia said, crossing her arms. "I want to keep him around. He's not getting away *that* easily." What? From the look on her face, no one would be able to tell. Since when did Phelia want a cat?

What's going on around here anyway? Zane thought to himself, bewildered. *Does this have something to do with dad taking time off? Why's everyone so into this cat? And why's Phelia being so aggressive about it??*

. . .

At the hospital, Zane stopped by the gift shop. Seeing nothing of interest, he decided to leave and made his way to Bailey's room. Inside, he recognized Charlie, Grandma Trinity, and Belle's voices. To his surprise, they were surrounded by too many flowers to count. So many that Zane could hardly see them sitting in their chairs. "*Whoa.* What happened here? Did a *magical florist* puke all over the room or something?" Zane laughed.

"Zane," Charlie called, shifting in his seat, parting a bundle of flowers and peering through. "It's been a long while. You've grown."

Zane nodded, offering a smile in his direction. "Nice to see you again, Charlie. Well, *sorta*..? Honestly, it's hard to see in this mess."

"I oughta *kill* those little punks!" Belle hissed from somewhere to Zane's right.

"Don't go on throwin' a fit, Belle. These here are Bailey's gifts." Grandma Trinity spoke quietly.

Zane was glad he hadn't decided to buy flowers from the gift shop on his way up. Curious, Zane shifted around the room to look at the flower tabs. Once he saw one from Sydney, his interest faded. From Bailey's reaction at the café that day, it didn't seem like she and Sydney were very close. Which was a relief, all things considered. Even so, Sydney sent flowers. Zane didn't recall there being an announcement about Bailey's hospitalization at school, but he supposed he could have missed it.

"You say that but look at this room, look how **huge** these things are! It's *ridiculous*!" Belle shouted, rising in anger, causing the flowers around her to rock noisily in their vases.

"Not to worry. I'm gonna to start linin' them up in the hall now and get them outta here, Belle." Charlie attempted to reassure, her in an accent much lighter than his mother's and made his way to his feet. He stood and bent down to pick up an armful of flowers.

"As if we even have anywhere for all of this to go." Belle sighed, frustrated. "Do whatever you want, Charlie, but I want nothing to do with them. And you're *crazy* for volunteering to mess with them in the first place. You didn't come all these days away to deal with plants." As she zig-zagged through the flowers towards the door, she grabbed hold of Zane's arm. "I'm going for a walk and I'm taking him with me!"

"Wai—what?" Zane stuttered as he was pulled roughly behind her and out of the door.

"Just hush up and *walk*." Belle ordered. He trailed behind her in an awkward silence, almost certain that he hadn't heard her say more than a few words since they'd met. He began to wonder if he preferred her quiet demeanor in favor of this brazen, fuming one. Zane didn't know why but this woman frightened him. It wasn't as if *he* left a nightmare of plants in the hospital room. Why was he getting bossed around? Why had she forced him along?

"Where are we going?" Zane asked finally, worried that it would send Belle into a fit. He thought she might punch him.

Surprisingly, she took a deep breath and answered through a sigh. "I don't know. I saw a balcony down the hall, so I figured over there." She said, leading the way. Sure enough, there really was a door that led to a balcony. One overlooking a small hospital garden. It was then, as he looked down at the icy flowers, that Zane realized he'd witnessed this view once before.

It was some time ago, now. The morning after his mother's accident, in fact. The day the hospital staff pronounced her dead and changed his family's life forever. It was here that his father first began to break. If Zane thought about the memory hard enough, if he lost himself in that terrible moment, he was sure he could make out the sound of his father's soul cracking.

"I don't even understand how they were able to fill up the room like that!" Belle's voice called out, forcing his attention back on the present. "I mean, shouldn't they have been more worried about Mama Trinity and my sister's safety rather than a bunch of stupid flowers? A limitation policy? *Something!*" Belle hissed, stomping a foot as she spoke.

"Well, if I had to guess, I'd say that had something to do with Sydney. She's a girl—" Zane began, cut off before he could finish.

"That girl." Belle interrupted, rolling her eyes. "I *know* who she is. Bailey can't stand her. I've only met her a handful of times and even I hate her. She's nothing but trouble."

So, it was true after all? Zane wished he'd been more himself on their date. He should have been able to tell. No. Maybe he could have but he'd ignored it in favor of anger. He wasn't sure there would have been anything Bailey could have said or done that wouldn't have set him off that day.

It was almost as if he'd been searching for something to get upset about. As if he'd been looking for any excuse to leave her there in that café, confused and questioning. There was no excuse for his behavior. He wished he'd been able to let things go. He wished he could do it over, that he had looked past his anger. Looking back on it now, he could recognize how surprised she'd been by his insinuations.

"Well, she isn't always the most likable person..." Zane shrugged, trying to be polite. Belle shot him a silent, disapproving look in response. "Alright, alright. Maybe she gets on my nerves a lot nowadays, but talking about her behind her back isn't really a nice thing to do anyhow, right? I wouldn't like it, at least."

"Oh, *please*." Belle scoffed. "As if she doesn't talk about anyone and *everyone* behind their backs. I doubt anyone is excluded from that. *Probably not even the girl's parents.* Anyway, you're probably right. I didn't even bother to look at those stupid flower tags, but if I'd found any from her, I'd have chucked every last one of them."

"You must *really* hate flowers or something." Zane said, focusing his attention on a couple squirrels racing across the grass and leaping into a nearby tree. If he recalled correctly, Bailey once mentioned that her favorite animal was a squirrel. A Eurasian Red Squirrel, specifically. He'd thought it an interesting choice for a favorite animal. *I never did ask her why.* Zane thought. *When she wakes up, maybe I should ask her about it.*

"I don't hate flowers. No girl hates them-unless she's allergic or something. Some might think it's cliché, but to *hate* them? Very unlikely." Belle remarked, opening a small silver cigarette case and sliding one between her lips. "You mind if I light it?"

Zane shook his head and listened to the *click* of her finger striking the wheel. "I like flowers as much as the next girl. I just can't stand **this**. Yeah? This whole thing. Bailey laying in there like that and we can't help her. We can't do anything at all. Aside from showing up and looking pitiful, I guess.

"That drives me too. The waiting. I think we're all going crazy just waiting for her to move a toe or flutter an eyelash. Stupid stuff like that. I don't know if someone in a coma can hear a word you say. I have no clue—I never even gave it any serious thought before now and, I guess, who wouldn't in the current state of things? I thought it couldn't get any worse.

"Then these random people sent all those flowers. But it's not *really* the flowers, yeah? It's that they sent a whole store full in here and they're ***huge*** for no reason. As if they picked all those massive plants just so they could mock us—mock *her*."

As she spoke, she blew a white swirl of smoke towards the sky, her left hand clutched tightly around her black lighter. Zane took note of the pink and white skull decorating the front. "Not a single one of those people called or made an appearance." She smirked. "Although, if that Sydney girl ever showed her face at that door, I'd probably get arrested. Charlie's so overprotective he wouldn't even stop me if he knew what she'd done."

Zane wondered what she meant but couldn't bring himself to ask. Instead, he continued listening, watching Belle's expression soften. "Mama Trinity would definitely give us both an earful." Belle chuckled. "I don't know. I feel like Bailey would feel a bit better though. Maybe she'd get up and fill the room with that laugh of hers. *God*, I miss that girl's laugh already."

"It definitely has a way of leaving a mark on you." Zane nodded. Thinking back on it, it was strange. The fact that it was even possible to take something as glorious as a laugh for granted seemed ridiculous. Yet, he'd done that too.

He recalled so easily how carefree she was since the day they met. How Bailey could laugh the entire day away. Just watching her passed the time. When they'd been in class, when they worked on projects together, when she came over for his birthday. Even on their date, her laughter had a way of filling the air. He knew it wasn't that long ago, but it felt like it had been forever since he heard it.

For a moment, the two of them stood there just watching the sun dim in the sky, slowly giving way to sunset. It was cold. Even in her coat, Zane could make out Belle's shivering. Still, her face didn't express any qualms about it. "Those stupid punks." Belle said, breaking their silence with a shake of her head. "Who sends those kinds of plants to a hospital room—sends those *giant* things to the ***living?*** My sister is in there and she's still breathing. It hasn't been that long—I think just weeks, *right?* She's not dead!"

Before Zane could say anything in response, focused on the tears brimming her eyes, a chime sounded from the other side of the door. "Code Blue. Room 402. Code Blue. Room 402." A voice called over the intercom. Wasn't that...***Bailey's room??***

Without so much as a word, Belle's cigarette dropped clumsily to the floor. For a single moment time seemed to slow down as a sense of dread made a home of his stomach and panic coursed messily through his veins. He watched the slow wisps of cigarette smoke dance in the air as Belle bolted through the door and back into the hospital. Behind her, Zane caught a glimpse of a doctor and other staff disappearing into Bailey's room as Charlie carefully led Grandma Trinity to a seat in the hall.

"Charlie!" Belle cried through a breathless croak. Zane took note of the flowers neatly lined up along the wall. "What's going on??"

With a worried look, Charlie shook his head. "I don't know. The machine...and then all them doctors. They were goin' so quick and we had to leave the room. All they said was that she stopped breathin'. They're doin' CPR."

"*What?*" Zane asked in disbelief. There's no way. Did Bailey...***die?***

Fourteen

Eustis...

SECOND CHANCES.

Eustis decided that was that. He was going to do better now. *I can do it*, he reassured himself. *After everything, I owe it to Grace to be a good person.* Even more than that, Eustis wanted Grace to view him different than in the past. As someone worthy to be around. He didn't want to pretend anymore. He hadn't been able to get it out of his mind, what the boys had done to her. It was too much. Just one thing of a very long list that Eustis wanted nothing more than to end.

That day, after he embarrassed himself by going into the girls' bathroom to give her his jacket, Eustis followed her, but he didn't have the courage to speak. He couldn't blame her for being terrified of him for more than one reason—and going into the girls' bathroom was bound to give the opposite impression than what he was trying to leave her with—but it had been the only way he could help. It was his fault that she was treated that way in the first place.

Eustis had heard that Grace never turned in her permission slip and couldn't imagine how lonely it could be to be stuck in school while everyone else was having fun. He couldn't imagine how much more it would hurt when everyone talked about the trip for days on end and she never even got to enjoy it. He considered the possibility less likely if he stayed. Besides, he hoped it would also be an opportunity to talk to her, to apologize to her for everything. He didn't manage it that day, but today would be different.

As Eustis strode along, yards behind her, he was reminded that he'd tried to follow her a few times and it always ended in failure. Like the day Grace fought Randal and Morris. That day, Eustis thought that if he decided to leave and go home, the others would follow. Only, that hadn't been the case. The next day, he worried that Grace had been rendered blind. Just thinking about how the boys had laughed and boasted to him that they threw rocks at her made Eustis sick to his stomach. He'd never hurt a girl, much less Grace.

He didn't say it at the time, but Eustis had thought they deserved more than bruises and a broken pair of glasses. Since then, it was almost like they had a personal vendetta against Grace. One that was never satisfied. Even after something as cruel as snipping her skirt in class. That glue hadn't just been cruel either, it had been *dangerous*. What if it had ripped her skin? What if her parents had to shave off all of her red-brown curls? Eustis couldn't imagine Grace without them. He didn't even want to try.

He ruffled his hair in frustration at the thought. Two incidents of danger were more than enough. It had gotten to the point that Eustis almost wished Grace was her usual self. Not the person that stood in silence with a painful look on her face as her bag was unzipped and all its contents thrown in the bin only to be drowned in spoiled milk. Not the person who didn't complain when her homework was ripped to shreds. Or the person who turned her back to cry after being pushed in the dirt.

These days, Eustis almost wished he'd never been born. If only he'd stood up for her at the start of it, Eustis often thought. If only he'd told the truth that day in front of the tree when she left him with a bloody nose and *every day* since then. Wouldn't things be different? When had he gotten so used to doing everything everyone else wanted of him to the point that he lost sight of what mattered? *Kennet would be disappointed in me. If he knew everything, maybe he'd hate me. Maybe he'd never speak to me again, and I'd fully deserve it.* Eustis thought sadly.

When Eustis pulled himself from his thoughts, he realized that he'd followed Grace the entire distance to her home. He remembered going there once, when his parents stopped by briefly to pick up some pie or other, and he remembered well what was said of them. How his mother said that the only entertainment worthy of attention in their home had been how eager they were to please. That, that family would make fools of themselves just to be in the same circles, which they often tested for their own amusement.

Most conversations were similar when it came to his parents, but Eustis had pitied the couple. He opted not to so much as step outside of the car, simply turned off at the thought that his parents would do or say something just to drive their point home. Now, he was there again, with an entirely different situation to face. He'd planned to speak to Grace a long while ago, but now what? Nervous, Eustis hid behind a nearby tree and watched Grace enter the white fence. Even from the distance he could see her unhappy expression.

It only took a moment for her to disappear inside, but she seemed to leave almost as quickly. A loud bang caused the front door to rattle and a variety of unintelligible clamors could be heard between shrill shouting. What was going on?

Before Eustis thought to make his way to the door, a light shuffle came from inside the house as the door swung open and Grace fumbled down the steps. Taking note of the panic on her face as she shot passed him, Eustis's heart thumped away in his chest as if in a bout of its own panic. As he followed her, he could hear the sound of something shattering against the concrete behind them.

Without looking back, Eustis raced behind Grace, hearing a woman's voice shouting towards their direction. "To the ***room*** with you the moment you get back!" As they rounded a corner, he could just make out the sound of a door slamming shut. Eustis wasn't sure how long he followed at Grace's back before he was led to a dead-end with no one in sight. Where did she go? Did he lose her?

Hunched forward and attempting to catch his breath, he groaned, frustrated. "Why is that girl so fast anyhow?" Eustis complained. "If she ran like this all the time no one could even catch up to bully her!" Suddenly hearing Grace's voice at his back, Eustis spun around to look in that direction. "What are you, a *ninja*? If you run like that you could be a track star." Eustis sighed.

"And if anyone sees you running like *that*, you're bound to get bullied next." Grace retorted, displeased. "And you're ignoring the question!"

"Fair enough. My endurance is terrible, I admit, but I've never even thought to chase anyone in my life." He said, truthfully. "I didn't quite catch your question between trying not to pass out from lack of oxygen."

"As *if* anyone would pass out from a little running." Grace said, rolling her eyes. It was then, as Eustis met her gaze that he saw the thick streak of blood sliding down her cheek. "I asked why you were following me." She frowned.

"I didn't come to hurt you or anything." Eustis said, lifting his hands slightly in the air as he spoke. "And there's no one with me. I promise."

"As if I need your promises. If this is about your jacket, I don't have it." Grace said quickly. "I left it back at home."

"I didn't come about the jacket. Although, you should have worn it. It's cold out here." He tried to reassure her. "It's freezing."

"Well, I'm not cold." Grace shrugged. Eustis tried to hide his disbelief. He could see her from there and she was already shivering.

"I came here because I need to talk to you." Eustis said, taking a step towards her. Grace took a step back, untrusting. "I just want to talk. Maybe we can take care of that cut on your cheek? I promise. If I do something you don't like you can scream or lie. Just like we did to you. I'll admit to almost anything as long as it isn't murder or something."

Grace raised an eyebrow. "Did you just say...like you did to me? What's *wrong* with you?" Grace frowned. "Did you catch a cold or something?"

"I did say that, but I'm not sick." Eustis said, shaking his head, still showing her his hands as he lowered them to his sides. "It's freezing out. Can we just go somewhere close and sit, please?"

Grace's mouth dropped and she quickly looked around as if to find something. "Did you just say please? To *me?*"

"What are you doing?" Eustis frowned.

"Looking for cameras. **Duh**." Grace answered quickly.

"There aren't any cameras. I didn't bring anyone with me, Grace." He sighed.

For the next few minutes, they simply stared at one another, encased in the winter air. When Grace made no effort to move or respond to him, Eustis decided he'd leave. "Fine then! Forget it. Just stand here forever and freeze to death. See if I care! You'll be the one getting sick out here!" He shouted as he stomped past her.

He willed himself to give up. Didn't this at least prove that they were destined to be on opposing sides because of his past mistakes? He couldn't blame Grace for not believing him nor not giving him an answer. Maybe, if the situation was reversed, he wouldn't answer either. Maybe, it was just too late. As much as he didn't want to believe it. He'd dug his way into this mess.

Still, didn't she want to get out of the cold? What about that cut on her face? Did she need stitches? Could he just leave her there? Frustrated with himself and a little with Grace's stubbornness, Eustis turned around and walked back toward the dead end. As he made his way closer, he could see Grace still standing there in the same position as when he left. Was she really just going to stand there forever?

Without giving himself time to think, Eustis grabbed hold of Grace's hand which felt terribly cold in comparison to his own. "You can hate me for it later, but we have to get out of this cold." He tried to explain. When she said nothing, Eustis tried to think of what to do. He didn't really know anything about that area of town. Realizing in that moment that of course he had another option, Eustis took out his cell phone and called Kennet. Why hadn't he thought of that before?

As always, Kennet, the Schmidt family's youngest driver, picked up on the second ring. Eustis wasted no time asking to be picked up as quickly as possible and Kennet wasted even less to head his way, even with Eustis' bad directions. Kennet, as per usual, seemed confident. Eustis liked that about him.

Sometimes, he wished it was possible to borrow such feelings so he could put them to use in his own life. Contrary to what people assumed when it came to him, Eustis didn't feel very confident. Even though he shared his parents' name and wealth, he hadn't seemed to inherit their pride or their unwavering sense of self-worth.

. . .

It wasn't long before Eustis saw the dark car in the distance. A few minutes later, he ushered Grace into the car and closed the door behind them. Without a word exchanged between them, Kennet looked towards Eustis and Grace in the back seat, turned up the heat, and lightly tossed a blanket to the back. There were many secrets sitting between them, a lifetime of them as far as Eustis was concerned. *Now*, Eustis thought, *Grace will simply have to be one of them. Although Grace would be a dangerous secret to keep, wouldn't she? Can I really ask Kennet to keep this from mother and father?*

After all, his parents often referred to her and her foster parents in the worst of ways. When Eustis brought her up in the past, the entire house was tense. All the staff knew this. This secret weighed more than most of those of the past combined, but Kennet was one of the only among the staff that he trusted.

More than that, Kennet may have been the only true friend he had in all of Snowville. He didn't know why the situation with Grace would have made him question the bounds of their trust. If it weren't for Kennet, Eustis wouldn't even survive living with his parents.

"Kennet, may I have a wipe? Also, it is probably best that you tell mother and father you're taking me out of the city for the moment." Eustis instructed. He took the wipe and passed it to Grace for her cheek. She was shaking less now, but her eyes met his, wide and frightened. Did he do something wrong?

"What do you mean, out of the city?" She muttered.

"Well, I'm not kidnapping you, if that's what you mean." Eustis replied.

He didn't want to tell her that he didn't want to risk getting caught with her in Snowville before he could speak with her and taking her home was out of the question. From the looks of things at her place, she was in trouble there too, even if Eustis didn't understand why that was. Maybe the boys were responsible for some other surprise and her parents had been informed? Or maybe it was something else. Trying not to put too much thought into it, Eustis searched for a different excuse.

"Well, Kennet has a first aid, so we'll check your cheek and I'm hungry. I'd like something to eat from outside the city. What time is your curfew?" Eustis asked, hoping to figure out how long he had before they had to bring her back. In his case, Eustis was allowed to be gone all night with Kennet if he wanted and even longer if they had his parents' permission for a trip, but he knew that wasn't a privilege most people could enjoy.

Grace shrugged and Eustis shifted slightly, trying to bury the questions in his head. He wanted to ask if she hated him, if she blamed him for all her problems at school. He wanted to know how she dealt with everything. Did she like her foster parents? What happened in her house? Instead, he focused on his relief. She had stopped shaking and asked a different question. "Does it hurt?" He asked, motioning to her cheek.

"It stings a little," Grace shrugged, "but it was just glass."

"*Glass*? What do you mean?" Eustis asked quickly, leaning forward, almost ready to remove the wipe in search of any remnants. In response, Grace shrunk into the door, as far away from him as she could. He realized he might have frightened her.

"It was just a plate, is all. A piece cut me. It's no big deal." Grace frowned.

It was in that moment, as Eustis was about to chide himself for overreacting that he made out dark bruises and cuts on her inner arm. "Did a broken plate make those marks too?" Eustis asked, displeased. He watched as Grace shifted her eyes and sat up straight against her seat.

She silently placed a hand over the bruises and cleared her throat. "I'm clumsy sometimes. That's all." Grace said, dismissive. "It's no big deal."

Eustis wanted to argue but couldn't. How was he to know? His plans to befriend Grace were foiled a long time ago. He knew nothing of her home life. Still, the thought that Grace's foster parents could have abused her sent an unexpected wave of nausea through him. A feeling only amplified by his guilt. If what he suspected was true, he'd contributed to that abuse with every single thing that happened at school. It was all his fault.

"Grace," Eustis started, his thoughts on the woman's voice he'd heard calling at their backs, "That woman must have been your foster mother, MaryAnne, right? Yelling at you."

"Just how long were you following me?" Grace asked with a hint of disgust.

"I didn't mean to follow you all the way there. I was just trying to talk to you." Eustis tried to explain, swallowing his nerves. "I'm not a stalker or anything."

"Could have fooled me." Grace retorted, shaking her head.

"I'll apologize for that later. There are other things I want to talk about first, but...she said you were going to go to a room when you got back. You're on punishment? Are you being grounded for something at school?" He asked awkwardly.

The speed at which Grace turned her head in his direction frightened him, though much less than the petrified expression that flooded every contour of her face. The sudden presence of tears clouding her eyes led Eustis to believe that he'd asked exactly the *wrong* question. "I guess." Grace stuttered, turning her entire body to face the window. "They'll be upset. They are always upset. Especially when I ruin my clothes, or they think I've been stealing."

Eustis felt he'd been struck with a knife. He'd lied so many times since they'd met, and the others accused her of something almost every day. Just how much of her suffering had he been causing? "You didn't do it. You didn't steal anything. We both know that." Eustis said, as if he could defy every lie they'd ever told, as if it would change time and fix all of his mistakes.

"I don't know what's wrong with you today," Grace said, her voice hardly more than a whisper, causing soft wisps to form near the frosted window as she spoke, "but we're the only two to admit it."

"I told you," Eustis shook his head, "nothing is wrong with me, Grace. I just want this to stop. I've been stupid and I'm probably the worst person I know. I wanted to be friends when we first met by that tree, did you know? I didn't know nearly as much as I thought I did back then. You taught me to come to my own conclusions and search for the truth even if that meant questioning my parents. I can't even begin to imagine how or why you learned that—imagine what you've been going through.

"I've been afraid because everyone said so many negative things about you and my family shamed you, but that's not how I felt. I thought I was doing you a favor, that I was toughening you up so other people couldn't bully you and make you cry again like the day we met. Now, I guess that was an excuse. Because I was afraid to stand up for you." In his frenzy of emotions, Eustis was hardly aware of Kennet parking the car or telling them that he would return shortly.

"I'm ashamed that I have let things go this far. I never hated you or anything like that. I'm sorry for everything I've done. I want a second chance, if possible—and maybe I'm stupid just for asking but I want to be your friend."

That was right. That was what he wanted more than anything. Tomorrow, he wouldn't be a coward. He would stand up for Grace, even to everyone at school. He would at least try to make it up to her, to become someone she'd be proud to call her friend no matter what the cost. *Tomorrow will be different,* he thought to himself sternly. *I can't stay afraid forever. Grace has always been herself. I want that too. To be comfortable just being me, and to pick my own friends.*

"I know how it sounds but...I'd rather everyone hate me than to keep going like this. Even I hate me, but somehow it feels a lot worse if you do." It was then that Eustis took notice of the slight movements in Grace's shoulders and the sound of her sniffles and cries against the window.

"I won't forgive you just like that. Even if you did say sorry." Grace sobbed. "I won't!"

"Then, if there's even a little chance, I'll prove it to you." Eustis nodded, solidifying his resolve, conscious of his own tears threatening to fall. He didn't know why he was getting so emotional. When was the last time he cried?

"You stupid elephant!" Grace shouted, frightening him.

"What?" Eustis asked, suddenly less emotional. "Did you just call me an *elephant*?"

Fifteen

Twister...

MISSING FAE.

"You're saying that Faeries are disappearing again?" Twister swallowed the lump in his throat as Father Wing nodded, his ancient eyes seeming to pierce through him. Almost as if Twister were made of nothing at all. Else, Father Wing's gaze was made of everything there ever was. He didn't know what to think.

"Fae have vanished for some time in other worlds. Least a number of them return, and makes their disappearances difficult to judge. Of course, we are all aware of how often Fae visit other worlds. Which would be easy to dismiss in that regard. However, this figure has surged in mere days. Not only in occurrence, but in number. Many Fae report that their loved ones have gone, more worrisome still, without a single word of warning."

Father Wing's voice echoed around them as he shifted in his bath. It occurred to Twister that since the Fae welcomed Princess Aurelia, they'd seen Father Wing less than usual. Looking at him now, Twister still couldn't view him differently, even given his current state. There was something in the space between them that would not let him forget, even for a moment, that he was nothing like a child. Twister watched him silently as he rested his head above the water, relaxed against a pillow etched with woven flowers and shimmering leaves.

"Tis is not the way of Fae. Many of the missing disappeared in the Human World. Nearly the lot of all other worlds combined." Father Wing frowned. "Of all ironies. The Human World again."

"What does that mean?" Twister asked, trying to rid himself of his awkwardness. He never imagined speaking to Father Wing, conversing as if he had every right to be in the room. Even less, during his personal time.

Although his parents stood behind them, they were utterly silent. Almost feeling so far removed that they could be worlds apart. It occurred to Twister that this may have been perfectly normal for them. His parents likely spent a great deal of time around both The Princess and Father Wing. Even around this time of the day. They could very well feel more comfortable around the two of them than their own son.

"I believe it to be consequence of everything we have feared." Father Wing sighed. Such a sigh that Twister could almost feel the very weight on his shoulders, could hear his exhaustion. "I gather even what you've described to be pieces in the great scheme of things, Twister. The probability that The Darkness has gained confidence and active once again, is incredibly high. Something has changed. Why and what is to come, are the greatest questions."

"You don't suppose it's my friends?" Twister asked nervously, fiddling with his scarf. What happened before through the door and what was happening now with The Darkness couldn't be a coincidence. Right? The first time in forever that a group of humans enter FlareWing all at the same time and Fae are going missing? It just couldn't be.

"We cannot say they've nothing to do with it, but the timing for the start of the disappearance of Fae does not coincide with their appearance. That is to say that the problem began before they crossed the threshold of FlareWing."

At least that was a relief. Regardless of timing, Twister was certain that the others were caught in the same web as the rest of them. Struggling and confused. What were they to do? As if to answer his question,

Father Wing sat up in his bath, his hair pooled around his small frame, and his red eyes blinked slowly in Twister's direction. "I do not deny the fact that your friends may be involved in these troubles, or that the very fact that they've traveled to our world without assistance of the Fae is of importance. However, we have other matters that take precedence. Most notably, we must know what is happening to the Fae that have vanished. Tis the place to begin."

Twister thought that perhaps there was something to be said of True's statement before. Of a mind-reading Faerie—perhaps of a mind-reading Father Wing. He questioned the possibility of Father Wing telling True where to find the door out of FlareWing. Could it have been the truth? Did he communicate with her without ever leaving his seat?

Chills ran down his spine as the corners of Father Wing's lips slowly pressed upwards to something akin to a smirk, though his eyes never left Twister's own. Even his eyes showed hint of a smile. "To find out what's happening to the Faeries," Twister began, itching for anything to take his mind away from thoughts of Father Wing, "what do we do?" He fiddled with his scarf folding and unfolding its end, hoping to calm his nerves.

Father Wing sighed again as he pulled his hair from the water in bunches, taking a handful of hair at a time, squeezing the thick red strands. Twister watched as the water poured and dripped back into the bath as Father Wing laid his hair over his shoulder. "You are not expected to do anything in particular. I advise you to be aware, keep your wits about you, and your wings quick. More so if you are so intent to travel back to the Human World. Thorne and Rune shall gather a small force to investigate in the meantime."

Minutes later, Twister was led out of the Grand Tree. His father, to his surprise, lightly laid a hand atop his head. "You did well." While he offered no hint of a smile, Twister felt warmth from the simple gesture. His mother, however, was already smiling at him when he looked in her direction.

"Thank you, I guess. I was nervous. You aren't going on that mission, are you?" Twister asked, unable to help himself. He knew that his parents led the Fae Army, so was there any point in asking? They must have been used to missions like those now. Maybe even more dangerous ones that he'd never known about. It just so happened that today, he had been there to know anything at all.

"We will, unless Father Wing gives an order otherwise. If there is danger of The Darkness being involved with the disappearance of Faeries, we cannot simply stay put and keep ourselves safe. Those are our Fae going out there. Family. Friends and all." His mother smiled softly. Twister knew she was right, but he still didn't like it. They were adults, but he couldn't help himself.

"I understand. Still, you two should be careful." Twister frowned. "Who knows what The Darkness is up to."

"Says the child who may have attacked the very Darkness without his parents having a single clue he could have been in danger." His father scoffed, bitterly.

"We should talk." His mother chimed in, interrupting Twister as soon as he planned to defend his actions. "Why don't you come back home? To live with us?"

Not knowing what to say, Twister fixed his eyes on the bright leaves of The Grand Tree in thought. "I don't know, mother. A lot has changed and I'm a little old for that now, don't you think?"

"You've always been independent." His mother chuckled. "But there are plenty of families that still live under the same roof. Are we so different? Still, we have lost so much time together. What is age when we need to learn of each other again? *Better*, this time."

Promising to discuss the matter, and reassuring his parents that he'd be careful, Twister said goodbye and decided he would head back to the Human World. He didn't know what to make of everything he'd heard. He didn't know what they would find out about the missing Fae, or what to do for that matter, but he had to tell the others what he knew.

Sixteen

Quill...

IT VS HIM.

"You should rest, Quill." Opal suggested. How could she rest when they were getting so close to the end? How many more creatures did she have left? 100? Less? Deciding to stay quiet, Quill ignored her. "As strong as you are, even you need proper rest." Opal whined.

"I have a meeting with ***HIM*** tonight." Quill directed at Opal, watching the smile on her face fade away before any hint of emotion vanished in an instant. "***Father*** will be proud of my progress, but I want to finish quickly. So that we can return and start the final phase." Still, her expression remained unchanged. Just what was it about Opal?

"You can be of no use to ***IT*** if you're exhausted. If you want to hurry so badly then you need to rest adequately." Opal sighed.

"Why do you insist on calling my ***father*** an it? That's very rude." Quill directed at her bitterly. She was always saying things like that.

"Just as you believe you've reason to call ***IT*** your *father*, I've my reasons not to do so. I will call ***IT*** nothing besides what ***IT*** is."

Quill felt a rise of anger bubbling up inside her. 'Believe,' she'd said. As if her relationship with her own father was a child's game. As if their bond meant nothing. Was it because Opal didn't have parents that she couldn't understand? As much knowledge as Quill had, she did not understand Opal. "Why are you loyal to him if you have any doubts of him? Why, then, should I not simply tell him that you don't believe he deserves respect? He *saved* you!"

It was as Quill looked angrily into Opal's eyes that she saw her blank expression fall away. She sighed as her eyes began to water. "Quill, regardless of anything in the entire universe, as we understand it, I can't imagine a world without you in it. My loyalty lies with ***you***—only you, not anyone else. If you decide to tell ***IT*** anything, then so be it. I will do nothing to stop you, but you will never learn the truth from ***IT***. If you report me then there would be nothing left for me here anymore. There would be nothing worst that ***IT*** could do to me."

As she watched her fly away, Quill understood her even less. Why was she loyal to her? Her father told her everything, so there was no other truth to be heard. Why did her father keep her around? Was someone so ungrateful worthy of his kindness?

Seventeen

Opal...

A HUMAN?

Opal found herself flustered and frustrated as she put distance between herself and the park. She hadn't known she'd come up with an excuse like 'gathering intel' just to get away. Even less, from Quill. She was disappointed in herself, but what else was she to do? To think that Quill actually believed that ***IT*** had done her some sort of favor—***IT*** saved her life? *Ridiculous*! ***IT*** took *everything* from her.

Opal's stomach churned every time she had to listen to Quill call ***IT*** her father. By whatever means ***IT*** had acquired Quill, she knew it had done something unspeakable. Maybe something even worse than what happened to her own mother. Maybe even, something worse than what **IT** was making the two of them do now. Opal was certain that that ***thing*** was not her father, even if she didn't exactly know what ***IT*** was.

She quickly realized that she hadn't thought very far ahead when she left Quill's side. Would Quill care that she wasn't there or would it make no difference to her? Was Opal only fooling herself? In defiance to her own thoughts, she shook her head, willing her negative thoughts away. *Think.* She demanded. *I must make myself useful! Information on these humans would be valuable to Quill.*

Even though she thought so, whoever these humans were that Quill mentioned, Opal wanted nothing more than to defy any plan ***IT*** had for them. She almost wanted to provoke ***IT***. She knew well enough that ***IT*** could let bits and pieces slip when it harmed her, when ***IT*** seemed to most enjoy itself at another's expense. And before she could talk herself out of it, Opal took a deep breath, fortified the blank space in her mind to guard her thoughts and feelings, and forced her way back below the surface.

The moment she found herself pressing through that cold blackness, surrounded by ***IT***, she wondered if she'd made the wrong decision. Had she been too rash? Was it because she thought she had a fight with Quill? Was she really willing to possibly throw her life away for something as small as information she might not even be able to leave with? For information ***IT*** might kill to keep secret? There was no way to know what ***IT*** would do to her.

As soon as Opal decided that she'd turn around and make her way back to the surface before ***IT*** could notice her, she became aware of a faint voice. Confused and cautious, she made her way towards the voice echoing in the dark. Who could it be? Was it possible she'd found her way to a different area than where she'd intended? Was there even a 'different' area there in the first place?

The closer she became to the strained, oddly familiar voice, the more Opal became aware of a river of vibrations. Of a strong rhythmic pulsing that seemed to come from every direction. Was it possible? Did ***IT*** have a heart? A physical heart by which ***IT*** could be destroyed? *If so*, Opal thought, *I'm more than ready to get rid of it. No matter the consequence.* No matter what would come of her relationship with Quill. Was today the day they'd truly be free?

Further she ventured, until the vibrations and pulsating felt akin to torture, jerking her entire body. Until she found the source of the voice. ***A human?*** What was going on? She could just make out the figure suspended above her. Upon closer inspection, Opal could make out the man's outstretched arms, his ankles pressed together, and the black tentacle-like shadows wound tightly around him.

She took note of his flickering eyelids, a line of blood running down the length of his face and the low groans that escaped his lips. He seemed to be in pain, but what was this? Didn't this ***thing*** swallow anything it took in? How could a human possibly survive? Not knowing what else to do, Opal decided to question him, not sure that he would even hear her.

"A-are you alright?" Opal asked, quiet and cautious. Almost afraid that ***IT*** would hear her. "Are you alright?" She asked again, wondering if the human was even conscious. "Can you hear me? Can you speak? Who are you?" Opal asked, recalling then that ***IT*** was probably responsible for his current state. After all, look at what happened to the Fae. Surely a human would be no match for ***IT***.

Suddenly the man's eyes opened startlingly wide. Upon closer inspection, he hardly seemed aware of her presence. Opal felt momentarily that she recognized him but ultimately dismissed it. Still, there was something there in his eyes of his that made her want to save him. "You remember who you are?" She asked.

A strange series of vibrations shook the space between them as he opened his mouth. The man looked off in the distance as if there was something beyond. When Opal followed his gaze, however, she saw nothing. Before she could ask another question, she heard a scream. A blood curdling screech that seemed to come from every corner of the space around them.

A sudden spark of light engulfed them, and images flew into Opal's mind, effectively blinding her and casting away all of her focus. She could make out the image of a beautiful field. Rows of bushes full of budding flowers on either side. A familiar place. "My love. I've missed you." A soft voice called from somewhere in the distance.

"And I you." A different voice replied, then faded away.

As quickly as it had come, it was gone. The field and flowers faded from her vision and her eyes could make out the black space around her again. Opal could feel herself being flung towards the surface. With such force that the pressure nearly rendered her unconscious. To her surprise, the human that had once been wrapped in quivering, dark tentacles was beside her. His body shook and his eyes were open and red.

She tried to open her mouth to speak, or to move an arm in his direction but found she could do neither. A wave of nausea struck her and she became too dizzy to focus her energy on the human or what possible things he was suffering beside her. This was a pressure she'd never felt. Was the human responsible or had ***IT*** done something? Had ***IT*** been aware of her presence?

Until the very moment the two of them were hurdled above the surface, they lived a nightmare. One Opal didn't think she'd ever forget.

Eighteen

???...

MEMORY.

He could tell that something had happened. Something that diminished his pain. Was he asleep? Could a person be asleep and aware that they were dreaming all at once? *Yes*, he thought to himself. *If everything else I know is possible then surely something as simple as awareness must be, dream or no dream.* Everything he knew? He couldn't believe it.

If he was awake, he'd have laughed. Likely the laugh of a maniac if anyone heard it, but truly pure joy in essence. How amazing a feeling, to be aware, to ***know*** things. And know them, he did. In that moment he was warm and comfortable, which he knew he hadn't felt for some time. He was completely aware of his own thoughts, his body and his other senses. He could smell a fire burning lowly nearby.

. . .

"Good. You're warming up. Maybe you'll remember something when you wake." A small voice whispered near his ear. It was a voice he'd heard before somewhere, but couldn't place. He tried to speak again and then attempted to move his arms but failed. "I must go," the small voice spoke again, "but I'll return. If you wake while I am gone, you ***mustn't*** leave. You can't go until we speak."

Don't worry, he thought, *I've nowhere to go*. Suddenly, he was overwhelmed with a feeling of misery. An almost unbearable sadness and fear of being alone. *Do you have to go?* He tried to ask, but he heard nothing but the sound of shuffling and a light creak. He knew then that the small voice was gone, but at least he could still make out the crackling of the fire and the soft *thunk* as a piece of firewood fell in the flames.

He knew the sound well as he'd heard it often as a boy in his father's study. Surprised at his own thoughts, he attempted to inspect them, to turn them over in his mind and prod them, trying to understand from where they came. It was in those moments where he focused his energy on this one pure thought that pieces of memory began to take shape in his mind again. He saw himself, a young boy, sitting in the classroom. Slowly, he began living through that moment again. Taking the place of the boy in the memory.

...

There was a different creature in the classroom that day. His teacher, Mr. Boone had often told him not to bring anymore nonsensical notions to his attention. No more discussing odd creatures and spirits no one else could see. Mr. Boone had said that if people heard him talking in such detail about invisible things, they'd be sure he had an 'unhealthy' brain rather than an 'overactive imagination.' The man had, on several occasions, spoken to his father. What Mr. Boone failed to realize, however, was that his father did not chide him; his father saw them too.

It was that day when the furry green creature with the dragonfly wings sat on Mr. Boone's head, that he'd first seen ***her***. His first sighting of a Faerie. He had been crossing the field of wildflowers with the broken shed when he'd noticed. That day, the wood was not old and weathered, the door was not broken off the hinges, and the large hole in the roof on the left side of the shed was gone. In fact, the dusty, aged shed had never looked better.

He'd felt no desire to resist his curiosity. He immediately stopped walking the vertical line out of the field in favor of the diagonal splintered path to the shed. Curious but uncertain, he ventured forward as quietly as he could manage. As two figures floated above him out of the shed window, he ducked down hoping not to be seen. A woman and a man, both with hair whiter than the clouds seemed to hover there for just an instant before they disappeared.

Quickly, he made his way through the door and closed it behind him. Inside, the shed was also in perfect condition. The cracked and leaning shelves were upright and affixed, the thick dust was nowhere to be found, the broken stool in the corner had all four of its legs, and the random assortment of tools were nowhere to be seen. Standing where those very tools should have been was a small girl with a mallet.

Her hair, too, was white. It fell straight to her shoulders where her silver robe met her...*wings*? They were beautiful fluttering things, enticing him as she worked on something in front of her. She quickly turned to face him, likely having heard the dragging of his feet, and he stared into her large peach-colored eyes. An eye color he'd yet to witness of any creature he'd seen before. What a wonderful color.

"Hello." He smiled. As if she'd been in complete shock, the Faerie's wings stopped moving and her eyes widened. "Oh. I didn't mean to scare you." He said apologetically, pushing up his glasses. He took note of the heart shaped beauty mark on her cheek, not too unlike his mother's oblong shaped one had been. He watched the girl look erratically to the side and then back at him.

"You can see me?" She asked almost as if she'd been holding her breath. "That can't be. I'm *cloaked*."

"I can." He nodded. "You're very pretty. I've never seen a real Faerie before!" He exclaimed excitedly. Not a moment later, the color drained from her face and seconds after, she disappeared. Not knowing what to do, he sat there waiting for another sign of her. When the sun began to set, however, he knew he couldn't stay any longer and continued on his way home to tell his father.

That night, as the two of them talked about his encounter, his father shot up from his seat. "Come! Oh, my boy. I understand!" His father laughed suddenly. His father, Morpheus Engel was generally a happy man but it was rare for his excitement to seep into his behavior. It had been such an unexpected bout of emotion that he thought the feeling was contagious. He followed giddily after his father as they went into the study—his father's study was somewhere he would spend all of his time, maybe even more than his father, if he had been allowed to do so. A home within a home.

They made their way past the heavy carved doors and his eyes immediately examined the room. He surveyed the perfectly preserved books lining the wall furthest from the entry, the dark amaranth desk and chair covered with large stacks of papers and the box of photobooks beside it on the floor. He inspected the glass on the coffee table and could just make out their fat cat Butter slowly making his way towards his feet to demand his daily massage.

"We really ought to get him that kitten. Butter's always grumpy now." He'd called to his father as he emerged from the storage room. Taking note of his full arms as he spoke, he tilted his head to the side. "What do you think, father?"

"It's easy to be grumpy when you're old. Maybe we ought to stop his diet too, before the poor old bat wastes away. The kitten might give him some life back." His father smiled, rummaging through a photo album.

"Can they do that?" He questioned; brows raised.

"Likely not." His father replied with a chuckle.

"A pity. I'd have liked to see it." He clicked his tongue. "What are you looking for, father?" He asked as Butter complained about his lack of attention. His question faded when his father's smile widened, practically from ear-to-ear.

"I found it." He beamed, flipping through pages of a plum book as he made his way towards him. "My first love was a Faerie." He sighed. "You must be following in your father's footsteps, Gunny."

"I thought you loved mom."

"Of course, I loved your mother. Oh, Gunny. Your mother used to get jealous when I talked about Fura. She'd say, 'Morpheus, you've a perfectly beautiful wife here in front of you. Your imaginary magical girlfriend is *nowhere* to be found.' Just like that." He watched his father's mustache twitch as he laughed, his gaze unfocused as if he had been lost in the memory.

"I thought mom believed you." He said, pulling Butter onto the lounger.

"She did, Gunny. I'm sure she didn't want to believe me sometimes, but she did. Your mother was taking whatever jab she could because she was upset with me is all. I'd kiss her and she'd say she was sorry. Your mother wore her heart on her sleeves like most young women did."

His father often mentioned young and old. He'd said it was to remind himself to put things into perspective. To remember that he was starting to age. His black curly hair, which he passed on, had begun to gray. Ironically, his mustache had beaten his hair and beard to it, losing all of its black sheen in favor of silver. Even his eyes seemed a little less blue as the days went on.

Even though he knew his father was aging, in moments like those, as he smiled showing him a photograph of a bright light in the shape of a person, he often thought his father was younger. He could look past the slight wrinkle of his skin and the color of his veins that he couldn't see a year before.

"I asked Fura for a picture that day." His father sighed. He studied the photo more closely. He could just make out the Faerie's white hair and the long fabric of her clothes. "It was our last day together. Fura was getting married the next day to a man she didn't love. A Faerie she was arranged to marry. It was the most joyful yet pitiless day of my life."

"She didn't say no?" He'd asked, not understanding.

"Things weren't so simple. The two of us were never supposed to be together. Fura often reminded me that views were complicated when it came to non-magical creatures. Humans have a bad reputation, you see. She often said I was special because I had magic in my eyes, like you do. We can see the beings of other worlds."

His father had often told him how his parents never believed him. How they'd forced him to keep quiet and hurt him if he mentioned the creatures. How he ran away from home so he could write in his secret journals. The very journals, all but the small one tucked into his shirt pocket, were tucked away in a chest in their storage room. One day, his father had told him, when he was older, he could read them all.

"I saw Fura only once since that day we were forced to end our forbidden relationship. Years after her marriage, she appeared next to my bedside. I had only just begun my relationship with your mother then. Fura showed me a beautiful little girl with the sweetest smile. She told me 'I've named her Morphia. After the only man I have ever loved,' and kissed me goodbye.

"Your mother awoke to my childish sobs and consoled me for hours. I didn't tell her the truth of what happened that night until after you'd been born. I was worried she'd leave me." As he spoke, he wiped a tear from his eye, kissed the photo and slid it back in its original place. "Perhaps, Gunny, you'll see her again." And he did.

Eventually, after going back to the shed every day and waiting until dark, after a long year of disappointment, she reappeared. For just a few minutes he was able to see her again. Just long enough for her to offer her friendship. Long enough for her to explain that she only traveled with her family to the Human World before she was gone again. The next time he saw her again, it had been over four years and on his fifteenth birthday, he learned her name.

"I'm Lily." She said with a smile and held out her hand to greet him. As he took her hand in his, he realized anew that she'd grown too. Even though he'd only envisioned her at the same age in the time they'd been apart. When he pulled her into a light hug, he was surprised by her warmth. "I'm Morgan." He smiled, taking in the sweet smell of her long white hair. "And I've missed you."

"Yes." She smiled, her bright eyes blinking at him beneath long, snow-kissed lashes. "It's been a long time, hasn't it? Too long."

The memory faded away as he opened his eyes. He could make out the dying fire ahead of him as the flickering orange glow cast streaks of light around him. *That's right*, he thought mournfully. M*y name is* ***Morgan Engel***...

Nineteen

Grace...

IMPOSSIBLE.

Grace had never felt so conflicted in all her life. Between Eustis sticking up for her in class and the warmth in her chest constantly making a reappearance, somehow managing to put her at ease during the days of her punishment, nothing in her life was making any sense. Was she dreaming? How had she passed so many days in ***That*** room without being aware of the cold or the pain?

Was it because things with Phelia and Zane had become less awkward? Was it because her mind played back her conversation with Eustis and his apology? Could it be she'd felt better because Eustis had gone against the other little monsters and told Miss Pine that she hadn't been responsible for the slimy mess smeared over her desk?

Had those peculiar dreams of rainbow silhouettes somehow improved her mood? Was it having the crystal by her side? Or was it that feeling of warmth that filled her chest—the same exact feeling she'd recalled having several times before, like the night of her long bath when MaryAnne and Duke were away?

Whatever the case, Grace had been grateful for it all. More so because her foster parents' punishments were getting worse every day.

They were longer, more painful, and twice as frightening. It was as if their anger had no bounds. As much as Grace tried to tell herself that she'd been through these kinds of things before, she knew otherwise.

She'd told herself that she'd been too careless that day with Eustis, and that she'd made him suspicious, but now, she was running out of options and excuses. It was almost as if MaryAnne and Duke stopped caring. If things continued the way they were, she wouldn't be able to cover it up. And if she failed to do that, then what?

Would everyone in Snowville know? Would anyone even care? What would Phelia think? Would she be ashamed to be seen with her? Grace was terrified of the fall-out. After all, if everyone were to find out, wouldn't she end up back where she started? She could be back in the system and away from Snowville—away from Phelia, Zane, Dr. Brand, True, and Victor. With her luck, maybe she'd be adopted again, by a couple much worse than MaryAnne and Duke.

As always, she felt horrendously doomed to repeat the same cycle until the end of time. Only, this one could be worse because she'd managed to make friends. If that was true, Grace wished she could fix it. Whatever ancient Gods she'd angered she wished to make amends. Whatever her curse, she wanted nothing more than to break it. But Grace had no experience in going against ancient deities or shattering dark magic, and ultimately, she was unconvinced that someone like herself would ever be strong enough to cause a single ripple in the bounds of her own world. Regardless of her fiery red crystal and its mysterious power.

Discouraged, Grace readied herself for the walk home from her favorite nameless pond. She knew nothing good would await her at home. If only she'd had her walkie-talkie, she could at least have a short conversation with Phelia. Grace would have welcomed any brief excuse to feel happy or hopeful. Knowing there wasn't one and it was getting late, she turned around, took a deep breath and tried to count the snowflakes falling onto her palms. And continued on her way.

Not long enough after, she'd made her way past the white fence covered in snow, and through the front door. Grace slipped off her shoes and turned around to see MaryAnne and Duke waiting for her, motionlessly standing in the hall nearest the kitchen, anger coating their faces. For a long moment, Grace stared at the wisps of smoke flowing from Duke's cigarette and the bright rubber gloves laying across the rusted tin bucket at MaryAnne's feet.

She knew what would happen the moment Duke's cigarette reached the end of its bud. She knew what the appearance of that rusty bucket meant, too. As she listened to the sound of her foster parents' footsteps closing the distance between them, Grace's heart thumped away in her ears and panic shot through her veins, completely immobilizing her. If ever she could break her curse and please the ancient Gods, now would have been the time.

The moment that MaryAnne's hand struck her face, Grace didn't know why she ever entertained those kinds of thoughts. As if there was something to be done. As if she would ever escape the fists that would strike her, the burns that would continue to make its abstract painting on her skin, or the blood that would pave her way to ***That*** room again. There was no point in imagining the impossible.

Yet, for a single second, as her tears stung her eyes, she remembered that she'd made friends she thought she'd never have. She'd seen the existence of other worlds since she'd found her strange, beautiful crystal, and she'd even gotten an apology from someone like Eustis Schmidt. And it was in that moment that Grace made out a shimmering floating figure beside her, flying towards MaryAnne and Duke at an impossible speed, knocking them onto the floor.

It was then, as Grace's panic made room for confusion and surprise, that she saw a cloud of dark smoke cover her foster parents and she could make out the culprit. Her eyes followed the shape and traced its multicolored scales. *No* way, Grace thought in disbelief. That thing *couldn't be...**A DRAGON??!***

Twenty

True...

UNCOMFORTABLE.

True rounded the corner on her left, turning her head to look over her shoulder. She knew it would only be a matter of minutes before the others caught up to her. As she focused her attention back ahead of her, she hardly had time to step to the side and avoid crashing into Mrs. Burroughs. *Could there be a worst time to run into the gym teacher?* True groaned. She'd been doing everything she could not to think about gym, let alone to have Mrs. Burroughs in her field of vision.

"I-I'm sorry!" True called in the silver haired woman's direction, taking note of the displeased expression clouding her darkly painted face, as she ran past her and down the hall. Lately it seemed as if nowhere was safe. True had lost all her spots to Sydney and her 'lipstick lackeys.' Or at least, that was what Zane often called them. Not a single day went by that True didn't find herself running through the halls of the school, practically desperate to find a moment's peace. Many days she slipped her way into one of the teachers' private restrooms until the end of lunch just to escape them.

True missed taking the lunch break outside. Specifically, in what used to be her hidden corner. It wasn't until Sydney spotted her sitting between the trees on the edge of the school property that those days came to an end. At the time, True was more relieved than ever that she never ate at school. And it was that day that her torment at school really began.

No amount of name calling, desks scraping loudly across the floor, or hard shoves to the shoulder could have prepared her for the cruelty of teenage girls. Like a pack of maddened wolves, those girls sniffed her out—their prey. Until recently, True had made the mistake of thinking that the incident in the locker room and Sydney and her lipstick lackeys were unrelated happenings.

That was, until Sydney's sudden appearance a couple days before. A moment of being shoved into a locker where Sydney proudly showcased all of True's belongings the rest of her pack had managed to steal. Pens, notebooks, books, her thermos, and even a pair of her shoes. Today, they'd added another pair, her snow boots, to their collection.

When it became apparent that any free moment in the halls would end in her being cornered, True opted to stay in her classroom right until the last minute and rush to her next class. It was the best she could think of. The only effective strategy that had worked thus far, even if it left her feeling more exhausted as the day went on. With all of her running, her ankle wasn't getting any better. It was red and inflamed. It stung when she put her weight on it and throbbed when she didn't, but True had no real moments to nurse it.

That included now. It was the end of the day, the wolves' last opportunity to strike, and they weren't wasting it. Ten minutes from now the school bell would ring, but True had wanted to leave before any of those girls had the chance to see her. Unfortunately, it seemed that a few of them had plans of their own. How they'd managed to get permission to come to her class, she didn't know. Whatever excuse they'd given, True had been excused before she could ask for it herself.

She was guided towards the door and purposely tripped into the hall. The two of them made a big show of being worried about her as they shut the door behind them, but once they had her surrounded in the soundless hallway, they immediately tried to strip her of all her possessions. In the struggle, they'd managed to take her boots, but she'd gotten away. Of course, the girls were only steps behind. True wasn't sure if Mrs. Burroughs' sudden appearance had scared them off, but she was determined to make her way outside, regardless of her missing boots.

As she pressed forward and listened to the metallic press release on the door, True stumbled her way through the snow. "Well, well." A voice called from her right. "I spy a little *freakling*." True turned her gaze to her side. She couldn't particularly place the girl, but all of them had begun to look too much the same to tell them apart these days. As she rushed forward, ready to make her way to the school's parking lot, something smacked into her back.

Falling forward from the pain, True turned around to see two nameless girls and Sydney walking towards her. Beside her, she recognized the culprit of her attack: her pastel thermos. At one point her name had been etched on the front but there was no hint of it now beneath the dark, jagged lines. "Who knew it would take so long to get ahold of you?" One girl scoffed.

"You're a fast little circus freak, give you that." One laughed.

"Fast or not, your punishment will be slow." Sydney smirked.

"Punishment?" True asked, not understanding. "Why should I be punished?"

"Don't play dumb!" The first girl shouted. "All this special treatment. Since day one, you have been getting off easy by everyone. Now, you think you're so special? Hanging around with people out of your league?"

"You have eyes under that mask of yours, don't you?" One of the girls called.

"Let's not play games. There's only a handful of guys in the entirety of Snowville that are even worthy of a second glance. You think that you could go around with two of the hottest guys our age and not get caught? We've seen you having lunch with Zane and Victor. The girls even tell me that you and Victor walked into school together." Sydney smiled as True grabbed her thermos, taking note of its unnatural weight. “You like? Your back must hurt, right? It’s filled with rocks and dirt. Whatever we could find really.”

“You hold random people to such high pedestals?” True asked, somehow surprised by Sydney’s words given her inflated sense of self. These girls sounded obsessed.

“See? This is *another* reason that you obviously need to learn your **place**.” Sydney scowled. “Random people? We are talking about the two hottest guys in our grade. Who also happen to have plenty of great qualities? We’ve been around them since day one, so who are you to say? You just *got* here! What *is* it with you?!”

“Are you friends?” True asked, not feeling any less confused by Sydney’s answer. “Victor and I are friends.” She continued, feeling the icy air against her feet and all too aware of the pain in her back. “Zane and I are starting over.” True said truthfully. She wasn’t sure what to say to people like Sydney and her group. Perhaps if Sydney and the rest of them were friends of Victor and Zane, she could tell them that they had this in common and everything else would stop.

Instead, True did not see a hint of remorse in any of the girls’ faces. Much the opposite, in fact. If they’d truly been wolves True would have witnessed bloodied fangs, ready for their next kill. “*Friends?* How can you be so stupid? ***Victor pities you!*** Consider yourself lucky that someone as perfect as him didn’t ignore you entirely. As if we’ll just stand around and let you drag them down with you!”

“No one is perfect.” True frowned from behind her mask. She knew what it meant to delude oneself. She knew all too well the consequences of building up a concept like perfection. True could admit that even in her own eyes people like Zane and Victor seemed a galaxy away, but she knew they didn’t consider themselves without flaw. They were not those kids of people. Moreover, searching for perfection in someone else only led to disappointment.

“You stupid little ***freak***!!” Sydney shouted as the girls began to surround her. As the distance around her lessened, True tried to ready herself for a situation she wouldn’t be able to escape. She didn’t know if she was shaking so violently from the cold or the fear rising inside of her. Was this it? Was this the moment she'd be beaten and humiliated? Unmasked?

As True shut her eyes and pressed her palms to her mask defensively, the school bell rang, and the familiar sea of voices filled the halls. The moment that Sydney and the girls began to complain about the horrible timing, True slipped past them. She staggered towards a nearby tree and a voice called out to her over the wind.

True quickly turned around, anxiously scanning the area for Sydney and the others only to see Victor crossing the snow-covered grass. The girls were gone. At least, for now.

"Where are your shoes?" Victor asked, looking concerned. As his gaze shifted downwards to observe her feet, True pressed them into the freezing snow to hide her ankle. This action seemed to make him more apprehensive. Victor immediately kneeled to inspect her feet and the sudden pressure of his palm around her bruised ankle caused her to jerk away from the tree and topple into the snow.

"Oh my God, True." Victor called apologetically. "Are you alright?"

"Y-yes. I'm fine. I apologize." She murmured. "I didn't mean to frighten you."

"I'm fine, but you're not. Where are your shoes? What happened to your ankle?" Victor pressed, taking her bag from her arms as she tried to cover her feet again. It was embarrassing, somehow. Being caught right after Sydney, barefoot in the snow in the midst of winter.

"I think I twisted it." True answered quietly. "I don't know where my boots are now." She murmured truthfully. Who knew what Sydney decided to do with them, or if she'd ever see them again. She'd have to get another pair.

"I've never heard of someone losing their boots at our age," Victor said, shaking his head as he reached into his bag. True watched quietly, trying not to focus on the pain shooting through her body or the air blowing icy kisses across her neck. As Victor pulled out the orange and brown thermal socks, she found herself smiling behind her mask.

"They've been washed a few times. I was planning to give them back to you. I guess today's as good a day as any." Victor chuckled, lightly scratching his head. "Maybe even the best day, all things considered." As True reached a hand towards him to accept the fox socks she'd slipped onto his feet the cold night they'd had tea, Victor frowned as he put her hands back to her sides. "I'll put them on you, just try not to kick me."

True obediently sat still as Victor slid the socks onto her feet, taking note of his careful movements around her swollen ankle. Surrounded by such cold, she could immediately feel heat radiating from his palms. Which made True more aware of the chill settling into her body and her tremors. Seconds later, Victor wrapped her arms around his neck and lifted her out of the snow.

"What are you--" True started, before Victor shook his head.

"It's freezing. You're cold. Your ankle is busted. I'm carrying you. I'll go as quickly as possible." True wanted to argue but quickly realized that if not for him, she didn't know how she'd get home without freezing to death. The sharp pains in her feet were already warning her of what was to come. She could have found herself in the hospital with a bad case of hypothermia.

"Thank you." She said finally, not knowing anything else to say. As Victor treaded through the snow, True wondered if she was heavy. Compared to the day Victor had carried her out of *Snowville Temporary Infirmary*, his movements seemed sluggish. Had she gained weight? She didn't think so. Before she could get lost in her own head, the sound of Victor's voice forced her out of her thoughts. "I'm sorry?"

"I was saying that when the bell rang, I thought I saw you outside with someone. You've been jumpy lately and rushing around the school like your feet were on fire. Now this thing with the missing boots?" True could hear her heartbeat in her ears, pounding its way to a crescendo. Even in the cold she could feel the sweat on her palms as he spoke. "True," Victor called, his pace slowed, almost to a stop, "are you being bullied? Is someone hurting you?"

Twenty-One

Victor...

AGAIN.

Victor could almost feel the awkwardness more than the frosty air cutting its way through his clothes. True never said a word in response to his question. It was times like those that he wished he could see the expressions on her face. He wondered if he ever would. A thought that made him remember their time in FlareWing.

He could not forget her long bright hair and the hint of her pale skin as she shifted on the ground, taking some kind of instruction from Twister. If he shifted his hand against her back, he was sure he'd be able to make out the feeling of her braid beneath the jacket. Likely not decorated with buds and flowers, but beautiful all the same. He swallowed at the lump rising in his throat and inhaled the cold air in hopes of calming the heat rising inside him.

Recalling that those thoughts were taboo—or at least, he'd forbid himself from thinking on it. Victor willed his thoughts in another direction. There were more important things to think about. Like if True's silence was an answer in itself. Was he overreacting? After all, it wasn't like it was impossible.

Look how she'd been treated before. How she was spoken down to that day in homeroom. And by Sydney, no less. Surely it was possible that other people had gotten comfortable with making her miserable because she was different. Regardless of that, was their friendship to a level where she felt comfortable enough to tell him something painful? Was it too new?

Victor wasn't sure how to go about asking such a question. And even if he could manage, he didn't know if she would answer after his insinuations. Right now, he had to get her home. Whatever did or didn't happen was less important than getting her out of the cold. He couldn't imagine that those socks were offering much protection.

But getting her home was proving difficult. Even more than his walk to school. He was exhausted. With every step forward he felt his grip weaken and the slow buckle of his knees. The cold wasn't responsible for this. Still, he was nearly there and he was more than resolved to not let her feet touch the ground until they'd reached her front door.

He wanted to make the trek to Zane's place. He wanted to ask Dr. Brand to take a look at her ankle, but he didn't know how True would respond to that. Perhaps more important, he knew he would struggle to make it back home, let alone carry her the entire way to Zane's. *Ugh.* Victor frowned. *Where the heck is Zane anyway? If ever there were a time to need him around it would have been today. Who told him he could play hooky from school?*

Looking up, Victor could make out the large dark mansion and sighed with relief. Almost. Just a little further. As he crossed the street, he realized his gaze was unfocused. The iron gate posts almost seemed to sway from one side to the next. Victor shut his eyes tightly and opened them again, blinking until they were in their correct positions. *What was that?*

Determined not to keep True out in the cold for longer than necessary, he pushed the thought to the back of his mind and made his way through the gate. Then up the stairs to the door. As gently as he could manage, he lowered True to the ground. Watched her shift her balance to her other leg. As he continued to stare, taking in the size and color of her ankle, he worried that she really did need to see a doctor.

Seemingly aware of his stare, True slowly hid her ankle away behind her good leg, forcing Victor to awkwardly focus his attention elsewhere. When True opened the door, he realized no one was home. "Where are your aunts?" Victor asked, recalling how one or both women would welcome her home almost daily.

"They must be working late tonight." True answered softly.

So, she speaks, Victor thought with a sigh. Something about his question must have been an issue. Otherwise, she was getting bullied, right? Was there anything else it could mean? Seeing her limp her way down the hall, Victor frowned. "You should rest until they come home. Let me at least help you put the fire on." Victor more told than asked. "Then I can get you some ice for your ankle."

As he stepped into the hall, he felt the sharpness of his vision fade, giving way to a blurry wave of misshapen objects. And in his confusion taking steps forward, he felt his body hit the floor. "Victor!" True called, her voice full of surprise. He heard the sound of her shuffles but couldn't make out her form properly enough to distinguish her from the rest of the space around him. "Are you alright?"

"I'm fine." Victor sighed. He did not to worry her. After all, he was fine. Wasn't he? He closed his eyes, trying to push back the wave of dizziness and nausea making its way through him. When he opened his eyes again, he could see True beside him. "I'm a bit clumsy today."

True tilted her head to the side, pointing to her mask. "Your eyes are red. Are you sure you're alright?" Victor managed to nod his head, quick to tell her they were just dry from the wind.

He made his way to his feet noting the doubled weight in his limbs. "I'm fine, really. Go ahead and rest." Victor said with a slight nod, noting her hesitation before she made her way to the living room sofa. When she was under the throw, he tossed wood into the fireplace and used the nearby scrap paper to light the flames. Then, he crawled his way to the kitchen in search of one of the ice packs he recalled seeing the last time he'd carried True through the door. It seemed to Victor that they were developing a pattern.

A few minutes later, he had written his home phone number on a slip of paper and placed it on the coffee table, said goodbye to True and her ice-covered ankle, and used her key to lock the door before sliding it through a mail slot and safely on the other side. It was there, as he turned his back to the porch and sluggishly found his way down the steps, that Victor allowed himself to look his nerves in the eye.

What was going on?? Was that really the best excuse he could come up with? He was clumsy today? What was that even about? Still, it had seemed to be accepted by her well enough. Or if it didn't, she at least didn't voice it. Which Victor supposed posed a different question. He'd wondered if she felt close enough to tell him something like potentially being bullied and yet, he couldn't manage to tell her about something as simple as blurry vision? *Then again, I wouldn't want to tell Zane either.* Victor scoffed. *Not with his Mother Hen tendencies.*

. . .

Having finally made it home, Victor found a note from his mother about dinner in the fridge. She'd been so busy at work lately; he didn't know when she even had the time to make dinner. Not that it mattered much, he hadn't had an appetite lately. Enough that in his reluctance to worry his mother about it, he'd taken to secretly packing the food away in Tupperware and giving it to Zane for his visits to the hospital. Since he was nowhere to be found today, he'd decided to give it to some random kid from school whose face at least seemed somewhat familiar.

After making his way upstairs, Victor looked at his eyes in his mother's mirror. They really were red. And he could see dark circles forming beneath them. It didn't seem to him that anyone noticed at school, but Victor attributed that to him keeping his head buried in his arms. Lately, he'd found himself more irritated that he couldn't find solace from his sleepless nights at home in the confines of his classrooms. Nothing was working.

He made his way to his own bathroom and rummaged the medicine cabinet. There he found an unopened bottle of eye drops and put them in his pocket. What to do about the dark circles? Deciding to look on the internet, Victor made his way back downstairs despite his body's stubbornness. In his mother's office, he typed random keywords into the search bar and read articles.

"Sleeping can fix dark circles? *Great.* The solution to my problem is the thing I *haven't* been able to do." Victor scoffed, deciding to move on to videos instead. *Make up tutorials?* He wasn't sure how it worked but if it would keep his mother from freaking out when she saw his face, maybe it was worth a shot.

He clicked the video description to see a list of products and went in search of the same types from his mother's things. Satisfied that he was able to find most of the list, he grabbed his mother's handheld mirror from her dresser and made his way back to the desk. After two hours of videos, however, Victor was sure that he would never accomplish such a feat.

He discovered a newfound appreciation for women as he watched them masterfully paint their faces. All their blending, patting and whatever contouring was supposed to be, sometimes able to work such masterpieces that it would give a plastic surgeon a run for his money. Whatever the case, he'd ended up in some strange rabbit hole, completely in awe just as much as he was frustrated.

He'd never seen his mother do all of those things to her face. Was she doing it all along and he was simply unaware? Or did she buy the products hoping to mimic women like the ones from the videos? Did *all* women aspire to do this? Did True?

Soon enough, Victor had put his mother's things back into their place, made his way to his bedroom and angrily stared at his ceiling. Again, his mind would cycle through events since they'd found the crystals. Again, he'd find himself turning over his relationships with others in his mind. He would find no peace. And before long, he'd turn his head to see that it was time to get up for school and try all over again.

Twenty-Two

Phelia...

WANT.

Phelia pointed to the other side of the sofa, instructing Fayth to sit there quietly. She shot him a disapproving glance as he attempted to lay a paw on her lap. "No." Phelia said sternly, shaking her head in his direction.

Are you still upset with me? Fayth whined in her mind. *Surely, I can speak to you this way, can't I? Technically I'm being obedient. I'm quiet.*

Of course, I'm upset! Phelia frowned. *You gave me no choice but to lie to my father, to Zane, and Grace. Getting upset about being a stray of all things? All of which you did after being disobedient.* She brushed away his soft paw, willing herself not to be taken in by temptation. It didn't matter how soft he was. She ignored his large blue-eyed stare as he slowly laid his head on his paws.

I admit that I made a mistake, speaking up so suddenly. But I made a calculated decision in leaving your bedroom. You appeared conflicted, trying to figure out what to do about my presence. How to keep me a secret and things of this nature, so I took care of it. Besides, only being allowed to sit in one spot underneath the bed grew tiresome. Fayth expressed, emphasizing his boredom in her room.

Phelia sighed, attempting to relieve herself of her frustrations. All in all, Fayth did have a point. His sudden appearance in the house had gone over incredibly well with their father. He hadn't seemed suspicious. Grace had been excited. And Zane had been...well, Zane. Still, he'd made a liar out of her. And the day before she and her father went around almost all of the town trying to ensure he hadn't had an owner.

As if that wasn't bad enough, a young girl, who Phelia could only assume was excited at the thought of getting a free cat in some odd misunderstanding, had decided to pick him up and claim him. Amid their surprise and Phelia attempting to come up with some explanation for her father, Fayth decided to scratch the girl. When she asked why he would do such a thing, his only reply was that he belonged to only her and he could have done worse; he could have bitten her.

Her father spent the next half an hour apologizing to the girl and her family and putting his doctoring skills to use bandaging her up to make it up to them. Had Fayth not acted out, they would have never been in such a predicament. Even more, it made her question if she'd made the right decision bringing him home.

Did he have a bad temper? Had he lied to her? These types of questions filled her head. Fayth was quick to dismiss them all. Assuring her that he did not have a temper, he had not lied, and she most definitely made the *right* decision. Even if she hadn't brought him home those days ago, he had stated matter-of-factly, he would have found her no matter the costs.

You're harping on unnecessary things. Fayth yawned. *Would you forgive me if I made it up to you? I don't like it when you're upset with me.* Fayth offered.

Made it up to me? What could he possibly do to make it up to her? She tried not to focus on the sad expression clouding his face. *I'm not sure. It could be a ploy.* She directed at him.

You sound like your brother when you get upset. Fayth huffed. *Won't you stop insinuating things of me? I have no negative intentions. I aim only to aid you, to fulfill my purpose. Which includes the things you so desire. I've no reason to offer you empty words.* He sighed heavily. And somehow it evoked a lonely, sad feeling inside of Phelia. One that buried the last of her bitterness without warning.

What are you offering? Phelia asked, uncertain but curious.

Something you want. I hoped to wait, to have more time with you- some sort of peace for now...but I suppose there's no other choice. Fayth spoke waves into her mind. His voice was soft, with an almost miserable weight to it. As if he were also overcome with a certain sadness. For some reason, it filled her with guilt.

"Yes, well, he *is* my brother after all. Tell me, what is this thing that I want? When will I receive this?" Phelia prodded, not wanting to be left in her state of wonder.

"*Answers.*" Fayth spoke quietly. His large blue eyes blinked up at her as she shifted in her spot on the couch. "Gather your friends as soon as you are able. It is time to meet your **predecessors**."

Phelia's eyes widened in surprise. Surely, he could only mean one thing.

Twenty-Three

Zane...

RABID.

Zane flopped down into the seat beside Victor, who hadn't come down to the cafeteria for lunch. He attempted to hand him the extra tray he'd brought with him, but Victor refused to lift his face from the gap in his arms. "You really don't want anything?" Zane asked with a sigh.

"I don't. Especially from someone who played hooky." Victor replied, motioning to his bag. "I brought you something else for your visit."

"Hmm? Another one of your mother's home-cooked meals?" Zane smiled, peeking into the container. "I'll have to remember to thank her. Since Dad and Phelia aren't great in the kitchen no one ever cooks for me."

"Stop that." Victor huffed. "You're avoiding. Why'd you skip school? And you got here right before lunch." Zane shifted in his seat, slowly scooping the food from Victor's tray onto his. He had barely managed to tell his dad what happened at the hospital. But what if it happened again? He surely hoped not.

"At the hospital, Sydney and who knows who else pulled some strings to fill Bailey's hospital room with a bunch of plants—flowers.

Huge ones. So many that it was hard to even see anyone standing in the same room. Belle was pretty upset by it. She ended having me follow her down the hall. I think she just needed to vent. And we went out onto that stupid balcony where my dad...the same place we went when mom was pronounced dead that day.

"Maybe that was bad enough. But Belle said that no one should send those kinds of flowers to the living. That it was like saying Bailey was gone. I guess the larger the banquet the more serious the condolences? I remember accepting a bunch of large flowers and stuff on dad's behalf too, but I didn't give it much thought until now.

"Belle was probably right too because while we were talking, they called a code for her room. I can't even explain that moment. The fear on Belle's face, and I thought my heart was going to jump out of my chest. We just bolted down the hall like maniacs. I am pretty sure that I heard some staff yelling at our backs.

"We got to the room and found out that they had to do CPR. Bailey...she actually coded—But! They brought her back." Zane took a deep breath and tried to calm his nerves. He didn't know why he had been talking so fast. "They brought her back, but none of it makes any sense. I kept thinking that kinda thing. Tried to put the parts together. I'm not doing very well in that department.

"She doesn't have any brain injuries, there's no abnormal swelling. I mean, aside from a few cuts and bruises from the fall, there's *nothing*. The doctors don't understand it either. If her readings are normal and they checked her entire body, how's she in a coma in the first place? I keep wondering about seeing her there in front of The Death House when we saw all those spirits and everything else. I keep thinking that I won't be able to apologize."

Zane tried to center himself, realizing he was holding his utensil and tray so hard that his hands hurt. He could hear Victor's apologetic tone but still, he didn't lift his head. It wasn't like Victor not to look him in the face when he was being sympathetic. Was the news so difficult? That didn't exactly sound like Victor. *Is he just that tired? Is his mom doing another bout of cleaning? Couldn't she wait another week or so? It is almost Winter break after all.*

"Anyway, there's something else too. Some weird stray cat which I realized I forgot to mention. You haven't been over lately, but Grace has seen him. I don't know if dad was so accepting because he is happy to be staying home for a bit or what, but Phelia agreeing to the whole bit was a surprise. She named him Fayth. I'm telling you; something is off. I still gotta figure it out but, there's something *weird* about that cat."

"I thought you wanted a cat. Didn't you say that when we met?" Victor asked, and Zane had the feeling he was poking fun.

"You sound like my dad. Even if I did back then, I haven't thought about that in forever. And nowadays we've got so much going on that it sounds even less like a good idea. Between these strange crystals, other world stuff, and Bailey...I don't know why they want to take care of a cat in the first place."

After a long, grueling silence, Zane shook Victor, all but sure he'd fallen asleep on him. If there was a time that he needed a few words of his weighty, caring guidance and opinions, now was it. That was, if the guy could stay awake for even a moment to give it. To his surprise, Victor sprung up from his seat, with such an expression that Zane stumbled backwards, and crashed into the desks behind him. "**Don't touch me!**" He shouted. Zane groaned, careful of his own movements on the floor as he met Victor's eyes. Only, they could hardly be called the eyes of his best friend.

It looked to Zane as though he was staring a rabid, wild animal in its face. His eyes were bloodshot. He could see dark shadows resting beneath them. Could hear his sharp, quickened breaths, following an even quicker rise in his chest. Had he been closer he was sure he would feel his breath on his face. Maybe if he'd been closer, his face would have been ripped to shreds.

Zane watched Victor take a step forward and swipe angrily through the air. Considering that he was heading in the wrong direction, Zane had no way to know if he was after him. Cautious, he slowly made his way to his feet, watching Victor's uneven, trembling steps. *What's going on?* Zane questioned. *What's wrong with him?*

"Victor?" He called and followed his angry erratic movements. In his frenzy, he almost didn't seem to notice his collisions with the desks and chairs. The force sending them quaking or crashing nosily to the floor.

"Victor? *Victor!*" Zane shouted. Willing himself to take him by the shoulders, turning him around to face him. He tried to make sense of Victor's mumbles before he gave up and shook him again. "Victor! What's wrong with you?!" He shouted. And in a moment akin to clarity, Victor's eyes met his and he glanced around the classroom before letting out a shaky sigh.

"Did I...do this?" Victor asked quietly, almost as if he were afraid.

"Unfortunately." Zane nodded. "You scared me--" He began, his thoughts being cut off as Victor pulled away, struggling towards the door. "W-wait a minute!" Zane shouted, wondering in the back of his mind if their ruckus had alerted any students or faculty. "You can't just leave like this. You hardly look like you can stand. You *gotta* tell me what's going on."

As Zane messily pushed furniture out of his way, his heart thumped away in his chest as he watched Victor stumbling forward. His breath caught in his throat as he recognized the exact moment of his descent—the exact moment his head hit the floor. Upon making his way to his side, Zane realized he was unconscious. *Please, no.*

"Victor? Hold on. Please, just—*someone*!" ***WHAT A PITY***, the voice called from the back of his skull. *Great.* He'd almost forgotten about that during his chaotic life at home and the hospital. He hadn't heard a peep from it during all his visits with Bailey. In fact, he wasn't sure when exactly he'd heard the voice last.

"Somebody help me!" Zane shouted, calling to anyone who could hear. He didn't have a clue what was going on but the thought of anything happening to Victor—of him ending up in the same state as Bailey sent waves of fear down his spine. "HELP!"

Twenty-Four

Eustis...

TRUTH.

Eustis knew the moment that he had started telling the truth, he'd opened a floodgate. He knew that he wouldn't be able to help himself anymore. He knew that with every word of truth he was also betraying the people who he'd labeled his friends. Although, it was not the first time that Eustis was made aware of just how untrue that was. If he were going to be honest, it might as well be with himself too.

It felt good before, just being able to call other people his friends, but he'd felt completely alone surrounded by them at every moment. Even when they smiled in his direction or gave him a pat on the back. Their compliments felt empty, void of anything genuine. When they spent time together, he'd found himself bored and wishing to be home with Kennet or in his own thoughts. And yet, he still did it anyway. Because they were the type of people his parents thought highly of, at least for their backgrounds.

Now, against all odds, it felt good—*really good*—to tell the truth. To tell Ms. Pine everything had been their fault, even if he'd pointed less blame at himself. She'd even called him brave for speaking up. She had no clue that he lacked any sort of bravery at all. If he had been brave, he would have told the truth from the very beginning. What he did by telling the truth was nothing more than being a decent human being. Or at least, he was trying to be. Grace deserved that much.

Grace, Eustis thought with a bittersweet sigh, *what would she say to me now?* She'd said he'd have gotten bullied if anyone ever saw him run, but what would she say if she knew it was telling the truth that led him to this space between the trees? To him being sprawled out on the ground in the freezing cold snow, taking blows from his ex-friends?

He'd lost track of whose fist or foot was striking him now. He felt the sharp pains all throughout his body as they struck him, in what seemed a relentless pursuit to pummel every ounce of their anger beneath his skin. Probably so he'd never forget. As if that would have been possible. He could never forget the sound of gasping for breath, the pain drowning out his senses, or the odd crackling sound when he exhaled.

He wasn't much of a fighter. Against all of them he knew even if he managed to take a single swing back, he'd still have been met with the same end. He'd still be swollen and hurting. His face would still be smothered in a mound of snow in the bitter Winter air. More than that, Eustis knew he deserved this.

Who knew what pain they caused Grace before? How many times had these very same people struck a blow to her? With how many rocks did they strike her? How many days had she gotten punished at home because of everything he started? He didn't know how accurate it was, but he imagined this was what she had felt. *Yeah. This is the* ***least*** *I* deserve.

. . .

"Did you just call me an *elephant?*" Eustis asked in disbelief. Suddenly feeling less emotional than moments before.

"What?" Grace had asked, blinking in his direction, almost as if she had been as surprised as he was. "No, I didn't."

"I'm pretty sure you did. I'm certain your exact words were actually *stupid elephant.*"

"W-well then, maybe I did. Stupid elephant, Elephant Spit...both fit. You've been a total jerk." Grace admitted. When Eustis began to chuckle, Grace's eyes met his skeptically. "What's so funny? Don't laugh!"

"Sorry. It's just, out of anything you could have called me, even the scum of the Earth, you called me something like that. And it rhymes." He laughed, unable to hold it in. To some extent, he found himself relieved. It was almost a weird nickname more than an insult. And he had no idea what Elephant Spit looked like, he was sure he never wanted to know, but he *had* been stupid. He acted like an idiot since the first day they'd met. Worse actually, and yet that's what she'd been calling him? Grace might very well have been a Saint...

...

"Eustis?! Eustis??" Someone was calling him. Forcing his eyes open, he wondered when he'd started thinking back on their conversation. He couldn't feel his face but registered the pain in the rest of his body. He could hear his teeth clatter as he groaned. When he turned his head, a wave of snow slid down his face. He could just make out Kennet's horrified expression mouthing words he could hardly understand. Had he fallen asleep somehow? How did Kennet find him? Did he manage to phone him at some point?

Soon, Kennet lifted his head to place it on a pillow in the back seat and tossed blankets over him. He could faintly smell his cologne as he leaned over him, touching his face, which was now beginning to hurt too. "What happened to you, Eustis?" He directed at him, his face full of a mixture of pity and worry. In that moment, he looked much older than 30.

"Where you found me...please don't tell." Eustis croaked. It was a horrible favor to ask, but he knew his parents. No matter what happened, Eustis couldn't tell them the truth. At least not yet.

"You can't be serious!" Kennet frowned, "Look at the state of you. I have to take you to the hospital and your parents are going to come. You were bloody and unconscious in the snow! And you are worried about them knowing where you *were*? Tell me. Who did this to you??"

"**Please**, Kennet. They'll blame Grace. I can't let them do that again. I'll tell you everything later. Promise." Eustis could see Kennet's anger and confusion rising while tears brimmed his already messy vision. "I have to fix it." He sobbed, the weight of it all settling on him. He couldn't undo the wrongs he'd done. But he couldn't let his parents get involved. It felt like this was the only chance he'd ever get to fix things for himself and his relationship with Grace.

Eustis felt the itchy sensation of warmth forcing its way into his chilled body and heaved painfully through his cries. Which only made things worse. He never knew crying could hurt so much. He felt younger than his current self, almost hopeless in his situation. Guilty too, for the things he was asking of his friend.

Eustis could hardly make out the deep-set wrinkle in Kennet's forehead as he heard the clicking of his tongue, a habit he'd witnessed in tense situations of the past. If nothing else, he was truly giving it thought. Which was more than what he should have asked for. But Eustis needed Kennet to be on his side. He had no one else.

"Ugh! ***Fine.*** You tell me when you're well enough. I think you've broken something. Just look at your face. You're an absolute mess. Your parents are going to kill me when they find out. I've got to get you to the hospital." He sighed and dragged his fingers through his hair. "What do you want me to tell them?"

Twenty-Five

Twister...

MAGIC AND PRESENCE.

Upon his return to the Human World, Twister's happy, albeit short, embrace with True was met with a bitter end. She quickly explained a few missed events, and when he'd asked about her ankle that was resting under ice, she asked where he'd been instead. "Here and there, I've had many little stops. FlareWing. Which is one of the reasons I rushed back here. You said that Victor's in the hospital?"

"Yes." True nodded. "Since yesterday, I think."

"I need all of you. Unfortunately, I don't think this can wait. Is he alright? Would he be well enough to speak with us?"

"Zane came by yesterday, saying that they would visit him today." True responded, fidgeting with her bedsheets. She was worried, Twister couldn't blame her for that. In fact, he felt as if his news was bound to make the feeling worse. For True, as well as the others.

"What about you? Can you stand?" Twister asked, pushing the ice off of her ankle to inspect it. True nodded, but her hesitation left him unsure. "Let me have a look."

He was tired and running on little rest, but he was sure he could manage something. With a nod, Twister instructed True to sit still and he slipped his left hand under her ankle. The other, he placed right above it and slowly nurtured the light in his mind. Until it grew with a warmth that traced his body down to his fingertips and water slowly took shape below his palm. He recognized the fluid shape taking form and filling with a green light as it flooded her ankle below.

When he was finished and the light dissipated and the water receded, he glanced over at True to see her eyes full of wonder. She slowly picked up her ankle and worked it in circles before sliding down to her feet. She pressed her weight into the floorboards and smiled. "It's sore, but much better. That was magic?" She asked, sporting a small, grateful smile.

"Yes. Magic properties are difficult to explain. This was a type of magic, that works by working with other liquid forms and their natural accompaniments. In this case, the blood and its cells already at work in your body. It isn't much, and it is limited, but it can come in handy. In a way, I suppose you can say that I flooded your ankle with more of your blood—it is a liquid in itself after all—encouraged the cells to work a little faster." Twister shrugged.

"It's amazing either way." She smiled again. Flooding him with a warmth that he was grateful to feel considering all the negatives he had swirling around his head. "Can all Faeries do this?"

"All Faeries have magic but only Faeries with certain types can heal. Although I'm capable of much less magic than other Fae because of my form, I can do this much. Even so, there are others much more apt at utilizing healing forms." Twister nodded. "This is not nearly so impressive as those."

"It seems fitting that the son of Faerie Generals would be able to heal. I think it suits you well, Twister." True said softly, making him blush. He wasn't sure he was worthy of such high praise. Would his parents have been impressed by such a little thing? He wanted to tell her about his parents' proposal, but there were more important things to discuss.

"Thank you kindly. But if you think you can manage, we should go to the hospital. Especially if the others will be joining." Twister frowned, trying to focus. "There are things I found out at home that you all should know."

"This is about The Darkness, isn't it?" True asked hesitantly. Looking at her drooping shoulders and hearing the tone of her voice, he wanted to tell her otherwise. Neither of them could forget what happened when she traveled through the door. He was sure that for some time neither were sure they would make it out back then. But they had and it left much time to remember. Telling lies would have done nothing, probably not even offer a false sense of comfort.

"Yes." Twister answered finally. "And then some. I'm sorry."

...

At the hospital, Twister sat tucked away into True's jacket pocket as she waited to visit Victor. It was a bit stuffy in there, but he stretched out as best as he could, happy her pockets were so deep, taking bites of some organic ginger snack she offered him. Or at least, that was what True had called it, though he had no clue of its name. What did organic mean anyhow? Was that not the natural way of things? Aside from their unholy slaughter of animals for meals, was there something else wrong with food in the Human World? Just what would be inorganic?

As he snacked away, opting not to get lost in those thoughts, he became aware of True's light shuffling as she exchanged a few words with someone. Interested, Twister focused his eyes and slowly looked beyond the bounds of the fabric. Such things could never bind a Faerie's eyes. After all, they were eyes borne of magic.

A couple minutes later, they were ushered down the hall and into a room. Inside, Twister could make out a couple of his other companions. Also in the room was a woman whose gaze was riddled with concern, fidgeting with her purse. "Mom, will you stop worrying? I'm only in here for another night." Victor's voice called from beneath a bundle of sheets on a large bed across the room although Twister could see the gloomy expression on his face.

"How could I not worry? You passed out at school, Victor! And what else did they say? Not only have you not been sleeping but you were dehydrated and were slightly malnourished? How could that be possible? You, who slept throughout most of my pregnancy and gave me frights. Half of your life you've spent asleep, I'm sure of it."

"Wait. You haven't been sleeping?" Zane's voice chimed in as he slid open the door. "And don't tell me those meals weren't for me." He frowned, looking equal parts worried and cross.

"I'm sorry." Victor sighed, sitting up in the bed with a look of surprise and embarrassment on his face as he looked around the room. "I wasn't hungry and I didn't want to waste it. I didn't want to cause a fuss and—" His voice faded as he looked in Twister and True's direction. "True? You too? What are you doing here? What about your ankle?"

Before he could get out of his bed, Grace grabbed hold of his wrist from his side and pulled him back down into his sheets. "No way, Mr. You're supposed to be resting!" As she spoke Twister became aware of a distinct presence nearby. Could it be...?

"Grace, I'm fine. I've eaten. They gave me that medicine and I went to sleep. You should be worried about her ankle. It looked so—"

"My ankle is much better." True nodded through her mask. Garnering the attention of Victor's mother and the others.

"Oh, hello True. It's been some time since I've seen you. I do hope you and your aunts are doing alright? I never did get to properly thank them for helping Victor."

"Mom, don't get so close. She gets nervous. Don't corner her." Victor chided lightly. Grace pushed him back down into his hospital bed. "Geez Grace. I'm not going to die if I get out the bed. True," He called looking back in their direction, "your ankle is really okay?"

True nodded. "Yes. Actually Twist--"

"I can hear you outside the door." Phelia cut in, appearing in the doorway with a basket. Twister immediately felt a similar sensation again. "I take it that you're feeling better, Victor?"

He gave a slight nod in her direction. "Well enough at present. The doctors keep giving me things and putting me to sleep and I have three mother hens. How could I not be?" Phelia chuckled and gave Victor's mother the basket she was carrying before making her way to Grace to exchange greetings.

"I am not." Zane scoffed, crossing his arms over his chest. To which Phelia and Grace giggled in response. "Don't laugh!" He directed at them, hardly able to hide the twitching at the corner of his own lips before Victor's mother offered a light kiss on the cheek.

"Victor can always use an extra parent around." She chuckled.

"Not you too." Zane whined, shaking his head as she asked Phelia if the basket was from their father.

Phelia nodded. "He said he was going to the cafeteria. I think he means to stay with us until visiting is done."

"That sounds perfect." She nodded, her brown eyes looking less worried. "I have some questions for him about Victor. Maybe he could help."

"Oh no. Mom. I'm fine. I told you already. You don't have to go seek out Dr. Brand. And you've been here all night. Why don't you go rest yourself?"

She looked at him as if contemplating his suggestion for a moment before making a tsking noise. "You and I will have to talk about this, but your friends are here so it's better to let you enjoy the company. They seem like they are worried too, but in the meantime Dr. Brand and I will have an adult conversation. One where you may or may not be a topic of discussion."

Whatever point the woman attempted to convey to her son seemed to have worked. Victor frowned but nodded his head with a sigh. Instead of words of opposition, he simply apologized as she made her way out of the door. Still, the slightly cheerful air about the room hadn't fully diminished. Twister felt a sense of bitterness set in as he would be the one to ruin it.

Slowly, he made his way out of True's pocket. He swallowed the last bite of his ginger treat and made his way to her shoulder. Victor was the first to notice, his voice making the others snap their attention quickly their way. "What are you doing in Snowville?"

"Twister? True said you'd been around." Victor said, a slight hint of something in his voice that couldn't be placed.

"No way! What are you doing here in our world??" Grace shouted, cupping her mouth with her hands. "Wait! Does that mean you really came back then like True said?"

"I'm ashamed to admit that I didn't exactly believe it." Zane said, scratching his cheek. "Sorry True."

True shook her head gently, showcasing her forgiveness. "It's okay." Twister couldn't ignore a separate sense of guilt rising up in him. Had he known he'd somehow manage to make True seem less believable because of his disappearances he would have made sure to see the others first.

"It's nice to see you again Twister." Phelia said politely, though he could feel a sudden surge in energy from her. One could only imagine the questions brimming her mind. He could even make out the fire beneath her gaze as if his presence signified some feast waiting to be devoured. Curiosity sometimes seemed its own kind of magic, in a way. A magic created in the form of wonderment and questions. Intricately balanced between innocence, hope and life. Phelia, as far as Twister could tell, often sprouted this magic like weeds.

"He healed my ankle." True said softly, still offering Twister more praise than he thought he deserved. It wasn't such a great feat.

"Ooh! That's so neat!" Grace beamed. "Can you heal Victor too?"

"Grace, I told you already—Sorry, Twister. I'm fine. Really."

Twister shook his head. "I get it. Considering what I overheard, I may not be able to offer you too much help."

"That's too bad," Grace sighed, flopping down into her chair. "Too bad we missed it."

"But what are you doing here?" Phelia asked. "Why'd you come before? Why didn't you say anything to us? What made you leave in the first place?"

"It seems like there's a lot to discuss. I hate to ruin things but my news isn't very good. And I'll explain everything I can, but first thing's first. I wasn't certain of it before but there are two other presences in this room."

"Oh, you've gotta be kidding me." Zane sighed, rubbing his palms across his face. "Phelia tell me you didn't bring the cat." He directed her way, to which she offered a guilty smile, slowly pulling a fluffy black animal from the other side of her jacket.

Twister silently studied it from his place across the room. When its eyes met his, he blinked away his surprise. "That's not a cat." He said through a breath. Though he wasn't sure how to describe it.

"He said there were two of something. Where's the other one? Is it another animal?" Victor asked aloud. To which Grace shifted uneasily in her seat.

"W-wait. What do you mean it's not a cat?" Zane asked, his face quickly clouding with suspicion.

Twenty-Six

Quill...

GOLDEN INK.

With limbs of lead, Quill dragged herself forward, beyond the cascading hills, passed the streaks of blood, empty homes and nameless fields. In the near distance she could see the temple taking shape. More clearly, a staircase forming a few yards ahead of her. The very staircase that was built into the base of the mountain which would lead her to the large, ornate crimson doors she sought. Finally, she was almost there. How many protectors had she faced in that mirage-like town? How many tried to keep her from fulfilling her ***father's*** wish? Whatever the case, they failed. Victory was hers now.

By nightfall, Quill had climbed the dreaded steps and made her way to the immense red doors. A large metal bar was attached to the top corner of a nearby beam and wired trinkets fluttered in the wind. As they swayed past each other she became aware of a peculiar tune. Of unnatural voices humming an unintelligible melody. One that, beyond all reasoning, rooted her where she stood. It was then that an echo of warnings filled her head.

Do not enter. Turn back. You seek nothing here. This is no place for you. Only unimaginable danger will befall you inside.

But these warnings meant nothing. Not even this strange energy would keep her from righting the wrongs of the past. She would not leave. Having renewed the flames of her resolve and scoffed at her nonsensical momentary pause, Quill placed her palms against the door. It was then that she recalled the previous mission and her arms fell to her sides against her will.

. . .

Opal seemed hesitant; Quill noted for the hundredth time that day. How many times did one person have to bark the same instructions for them to be followed? As the two of them lay the jagged gold spheres on the ground, Opal frowned and looked over at her. "Quill," she'd said in a smaller than normal voice, "why don't we stop this? Before it's too late."

"What are you talking about now?" Quill scoffed, not hiding her annoyance. They needed to hurry or their trap would fall to ruin.

"All of this. Finally, we are up here with access to all of these worlds, all of these beautiful things. Real food. Fresh air. Yet, we are running around doing these things. *Unspeakable* things in every world we step foot into—just look at this situation we've found ourselves in now. Setting gold for ***bait***. Readying ourselves to ruin the life of another being. Again. If we return his gold and leave, turn back, nothing else has to happen."

"Are you suggesting that we **fail**? That I should care about the lives of anyone else above my family? How can you utter such words? We've lived as if our existence meant nothing. While all of *them* ignored the fact that we existed at all. My ***father*** did what he could for us. I'm not abandoning my life's purpose to live in a world of lies."

"How can you know truth from lies if you never question it? Aren't you afraid of what you are doing? Of consequence? What if you're ***wrong?*** Does my life matter to you, Quill? In this grand plan... does it matter if I live?"

"You are always sputtering nonsense. You don't know enough. He hasn't told you things so you have too many questions. Your life? Hmph. If you keep talking like that it will matter very little."

It took only a matter of seconds for Opal's face to express something unfathomable. Before long, that look disappeared as they often did. She mumbled something under her breath and quickly scurried away. Quill did not fret over it.

That Faerie was too much of a distraction. Surely, she would have to face reality. She was too coddled below the surface. *If she says something like that again I'll report her*, Quill thought through a frustrated sigh. *Now where's that stupid Leprechaun? He won't get away again.*

. . .

Quill looked down at her blood-soaked palms and the quaking of her fingers caught her by surprise. She wanted to say it was the excitement of finishing her tasks that was sending ripples through her. Or perhaps this was the aftereffects of not eating as much as she should. Didn't Opal say that sort of thing could happen?

And yet, neither of those things felt like the case. She'd eaten plenty right before entering that town below because she dreaded the thought of more hunger pains. Beyond that, she couldn't manage excitement when she was so utterly exhausted.

Opal. Where was that ungrateful little Faerie anyhow? At a time like this she could have been useful. If nothing else, to help her discern the feeling swimming through her body and the shaking of her extremities. Hadn't she told her that she'd follow her everywhere? Yes. Those had been her words. So, where was she now?

When it came to that strange Faerie, Quill had no clue what to think. Is a loyalty to her but not the man responsible for her life disloyalty? Every time she broached the subject of her father Opal was mute and refused to say another word for hours. Else, she'd fly away with those double layered wings of hers. But thinking of her or her words were a waste of time. Something that if nothing else, she couldn't afford.

Quill frowned, cleared her mind of anything besides her goal, and looked at the temple towering above her. If the trinkets and the double doors had been responsible for those thoughts, she would not give them another chance. With a small sense of pleasure, Quill smeared her bloody hands against the thick wood, immediately aware of heat forming around her palms.

Before long, she recognized what was happening. This door was intent on burning her away to nothing. Now that she could feel its magic, however, whatever protections it could muster would be futile. It was drained thanks to her recent success in the town. *Wither away to nothing.*

It was almost a disappointment really. How easy it had been to destroy bodies imbued with magic much older than her own existence. It was only a matter of time before Quill could feel the magic caving beneath her fingertips. Before the temple began to crumble and the searing heat that had been trickling up her arms faded with it. Floating above a podium, a mere 10 feet ahead of her, stood today's prize.

Upon closer inspection, Quill found herself less impressed by the jagged lines of ink on the old parchment. She could make out the fox and its neck decorated in large beads but hardly any detail to the rest of its features. Wasn't it supposed to be some grand painting? Clearly more than a little had been lost in translation and time. There was nothing grand about what she was seeing. This simple drawing inspired no ounce of wonder or excitement. Still, the fact that it was there meant her last mission was not in vain. Assuming it would work.

If nothing else, she could feel the pressure of magic around it. There was nothing else to do but attempt. Quill reached in her pocket and retrieved the swirling golden ink. This was her prize for treacherous days of Leprechaun hunting. She still understood very little of the ancient secret magic bonded with the ink or the other components besides liquid gold that were mixed to create it. What she did know, however, was that this ink took thousands of years to procure a single drop whereas she gained an entire inkwell of it. It would undoubtedly hold enough magic to bring the ***Kumiho*** to life.

Quill dipped the silken wrapped brush into the warm, bright liquid before pressing it to the end of the fox's body. Slowly, she painted the first tail. The second, then the third. Fourth, fifth, sixth, seventh. Eighth. Ninth.

By the time the final stroke etched the crinkled paper, swirls of ink, black and gold, drifted through the air. It stretched slowly from the parchment and swirled in a rhythmic pattern near her feet. Eventually taking an animalistic shape. Turning into something beautiful enough to be a painting.

A white furred fox with golden eyes blinked at her. Black waves of fur intricately danced down the middle of its back. Stout orange and black beads hung from its neck and a jewel of similar design rested atop its forehead. Surely, they should have gotten the services of a better artist. The messy inked drawing had done the beast no justice.

Even the constant rage flickering behind its eyes and the saliva brimming its lips could not take away from its beauty. Quill had been prepared for this. She wasted no time placing her bag on the floor in offering. It had just been awakened and it needed to feed. Supposedly on 100 livers.

"I've come prepared," she smiled. But her pride would be short lived. The beast only devoured two. Deemed the rest unacceptable. It bared its fangs as it looked her over, almost in warning that her own liver was ripe for the taking. Who would have guessed that the ancient fox who sat trapped in paper for hundreds of thousands of years would be picky with its food?

Twenty-Seven

Opal...

LOST.

"You can't speak?" Opal asked, slumped over one of the fruits she'd acquired for him that morning. The man shook his head, defeat painting his features. *How unfortunate for us both,* Opal thought. *I'd hoped to ask about those images from before. Those words. If they were a memory—his memory. It felt so, at least, it was similar to what it is like when my parents' memories are at the forefront of my mind.*

She'd already asked him if he recalled being thrown to the surface. Apparently, he did not. How it was possible that he recalled nothing at all concerning it was beyond her. Perhaps the man had really lost consciousness well before they made it out. But how had they? Opal had days now to figure out what had happened. Although she supposed she'd also had days to try and squeeze information from this human with the familiar blue gaze.

Still, she couldn't bring herself to push him. He'd seemed confused. Tired. He was thinner than she knew he should have been. Overall, he was in a poor state. She'd managed to collect a lot of fruits and vegetables for him, firewood for the tattered cabin, and extra blankets. All of which took a great deal of time the last few days.

The first couple of days he'd weakly eaten food but had little strength to do more before falling asleep. Not even the sound of the train in the distance could wake him. Yesterday, he had gently looked over the food and managed to use a blade to chop a random assortment of ingredients together in water to make a soup. Although Opal couldn't call it much of one. This also exhausted him to the point that he didn't so much as stir again all night. That morning, however, had been a different story.

He'd woken and began the fire. Rinsed his bowls from days before and gingerly went about the dusty table with a ripped piece of cloth he'd found, cut fruits and vegetables, and chewed a stem as he moved about the rest of the place, exploring for the first time. Opal left him to find more wood to feed the fire. Upon returning, she found him napping on a stool in a corner near the flames, tears streaming down his face with a painful expression.

That was a handful of hours ago now, and though he had seemed surprised by the state of his own reflection in water from the bucket, he'd regained some sense of a composure and went behind the old curtain to wash himself. After which, he'd taken to eating as if he were having food for the first time. Not too unlike herself, in hindsight, when she and Quill had their first meal above the surface. To have anything other than sludge and filth. To recognize real texture and form, smells, of a meal, let alone taste. It had been glorious.

How long had this man been below anyhow? Had he always...? "Could you speak before or have you always been mute?" Opal asked abruptly, her curiosity forcing her out of her own head. His nod surprised her. "You could speak?" Another nod.

She couldn't place the sour taste knowing had left on her tongue. Had *IT* done something? Just who was this human? Every time she looked at him, she could feel nothing dark about him, in fact, she could hardly tell that anything afflicted him at all as the days went on. The residue of *IT*s energy had waned. And the more she looked at his forlorn eyes, the more she felt something there. Almost, if she had to guess, like the faintest hint of...*magic?*

Whatever the case, she couldn't afford to spend much more time trying to piece together that puzzle. She'd spent a suspicious amount of time away from Quill and knew she needed to make a reappearance. Even though Quill's words still echoed in her head. Even though her words still hurt her heart. She couldn't abandon her now. *She is merely lost*, Opal thought sadly, in need of further convincing, *and if one is lost, they need only be shown the way. One day Quill will see things clearly. She must.*

"I'm sorry, but I must leave you for now." Opal said, gently taking flight to eye level. She watched as he turned his head to watch the flames of the fire before eventually meeting her eyes with a pitiful smile. She wished it were even a little reassuring. "I wouldn't like to leave you this way. You're hardly recovered. Everything you do seems to exhaust you. I'm sorry.

"You have to build your strength so you shouldn't overdo it, yes? It's freezing out. I've found a coat but it's laden with rips and probably won't fit you well. Still, it may offer a little extra warmth with the other blanket. If you go out there you might just freeze to death in your state, so stay inside. I will return in four days, five perhaps. But this should be enough to last you in case I take a little longer. And I'll find paper. You can write and read, can't you?"

Silence. A curt nod and an expression she couldn't place. Still, at least he understood. "Good. That's perfect. Then we'd be able to talk to each other then. I have questions and I'm sure you must as well." Another nod. "It doesn't feel right, leaving you on your own like this. I really wouldn't go if I had any other choice." She knew she felt guilty, but Opal truly meant every word. She couldn't imagine the fear he must have felt, somehow surviving under the surface and above, knowing nothing. Almost every question she had asked since she brought him there had ended in no or a slight shrug.

Now, he was even stuck in a small cabin with a fraction of it usable. Unable to speak when at some point he'd been capable. She knew nothing of what he'd been through or who he was, but no one deserved to live such a life. She could offer him no comfort in his situation nor in the future. And she was leaving him completely alone for more than a few hours this time. After all, she couldn't tell Quill. She was devoted to ***IT***. If she'd gone back immediately to tell her the truth, would Quill have even hesitated to report her?

Suddenly aware of a light pressure on her shoulder, Opal realized that she'd been distracted by her own thoughts again. She must have worried the man because he tilted his head ever so slightly to the right and turned up the corner of his lips as if to reassure her that he would be okay.

When she thanked him and headed towards the door, he stood and walked her out, peeking around the doorframe to the perfectly laid snow around the cabin. Opal watched as the chilled air ruffled the man's black curls before she shuffled through the door with a shiver and urged him to close it behind her.

Now I must find Quill. Who knows how much progress she's made by now. Or where she's run off to. I am coming back empty-handed. What excuse could I give her? Do I even need such a thing or...?

Twenty-Eight

Morgan...

AN OSETT AND THE FREIGHT TRAIN.

Morgan wondered what the Faerie, Opal, thought when she looked at him. Which thought explained the pitiful look that clouded her face those moments before he shut the door? He did look rather worth pitying. Or at least, he'd thought so upon seeing his reflection. If he'd managed to be any thinner, he wondered if his cheekbones would have sunken in. Or if his ribs would be seen through his ragged clothes.

He was tired again. Which seemed a consequence of his current physical state. The fog in his mind had lifted and his thoughts were clear. So clear that he should have been able to voice them—he didn't have a voice anymore. *Somehow.* Though he could almost remember the sound.

It terrified him to think on it, so he focused on other things. Like what he was capable of instead. Simple meals, though his taste buds missed seasonings. Even the simplest of them like salt and pepper. He remembered those, and how to tend to the fire. Cleaning and washing. His body knew them before his mind.

He remembered books that he'd read as a boy and conversations with his father. He remembered meeting Lily. His name. But everything else seemed to dance away from him. Prancing around the back of his mind, shuffling in and out of reach as soon as he took a step towards them. Moving to their own rhythms as if to taunt him. Still, it felt better to know things and to think. Even if it wasn't enough.

And it wasn't. He needed to jog his memory. He didn't know the day or the time, but surely there must have been something, anything he could do. For a long moment he watched the flames of the fire and put his feet as close as he dared without getting burnt. Thinking again on his few memories and cried again at the thought of Lily. Where was she? Where was his father? He didn't understand why he was filled with such grief. How long had he been away?

Away **where**? Suddenly, a chill ran down his spine. He saw the flames swaying ahead of him but couldn't feel their warmth. His insides frosted over and he was struck with a sense of fear unlike he'd ever known. His teeth clattered, and he pulled his legs to his chest in a moment akin to infancy. For in that moment, he felt like a child again. Spooked by some unknown thing from the closet. And yet, something altogether worse...

...

By the time his fright had subsided, and the chill of his spine made way for the slight warmth of the dying fire, Morgan had decided what he would do. If nothing else, returning to some of the places in his head could calm the incessant waves of anxiety washing over him. And if he was lucky, perhaps the rest of his memories would make an appearance. As he slowly tossed a single log into the flames, he found himself apologizing to Opal from their distance.

She'd warned him that going out was dangerous. Even he knew that in his current state he would be asking for trouble but sitting there and doing nothing was no longer an option. Morgan refused to wait for that terrifying feeling to grip him again. Making himself busy and solidifying his resolve seemed much better an idea.

He recalled the noisy churning of the trains in the distance. If he was going to find his way away from the cabin, this was probably his best bet. So, he went about the place and packed most of the food, took the cup, the small pot, a few utensils and some of the firewood and wrapped them in a bundle of old cloth. He slid on the aged pair of oversized socks, the other shirt and trousers folded neatly in the corner, the weathered shoes, and tattered coat. He fumbled weakly at both blankets, tossed them around his shoulders, and tied them into a knot to hold them in place.

Slightly out of breath, Morgan wiped at the beads of sweat forming at his brow and made his way back in front of the fireplace. He was more than a little annoyed by his lack of physical strength and endurance. It unnerved him to think about the journey he would need to make through the snow on the other side of the door, so he opted not to think about it. Opal had said she wouldn't be back for days. If he was going to do anything on his own and possibly offer the Faerie more information than his current state afforded him, he needed to start looking for his own answers.

He sat pensively gazing into the fire until the flames extinguished and the cold air began to make its home in the broken structure. Then, with a face that mirrored his determination, he stood and made his way out the door. He looked down at his two fresh footprints in the snow, turned his attention to the left and nodded. *The trains were definitely in this direction. If I keep going, I should come across the train tracks. Then I'll follow those until another train appears.*

After what felt like an eternity, Morgan's deductions proved true. By the time the frigid cold rendered his face numb, he'd come across the tracks. And when he felt he was nearly out of strength, he heard a train in the distance. When the Engineer eventually passed him by, Morgan turned his body towards the train, eyeballed a couple of good options, slightly bent his knees, and readied himself for the leap.

His stunt nearly knocked the wind out of him. His fingers messily clasped onto a metal bar, his breath caught in his chest, and practically tumbled onto the rest of the car. For a moment he thought he'd missed the bar entirely. Morgan laid uncomfortably against his back, waiting for his heartbeat to return to its natural rhythm. More uncomfortable by the second, he opted to sit up with his back against the cold metal. Better that than removing the bundle. No matter how relieved he was to have managed, Morgan couldn't escape his frustrations.

None of this felt right. He was certain that he should have had no problem with a simple leap onto the train. He had been stronger before. And as much as he wanted to probe that thought, wanted to explore the very depth of what 'before' meant, and thus his situation proceeding the cabin, he dreaded the thought of having that sad, dark and crippling feeling creep over him once again. So, all the next day, he passed his time in an unwilling, frustrated silence. Hidden in a corner of the freight car, exposed to the winter air but too worried to start a fire for warmth.

Feeling a slight weight on his shoulder, Morgan groaned and tried to nudge it away. "*Wake **up** already!*" An unknown voice shouted. "How did you even get in here??" Suddenly realizing that he must have fallen asleep, he forced himself awake and opened his eyes. Ahead of him were two stout men, likely in their 30s, glaring at him a few feet away. Identical twins working the freight train? Morgan jumped to his feet. The items on his back rattled noisily behind him. *Where are we?* He wondered nervously inside his head. He tried to peer around their wide frames.

"What're you looking all lost for? You're obviously on one of our train cars, a little stowaway." Frowned the one on the right, looking more displeased by the second. "With those overnight temps how are you conscious? Should've frosted you over."

Morgan motioned outside the doors and shrugged his shoulders. He understood that he was interrupting their work, but he had no clue where they were. He hoped they hadn't passed his destination.

One of the men scoffed. "Well, whatdaya know? This one's a dummy. Can't talk?" Whatever twisted pleasure he'd gained in the moment made a home of his features. It increased tenfold as Morgan sheepishly nodded his head in response. He motioned again.

"You stupid bum! What's more important? Knowing where we are or my *fist* making a map out of your face?!" The other shouted, as he stepped closer. Morgan frowned. Weighed his options. Attempted to ignore that he couldn't feel his own hands and feet, let alone his face.

In all honesty, knowing where we are is much more important. He sighed a silent sigh. Repeated the motion again. Watched the man's breath swirl in the space between them. The man inched closer; his face packed with anger. Morgan made out a silhouette taking shape behind the two men. *What is that?*

His mouth moved to shape words, but no sound came. He'd seen something just now out of the corner of his eye. Some form shifting into focus in the background. He pointed frantically behind them in warning. *There's something--!* An instant later, the enginemen fell to the ground with a loud thud. There had been no time.

"My goodness. Humans are quite *noisy*, aren't they?" A voice called as Morgan's eyes were drawn to the large brown circles blinking back at him, floating in midair. "These two also don't seem to have a very good sense of judgement either. So quick to pick a fight rather than showing kindness. Such a shame. What wasted potential." The voice filled the air as the silhouette bobbed into view again. It slowly took on a human-like shape.

Not exactly a person, Morgan noted silently, *surely a creature? It almost looks familiar somehow.* Just as he was able to take in the long, silky-white hairs covering its body, it changed, mirroring the twins in nearly an instant.

"There. That's a bit better, at least now no one will be suspicious. I'll just tidy things up here. Why don't you go on ahead to the cab? I'll meet you there in a short while. Won't be long."

Do we know each other? Morgan asked cautiously in his mind, unsure of what was happening. How he wished he could talk.

"Oh. Forgive me. We don't--not personally. You saw me earlier, hadn't you? Before, when you'd hopped onto the train and missed the bar, I pulled you up? I could have sworn you met my gaze directly. And just a moment ago as well, you locked eyes with me then too. Was I mistaken?"

So, he had missed the train after all? He didn't recall seeing the creature, but he could have been too distracted. He'd been upset and exhausted at the time. It was no surprise he'd thought it familiar. Perhaps a small part of him recalled the events subconsciously. Wait. Could the creature hear him?? *You can hear me??*

"Of course, I hear you very well. Though I *do* wish you'd stop shouting. I'm not a fan of loud voices. It's a natural ability of mine."

Morgan tried to contain his curiosity and excitement. For the first time he could communicate with someone as if his voice had never left him. He willed himself not to be overwhelmed. He almost thought he would cry. To distract himself from those feelings, he shook his head and thought about what he'd been told before. Had their eyes met before? *I don't quite recall given the state of me, I'm afraid. Thank you for giving me a hand. And you've helped me yet again.* Morgan said apologetically. *May I ask why?*

"I suppose because you looked in need of a hand?" It was strange to witness a small, sympathetic smile on the face of a man who had only minutes ago been ready to bash his face in. Whatever this creature was, he'd done a little too well of a job imitating the pair. If they'd been standing together no one would be the wiser. If not for its kind tone, not to mention witnessing the change himself, neither would he. "I must handle this drop-off now, if you don't mind? Why don't you have a seat up front?"

Is he really going to do their job? This creature seems very kind. Oh. Of course, I will find my way then. Although a part of him worried about the men, the creature's courteous demeanor eased some of his worries. Even if he found it strange to think the creature so polite after witnessing it render two large men inert.

He slowly climbed out of the car and tried to work warmth into his hands. He glanced about, unable to make out much in the blanket of fresh, white snow. *Perhaps the creature would be able to provide some answers*, he thought to himself, as he made his way past the other cars and entered the doors of the train. Not knowing what else to do, Morgan sat down on the seat, thankful for the warmth that was already seeping into his stiff blankets.

When the creature offered him that kind smile again, sliding past him, the way it fondled the controls made it seem as if it had done this kind of thing before. The creature glanced at him with a knowing glance as the train pulled off, looking quite pleased with itself. "I do very much love trains." It sighed, almost giving the impression that its head was filled with fantasy, and it wasn't currently guiding the freight train at all.

I can see the happiness in your eyes. Pardon me, but where are we? Morgan asked, taking a couple pieces of fruit from the cloth on his back and gently offering one in its direction. In his experience, most magical creatures enjoyed a piece of fruit. Had he just remembered something new then? *I'm sorry I don't have much else to offer you at present. But this fruit is fresh if you'll have it.*

"What an interesting person. You aren't going to ask what I am? There wasn't even a tickle in your throat back there. I registered a bit of surprise but even so, you didn't scream. Don't you have questions?"

Unfortunately, Morgan sighed, slumping down against the cushion, *that is all I have as of late. In this case, you've already saved me twice already—would it be three considering you're driving the train? There's no reason for me to bother you more than necessary.*

"Nonsense. If I thought you'd be a bother I would have let you fall from the train." It chuckled. How nice those twins would look if they'd met him with such a warm smile. *Where are they now?* Morgan wondered. Inside a closed car perhaps? Should he ask? Did it matter?

"I wonder if it's because of those eyes of yours that you're such a kind soul. And yet, part of me is sure that you likely were meant to be so even without them." As the creature spoke, it reached into its pocket and gently passed Morgan a sheet of paper. "This is the schedule for the train. If you are in need of a ride in either direction on these dates, I will lend a hand. No thanks required. I get a legitimate excuse to thieve the train after all." Looking at the light, steady strokes of ink on the paper, he was sure that the handwriting of the two original enginemen probably couldn't compare.

"I am an Osett." The creature spoke softly, inspecting the fruit carefully before swallowing it whole.

I suppose you can feel it too. The 'magic' in these eyes. Perhaps all magical beings can all do so. I don't remember much, but I don't recall knowing of any Osett. Morgan attempted to reach the memories floating to the surface of his mind but became too distracted by the pain in his feet as the warmth spread.

"Ah, so you're aware of the magic. I am a being whose people are mostly forgotten to time now, rightly so I suppose, as there aren't many of us left. Although normally no one can see us at all. My people are well-known for their ability to read a person's feelings. Feelings are everywhere—universal, in a sense. And when feelings are strong enough, one can almost hear them like words echoing on air."

If that was the case, Morgan felt that his confusion and mixed emotions must have been overwhelming for the Osett. They were nearly too much for him as is. Hearing emotions. It seemed a burden-stricken ability if nothing else. *Your people are known for that and not that you change form?*

"Heh!" The Osett let out an airy laugh. "This is nothing more than a simple spell. Just a trick. But with eyes like yours, surely you could see through it?"

See through...? I haven't a clue. He replied thoughtfully.

"Not to worry. You can try it again another day. You'll find your way, I'm sure. You're on a very important mission after all, aren't you?" The Osett more stated than asked.

Yes. I'd say so. I have a home I must go to. Surely there must be answers there. There are things I have to see. I hope to remember. It is all so complicated. Speaking of home, if you don't mind my asking, do you live here on this train? Considering your mention of the schedule I thought perhaps--

"I do, of my own volition. Oh, I do enjoy trains very much. My own home was destroyed a very long time ago. I am glad this train can help you return to yours. How fitting."

--I see. I'm sorry. I can't imagine.

"It's quite alright. I don't know why I told you really, perhaps because there's not many I can tell." The Osett's lip quivered, slightly masked by the enginemen's curled moustache. Morgan tried to imagine being one of the last of one's kind but also, as if by the cruelest of fates, being sensitive to every creature in existence yet incapable of being seen by most of them. If feelings were like words echoing on air, then it was screaming loneliness.

If you're willing, I would like to hear your story. Morgan smiled sadly.

The Osett's eyes met his, for a moment appearing large and brown, mirroring the disembodied ones he'd seen before its apparent spell took effect. When Morgan blinked again, however, he saw the engineman's green eyes looking him over, silently assessing his offer. Else, his feelings. "You truly are a kind soul, aren't you? I would like to take you up on the offer, assuming that the upcoming town isn't your destination."

Morgan raised his eyebrows, turning his head to watch the hills give way to a cluster of cascading buildings slowly being covered in a fresh blanket of falling snowflakes. What a beautiful scene to witness. It sparked a familiar feeling in him, but it wasn't home.

"Not yours I take it?" The Osett asked, clicking its tongue. "My apologies. Perhaps the next one?"

It's alright. I'll get there. Morgan replied, wanting to stay optimistic. *Now, I can hear your story while you work.*

"I suppose that's true..." The Osett nodded, gesturing to the town outside the frosty glass window. "Do you know the name of that town below?"

I wonder if it should. It does seem distantly familiar to me but I haven't the slightest...

"Funny thing, that." The Osett smiled, "It's a name befitting this weather, in a way. I couldn't tell you too much more about it since I've only been to the station, but...*Snowville*."

Oh. Morgan thought. *I'm sure I've heard that name before. It looks quite beautiful from up here, have you a stop to make? Some delivery perhaps?*

"Not today I'm afraid." The Osett shook his head apologetically.

Snowville, huh...? Morgan shifted in his seat as he watched the town slowly disappear from view.

Twenty-Nine

Grace…

DIZZY ENOUGH.

Grace guiltily looked at the others after a poor explanation of Blitz's presence, in which she left out the entire issue with MaryAnne and Duke. She didn't know how to explain the events that led up to seeing Blitz, or that she was currently staying with a Snowville police officer. A nice woman who had the unfortunate luck of getting stuck with her while MaryAnne and Duke were being investigated.

Even more than that, Grace hadn't prepared for a pet dragon, a term that Blitz had not seemed fond of. Especially one who had been attempting some strange magic on her foster parents. Whatever the wispy black smoke with the sparkles were, Grace never imagined that by the time MaryAnne and Duke stood up again, neither of them would remember her. In fact, they were immediately horrified by finding her there with the rusty bucket, let alone ***That*** room.

At first, she thought it a strange trick. Something to test her, even. That was, until they'd called the police. Unknown to the others, her foster parents were now under investigation and forced to submit to some sort of psychological evaluation. Part of her was sure it would only be a matter of time before this knowledge flooded the town. Under temporary custody of an officer or not, what would happen to her now? She wasn't sure she was ready to face the others when they found out what she'd been hiding. Would she have to leave Snowville forever?

"So, you're telling me you have a pet dragon that just showed up outta nowhere?" Zane asked, forcing Grace to give attention back to the current tensions in the hospital room.

"Well, sort of...? I mean, Blitz doesn't seem to like it when I call her a dragon. She gets all huffy and whatnot. And I think she was in my dream first. Or at least, I am pretty sure she was." She tried to explain, feeling more than a little awkward. "But I could be wrong."

"Are you saying she appeared via your dream? Was the crystal responsible somehow?" Phelia asked, already seeming to beam with curiosity as she lightly touched Blitz's tail.

"I don't know about that. It isn't like the crystal did anything else for me." Grace frowned. It had definitely neglected her, if this was some sort of happening through crystal magic. She'd wanted Eustis' head to blow up like a hot air balloon, even wished he and the other boys would disappear. Which were most definitely not the only things she wished for since she'd found the crystal that rainy night. Although, now she thought it might have been bad if Eustis suddenly didn't exist. Or at the very least, if he weren't around, she would never have experienced that apology or had someone else stick up for her.

"And you already named it. Aren't you worried about getting attached? Or I don't know...questioning why the thing is following you around in the first place?" Zane raised a brow, looking more than a little tense. "I don't know how much you can trust it."

"I guess I do a little. But I don't know what else to do. The name just popped up in my head. Besides, Blitz seems like a good girl. And she's really, really cute." Grace sulked.

"I think it is a wonderful name." True chimed in. And as if understanding her every word, Blitz made her way to True's side and gently circled her, coming back to press her forehead to her mask.

"See?" Grace giggled, unable to fight the urge to take Blitz into her arms. "She's just *so* cute!" She beamed, embracing her. Like Fayth, but bigger, with wings, and a lot more colorful."

"Can she speak?" Phelia asked suddenly, looking at Fayth in her arms. To which Grace tilted her head. Could she speak?

"Of all the things you could ask, that was a bit unexpected." Victor chimed in.

"Not as much as you think." Zane said quickly. Shooting Phelia a stern look. "You have got to be kidding me. Does that mean what I think it does?"

"Guilty..." Phelia replied lowly.

"What are we missing here?" Victor asked.

"Wait a second. Are you saying that the kitten was actually *talking* back at the house??" Grace asked, trying not to raise her voice and attract attention.

"I knew I wasn't going nuts. Well go on then, have the cat say something else." Zane scoffed.

The room fell silent as everyone's eyes rested on Fayth. After a few moments Phelia sighed and turned to her brother. "He doesn't want to talk yet because everyone keeps calling him a cat. Although I thought him some cat-beast or other myself at first. He's so stubborn about it. He did it to me too, quite recently. Fayth wants to be called by name."

Zane furrowed his brows. "What's that supposed to mean? He looks like a cat to me. What's the big deal?"

"Well, he isn't a cat." Twister shrugged. "I've seen these 'cats' from the Human World. Fayth is something else altogether taking on this particular form. Likely, to blend in."

"I knew something wasn't right. I called it." Zane shook his head. "This entire situation sounds creepy."

"But if he isn't a cat then...what is he?" Grace asked, looking over Fayth's features. He looked like a cat. Felt like one too. She was sure she recalled a purr when Dr. Brand pet him.

Twister rubbed the end of his scarf under his chin in thought. "I feel a great deal of magic flowing from him. If I close my eyes and focus, he doesn't have a shape. It doesn't seem like you have anything to worry about. His magic even feels purer than mine. Whatever he is, he feels...*ancient*." As she listened to Twister's words, Grace found herself silently watching Fayth. Catching what seemed to be a twinkle in his eye. Maybe even the faintest hint of a smirk on his face. "In any case," Twister continued, gently clapping his hands together, "he could tell you much more than I."

Things seemed to get more insane by the second. Of all things, there was a talking something or other taking the shape of a cat to blend into society, and Blitz the dragon-not-dragon who showed up just as suddenly into her life. It isn't every day that a girl gets saved from her foster parents by a mythical creature. Anxious, Grace tried to focus her thoughts elsewhere. After all, Victor ending up in the hospital from lack of sleep of all things, seemed much worse than her situation.

Didn't the doctor say that without REM sleep, the brain starts shutting down one part after the other? They'd been in awe that he hadn't just gone insane. And Grace couldn't escape the feeling that Victor wasn't willing to tell them the full extent of the issue. As if he skipped over something, or multiple somethings. Maybe she recognized it because she was developing the habit herself, as much as she hated it.

As if the day hadn't been dizzying enough, they soon found themselves sneaking out of the hospital to make their way to *Snowville Temporary Infirmary*. Nearly caught rounding the corner down the hall from his room. Since then, Twister had taken the lead, going ahead of them and signaling when they should follow. Meanwhile, Blitz had been tucked away in her backpack again and Fayth hid away in Phelia's jacket. When Grace asked why no one freaked out seeing a small winged man flying near their faces, she heard slight chiding about her verbiage from Zane while Twister chuckled.

"Remember our conversation about crossing the veil? I simply cloak myself from time to time. Until I need to signal you. It's quite handy, don't you think? Especially, around humans."

"Aww beans. I totally forgot about that. I wish I could do that." Grace pouted. "I wanna disappear and do cool stuff."

“It does sound like it could come in handy.” True voiced from somewhere on the right.

“Why? Is there some reason you need to disappear?” Victor asked, and the tone of his voice immediately caused Grace to glance back in their direction. True gave no response. What was that all about? Grace turned her attention back ahead of her but there was no denying some strange bout of uneasiness in the air just then. Although, she couldn’t be entirely sure she wasn’t just jumping to conclusions.

Thirty

True...

SORRY.

True felt a slight sense of panic rise in her as they left the hospital and quickly made their way to *Snowville Temporary Infirmary*. Victor's question had unnerved her. And while she had an answer, she couldn't bring herself to mouth the words, let alone actually say them.

For the majority of her life True had wanted to disappear. Since the day her mother passed away and a million times over every day thereafter. It just so happened that now, she had more troubles atop the ones of the past. All equally deserving of escape.

Every day, True wished for a moment to disappear from the hallways of the school or its classrooms. Almost to cease to exist just as suddenly as she'd been born into the world, and thus, end her torment with Sydney and the others. Victor's questions echoed in her head. When he had asked if someone was hurting her, if she was being bullied, why hadn't she been able to say a simple three letter word?

At the time, she had noticed it. That something had been different with Victor. She had wondered if she'd been too heavy to carry through the snow, but in reality, Victor had been suffering. He even fell to the floor near her door and still managed to help her start a fire for extra warmth and iced her ankle. She'd memorized the number Victor had written on the slip of paper and thought often to pick up the phone and dial it. Just to make sure he had gotten home safe, that he was alright. And yet, she hadn't managed that either.

Why did she let him leave? Why hadn't she insisted on a doctor? Or at least him staying until her aunts returned and could take him home? True believed her ignorance to Victor's troubles were largely her fault. Not only because she ignored her instincts but because she'd been so caught up in hiding away her own troubles.

Even worse, she often mused over the existence of their friendship without questioning if Victor felt he could come to her with his problems. If he had, would she have realized how dire the situation was? How could she have assumed he could come to her when she hadn't managed to do the same?

True found her gaze trained on Victor as they entered the weathered, stone building and traced the familiar steps to the staircase. And while lost in her regret, she hardly realized they'd made it to the space on the wall and already a door was forming ahead of them. Victor's eyes weren't red anymore, he hadn't seemed to struggle taking steps forward on their way, nor did he stumble through the window or up the stairs. Whatever they'd done at the hospital had gone well, but she still worried.

Would he go back to normal? Was he upset with her for acting so selfishly? For being a bad friend? She didn't know if she'd been meant to join the conversation in the room, let alone what it was about as the light started to fill her vision. But she'd been acutely aware of the sadness and worry coiling around her insides like a snake. And the moment she'd thought these feelings would consume the warmth of the light surrounding her, she took hold of Victor's hand before she could stop herself. Fully registering the look of surprise in his green eyes as he spun around to face her.

. . .

A few moments later, True found herself on the other side of the door, Victor's hand still clasped between her fingers. She ignored the quick thumping of her heart in her chest and another wave of panic in favor of the other emotions that had led her there, standing in some unfamiliar place, still holding onto him.

"True...?" Victor called, in a voice hardly more than a whisper. As she looked at his eyes again, still full of surprise, True realized she didn't know what she wanted to say or how to say it. She fought the thought to let go of his hand and say nothing, to simply turn away and pretend she hadn't done anything to warrant the look on his face.

"I'm sorry, Victor." True said, finally finding her voice. Even though I'm sorry didn't seem nearly enough. How could she express how rotten she felt for failing to be there for him? For not finding it in herself to talk openly about the situation at school? For still not being able to admit it now?

"Sorry? Why are you apologizing to me?" Victor asked, before their conversation seemed to catch everyone else's interest and True dropped his hand.

"Where are we?" Grace asked, in awe as she opened her bag and allowed Blitz to hover at her side. Regardless of if she was a dragon or not, True found it a curious thing that she was not displaying any wild behavior. The little beast almost seemed trained. And considering what Grace said before, she wasn't responsible for it. Especially if they've only just met. But then, who was?

"In a place known as *The Ruins*." A voice answered in an even tone. At which moment True realized was the voice of Phelia's pet, Fayth. Immediately followed by a loud yip from Grace's direction. A sound unexpected enough to frighten the kitten-lookalike to the point that he hunched his back, and hissed as his tail shot up towards the sky. Zane had been right, Fayth certainly seemed like a cat.

"Whatever's the matter with you?" He directed at her, slowly relaxing his body.

"You talk!" Grace shouted.

"Was that not previously confirmed? There's no need for you to shout." Fayth said, sounding particularly disapproving. "You gave me a fright." He sighed, closing his eyes.

"Don't worry Grace." Zane cut in, "I'm screaming internally, I assure you."

"Thanks...?" Grace said, raising a brow. "Sorry, but a talking cat will take some getting used to."

"I am not a cat. Just Fayth—please. So long as you won't yell out every time I speak I can understand. Apology accepted."

"A talking cat isn't so surprising after a world like Mirror." Victor shrugged. "As long as you don't want to keep us, I don't think we will have any issues."

"When we met, I thought Fayth came from Mirror, ironically." Phelia chimed in. "Actually, this size is—"

"I'd like to keep Phelia. Would that be an issue?" Fayth asked, and from what True could tell he meant it.

"Of course, it is! You can't *have* my sister." Zane scoffed. Their conversation faded away almost to something of white noise as True took in their surroundings.

Ahead of them, she gazed upon a land almost entirely devoid of anything signaling life beyond the random patches of grass. Save for those, the land was barren and dry. Much of the ground was uneven with small mounds and indentations as far as the eyes could see. Staggering sized boulders lay astray, some of which appeared almost cleaved in two. True went to inspect one more closely, her eyes following jagged skid marks. With a hand to the rock, True took notice of several scorched specks on its uneven surface.

"Perhaps you can guess why this land is called The Ruins. At one point it was beautiful here. A long time ago now though." A light, unknown voice spoke from the distance.

"Ah. So, you've arrived." Fayth yawned. In a matter of moments, the others fell in line at True's side, their eyes trained on the sudden appearance of several figures taking shape mere feet away.

"We have." A young woman smiled softly in their direction as light skated across her brown eyes on the other side of her glasses. "It's an honor to see you again, in whatever way that may be." True took note of the necklace hanging at her collar bone with a curved letter U sparkling of silver. Behind her stood a boy with dark hair and glasses, a pair whose face almost mirrored each other, and a blonde with blue eyes sporting hair clips. Could it be?

"My apologies for the loss that bore me." Fayth said, bowing his head slightly. "I'm afraid that under current circumstances my recollection of you is lacking."

"As to be expected. No reason to go crying about it now." The blonde frowned, only to turn her unpleasant expression upon the rest of them instead.

"Are you...Uriel, by chance?" True asked as the woman smiled again with a nod. She almost couldn't believe it.

"I am." She said, motioning to the boulder True had been inspecting. "The damage you see here is from a battle fought long ago. But the war itself still wages on, possibly to the end of time. And in some strange irony, the sun is always shining here now, and the sky always blue."

It was then that True took notice of several starkly different hues of blue painting the sky. And the light beaming down against the landscape effortlessly even though she could find no hint of a sun. Both seemed incredibly impossible and beautiful all at once.

If everything they saw before them was the result of a difficult battle, True found it almost in bad taste. The bright sky mocked the tattered, crumbled land below. Almost as if it aimed to trick one into thinking nothing had ever happened there at all. A narrative she could nearly believe if they'd found themselves standing in the clouds instead of on the broken ground. What kind of battle could leave such large boulders? Let alone split them in two?

Thirty-One

Victor...

CIRCLE.

"If you are Uriel then, you must be Mathew?" Victor asked, looking the group over, his eyes landing on the dark-haired man slightly to Uriel's right.

"I am. Nice to finally meet you, Victor." He smiled.

"You know my name?" Victor asked, suddenly a little off-put by his warm smile. Did that mean he also knew that Victor had seen his letter? He attempted to clear the lump slowly forming at the back of his throat.

"We know all of your names." Uriel chuckled. "We've known since the moment you were chosen. Even a little about your Faerie friend, Twister, as well."

"How nice to be known, I suppose. I *must* say that you all look particularly familiar to me." Twister smiled politely, looking as if he had a few questions of his own to ask.

"What's all this nonsense about being chosen anyhow?" Zane asked.

"Nonsense, huh? *You* ***wish***." The blonde spoke, crossing her arms over her chest. Victor didn't think the woman's frown could get any deeper. He was wrong.

"**Ohh!!**" Grace suddenly yelled, overcome with some sort of epiphany. "Ohh! I *knew* it! You're the mean one—Brilla, the one who doesn't like anybody!" Victor found her lack of filter amusing and stifled a laugh, but he could already see Zane's fingers sliding down his face from the corner of his eye.

"What did you say?! You little--" Brilla started, looking ready to charge in Grace's direction. But the moment she took a step forward, Mathew quickly grabbed ahold of her arm to stop her. "Let. Me. Go." She hissed.

"Come on, Brilla. That's *not* why we're here." Mathew said in a stern tone. "We're short on time as it is. We must prepare them." Victor took note of Grace's red hair poking out from True's side as Brilla shot a menacing glance in her direction and scowled.

"Shall we take a seat?" Fayth yawned, almost immediately making Victor wish for another nap. Momentarily, he lost himself in thoughts of guilt given his very recent trip to the hospital. He tried not to think about the worry on the others' faces, or the fear and anger that had clouded his mother's expressions every hour she sat at his hospital bed, but he was unsuccessful. He found himself hardly aware of following everyone else's lead as they crossed their legs on the ground and Vale and Vick introduced themselves.

At the sound of Twister's voice, Victor willed himself to pay attention, opting to rest his gaze on his small frame sitting between Fayth and Blitz. The two of which looked particularly comfortable resting in the middle of their circle. "This land, it is ever so faint but, the battle here...was it with The Darkness? You mentioned preparing them for something, what would that be? And how did you know of me? Have we met before?"

"Yes, that is correct. Considering the residual energy here, you must be able to tell how much was here in the past. This world used to be much more striking, but now only this much is left. The rest was destroyed. Long before the last war in the Faerie world." Vick nodded, gently resting his elbow on his lap with a sigh. "It's a shame. We didn't even get to see it in all its former glory."

"We know only small details about you," his sister shrugged lightly, "but we haven't *exactly* met. It's possible you may have seen us a long time ago in the Faerie world. We've been doing this for a while now. But as far as knowing your name and the rest, our Master told us you would play an important role against The Darkness, alongside the others. Of course, that was before he..."

Uriel gently laid a hand on Vale's lap. "We cannot offer much. Our power is nearly gone, so we have no choice. we won't be able to continue as we are now. The best we can give you are some answers and prepare you for this struggle by completing the ritual. Though that is not exactly something that *we* do. Unfortunately, the crystals' powers aren't something we can teach you to use, specifically."

"Wait. You said something about a Master or something when we were in FlareWing, didn't you Twister?" Zane asked, his brows creased.

"What struggle? What's all this about powers?" Victor wondered the same, but he almost didn't want to know. Something about this conversation was already filling him with dread.

"I did." Twister nodded. "The Master of the Keys."

"The same one that created the veil that protects FlareWing..." True said lowly, her hands shifting on her lap. Victor struggled to look away from her familiar, slim fingers. His mind flooding with the thought of her hand suddenly taking ahold of his before they went through the door. What was that anyway? Why did she apologize to him?

"Yes." Uriel said, her gaze suddenly focused on Phelia. "I'm sorry. You're very young. I wish things had gone differently, that we had done more. Or at least, that we weren't running out of time."

"This Master again. Just what kind of Master is he? He's gone, I take it?" Phelia tilted her head to the side.

"No, no, no. Wait a sec. Why did you just look at my *sister* when you said that?" Zane asked abruptly.

"You don't know?" Uriel asked, shock present in her features. She slowly looked to Fayth, who closed his eyes.

"There's been very little time. I've only just found her. These children know nothing." Fayth spoke in a disappointed tone, burying his face under his paws. "They have been able to open doors, yet that seems the extent of it."

"This is *insane!*" Brilla huffed. "You can't possibly be saying that we are still going on with the ritual to awaken their powers. It'd be like repeating the past all over again!"

"We don't have a ***choice***." Mathew sighed; his expression pained. "Our Master is gone now. Our powers are dwindling too quickly. We wish it were different, honest. But we have done what we can." Mathew's eyes met them all, one after the other before he cleared his throat. "We can't teach you how to use the crystal power, because they aren't always the same when they are passed on. But you will need them to fight. Your sister, Zane, is the ***new*** Master of the Keys."

Thirty-Two

Phelia...

UNEXPECTED ANSWERS.

"What?" Phelia mumbled, a mix of confusion and curiosity overtaking her all at once. "I don't understand. How can I be a new Master of the Keys?" Was this some sort of joke? An attempt to test how gullible they were?

"I will try to explain as best I can." Uriel said thoughtfully. "Please listen carefully but bear with me. This is my first attempt. The Master of the Keys has always chosen their own successor and even the World Knights—or so, that is what people have called us. And, considering that you all have crystals, you've been selected to take our place.

"The Master is many things. One of the most notable being, a person most responsible for the balance between light and darkness. The effect of these on worlds...? The only human being that has direct contact with, well, *the universe.* They get to intervene in these worlds, this universe, but we never quite understood who gives the Master permission for anything.

"Our duty, as a whole, is to protect those in these vastly different worlds from major threats. Almost entirely, in our experience, pertaining to The Darkness. So, we fix, restore, and keep the balance through direct conflict."

"By direct conflict, you mean, you *battle* The Darkness? And the Master of the Keys just watches?" Phelia asked, not particularly fond of what she was hearing. She could almost hear the sound of wheels turning in the silence. Everyone was attempting to put the mysteries together. How could she have anything to do with the entire universe? She couldn't manage her own difficulties as is.

"No. The Master's mind is their greatest asset. Their knowledge from all of the ones who've come before them, their intricate plans and alerts to troubled areas are imperative to everything we do. Not to mention that the Master has been able to shield worlds like FlareWing. There are many things that the Master of the Keys does and understands that we cannot even pretend to grasp. Fayth and you, yourself, Phelia, would best understand this."

"But I don't have these memories of previous Masters. I don't have any such power to protect some world. I've never created a veil in my life. Least of all think I have any such capability to do so. I can hardly make a *sandwich* in the kitchen. You must have the wrong person." Phelia voiced in disbelief.

"There's no mistake, Phelia." Fayth said. "My connection to you, and my existence alone is proof enough of that. You don't yet understand, but you will. The memories you speak of are locked away for now. A new Master of the Keys can only be awakened after the last one dies. You and I were born the day *their* Master lost his life."

"You've said something like that before. Awakened…us sharing a birthday."

"I did." Fayth nodded.

"Wait a second. You're saying my *baby sister* is some kind of magical reincarnation of several dead guys?? And we are some kinds of knights in shining armor who are gonna fight *The Darkness?* As in, the-evil-something-or-other-entity-that-massacared-a-bunch-of-magical-Faeries-blasted-a-*freaking*-**crater**-in-the-ground-and-*literally*-

destroyed-most-of-the-world-we-are-sitting-in Darkness?? Have you people lost your minds?!"

"But..." Grace's voice trembled. "I don't ***wanna*** fight The Darkness..."

Thirty-Three

Zane...

REASONS.

Zane didn't know much, but he knew he didn't like a single word coming from these people's mouths. Maybe they were deranged. Maybe they were preying on them. That's what he wanted to believe, even as he heard Fayth and several of the adults from the other side make note of Phelia's gifts. Even though he had always known since she was born that there was something *different* about his sister. It was true that she knew things she was never taught. And it was true that she felt a million miles away from where he stood most days, as if they weren't even part of the same orbit.

Some part of him in their younger days had made up outlandish reasons for their differences, but he'd convinced himself that things weren't as out of the norm as he had been thinking. After all, he knew that geniuses existed in the world. But there was no way he thought he'd be given a reason like this. If Phelia was what they said did that even make her ***human?***

Supposedly whatever these past lives and memories were, they were locked away somewhere. Even Phelia herself was in disbelief. Phelia was probably scrutinizing every word they'd been saying herself, in that super interested but skeptical, cautiously intellectual kinda way. How much was it supposed to matter in the first place? Phelia was his sister. And regardless of how different she was or whatever these people thought her role was supposed to be, she was still a kid.

"Even if she this so-called Master, she is a little *kid.* We're too young to be fighting evils in this world or the next." Zane said finally, interrupting whatever other explanations they were giving. "This stuff is dangerous! Didn't you say that the last guy died and because of that you all are having issues anyway? And you expect us to be okay with hearing that? You expect *me* to just say 'yeah, it's totally alright for my sister to take his place'??"

"No." Brilla spoke with a scoff. "Do you think we are stupid or something? Who expects you to be alright with it? We weren't either. We'd have to be a particular screwed type to think that, or down right sadistic to enjoy it."

"Then how can you ask this of us?" Victor said, offering a nod in Zane's direction. "If you didn't like it, and you yourself Brilla have already voiced today that this was insane, why put *us* through it? We went to Mirror and almost got captured and sold off without a single clue what was going on. Witnessed the ceremony in FlareWing, then something weird obviously happened to--"

"Speaking of, we have to discuss what I found out at home, what's happening to the Fae. I spoke to Father Wing..." Twister interjected momentarily, causing everyone to look at him in both surprise and worry. Why didn't he sound happy about it? What could be happening to the Faeries? As if they didn't have enough problems already.

"—Great. Sounds terrible." Victor sighed. "Point is, between all of that and going to The After Land or Land of the Dead, whatever it's called, this has already been dangerous. So, again, how can you ask us to do this? In fact, you're asking something even more dangerous."

"You don't seem to understand." Uriel said, shaking her head. "We are not the one's asking. If anything, the crystals, the universe, *they* are. However funny that sounds. We couldn't get all the way to the root of it, but maybe you can."

"All of that is still sounding pretty deranged to me." Zane frowned. "Are you trying to say that the crystals are alive or something? And even if that was the case and not just kinda creepy, that's still not a very good reason."

"OH. You want a *better* reason?" Brilla smirked in some almost inhumane way, her expression somehow mingled in between disgust and animosity. "Aside from worlds falling apart and countless lives being lost? Fine, because you don't know what it's like to see a world completely swallowed whole by The Darkness." As she spoke, she pointed a finger in Phelia's direction, "Your best reason is right *there*, idiot. Your sister will come into her role whether any of you like it or not.

"She *is* and ***will*** be The Master of the Keys regardless of you. Generally speaking, Master's tend to choose their people, but I'm sure there are exceptions to the rule. But hey, if you want someone who doesn't give a crap about her to protect her then that's fine. If you want her ***life*** to possibly reach its end before it has really even started, or for her to face The Darkness alone, then be my guest. I may not enjoy sending you off like we were but I'm capable of listening to reason. The question is, are you?

"We were tricked. Before Master June died, The Darkness had done something we'd never seen before. It *scattered.* Split apart and went to multiple worlds in this weird frenzy. We were worried about him, but we followed our Master's orders. Even though we *knew* he was weak...

"Previously, we had a pretty recent run-in with The Darkness and Master June said it left remnants inside him. You haven't yet witnessed the pure energy, light, or *whatever* you want to call it that's attached to The Master of the Keys. Let alone the crystals, but it is...otherworldly. It's powerful.

"So, for that thing to be able to latch on to him in any way, it must have been excruciating. Not to mention near *impossible.* It' not like what happens with the crystals. There's no fixing it. And he knew things were going bad. Probably even knew what was coming next. He still sent us off to protect those worlds while we were clueless. We split up; we didn't have a choice. Tried to protect worlds on opposite corners of the universe. Then, without warning, ***IT*** disappeared.

"We didn't get it at first. But then, we felt it. There're no words to describe how it feels for someone essentially more ancient than worlds to be fatally wounded by an entity like that. But that thing had attacked him in his weakened state. And while The Darkness took damage, our Master didn't make a recovery. He slowly became a shell of his former self. Hardly able to direct us at all by the time it was over. There was nothing we could do but watch him wither away.

"I don't know what a natural death for a Master of the Keys is supposed to be like, but that wasn't it. You all got chosen. I tried saying no too, before. I didn't understand that once you're chosen you can't stomach turning away from all those people. Or that you'd always be a target. Like the dark things in the world could sniff you out from a million miles away. At the very least, you can try to do what we couldn't. And this time, the Master is your sister."

"The Master of the Keys...crystal keys to the universe...?" Grace shook her head. "And the universe wants ***us*** to fight *The Darkness? If* we don't, worlds are going to get eaten by The Darkness, we'll be in danger anyway, and Phelia will have to face It alone?" Zane could see it in her eyes. Those feelings.

Victor's too. It was the same whirlwind of feelings swelling up inside of him. The uncertainty, the fear, the disbelief. The realization that if everything Brilla said was true, how could they refuse? Leave Phelia, his baby sister, alone to face something like that alone?

"And you're saying I don't have a choice? All of this because I'm not *normal*...? What if I don't want it? What if I don't want them to protect me? If the Master picks the World Knights, then I'm the reason they have the crystals somehow, aren't I? What if I un-pick them? If we pretend we'd never heard a single word of this? Gave the crystals back and simply went home?" Phelia said, her shoulders tense and her head down. She seemed determined not to look their way.

"Phelia..." Fayth called lowly, standing and walking to her lap, pawing her gently. It was then that Zane saw her hands clutched tightly to her legs, shaking. "World Knights have to be trustworthy and loyal. Their potential relationship to The Master of the Keys is crucial, but it doesn't mean it is your fault. They also had to be compatible. World Knights are chosen by soul energy. Just as your brother and your friends must have similar soul attributes to Uriel and the others to share the crystal. You didn't point them out and tell the universe that you wanted them to ride to battle beside you and put their lives at risk. Even you were chosen. Just like they were."

"I ***said*** what if I *don't* want it??!" Phelia huffed, suddenly shooting Fayth a cold look. "What if we went home and never touched a crystal again?" He hesitated for a moment. Took a small step back and casted his eyes cast towards the ground.

"You could attempt. But you are who you are, Phelia. Uriel, Brilla, Mathew, Vick and Vale cannot receive any power from your crystals and continue where they'd left off. It does not work that way. The Darkness will destroy everything in Its path. It is a greedy entity full of malice and altogether, a particular sort of *empty*.

"It will go after every world, one after the other, if left to Its own devices. Eventually that will mean your world too—anyone and anything you care about. I ***know you***, Phelia. You will not be able to watch and do nothing. Knowing you could have tried to save your father, that you could have helped your brother and your friends, but tried to run away instead. Nor will you be able to erase your role as The Master of the Keys. Ignoring the existence of the crystals will do nothing to help you, even if you do not utilize them."

Zane felt his heart breaking at the sound of his sister's cries. He didn't know what to do, or if he could offer her comfort. He wasn't sure how Fayth figured he knew her so well, but for the moment it didn't matter. He was right.

Phelia wouldn't be able to handle it. Maybe, none of them. What they'd been told was the stuff of nightmares, but he wasn't sure they'd ever sleep again if they gave the crystals back and had to watch their world fall apart. If they had to just accept it with their tails between their legs. All the while, knowing that there was something they could have done. Or at least, attempted to do.

"If you decide to do this, you're not doing it by yourself." Victor said, sounding particularly resolute. It seemed to Zane that he had been able to bury the feelings he'd seen mirrored in his gaze just a little before. Maybe it was that other side of him kicking in, the one that protected girls in trouble. Or maybe he was just stronger than Zane could ever hope to be. Maybe it should have bothered him, but it didn't. He only found himself glad that Victor was there at all.

"What he said." Zane nodded, determined to try and conceal his other feelings. Right now, he had to let Phelia know that, no matter how insane the situation, he would be there. "I'm not going to bow and kiss your feet or anything, oh *Master* of the universe. But, yeah no. The Darkness doesn't get to keep you either."

"If there's really something we can do then we should try, I think." True said, smoothing out a corner of her jacket. Even she would agree to protect Phelia? True really was kind.

"Awe beans! We'll probably be the worst superheroes ever. We'll probably blow an entire world to bits or something and I'm scared, but I don't wanna see the world gobbled up by The Darkness either. Plus, there's no way I'm letting my *best friend* fight that thing alone."

"Best friend?" Phelia asked suddenly, her tear-filled eyes directed at Grace in surprise. "Are we best friends?"

"Oh. Sorry. I mean—well, if you maybe *wanted...*" Before Zane could understand the sudden shift, Phelia excitedly wrapped her arms around Grace and smiled. Then, she turned to face him.

"I'm sorry, Zane." She wiped her eyes with the back of her arm, a slight child-like gesture. "But maybe the best way to handle this is to 'charge through the uncertainty' instead? Could I ask you to help me?" Zane noticed an unwelcomed feeling. A conscious, large amount of effort required to swallow a momentary bout of hate. One wholly directed towards Uriel and the others.

He tried to force away the intrusive thought; had it not been for this conversation with them, these predecessors, maybe they could have lived in blissful ignorance a little longer. Even though it didn't seem entirely their fault.

Besides that, he didn't know why but, as glad as he was to see his sister's smile and determination, he found himself a little annoyed by Fayth's proud hint of a smile beside her. Was anything about this a smiling matter? Just what had they gotten themselves into?

Thirty-Four

Eustis...

A CERTAIN SOMETHING.

Eustis felt like he'd crashed into the tip of an iceberg and his body was sinking into the depths of a cold, unforgiving sea. Only to realize, as he fell deeper, drowning wouldn't be his downfall. Meeting his end would be a million times more severe. Because somewhere near the sea floor, a more menacing threat awaited him: a monster with the mouth of a black hole just waiting to devour him, to expunge his existence from the world for all time thereafter.

But when he woke, drenched in sweat and cold enough to give Snowville's winter frost a run for its money, there was no sea to be found. No dark thing ready to swallow him hole. His eyes were met with the same mulberry-colored walls as usual. And the sound of his parents' nagging voices, taking their anger out on Kennet once again.

It was an almost daily occurrence now, in which Eustis found himself imbued with guilt, later to apologize in a corner of the house, room or even the car. After all, it was because of him that Kennet faced his parents' wrath and suspicions. It was probably wrong of him to beg Kennet to secrecy. And while Eustis had been healing from his broken rib and slew of other nameless injuries, his friend took blame for his silence. He deserved none of it.

His parents treated Kennet as if they didn't pay him only to be his driver. It was unfair of them, no matter how much time the two of them spent together, to expect him to do something out of the scope of his duties. Even if Kennet was often a friend, brother, and if Eustis so-dared to think it, a father figure to him.

Unable to handle a moment more of their spiteful yelling, Eustis shoved past one of the guards posted on the other side of the door, fumbled his way painfully down the staircase and took hold of Kennet's hand. "Stop blaming Kennet! You pay him to drive me, not to guard my life!" As he began to pull him away from his parents, he was suddenly aware that he'd heard Grace's name a moment before.

He quickly turned to his parents, their displeased faces showcasing a moment of shock. It was the first time Eustis had spoken a word to either of them since Kennet phoned them and sent them rushing to the hospital. How many days had it been? "What did you say just now? The thing about Grace?"

"It's her fault, isn't it?? With the ghastly things we've been hearing about her house and her wild behavior getting into fights with *boys*? We wouldn't be surprised! All you have to do is tell us, Eustis. Or if *Kennet* ***here*** remembered seeing a single thread of that *feral* hair of hers, we could-"

"What do you mean at her *house*, mother?" Eustis interrupted. He didn't care to listen to a moment more of her squawking than necessary. He could feel the cold leave his body as the heat set in and sweat formed on his fingers. He didn't know in that moment if it was from his anger or an acute sense of panic. "What's happened at her house?"

"—Well of course you hadn't heard. Perhaps if the girl was the reason for your injuries, she's already gotten some of her just-*desserts*," his mother laughed, "considering the *blood* and all they-"

"Kennet!" Eustis shouted at his back as he unintentionally forced him along, bolting towards the door. *Blood? What did she mean,* ***blood?!*** He heard his parents calling his name behind them as they rushed down the pathway and around the bend to the gate. Eustis eyed Kennet's dark car. "Grace's place—you have to take me there!"

"Well, don't just *stand* there you imbeciles!" His father howled. "We said he isn't to leave the primases. Go *get* him!!"

"Can you outdrive the body guards?" Eustis asked between painful breaths, sliding into the backseat. He clinched the rib responsible for most of his agony and instantly regretted it. "I'm sorry for causing you even more trouble. My parents are losing it. But if something's happened at Grace's place then..."

"*Can I outdrive mere bodyguards?*" Kennet scoffed. "Put on your seat belt and don't *insult* me again." Eustis met his eyes in the review mirror, noting an ever so slight hint of amusement, and clicked his safety belt into place. "These morons aren't even from town. We'll have lost them before the end of the *street*."

And it was there, on the drive that seemed to take forever, with Kennet closely eyeing the streets of Snowville behind them, that Eustis finally found the moment to tell Kennet anything that seemed to matter. Every conflicting moment from the time that he'd met Grace in the classroom, to every time he felt unlike himself and the weight of his parents, teachers and ex-friends' expectations. By the time he'd finished and Kennet pulled the car into the garage of an unfamiliar house, he had to wipe the tears from his eyes. Crying still hurt.

"Where are we?" Eustis asked, blowing his nose into a tissue Kennet had passed him from the front seat. He watched him leave the car and rummage through the trunk before opening his door. Without saying a word, Kennet slid a warm pair of thermal socks onto Eustis' feet, wrapped him in a blanket and then went to the trunk again for a pair of slippers.

"Put these on and stay put." Kennet said, sliding the garage door closed and opening a window too high for Eustis to reach even without a swollen face and busted rib. "We are at an old friend's place. I live here and look after the house for now. When I leave, they'll probably hire someone to do it instead. I'm sure he doesn't have any intention of living here again, even if he'll never admit that."

"When you leave...?" Eustis frowned. "I thought you were taking me to Grace's place—where are you going? Why would you leave?" He thought Kennet stayed on the grounds like most of the other workers. Especially considering how he appeared practically in a moment's notice to drive him about.

"You're growing up, Eustis. You won't need a driver forever. Besides that, I have a feeling that things with your parents are going to get worse from here on out. They won't like what's happened today. You know that."

Eustis knew he was right. Even he had mentioned that his parents were losing it. They were not above taking any frustration out on someone else, especially the hired help. It wouldn't matter that Eustis quite literally pulled him out the door. But the thought of him leaving felt like the worst punishment he never saw coming. And even worse... "You seem awfully prepared." Eustis said with a hint of bitterness. "To leave me."

"I'm an adult. It comes with the territory. Besides, have you ever known me to be *unprepared?*"

Eustis was starting to hate this conversation. "Never."

"Exactly. It's my specialty." He smiled, crouching in front of him and gently sliding the blue slippers onto his feet. "I told you to put these on for a reason, you know. It's freezing."

"I'm not cold. I'm practically suffocating now." Eustis frowned, knowing he was only taking the opportunity to be childish. To have Kennet do something else for him. Like usual, without complaint, he did it. Was that also because he was an adult?

"Well, you'll have to suffocate a while longer." Kennet replied with a smirk. "This house is close to Grace's. Less than ten minutes. I can't let you run around in this weather."

"You're saying I'll get in the way, aren't you?"

"Yes. I'm saying that," Kennet nodded, not even bothering to lie, "and you'd slow me down if we ran across the body guards while trying to make it back here. My plan is to humiliate them even further by getting you home afterwards without them knowing a thing."

"Aren't you worried? About my parents? You seem awfully amused." Eustis asked, somehow consoled and equally confused by his reaction. Maybe he was good at hiding his feelings and he took it all without complaint. If Kennet truly hated him, he'd never even know it. His self-control seemed as dangerous as daggers. How Eustis wished he had it.

"I am *quite* amused. You tend to keep me so." Kennet laughed. "I'm prepared for anything. I'm not worried about your parents. All they can do is fire me, maybe make it hard to work in town, as if that's a downside."

"Do you *want* to be fired or something?"

"Of course not, Eustis. I don't know anyone who wants to be fired in general. I am fond of seeing you grow up. And if I get fired, I'll miss all the fun."

As Eustis watched him unlock a door leading into the house, he realized he was suddenly afraid. Was this what it would look like when he left him for good? What if he didn't come back? "You'll tell me, won't you? What's happened at Grace's house? No matter how bad it is?"

As if seeing right through him, a friend, brother, father that always knew the right words to say, Kennet paused in the doorway and glanced over his shoulder at him. "Yes, I will. No matter how bad, I'll tell you every detail just like you did for me in the car. I'm not leaving, Eustis. I'm coming right back here. To this garage, to you, and taking you home after. Your parents will ground you, and I might get fired."

"You're a good person, Kennet. I don't really know many good people, but I imagine they'd be like you. You're loyal too...it's my fault. I'm the reason they are mad at you. I'm the reason they would fire you. Do you hate me?" Eustis felt tears stinging his eyes again. Stupid tears. Stupid ribs. Stupid swollen face. Stupid mom. Stupid dad. Stupid...*him.*

"I don't hate you, Eustis. I never have, probably never will. You're not the reason. I made my own choices and your parents will always make *their* own. You sound like you did before. While you were telling me all of that stuff about what you wanted, and how you felt on the drive. I kept thinking that I should have been able to see that more clearly before now. I was thinking 'what is a kid doing shouldering burdens like that? Feeling shackled to expectations and a family name?' You've got to stop doing that to yourself. You're not living for your parents, or for me. Your life is for *you.*

"And when you took my hand today and rushed out of the front door, I felt like it was the first time I'd ever seen you defy *everything*. Even though I've felt those moments from you, like the last time you brought Grace into the car. I understood it a little more when you spoke about her.

"How monumental she's been for you, how much you care about her. I've never heard you talk about someone else like that. Nor me either. I was touched. I want to see what you look like away from this place. I'm not here with you just because of the job, the money, or a sense of loyalty." He hummed in thought.

"Now that I think about it, I might've lied once. Just a minute ago. I said I was prepared for anything. But you know, I'm not really all that prepared to leave you behind. Is that alright?"

Eustis didn't understand how he could even ask a question like that. But it was in that moment that he realized something else that he'd felt in all his time with Kennet. A certain something that was hanging in the air between them, a feeling he'd never felt directed his way otherwise. Not from his parents, so-called friends, neighbors, teachers...not from Snowville itself. ***Love***.

Wasn't that what Kennet was saying? That thing that went beyond the job and his parents and money? "Yeah." Eustis nodded, as he watched him close the door. "Yeah, that's okay with me."

He listened to his footsteps fade into the house and further away from him and cried. So much and so hard that the pain made him cry some more. Until, before he'd even realized it, Eustis had fallen asleep.

Thirty-Five

Twister...

TAINT.

As Twister watched what seemed like another small moment of happiness, he felt the familiar prick of guilt pain him. Again, he would have to be the one to ruin it. "I apologize for interrupting but if I may, considering what was just said about your crystals and the like, you may need to know what I've found out in FlareWing all the more." Twister took a quick glance in True's direction before standing to stretch his legs.

"As I mentioned previously, I went back home to FlareWing temporarily. I had the opportunity to speak with my parents and Father Wing—"

"Your parents? Did everything go alright?" True asked, leaning towards him, sounding worried.

"Woah! That's a big deal, isn't it?" Grace beamed. "Wait, is Father Wing still little? How's the Princess? Did you get to go inside The Grand Tree? Was it massive on the inside too?"

"—Father Wing is still young, yes. He won't change *that* quickly. Or at least, it hasn't happened before and yes. The Princess is well. Sleeping mostly, like most infants do. I did find my way into The Grand Tree and

I'd say it's equally "massive" on the other side. As far as things with my Parents, they went very differently than in my head. My mother even asked me to move back home. Ah, but that's a conversation for later."

Twister sighed. The truth of the matter was, he would have preferred telling them everything that had transpired between him and his parents. A part of him wanted to vent and get their opinions, and the other wanted to tell them anything but more news concerning The Darkness. Even if his new friends were chosen to be World Knights, they were even younger than him. He had felt their fear and frustrations when they were told of their role. Still, he couldn't just tell them nothing. If they were in fact to be dealing with the dangers that threatened worlds outside their own, then surely FlareWing would be amongst them.

"I was told that Fae have been going missing at an alarming rate. According to Father Wing, the likelihood of The Darkness being responsible is high. So too, that all of you are involved in some fashion." Twister frowned.

"Latching itself onto Master June was no easy feat. I'd imagine that doing so to a Faerie would be considerably *less* difficult." Vick sighed. "Still, Faeries are high on the 'light' ladder, so to speak."

"Are you saying we are at fault?" Phelia asked.

"No. Of course not, Phelia." Twister shook his head. "And according to Father Wing, the disappearances begun before any of you ever came to FlareWing. So, no one would dare blame all of you."

"You mean it's happening again, right? Because the last time this happened FlareWing had a Cursed Fae epidemic." Victor scratched his head and leaned back with a heavy sigh. "Man, what a pain. I don't even want to ask how many are gone. We might be facing an army of them." Twister hated to think it, but Victor was right.

The best assumption to make was that every missing Fae was now an enemy. However unfortunate for him given his relationship with his parents was now on the mend, the Fae were lucky that The General had never relaxed their duties or training. To think, not long-ago Twister himself had been one to dismiss the army. He was wrong. They still needed to be battle ready. He'd had no idea.

"Those poor Fae." True sounded particularly downcast. "What do you suppose they feel as Cursed Fae, Twister? If it is anything like what happened before..."

"What do you mean by what happened before?" Victor asked, seeming suddenly more alert.

"You're referring to when you went through the door leaving Flare-Wing..?" Twister frowned. It had been his first time going through a space like that. It felt wholly unnatural and desolate. He'd doubted for a moment that he'd ever find his way out of it, let alone that he could save True. But he had to try. And somehow, they'd made it after all.

"That cold, dizzying...terrifyingly tenebrous space. Any ounce of pain...if that is anything like what they experience, it doesn't seem fair to cause them more." True began to fidget with her hands. The awkward gesture gave Twister the urge to comfort her, but he worried it would only make her feel worse. After all, True didn't favor being the center of attention.

Only, as Twister read the expression on the rest of the children's faces, he took note of their quiet realization. It seemed to click one after the other, like a series of bulbs. The fact that he and True had witnessed something harrowing on the other side of the door. That The Darkness had tried to do something to her. If he had to guess, It had planned to swallow her whole.

"So that's why you were the last to make it back." Phelia shook her head. "When we questioned you that day, I doubt any of us even thought to think such things. Again, my apologies."

"I'm sorry True," Grace said, clearly uneasy. "That sounds terrible. And I couldn't help thinking...it sorta sounded like the stuff that happens when we go through the door. Right?"

"What do you mean," Vale asked, her green eyes quickly darted from Grace to Uriel, "like what happens when you go through the *door?*"

"Hmm? You mean that creepy stuff? Every time we go through a door to some other place there's this moment that everything is pitch-black. You can't see each other or hear anything. You can't feel a thing until you get to the other side. It's *super* scary, but it doesn't seem to take as long to get through as it did the first time." Grace explained, talking with her hands before wrapping her arms around herself with a shiver.

"Now that you mention it," Zane agreed through a nod, a wrinkle creasing the space between his brows, "when we came here with the cat—I mean Fayth—it didn't happen."

"What is it?" Phelia asked as Uriel, Brilla, Mathew, Vick and Vale appeared stunned into silence. Twister had never heard of such a thing. Surely, he never experienced anything like it crossing the veil into the Human World, but then again, he had never faced what he witnessed with True either. Let alone bothered to travel to many of the other worlds in the first place.

"Phelia, why hadn't you mentioned this before?" Fayth asked, its front paws pressed against her abdomen, eyes wide. Even the winged beast quickly made its way to Grace's lap with a worried look behind her eyes. "All this time? You should have informed me."

"I don't understand. You never asked and it didn't seem particularly important in comparison. It's simply how things work, is it not? Why are you so worked up?"

"Because, there's nothing simple about it, you idiots!" Brilla shouted. "Who the heck thinks passing through The Darkness every time they open a door is normal?!"

"*What??* You're saying we have been somehow passing through that thing every time? You all go through doors, right? How's that even possible?" Zane exclaimed.

"We have never passed through anything like that. This is the first time I've heard of it. Don't have a clue what that means, but can't be anything good. Have there been any other incidents like that...?"

"Would being catapulted through a dark swirling something-or-other count as *that* sort of incident?" Phelia asked, glancing in her brother's direction. Twister was beginning to worry even more.What did it mean? How was it possible for The Darkness to be situated so close to other worlds in the first place? There was no way It could survive like that. Was It just lying in wait that day It grabbed True?

Were his friends in danger just opening doors to other worlds before they ever stepped foot in them in the first place?

"I told you, Phelia. I wasn't hurled through some hole." Zane scoffed. "Now stop it already because you're freaking me out."

"Freaking *you* out? How do you suppose I felt? One moment you were there, the next you'd disappeared altogether. You don't recall it, but my memory is haunted by it. I can't forget, even if I tried. I recall it and every second after. The next time I saw you, you were unconscious in bed."

"Wait, what are you two talking about?" Victor asked, shooting Zane a look Twister couldn't quite decipher. "When did you two go off somewhere and how exactly was Zane catapulted?"

"When I lost my crystal after True made it through the door. Zane took me to go look for it. It was there in *Snowville Temporary Infirmary*, in front of the wall that leads to the door. We don't know why it happened but we went through and were sent *elsewhere*. Zane was treating me like an infant--"

"You mean you were being *reckless* and I was trying to protect you. And I regret every moment of that place. I certainly wasn't *wishing* to go off to another world."

"See? You *do* remember." Phelia squinted her eyes, effectively throwing invisible daggers in her brother's direction. Twister wondered if that would be his fate if his parents ever birthed another child.

Zane scratched his cheek, "I could have sworn I said I remember things. I was just having a nightmare. You too, probably. Unconscious seems like an over exaggeration."

"I ended up in a room too," Victor cleared his throat, taking a peek in Matthew's direction for only a moment, "but nothing like that. No Darkness incident that I'm aware of. I didn't wish to go anywhere either. Then I ended going home barefoot."

"Doors open for many reasons. You don't always have to open them yourselves by wishing." Brilla said, tossing some of hair back over her shoulder. Twister knew very little of opening doors. Faeries don't use a medium like a crystal to do so. There was a lot of intent involved, but it was second nature. He could offer no explanation, but he found himself forever worried about these human children.

"Sometimes the crystals take you to a world you need to go. Other times they will do it to protect you." Uriel explained. "But if your crystal sent you there, it was for a reason. From the sound of it, *to* protect you. Yet, somehow The Darkness was able to find you and take you somewhere. That means it is very powerful right now. What worries me the most is that you have little recollection of it. Did anything change after that incident?"

"Everything did." Zane answered. From the look of surprise on his face, by accident. Twister watched him run his fingers down his face, a gesture he'd seen often since they met. "I guess there's no taking it back now, even though it's the truth. What I *meant* was...I had that nightmare and got worse from there. I went on a date with Bailey and I couldn't contain my anger, I lashed out." He looked towards True. "Then I went to True's place. I attacked her. Fought Victor. It was one of the worst nights of my life. That voice appeared in my head back then. ***Everything*** was different."

Twister remembered that night too. It was his fault True had been outside in the cold. His fault Zane had access to her at all. He wondered if Zane had been forced to knock on the door, if he would have had more time to see that something was very wrong. If he could have convinced True to shut the door, lock it and not see him. It was also that night that he'd panicked. He'd seen some dark shadow looming over Zane and Victor while they tussled in the snow.

"The Darkness is a formidable foe at every turn." Matthew chimed in, gently placing a hand on Zane's shoulder. "It finds a way to influence people, exploits *any* insecurity, and weakness It finds, and evokes the darkest parts of people's hearts. Even being scathed by It can change you. I'm afraid, however, that what you are describing *might* be worse."

"Until we went to The After Land, I didn't really even feel like me." Zane's lip quivered. Had that been the result of sadness, anxiety, guilt, or fear? He soon seemed to get ahold of his emotions. "I still worry that it might all happen again. Sorta like something else will go wrong or that I can hurt my friends. Cursed Fae turned on their friends and family too, didn't they? Somewhere in the back of my mind, I wondered if they were related."

"I don't think you're turning into a Cursed Faerie, Zane. You're not even evil. Plus, you protected Victor from that bad Enrich guy too." Grace huffed, "Still...I don't understand The Darkness. If It is so powerful, why is It taking Faeries in the first place?" Ah, finally at least a small explanation that Twister could offer.

"To The Darkness, Grace, everything outside of It seems to be collateral or a food source. If you guys have been stepping through It on the way to other worlds, then you know. That thing is empty. Kind of like a power hungry, putrid monster with no concrete shape. The Cursed Fae, I would guess, are a means to an end. But what The Darkness is thinking or how It plans to get everything It wants, well, that's something I don't think anyone can answer."

"That's another aspect of The Darkness I don't understand myself." Phelia shook her head, crossing her arms. "Everyone says The Master of the Key's most powerful asset is their brain. But The Darkness is some kind of entity that apparently exists without one. How am I—how are *we* supposed to kill something like that? A *thing* without form, that is capable of sophisticated thought which even you haven't defeated? It goes against the natural order of things."

"Yes," Uriel smiled. "Only, the natural order of things isn't dictated by rules of the Human World. It encompasses both physical and metaphysical. For all intents and purposes, everything you have experienced with your crystal has been out of the 'natural order' the Human World dictates. Our battle, as World Knights, has to do with balance. And even all I have said thus far is an oversimplification.

"The Darkness cannot be destroyed. Neither can Light. Or at least, we haven't a clue how to do so. But even if we did, all in existence would fall apart. We hadn't figured it all out ourselves, but the obvious weapon of choice against The Darkness is the power from the crystals. *Magic.* Which is also outside of the 'natural order of things,' no? Yet, fully capable of tipping the scales back in our favor."

"There's still something else bugging me." Victor sighed. "Going off what Grace was saying about the Cursed Fae, and The Darkness being empty, what's the point of using Fae specifically? Cursed Fae can't cross the veil anyway, right? Why doesn't The Darkness walk itself into FlareWing? Why not just create a body?"

"Perhaps that's one of the reasons It taints...?" Twister began. Suddenly feeling a chill creep down his spine. He wasn't sure what the criteria would be, nor if it mattered what world Its prey came from but...what if? Noting the intense expression clouding Phelia's face as she looked towards Zane, Twister knew she understood just where his mind had been headed. Hadn't Mathew said whatever had been happening seemed like more than just a run-in with The Darkness?

"You're suggesting that The Darkness doesn't need Its own body. It needs to ***possess*** one...?"

Crystal Storm, Book 2

CKBS

Part 2:
Ripple Effect.

Thirty-Six

Quill...

DARKEN THE SKIES.

Quill trudged lazily forward; her limbs attempted to defy her wishes. She was fully aware of exhaustion now. Especially after her trouble with the kumiho. It was not a feeling she enjoyed. Then had not been as bad as what plagued her now. Perhaps it was her finishing her goal that made the difference.

The realization hit anew and Quill dropped to the ground and spread her limbs out on the grass with a laugh. She would just rest a moment. This was her first time feeling joy. And as if the awareness of the emotion itself was enough to elevate it, she laughed some more. In her time of celebration, however, Opal did not seem much in the mood to rejoice. If anything, she'd had that ridiculously distressed look on her face. At least she'd learned to recognize one of her expressions, that was when she had any at all.

Quill was not sure when it happened, but she'd found herself less annoyed than usual by her talk since she met back up with her. Opal had also stopped interrupting her duties in the midst of their cultivation. Although she wasn't sure what caused the sudden change, she couldn't say she wasn't pleased not hearing her nonsensical notions.

Stranger still, Quill found herself debating her role where the Faerie was concerned. She'd at some point begun to wonder if she was supposed to silence the girl's worries. Ultimately, she decided that it would be a waste of time. Both because her worries were unnecessary blather and her goals had very little to do with babysitting the sentiments of someone else. And yet, the look on Opal's face still ate away at her.

Quill looked her over slowly with a sigh. There was something comforting in looking over her features during the day. Every glistening-colored speck that trailed around her even when she stood still. Her black wings hanging down behind her back. Every strand of her hair in stark contrast to the rest of the scenery around them. *Like midnight during the day*, Quill thought. Yes. That was what it was. In this bright land that stung her eyes if she didn't take time to close them and give herself a break, she was a reminder that the dark she missed existed there as well.

And it would soon darken the skies of many worlds. Could there be a more perfect revenge for their suffering? For her mother's death and their exile? Quill could not think of one.

She would occupy the throne of victory with her father. Nothing else mattered. Nothing would get in their way that couldn't be crushed whole. Soon enough, this joy she felt would be hers to share. Would Opal find a sense of happiness after it was all over? If she behaved, at least she'd find a spot at the foot of the table.

Behaved? Hadn't she been convinced that the Faerie's opposition was worthy of punishment? Perhaps her words of loyalty had moved her, but what need did she have for any loyalty of hers in the first place? Still, she hesitated at the thought of telling her father. He would not be pleased. If nothing else, she should give Opal the opportunity to redeem herself. All she had to do was follow directions. Aside from her moments of mouthing, she was doing so now, right?

With her glee dispelled, Quill made her way to her feet and turned to Opal. "It is time. We must go back."

"I... I'll wait. We can meet here when you're done reporting." That's right. Opal wasn't informed. What difference would it make where she waited?

Although these were the thoughts that crossed her mind, Quill couldn't ignore the frustration rising inside her. How many times would she refuse? Just what was it about being above the surface that pleased her so much she'd avoid going home?

"Suit yourself. We will meet here when I return."

"I'm sorry, Quill." Opal said, hardly above a whisper. Even her random apology bothered her. She still did not understand the Faerie. Although she thought to ask for an explanation, she decided against it. It would only waste more time and stir up more unnecessary feelings within her.

She'd said it before. Now, she repeated it to herself. Nothing else mattered. Nothing would get in her way. Not even Opal.

Thirty-Seven

Opal...

CHOICE.

Opal did not sit idle as Quill went to give her report. Of course, that had never been her intention. Although, she had felt a smidgen of luck on her side when she refused to travel back together. Quill hadn't asked a reason why, and she gave no protest to Opal's decision even if she had not looked especially pleased. It was a feeling they'd shared for different reasons.

Truth be told, the feelings stirred up in her had carried much more depth and conflict than mere displeasure. As she watched Quill cheerfully chuckling in the grass, she felt something unbelievably foul. Opal wanted to be glad to see the first of her smiles. She'd wanted to love the sound of her laughter. Only, she'd felt nothing of the sort. She'd known, with an uncomfortable certainty, the reason she was happy.

Quill had been laying there in the grass celebrating the heinous acts she'd committed across a number of worlds. She was relishing the deceit, the torture, the massacre she'd inflicted upon them. And of all things, she'd dared to look in her direction with some sickening expectation behind her gaze—Quill had been waiting for her to join in. Expecting her to be able to find peace in what had transpired.

It had not been the first time she'd seen something like that of her. Opal had unfortunately witnessed too many of them since they made it above the surface. Too many of those moments she unmistakably saw ***IT*** making an appearance in her. She'd been wanting to deny the influence. She'd been so sure for so long that it would be different when they got away. Even convinced herself that Quill would realize her mistake trusting that ***thing*** to guide her.

Opal had since lost most of her confidence in those things. She dropped to the ground, eyeing the cabin in the distance. Still standing, looking much the same as she'd left it save for the smoke dancing away from the chimney. The winter air was nothing compared to the chill coursing through her insides. The vomit burning the back of her throat on its way out was the only warmth she recognized.

She could hardly believe the disgust she'd felt towards Quill. Nor the petrifying instant she realized those feelings had begun to morph into hatred. For an *inconceivable* moment, she ***hated*** her.

A rustling behind her changed the path of her thoughts. When she turned, she had to blink away her surprise. "It's you, isn't it?" She forced a smile as she looked the man over and met his blue gaze. She was certain the human before her was the one she'd brought to the cabin. Besides, the area was all but abandoned for miles.

Had she been thinking of anything else the moment she laid eyes on him she was sure it would have been genuine. He was bundled up in a proper coat with leather gloves and a hat. Better shoes, too. He nodded. Suddenly conscientious, she mimicked her previous position on the ground and pretended to be in search of some missing item. Of course, she was successful in her pursuit of the imaginary. She stuffed the invisible item into her clothes. "Found it!" She said, as she made a show of dusting off her hands.

...

"Really, I hardly recognize you." Opal said as she sat on the table inside the cabin. At some point since her last visit, he had not only rid the place of any dust, but gathered some more food including bread, made a hot meal which was now waiting to be devoured, and gotten himself clothes that suit him. If not for the gaping hole in the ceiling and the unusable portion of the structure on the other side, she would have thought it an entirely different place than where she'd left him.

Not only that, but the man she was looking at now, almost made her last sight of him feel like a dream. He'd clearly had a bath, his dark curls had been combed and cut. His beard trimmed low and shapely. The painfully red, dry areas of his eyes had gone. He even sported a pair of round glasses. *Still a bit too thin*, Opal noticed, *but he seems healthier.*

He took a spoonful of food from the bowl beside him before he stood and rummaged through a bag in the corner. She'd never seen that before either. Just what had he been up to? Wait. Hadn't she told him it was too dangerous to leave the cabin?

When he turned around to face her, a smile lighting up his face, however, Opal sighed. How could she manage to be upset with him for putting himself in harm's way when he smiled at her like that? Besides, perhaps the man was more capable than she'd thought before. He clearly had managed to leave, retrieve necessary items, and returned in one piece. As he waved sheets of paper in the air, Opal gasped. She'd completely forgotten. It was her that was supposed to bring something for him to use.

"I'm very sorry. I'd forgotten completely about the paper and all." Opal admitted. He shook his head as he took another bite, completely unbothered. Then, she watched him press a finger against a button and begin to scribble across the paper. He crossed something out. Started again. Curious, she leaned forward to inspect the writing tool. This was not the same thing she recalled seeing from her parents' memories. "What is this thing you're using? You didn't have to use ink."

Seemingly amused, his smile widened. *It's called a pen. The ink is inside so there's no mess. I've witnessed a lot of new things since we last saw one another.* He wrote. *Some absolutely terrifying, but this is perhaps one of my favorites.*

"Ah. I see." Opal nodded. "It's a pen, then."

It's been a long time since I saw this world, so I must thank you. I have a lot more to learn. But you brought me back here. You saved me. I even remembered my name, Morgan.

"Oh, no." Opal shook her head. "As nice as it is to properly make your acquaintance, Morgan, I don't think I saved you. I haven't a clue how the both of us made it away in the first place."

Even so, you brought me here. You kept me warm, gave me food, spoke to me. Reassured me. You came back here again, twice. May I know the name of the person who cared for me?

She was beginning to feel embarrassed by his words, and still undeserving. He had made them sound so grand. As if she was wholly selfless and some sort of person worthy of praise. "I apologize. My name is Opal." She smiled awkwardly. "I can't say I wasn't worried, seeing you there like that. You seemed to be in pain too, but...part of the reason I helped you, I think, was also because of my curiosity. I wanted to find out how you were there, for what purpose. How you survived."

He shook his head, taking another couple of bites from his food as he scribbled across the paper. *You say that as if that makes you a bad person. I do not care if you had more than one motive for helping me. Because of you, I might get the chance to get the answers I seek—answers to questions we seem to have in common, at that. Unfortunately, I don't exactly recall where I was when you found me. Nor how I'd gotten there. Although I remember all too well the pain. An endless cycle of it, and drips of sanity that came back to me on whim.*

"You didn't know where you were?" Opal questioned, a little disturbed by the notion that he had been in such torture that he'd never had the time to take in his surroundings. Not that there was ever much to behold in the first place. Still, the thought unnerved her. He did not even know how he'd gotten there. He'd mentioned moments of sanity but how was this man sane at all?

If not for her own excitement looking at the outside world, Opal was sure she would have found every new experience terrifying. Possibly to such an extent that she would never venture outside again. How long had it been since he was in the Human World exactly?

Not in the slightest. I tried to remember it while you were away. I'm ashamed to say that something terrible took hold of me in my attempt. A kind of fear worse than fear itself. A kind of something unnatural and altogether repulsive. I want to explain it well but I'm afraid there aren't enough words for something like that. Even thinking of it now makes me feel unlike myself. I was never one to frighten easily and yet...

"That's not your fault. I know what that's like. That's because of that **thing**. *Whatever* **IT** is. If it doesn't make your stomach churn, there's something wrong with you. I don't know why ***IT*** would have taken you. Until you, I wasn't aware that anything human could survive down there. Usually, save at least for Quill and I as far as I am aware, ***IT*** gets rid of. One way or another. Still, ***IT*** was keeping you alive for something. ***IT*** fed you and gave you water."

Only, I've not a moment of recollection of it happening. Not of a single drop of water, food, warmth. Nothing at all.

Opal shuddered at the thought of it. "That's probably a very good thing. I wouldn't wish it on anyone. As for the warmth," she spoke as she took a bite into a small green fruit, "there was never any in the first place. So, that's hardly a surprise. You're much better off here where you belong. You were wasting away. But look at you now. I don't know what happened to you while I was away, I apologize for how long it took me to return, but you seem better for it."

I returned home. After some of my memories returned to me, I could think of little else. I took some of the things you gathered for me, and by a great bit of luck, caught a train that passes through. You were right to warn me of course. I nearly froze to death on an open cart. Two enginemen, the men who control the train, quite nearly pummeled me. Then, I met an ancient being, an Osett, if you've ever heard of them.

"I can't say that I have." Opal said thoughtfully, mentally shifting through her parent's memories as she realized she'd been right about his eyes—there *was* magic in Morgan's gaze after all.

For only an instant she savored the thought that she was free to do so without danger. Even if now was not the most appropriate time for it, she could let herself get lost in the memory of them. She could allow herself to feel every moment of sadness, joy, pain, laughter, every ounce of love. But would she have the time? After all, she may have been free to think without finding herself in danger, but danger itself would be following her. Something worse would befall everyone else. She should at least warn Morgan.

He took on the form of one of the enginemen and drove the train. He told me stories of his life and places we were passing by on the way. After a day or so of riding, we came upon my town and said our goodbyes. There were many strange looking vehicles on the roads. Many buildings, people, animals and such I did not recognize. Not far from my home the town began to look the way I remembered. Although it was much emptier and more broken than in my memories. Even my old school was shut down.

A woman I did not recognized called me by name. She looked human, save for her unnaturally bright white hair, but felt otherwise. And I soon found out that she was possessed by some sort of household spirit. When I'd asked her if we'd met before, she informed me that we had never met personally. She made a pact with my family to watch over our home. Which she apparently very much liked to clean while listening to the musings of some male musician who often sat in the field behind the house. My father, had been adamant that I would return one day.

It took some time for it to hit me. For me to understand just how long I had been away. We didn't expressly speak on it, but it was apparent. In all the changes outside the home, in my ignorance when she spoke about the world or showed me items I'd never seen. We walked about the neighborhood. I met new creatures I'd never heard of, entered shops that had never existed in my time. It was a wonderful and altogether horrifying experience. I learned too, that it was not just she who protected my home. My father had enlisted the care of many other creatures. For my sake.

It was in that that I tried to find comfort. That perhaps even, I gathered the other bits of lucidity left within me together. I knew that my father was long gone. And in the two letters he left me, he told me that he was too old to venture back and forth from FlareWing. But he'd known about the state of things from other beings. About the war coming. He knew I would return one day even if he didn't understand where I'd gone. He was worried but had faith in me. Because he knew I would never stay away with my child on the way.

The poor cleaning spirit had to console me the rest of the evening, but she fed me well. I spent the night calling upon her for this thing or that. To explain things. To ask questions about the rest of my father's life. My family's lives. She had very little to offer me.

Opal felt the sting of loneliness nipping at her and slowly the bitter feelings she'd had earlier began to make their appearance again. She pitied him. She understood what it was like to be left suddenly alone with only memories. But the terrible feeling looming over her increased the moment she realized what she was hearing. She didn't understand it completely, but Morgan had ties to the Faerie world. FlareWing. He'd mentioned it by name. And having sifted through her parents' memories a moment before, the name struck her again and again.

FlareWing wasn't just connected to Morgan. It was the place that Quill was...it was also Opal's father's...

I decided then that I would give myself the rest of the night to feel my father in that home. To peruse his work, his journals. My father kept very detailed writings; you see. And of course, he'd been right. I would have done anything to be with my wife, with my child. Nothing would have stopped me. And yet, ***something*** *did. I left there because we promised to speak, and I'd hoped you'd lead me to FlareWing. Since you are a Faerie. Because if nothing else, I could learn what happened to them there.*

She clinched her fist. It didn't matter that his home was protected. If she was right about what would happen, even his house would not be left standing. Morgan was probably safest staying in the cabin now. She didn't know what she could do, but she could probably tell Quill that she was attached to the place. She might be able to convince her to leave it unharmed and him within it. If nothing else, she could come back and would protect him herself. The only thing she did know was that leading him to FlareWing would put him in danger.

"I am a Faerie, yes. But there's something wrong with me. I'm not like normal Faeries. You spoke about war, vaguely. A war did happen in FlareWing before. Many Fae died, though I cannot say what happened to your family. You sound like you had an attachment to a Faerie or live with your family there. I can't imagine it, a bunch of humans being allowed to live in FlareWing, but things have changed since then. Even the likes of me cannot go there."

Even if we aren't supposed to go, I need to try. Morgan wrote, his quick strokes showcasing the urgency rising up in him. It felt undeniably cruel to refuse him. But what else was she supposed to do? She couldn't, in good conscience, send him to some place she knew probably could do nothing to help him.

"I'm sorry, Morgan. I cannot take you." Opal shook her head again. She'd barely managed to get the words out. Her last thought plagued her. She could not, in good conscience. Wasn't that true about everything else too? "Something bad is happening, Morgan. FlareWing is not safe. Your home, either. But this cabin will be. I will make sure that it is safe for you."

With her mind racing, her pulse skyrocketing, and unable to take the look in his eyes as he looked her way, she rushed to her feet. "I will be back, I promise." Opal said quickly, rushing towards the door. "Until then, unless you're sure it is me, please do not open the door. Not for anyone or anything. No matter what you hear."

With her warning, she hoped that he could understand. She wished only to protect him, Opal turned around and covered the front door in her magic. It would not last. But for now, at least, it would protect him from immediate danger. Long enough, she hoped, for her to return without him being in harm's way.

She'd told Morgan that even she could not go to FlareWing. The fact of the matter was, she could find her way there, but it was true that the likes of her weren't invited. FlareWing, as far as she was aware, was meant to keep people like herself and Quill far away from its borders. But she had to try something.

She'd been wrong to waste her time trying to convince Quill. She was resolved to follow through on her revenge. Even though Opal was sure that something about the entire ordeal with her supposed mother's death was questionable. If for no other reason than because ***IT*** had told her the story.

Truth be told, Opal had no idea who Quill's mother was. She'd never known. She might even have thought it made sense to destroy everything around her had her own mother's death been from anything but *IT*. She wasn't sure, really. She was sure of one thing; right now, she had a choice in what she did. She wasn't sure if it would be for nothing, perhaps she was too late to take action now, but she had to try.

Opal was sure that if she didn't make her way to FlareWing as fast as she could, she would live to regret it. And presumably, hate herself forever. If she was lucky, maybe, just maybe, she could ask some Faerie about Morgan's family too. Assuming that she didn't manage to scare them off the moment they realized that she wasn't like them. That she was the kind of thing that didn't belong. If, of course, she could ever get close enough to do so.

Thirty-Eight

Morgan...

LUCK.

Morgan stared at the ceiling, out of breath. He'd been trying for hours to leave the cabin. The door would not give. After his conversation with Opal, he knew he had to leave. He knew that he'd never personally seen a Faerie that looked like her, especially one that sported black wings, but it had not occurred to him that there might have been something more he was missing. She didn't explain what she'd meant when she gave him the warning. She had asked him to stay in the cabin, for the second time.

He knew that she'd meant to protect him. Genuinely worried, when he mentioned FlareWing. Since they met, he had yet to see the expressions that crossed her features today. Before he knew it, Opal rushed away in what he could only describe to be an emotional frenzy. She looked, if he were to tell it, equally terrified and determined.

There was some part of him that wanted to listen to her reason. He felt that she truly believed her words, and perhaps of more importance, that she knew much more than he did about what may have happened to him and the thing responsible. But if something bad was about to transpire, he couldn't stand to stay still. Considering his time with the

Osett, and even the beings at his family home, his eyes had not failed him. He would use his eyes to find FlareWing. Or so he'd thought before he realized he was trapped in the cabin.

Even if I stood on the table and jumped, I wouldn't be able to reach that opening. Even if I could, how confident am I that I could pull myself up and not come tumbling back down? He turned his attention to the table. It definitely would hurt if he fell on it.

"Well then. You're perfectly trapped down there aren't you Mr. Morgan?" A familiar voice called. When he made out the pale green eyes peering down at him and the stark white strands of hair falling around them, he quickly sat up. Even the snowflakes got lost in her hair. He'd thought it briefly when he saw her before, but now he couldn't ignore it. Her hair reminded him of Lily's.

What was the household spirit doing there? "You seemed positively torn when you left. It worried everyone. Since I have the most experience out in today's world, I volunteered to follow you. I suppose I've arrived a bit later than intended, but who'd have thought I'd find you trapped here?"

Morgan rose to his feet, beaming.

"Well, don't just stand there and *gape*, Mr. Morgan." She spoke, reaching a hand down in his direction. "Come along. We've managed to find an entrance to FlareWing as well. I'll escort you there myself."

As he climbed onto the table and interlocked their hands, Morgan thought perhaps his luck was finally turning around. There were undoubtedly many kind creatures in existence. He thanked his father's forward thinking for his current fortune. Surely his father had not anticipated these circumstances exactly, but his faith in his return had saved him many times over already.

...

"What you seek is there beyond the brush." The house spirit, Evelyn, smiled softly. Thankfully, she'd thought to offer it. "We hope that you find the answers you seek, however you can." Morgan stopped and turned to face her. She would not accompany him?

"It's very tidy there. If I can never clean, I won't be able to enjoy myself. And, if I hurry back now, I will be able to enjoy the boy's music and dust your father's old study." She smiled again. "We will be awaiting your return, if that's alright with you. I've grown fond of it, your home and the others alike." Morgan gave a nod. He sincerely hoped she would make herself at home, and that whatever bad things were on the verge of happening now, it would not keep him from returning once again.

He gently took hold of her hand and squeezed it then watched her wave him off for a moment before he bent forward and pushed his way through the thicket ahead. On the other side, as he made his way to his feet, he noticed a translucent budding flower pattern flowing horizontally across the mound ahead of him.

Vivid, multicolor gleams danced rhythmically across the surface and the moment his fingers grazed it, a comforting warmth spread throughout his body. Almost simultaneously, he watched a stream of the luminescent lights dart erratically across his vision and vibrations erupted beneath his fingertips.

As he began to question what was happening, a child-like figure emerged on the other side. Morgan's wonderstruck gaze was returned by a pair of olden, incandescent eyes. "So, you've returned, Morgan." The Faerie's deep voice spoke as soft hymns trilled in the distance.

Thirty-Nine

Grace...

ALIEN.

Grace dropped to the floor, exhausted. She'd done everything she could think of. No amount of wishing, jumping, striking the air, recklessly racing around or anything else she imagined could invoke magic, worked. What Uriel said before they'd left The Ruins made no sense. They had to be wrong.

The ritual had sounded so fancy, but the reality was somewhat underwhelming. Although Grace supposed that no one had said it would be a grand ordeal. She'd managed that thought all of her own. Phelia repeated some words, which Grace couldn't begin to remember now, guided by Fayth. And one after the other they heard those familiar chimes. A sound she was sure they'd heard very rarely since their first time traveling through the door, since that first time in Mirror. She'd forgotten to ask about that.

One after the other, the crystals slowly flickered—save for her own—and a beam of multicolored light swam through them. Grace had been enjoying the swaying of light between her fingers, it was pretty after all, but not close enough to what she had been expecting. A kaleidoscopic symbol etched onto the surface by a white light. And almost as quickly as it had begun, the ritual came to an end.

When Grace asked why her fiery crystal seemed to have missed a step, it had not blinked even once, they told her that this was because her crystal had always been "whole." None of their predecessors had a matching crystal, nor powers to give her. Why? Because as far as what they had been told, she'd had her own powers. Powers, as they understood it, which she inherited from her parents.

For an instant, Grace was excited by the thought. Until multiple realizations hit her. One, they had been in the process of telling her that her parents where from some other place, which made her what, exactly? An *alien?* Two, even if that was true, she literally knew nothing of her birth parents. Three, just the thought of one more thing being *different*—being wrong—with her bothered her to no end. It wasn't enough that she looked like this?

Still, Grace thought that she would know by now if she had powers. Right now, her own superpower seemed to be causing trouble. As she caught her breath, kicking her feet frustratedly against the floor, a warm feeling slowly spread through her chest. It happened right before they'd left The Ruins as well. Only, it had been so intense that Grace was nearly convinced she'd developed a dangerous case of heartburn.

She turned her head to look at Blitz who was watching her silently from under her bed. She could make out the shimmer of her blotches of rainbow scales on her otherwise white body, her short horns and her large eyes. If she had powers it would have been neat to do something like Blitz.

She wasn't sure what Blitz had done exactly, but if her foster parents' amnesia wasn't a ruse to escape possible consequences, it was most definitely the result of Blitz's magic smoke thingy. The thought of being able to make anyone and everyone forget something she'd done or even her entire existence seemed like a convenient kind of magic to have at her disposal right about now.

Whatever the case, what Blitz had done to MaryAnne and Duke brought her there. Officer Jane Nuri took her in. Gave her so much freedom and food. She'd even tried to protect her from the rumors quickly spreading around town. Grace was too scared to face it. And she couldn't help but wonder, what would happen when the Brands heard?

Phelia had never made mention of the crawlspace. In fact, they'd completely avoided the topic altogether. Why couldn't they do it forever? She didn't know if she could tell her everything that had happened when she couldn't admit it all to herself. The thought of even recalling it all, fully being aware and unable to excuse any of it, felt dangerous. As if there was something waiting on the other side of the wall, likely to turn her life into something too horrific for words, and her along with it.

Officer Nuri had been the first person to tell her that everything she'd faced under MaryAnne and Duke's care had been "abuse" and "wholly undeserved." She'd cried. Maybe the hardest she'd ever cried in her life. Validation of the smallest feelings hidden away from oneself, and yet still something that she couldn't exactly let herself believe to be true was a strange feeling.

As things were, Grace still felt like she deserved it sometimes. She still got scared of walking in the front door. She still expected her punishments. Still became fearful when she spent an hour in a hot bath. And a million other things she hated.

Officer Nuri, Grace thought, *will probably be a good mom one day*. But if what she'd heard with the others had been the truth, then what? She had many questions. If she had parents out there, where were they? And if they were born with powers, ***what*** were they? What did they look like? Sound like? Were they nice people? Some questions carried an ache to her heart the moment she thought them. The question that pained her most; why hadn't they wanted her?

Forty

True...

CONCERN.

True waved her aunts out the door with a smile. At least they hadn't seemed to notice. All morning she couldn't escape the battle waging on in her mind, constantly fighting to think of everything they'd heard during their conversation with Uriel.

True never got the chance to talk to her about the journal, but when they were saying their goodbyes, she tried to return it. And of course, apologize for reading her private matters. To her surprise, Uriel shook her head and told her that there was no need for the apology nor to return it to her. She'd said, it had been the start of a very rough first attempt and she'd gotten much better at it now. She had a new journal, albeit much more personal than that one had been. "Now," she'd told her with a soft look in her eyes, "it feels like a perfect memory. One that will hold up much better in *your* hands. Do with the journal however you see fit..."

...

"Can I eat some of these?" Twister asked, his voice taking her away from her thoughts. It had been more than a comfort to have him there. So much so, True was worried she'd miss his presence too much whenever he returned to FlareWing for good. Perhaps, after he officially accepted his parents' proposal to be a family again. If he so chose. Though True didn't know why he would refuse.

"Of course, Twister." True gestured lightly to the spread on the table. "Help yourself." There was no way she would be able to finish it all. Not even with Twister's help. Of course, the fruit and a few other things would be just as good tomorrow, so that helped. Her aunts always made a large breakfast when they got carried away in their early morning conversations.

True thought briefly to call Victor. It hadn't taken very long to memorize his number. She didn't know if he ever ate breakfast. Any time he came to her house, he hadn't come for breakfast. She imagined that on a day like today, Victor would much rather spend his mornings sleeping in than having a meal at seven am. She wondered how he was doing now. If he managed to sleep again after he snuck back to his hospital room with Twister's help. He'd said they'd probably get caught with all of them tagging along so he would make it back to the room with just the two of them.

"Everything alright?" Twister asked as he sat down on the table between an orange and a plate of eggs. She watched him wrap his scarf around his neck and inspect the orange. "Something on your mind?"

"I imagine many of the things that everyone's thinking." True sighed as she took a seat near him. She peeled the orange skin and pulled the fruit apart, having took notice of Twister's interest. "Twister?"

"Hmm?"

"Are you sure that you want to be here right now? The news from The Ruins was...unsettling. To say the least. And the look on Zane's face when you mentioned being tainted...do you think The Darkness really hoped to possess him?"

Twister chewed, swallowed. "Honestly, I think it makes the most sense. You saw it for yourself, how different he became. For all we know, The Darkness may have just saw the opportunity and took it. I didn't want to have the thought myself, but it isn't as if any of us gain peace by pretending the possibility never existed.

"Phelia being The Master...that was a *surprise*. I sensed that Grace wasn't exactly human when I'd first met all of you in FlareWing so that one was not so shocking. Though I can say little about what she is or where she's from. I don't have much experience with worlds outside of FlareWing and the Human World." Was that the reason Twister called her interesting when they first met?

"As for where I want to be, I'm already there. Aside from all this mess with you all facing The Darkness, I wonder if I will even get the chance to give my mother's proposal any true thought. If things go awry, I might miss any chance left at fixing the other aspects of our relationship. I keep wondering, what if? What if they were hurt and I never saw them again? What if *you* do or just...*any* one of you?"

True gently pressed a finger to his palm. She felt very lucky to have met him. Twister was much more than magic. Though it pained her to know he was so concerned. Not that she could say otherwise. After all, even she had many of the same feelings and thoughts. What if she was hurt...? The truth was, she'd never given it a thought.

"I'm not worried about myself. I'm not sure of any powers from the crystals, nor how I can be of any help. I feel the same as before. But if there is something I can do, something I can try, I will. I'm concerned about the others. Phelia had seemed truly shaken. Grace, absolutely confused—I had not known much of her and was clueless to the fact that she was an orphan altogether.

"Is Victor well enough to be involved? I'd mistakenly thought he was alright. I'd thought he seemed relatively normal. When I questioned anything, I hadn't thought it so bad. And Zane, well, I cannot even begin to imagine how frightened he must be now. I don't know what The Darkness had in mind for me, but he'd had something invading his mind and his body...

"You said you are where you want to be, but if you have these concerns with your parents wouldn't you rather tell them? Or, go back home to be with them now? Why torture yourself? It doesn't seem fair to keep you here."

Twister wrapped his arms around her arm, in something of an embrace. She'd felt as if she'd said too much. Or perhaps, she had let her emotions get the better of her. There he was again, spending time with her. Consoling her, where she could offer nothing in return. Why shouldn't he prioritize his own wants, his own happiness? True knew that if she'd had a single nanosecond to change her mother's fate, or to fix everything that ended up broken by her death, she would not hesitate. At least right now, his parents still lived. So, why?

"True, thank you. I understand what you are saying." Twister rolled a grape across the plate beside him. "Truly, but the truth is, even if I were to return to FlareWing this instant, there is *no way* that my parents would be sitting around idle—or would with me, for that matter. Nor would they have the time to spend with me. I know at least that much."

Her heart ached for him. Even his wings hung low on his back, as if they were willing to express the sadness he was so desperately trying to hide behind his green and white eyes.

"Besides that, I am certain that this is where I'd want to be right now, even if circumstances were different. Like all of you, I'm not sure how any of this will go. I don't know how any of us will be able to play some major role the way we are now. Still, I'm alright like this. Having a few moments to breathe and enjoy a meal with you.

"More than that, I want to help you. All of you. I don't know about you, but humans with new abilities that they don't even know how to control sounds pretty dangerous to me." He laughed and the sound of soft chimes echoed in the shadow of his voice. True very much enjoyed his laughter. "If they suddenly activate, I may be able to offer some assistance. I *have* had magic all my life. If nothing else, Faeries could make good allies, no?"

True felt the corners of her own mouth turn in the hint of a smile. Twister himself was a breath of fresh air. If only he realized it. A sudden knock at the door halted their conversation. When Twister stood to accompany her to the door, she shook her head. She wasn't expecting a visitor. "It's alright, Twister. I'll get it."

He gave a quiet nod, and helped himself to one of the ginger cookies behind him. She'd given him one before, when they'd gone to see Victor in the hospital, and he seemed to enjoy it. She wondered if other Fae would enjoy some, the thought crossed her mind to give them as a thank you to several of the Faeries they'd had the pleasure of meeting in FlareWing. As she slid on her mask and jacket, she wondered if Father Wing would approve. Did he even like snacks?

True unlatched the lock and opened the door. Mrs. Burroughs?? "M-my aunts left not long ago." True stuttered. She knew that skipping gym would catch up to her at some point, but she had never expected a home visit. Least of all, with winter break mere days away. True supposed there was no point in regretting it now. Was there ever any room to regret being away from Sydney and the others in the first place?

"Uh-huh. I noticed that I passed them on the way here." Mrs. Burroughs nodded. "That's not why I'm here. I came to have a quick chat with you, just the two of us, so whether they are around is of no particular consequence." Talk to her alone? True fidgeted with the lining of her jacket pocket. Should she be worried? The last thing she wanted was to have any semblance of this conversation. True looked over her teacher's clothes as a distraction for her rising anxiety.

Today, she wore velvet bottoms, and a black sweater with colored accents, and black boots. Her gray hair blew freely in the wind, her bangs held in place by black cat hairpins. The dark eyeshadow and even darker lipstick that painted her face reminded True somewhat of her usual sporty attire at school. A part of her preferred to see the gym teacher the way she was now. She knew that all teachers had own their lives out of the classroom, but all the thought brought her were questions about her home's décor.

"I'll get right to the point." Mrs. Burroughs crossed her arms. "Are you being bullied at school?" The wind whistled. True swallowed. Wished, in that moment, the freezing cold that rushed past her from her place in the doorway could ice her over. She opened her mouth, but the only audible sound was a strange, muffled whine.

If Mrs. Burroughs heard it, she didn't react. "Look, I was in high school before too. Surprisingly, I remember those days very well. And I've known the likes of Sydney's kind personally. It's her, isn't it? The ones with a crowd are usually the worst sort. I realize that as an adult, it's sometimes all too easy to forget how difficult it is being a kid. Balancing life. Trying to be perfect or do perfect things. Having so many people to answer to outside of yourself, while finding your way.

"It's easy to forget what it's like when you feel different, especially in a place full of so many of the *same* people. But this is something that can get better. I know I'm asking you something that would be difficult to admit—what I'm saying is, you can trust me. All you have to do is say the word. Matter fact, don't say anything. Just nod your little head and I will take care of the rest."

True hadn't imagined this outcome. She'd never expected to be offered a hand. She recognized the olive branch being extended in her direction. She understood that Mrs. Burroughs was being more than sympathetic. Her concern was genuine. Just the look on her face was enough to know that it was possible that this woman before her had felt her pain. At least to some degree.

But True didn't want to feel responsible for what happened to those girls. Nor give them the room to find her at fault and retaliate. And she didn't think she could manage to tell Mrs. Burroughs the truth before she had the courage to be honest with Victor or her aunts. In the long silence that followed, Mrs. Burroughs let out a sigh.

"That's alright," she said with a shake of her head. "Wait here a minute." She directed, as she turned around, made her way down the steps and the walkway, and out the gate to an old, violet colored car parked on the road. True took a few steps out of the door and closed it behind her as Mrs. Burroughs made her way back again.

"I'll offer you this." She huffed and passed True a brown paper bag from her arms. "You have missed a lot of my classes. Considering that I checked with the rest of your teachers and you're doing fine elsewhere, I will assume it has been for ***medical*** reasons.

"No one, least of all me, wants to do anything in this God-forsaken snow. So, I'll pass you for now. After winter break, when spring finally manifests its bright little head, I'll get the keys to the gym. You come with me and work your butt off for three days. You look kind of *frail*, so three days ought to do it. Can you handle that?"

True nodded. She'd give her a passing grade? "And I suppose I'll have to tell my aunts that I failed gym...?"

"What are you going on about?" Mrs. Burroughs scoffed. "I don't remember you *failing* my class." True watched the woman in surprise as she smirked and shooed her back inside the doorway. "Alright then. I'm holding you to that. Now get back inside before you catch cold." As she turned around and made her way back off the porch, True opened the bag.

Inside, she found each one of her missing items. Her shoes, her note-books, pens, even her old thermos next to a new item of similar design. She gingerly opened the folded piece of paper taped to the top. It read, 'this one ought to make a good replacement, no?'

True stumbled quickly down the stairs and raced to the gate as Mrs. Burrough's started her car and turned around. Her dark lips shaped another smile as she nodded in her direction.

"T-thank you!" True called, as she unintentionally crinkled the bag in her arms. Mrs. Burroughs was such a wonderful person. That was the kind of thought True had as her car sputtered down the street and out of view. "Thank you very much..."

Forty-One

Victor...

HONESTY.

Victor made his way through the halls of *Snowville Medical* and stopped as a nurse closed the door ahead of him. He watched her mark the chart on the door and waited. Waited, for the woman to walk down the hall and disappear around a corner before he turned the knob on the door.

The room was quiet, a few cards and a small bundle of flowers decorated a table beside the bed. Machines beeped on. Birds chirped musically in the distance. Their routine not impacted by the bitter temperatures outside, and definitely not by the lack of commotion in Bailey's room. Somehow, considering how lively the girl was, it didn't sit very well with him.

Victor pulled up a chair, and looked her over. The hospital gown was too plain for Bailey's tastes. Zane had been right; by all appearances, she seemed only to be sleeping. "I think I owe you an apology." He cleared his throat. "I might have accidentally let it slip that you liked Zane. Which I guess he might not have understood when you asked him out. Anyway, I'm sorry that I told him first. I think it would mean more coming from you though, if you thought you might want to tell him—officially, that is."

Victor thought back to the day they saw her in The Land of the Dead. Her being in the hospital and her appearance there was somehow connected, wasn't it? He wasn't sure he understood how that was possible, but he supposed that didn't matter now. As if The Land of the Dead hadn't been bad enough on its own. "I remember you complaining a long time ago that Zane wasn't paying attention to you. You'd said it was probably because we were best friends. Well, he's paying plenty of attention to you now. He's worried sick."

"Did Zane apologize to you yet?" Victor asked, of course, not expecting an answer. "You'll have to forgive him, Bailey. I'm sure you know Zane's an idiot." *But then again, so am I. I made everyone worry. Mom, Zane, Grace...even True.*

True. Victor sighted. He wanted to see her. He chided himself. Since when did he allow himself to think things like that? Just then, the thought swam through his mind without any hint of difficulty. *No.* Victor thought. No way. *You have got to stop this, you idiot.*

...

Victor soon found himself there anyway, and made his way through the black iron gate. Even though he'd explicitly forbid himself from doing so just a few hours before. Frustrated, he demanded that he turn around and go home. With his back to the door, Victor heard the lock unlatch. Felt the warm air from the house brush past him. "I thought it was you..." True called.

Victor couldn't leave then. At least, that was his excuse. He hadn't managed to knock. Was he becoming that predictable? "Yeah. It's me." Mentally, he kicked himself. This neediness of his was getting out of hand. And what was that 'it's me' bit? He really was an idiot. He turned around to face her, looking over the brown kitten mask with pointed ears covering her face. Was it just him or was her mask variation insane?

He felt a smile threatening to bury his irritation. "If you're busy I can come again some other time."

True shook her head, stepped to the side, and invited him to the living room. He made his way in and walked towards the fireplace to scan the photos in the frames. When he was there last, he hadn't had the opportunity to look over them. There weren't any photos of young True. In each photo, she sported a different mask. She was a bit shorter but guessing her age in them proved difficult.

True stepped to his side, and held out two plates of food out towards him. "Oh. So, that's what I've been smelling. Did your aunts have breakfast? I should probably say hello."

"They've gone to work." True said, again offering him the food. Gone again? How did he keep getting himself into this situation?

"Uh, thanks." Victor accepted the plates, placed them on the table, and then made his way to the couch. "I had been meaning to ask you about the house." He said, stuffing his hands in his pockets. "Since the whole ghost murder mystery thing. What did you mean when you said the house felt 'normal but empty' and all?"

"Oh." True tilted her head as she sat down on the other side of the sofa. "I suppose that things are different now. The house feels almost like any other one. There aren't any more pockets of sadness. There are no cold corners of the room. No hints of anyone else being here before or with us."

"There was a lot of that before?" Victor asked. He wasn't sure about the rest, but he definitely noticed the lack of cold air inside. "Mm-hmm." She nodded. Victor tried not to be amused by the mask. There was something about its stiff features and the bobbing of her head that tickled him. He leaned back on the cushion and rested his head against the pillows behind him.

"Weren't you able to rest?" True asked, suddenly closing the distance between them. She reached a hand towards him and Victor quickly shifted, surprised. True silently dropped her arm and placed her hands in her lap. "I-I'm sorry."

Crap. Victor shifted again. “No, it’s alright—just then, that was my own fault. I’ve been a little on edge.” *Such an idiot...* He sighed.

“Because of The Ruins?” True asked softly.

“To a degree, for sure. I didn’t sleep very much since we got back to Snowville but I slept. I’m sorry about making you worry.”

“I think I made you worry too, didn’t I? You asked me before if I was hurting. And back then, you even carried me home.”

“Yeah, I did ask you *something* like that.” Victor watched her fidget with her hands. As she spoke, the movements of her fingers became more erratic, more intense.

“Today Mrs. Burrough’s came to see me. That thing, me being hurt like that, I don’t think it will happen again. I think everything is going to be fine now. I’m pretty sure.” Victor didn’t understand exactly what she was saying. He knew whatever was happening now was incredibly important, he knew True wasn’t saying it for nothing. But it felt a bit vague.

The day he carried her in the snow with the busted ankle he’d been a mess. But it would have been impossible for him not to notice her ankle and bare feet. He’d asked her if she was getting bullied. If she was *being* hurt by someone. She never gave him an answer. Was this supposed to be an answer? What did it have to do with Mrs. Burroughs?

Victor wasn’t sure how to feel. On one hand, he didn’t know exactly what had been happening with her. He didn’t like that feeling. On the other, she was saying that there was nothing to worry about anymore, right? So, he should be glad to hear it but why did he feel so...? “That’s good, right?”

True nodded, but her hands still fumbled around, still slid across her jacket. Victor glanced down at her feet. Even they weren’t keeping still. “Yes, of course. I-I was also thinking, before you came, that I didn’t want to care what anyone else says about our friendship.”

“Our friendship?” What kind of things did someone else have to say? Just the thought of some clueless person daring to open their mouth to say a single word of opposition ticked him off. He might have been too sensitive when it came to True lately, he realized that. Still, the way she'd said it bothered him. "Were you having doubts? About our friendship?"

"Doubts...I'm not sure. I realized that I had been so distracted that I didn't notice enough. You were going through something. I didn't know: when we were in class, when you carried me through the snow, when you fell in my house. I never realized how bad things were for you. You weren't eating. You weren't sleeping. Y-You were suffering so much and I...

"When I understood what happened and that you must have felt that you couldn't talk to anyone about it, I did not enjoy that feeling at all. Even though I did not do a very good job being open with you either. I'm very sorry for being a terrible friend. Please forgive me."

Victor had never thought the sound of someone's voice could ever be enough to rip a hole through someone else's heart until that very moment. He had no words to describe the pain crushing his insides. He'd never heard her sound like that before. How could she talk about his suffering? If she was being bullied, he hadn't understood it when it counted, and Mrs. Burroughs had been the one to help her. Somehow. He was the one who tried to hide everything that was happening. And right now, he was the reason she felt like a terrible person.

He almost couldn't stomach the thought. True was already perhaps the kindest person he'd ever known. It was this kindness that made her believe that she could have ever been at fault for his own shortcomings. When he worried about hurting her, this had not been what he imagined. And to think, she was saying some of the very same thoughts that had run through his own mind time and time again. She *also* did not like not knowing.

Before he could think better of it, Victor placed his hands over hers, intent on keeping her hands still. He ignored the cat mask staring him in the face and closed his eyes so he could focus on his words instead. "The burden doesn't only lie with you. We agreed to be friends, so this is supposed to be a mutually beneficial relationship. Which requires mutual effort. You're allowed to think and be involved in other things, make friends with other people, and deal with your life outside of me.

"I was selfish. I was trying to avoid making anyone worry so I pretended to be fine. I took the opportunity to joke with Zane when I wasn't feeling well, I purposely gave away my mother's cooking when I didn't have an appetite, I pretended to sleep in class. I even tried those makeup tutorials. Which are *so* much harder than they look for the simplest of things."

"Make-up tutorials...?"

"Y-yeah. Never mind that." Victor shook his head. He hoped she would forget that part. Even if he found a new level of respect for women painting their faces, he didn't want True to remember him as the boy that tried it. Surely if anyone else heard it, they'd deem him emasculate. True was probably too nice to even have the thought.

"I'm also sorry, True. For making you worry and not being a very good, or honest, friend. I'm confident that we can do better so, would you mind if we start over one more time?" Victor slowly exhaled. He didn't know when he first started to hold his breath. His heart was beating like crazy. Why did the silence feel so eternal?

"Yes, alright." True agreed. When he felt her hands shift beneath his, he opened his eyes. She slowly turned over his hands until his palmed faced upwards. "But it doesn't have to be just once." She spoke tenderly as she placed her hands over his. "Or rather, if it's alright with you, is something different acceptable?"

"Something different? What do you mean?"

"Let's not start over. Can't we try from here, until we get it right?"

Somehow, Victor felt she was treating him too carefully. Not so unlike her pencils and pens she put away at the end of the school day. It felt like it would only make things worse. How was he supposed to talk sense into himself now? Every new experience with her. Every new side he'd never seen. Every soft-spoken word from the other side of her mask only made him more likely to seek her out.

"I didn't think about it that way." Victor answered truthfully. "I think that might be a better idea."

Victor ignored the incessant, vigorous thumping of his chest as he studied True's pale fingers. His eyes traced veins down her palms and his hands followed them to her wrists. He tried to recall how long ago she stopped fidgeting. How long ago was it that they'd met? Six or seven months? What a terribly short time for one's entire life to be turned inside out.

He allowed his mind to wonder. He recalled their unconventional first meeting and his suspension in May right before graduation, returning after his mother's cleaning fit into the next school year months later. Her awkward thank you and her warning about the rumors starting because of her. It was one thing for the school to talk. It was another for them to be physical. He wondered if he'd missed a lot of smaller things before her ankle. Had something like that started back then?

He thought of Mirror and his absolute certainty that he never wanted a pet again. Who knew that True had led them home without their notice? She'd helped the twins then too. He thought about True's creative presentation in Mr. Van-Dayton's classroom and her perfect handwriting. It was still hard to believe that she sought him out soon after, to talk about the crystals.

He wasn't sure how he felt about that, nor the journal's part in sending them through the door. But without it, they would have never seen FlareWing or met Twister. He wouldn't have raced Zane down the hills to the bridge like they were kids again. Or been fed dozens of spice flowers and buds at the market by True. He willed himself not to imagine her platinum blond hair buried somewhere beneath her jacket as she sat across from him.

He thought about the blows he and Zane traded in Snowville's November snow. The lavender sea he witnessed in his 'room' and the feeling of her hand in his, as she led him to the porch when he returned confused and barefoot. True had thanked him for protecting her back then. And the truths of The Death House were revealed days later at the beginning of December.

Now, Zane's birthday, their next break from school and the holiday were days away. With some sort of crystal, World Knights and Master of the Keys trouble right out of eyeshot. Looming there in the background. Victor frowned. Had that ceremony really given them some sort of power? Trained in martial arts or not, Victor didn't feel like he had any advantages as things were now. It wasn't like he could punch and kick The Darkness. If only.

"Victor...?" True's voice was so quiet he'd barely heard her.

He clearly hadn't thought any of this through. How was going to explain all of the things in his head to True? In the present moment, everything felt unbelievably complicated. How worried was she about the others? About the things they'd heard in The Ruins? Was she afraid? Victor feared being helpless. He hoped, more than anything, that whatever Phelia's words had done to the crystals truly bestowed some power in him that he could use.

Something, that could protect her and the others. "I don't know what we are supposed to do as World Knights or whatever it is. And I would rather none of us were even bothering with these things at this point, but it is probably too late now, huh? No turning back the hands of time. The least we can do is try to help each other..."

"Victor...a-are you alright?"

"I don't know, honestly. I'll let you know when I know."

"Is there something I can do?" True asked. He was starting to think that he should leave the room. Or at least let go of her. But she hadn't complained. She didn't shrink away from him. He was being ridiculous. Selfish, in fact.

"You've already done more than enough." Victor shook his head and slowly but surely, released her. He immediately regretted it. "Regardless of the crystals, I'll protect you." He tried to look her in the eyes to showcase his resolve. He'd nearly forgotten that it was impossible. The brushed features of the cat mask stared back at him.

"What about you?" She asked, in that all too familiar way that made him think her voice was too perfect for words. Was she still worried?

"What about me?" Victor asked, curiously.

"Well, aren't the *two* of you cute?" Twister smiled, suddenly appearing in the space between them. Startled, Victor jumped to his feet and watched crumbs fall from Twister's hands to the couch.

"Twister!" Victor noisily cleared his throat. The heat of embarrassment warmed his cheeks. "Don't sneak up on people like that." Victor huffed. "Free-loading at True's place again?"

"Want a cookie?" He offered. Victor watched him munch away as he held out an oblong shaped cookie in his direction. He didn't even bother to reply to the free-loading comment. It hadn't occurred to Victor that Twister had gone back to True's place again. Just how long had he been there, and exactly how much of their conversation had he heard?

Forty-Two

Phelia...

DREAMS AND SCREAMS.

Phelia had been glad to see Grace when she showed up on their doorstep. Even though she could tell something occupied her mind. After all, Grace was the kind of girl whose emotions were often written all over her face.

That said, that was also one of the things Phelia liked. Understanding Grace came easier than it did with her father or Zane. Last night, however, Phelia didn't have to question what her brother was feeling when he looked over to their father at dinner. She'd known that he'd wanted to tell him *everything*.

It wasn't as if Phelia herself hadn't had such thoughts. On more than one occasion she'd debated it. How would he take it? What could any parent say to their children if they were told some magic sent them traveling to other worlds? That their adventures had uncovered a harrowing situation with a dark entity for which their children were the remedy? Of course, one mustn't forget to inform the parent of everyone who died attempting to do just that.

Grace had experienced those other worlds and insane things. In fact, according to their predecessors, Grace was from one those worlds of insanity herself. Phelia had turned the thought over many times since then. There was nothing that outwardly suggested that her friend was from *elsewhere*, but Phelia supposed it could be true. Assuming so, she'd found it more than a little ironic that her closest friend was anything but human.

Phelia suggested that they have their conversation upstairs, as it would be away from her father's ears. Which Grace was more than happy to agree to. Apparently, Blitz was not a fan of staying in her backpack. Phelia suggested putting her in Zane's room, since it was much less likely that her father would enter it when he wasn't home. That way, if he so happened to come to her room, they wouldn't have to explain the dragon beast flying around. Meanwhile, Fayth had not uttered a single protest to staying in her father's lap.

For the first time, Phelia informed Grace of her dreams. Every reoccurring nightmare of the infant floating in the dark, the screams and the red fog. She even told her about her daydream from earlier that morning. Or at least, that was what she assumed it to be.

"It was such a strange daydream. One very similar to a dream I had before. The images filled every corner of my vision. I saw hands reaching forward, shards falling from the sky. They were beautiful bright pieces—like glass shards almost, but perhaps not exactly? The imagery was so beautiful, and yet, I felt fear. And the moment I registered that fear, I began to hear screams."

"Where were you?" Grace asked, holding her arms over her chest. "What kind of screams?" She asked hesitantly.

"I was in the restroom, washing my hands. I'm not exactly certain of the kind. Voices, piled on top of each other. More terrified than I."

"Sounds like a scary movie. The screams were in your head?"

"That is the part that confuses me most." Phelia frowned. "I've daydreamed before. Never like this. This was much too audio-visual an experience. The voices weren't coming from my head. It was as if they were coming from everywhere around me. Fayth hurried in to ask questions, but I was so shaken by it that I couldn't bear to answer him.

Even though he seemed uneasy himself. I had to know if anyone else heard them."

"And had they? I mean, did anyone else hear the screaming?" Grace asked. Her body was hunched forward. Her eyes lit up with interest. Even though her shivering clued Phelia in to her fear. "At least if Fayth came then *he* must have heard it. Right?"

"Zane had already gone. My father was sound asleep. Their voices had been almost deafening, Grace. It's impossible that father would sleep through it unless he heard nothing." Phelia shook her head. "As for Fayth, he said that my reaction had worried him so he hurried to find me. It seems he can feel much of my feelings, somehow. It is something I don't quite understand myself."

"Woah. I don't know if Blitz can do that. Are you okay?"

"I feel better at the moment. I just keep thinking about it. Perhaps I'm mistaken. Perhaps I was half asleep instead. Or, well, I don't know."

Grace leaned back and closed her eyes with a sigh. "I don't know, Phelia. That doesn't sound like a daydream or sleep thingy to me. I've relived things *inside my* head before, never outside it."

As Grace spoke, Phelia noticed a dim light slowly fill the room. Followed by a familiar resonant chime. "Oh no." Grace groaned. Phelia did not have to question her sanity this time. "This can't be good." Grace frowned.

As her bedroom faded away to white light, Phelia recalled Blitz tucked away in Zane's room, and Fayth curled in her father's lap. Panicked, she called to him in her mind. *Fayth!!* Could he distract her father? Else, keep him from finding Blitz?

Forty-Three

Zane...

CALM BEFORE THE STORM.

Zane stared down at the crystal in the center of his palm. Maybe he could find it in him to be a little glad it existed, this time. It had been the crystal that whisked him away to this room beyond the confines of *Snowville Temporary Infirmary* after all. To this seashore that looked mirrored the one in his memory. The place that he, Phelia, their mother and father visited years ago. Not very long, in fact, before their mother's death.

It was these same aquamarine waves brushing up his ankles now that he'd been reminded of before. That stormy day in Snowville when he'd found the crystals. This very sand beneath him that convinced him the other crystal, even with its blue so similar to his own eyes, was destined for Phelia's hands. Considering the ritual, he supposed he had guessed correctly. Even if that felt more a consequence of his own selfishness than anything else.

He'd almost forgotten what this sea air smelled like. Sometimes he'd even mistakenly thought he could smell sea salt from the town. After his bouts of panic, given what they'd heard in The Ruins and more self-reflection, he'd found himself there. *Elsewhere* as Phelia had coined it. And like a melody to calm a child's nightmare, the smell of the sea pacified him. He felt calmer than he had in a long time. For once, he felt safe to think.

There was no hint of any voices egging him on from the back of his head. Albeit it, the voice had seemed to leave him altogether recently. But Zane still felt something there. Like a whisper left behind, or a scar after stitches. Some cold space he didn't dare probe in the back of his mind, where it had once attached itself to him.

He'd drove himself almost insane behind his bedroom door. At dinner the night before it had taken almost everything, every morsel of self-control he had not to tell their father the truth. And he'd thought it before. Too many times to count. Before the voice had made a home in him and everything changed. Before they'd ever known anything about Phelia being some Master of the Keys, or that they were supposed to let her face danger.

Secrets. And now there was Fayth too. *So many secrets,* Zane thought disapprovingly. There was a word that fit more than most; compounded. The secrets were just piling up on top of each other. One after the other, endlessly, and without a moment to balance their weight. Like a tower improperly crafted. Some alluring thing on its surface but with danger lurking in the places he couldn't see. Zane couldn't help but wonder, how long until the entire thing came tumbling down?

What about the other repercussions of using the crystals, of being a World Knight even? Lately, he couldn't escape the nagging feeling that suggested the crystals were also somehow involved in Bailey's predicament. What was he to do? It wasn't as if he could conjure up Life at a moment's notice. Who better to ask, if not someone who guides those in The After Land? That had been where they'd seen her. Or at least, he was almost certain. The others had seen her, but some days he couldn't be totally sure he hadn't just dreamed it all up.

Maybe some part of him wanted it all to be a dream. Wanted it all to end and wake up in his bed, with his usual routine. To find a hairpin or band for Phelia's head, cook a breakfast for his family, see his father off, or better yet, have him sleep in. Since it was all his own wishes, he'd skip school altogether. Probably push Victor off the couch for falling asleep before the food was done. Grace could show up as lively as ever. True could...well, be True. Maybe even have Bailey over again, like they'd never began to grow apart in the first place.

As he looked at his reflection in the water, he watched it morph into Life's form. He recognized her black coiled hair and vivid peach-colored eyes staring back at him in an instant. "See?" Zane spoke to himself aloud. The crystal couldn't save him from his own madness in totality. "You're really starting to lose it. The crystal saved you but it cannot save you from yourself."

"If you are suggesting, child, that I am a figment of your imagination, you would be incorrect." Life called back to him from the dancing image below him. Zane scurried backwards, uncertain.

"Is this real?" He asked as he crawled slowly towards the shore's end.

"You summoned me, yet remain in disbelief. I am as real as the rest of what you see before you now." She replied.

"Well, I'm not totally sure all this isn't a figment of my imagination either so that's not so convincing." Zane sighed with a hint of frustration. He looked at the crystal again. Had it done this too, somehow? If it could summon up people for conversation, why not Bailey instead? Either way seemed crazy.

"Shall I leave you to your thoughts?" Life asked. Normally Zane would have taken that as impatience, but the look on her face suggested otherwise.

"Wait. No." Zane answered quickly. Determined to at least attempt to get useful information. Or maybe it was a rant to help himself feel better. He wasn't sure which was the truth, but he spoke anyway, however briefly. About feeling like he should tell his father that they've been traveling to other worlds. About his uncertainty in his own actions, his confusion with the reason they ever left their world in the first place and Bailey.

She responded in much the same way as when they'd first met. Calm and sweet-toned. With some strange sense of optimism that seemed entirely backwards to Zane, considering the horrors of The After Land in the first place. "There are many possibilities, all at chance by equal measure, that could be the reason for your travels. You speak as if the crystals have done you an injustice. Have you not considered other things?"

"I admit, I'm not totally following you. Do you mean like the fact that we saw Bailey there in the first place? Is knowing that supposed to be a good thing?"

"Are you saying that what you experienced here was only negative?"

"Well, let's see. There was the fact that we were taken away from my mother's gravesite. There were those people chained up and crying headed off to a scary swirly thing situated randomly off the ground. Now that was such a *beautiful* sight, no? Oh, let's not forget the horrific events that took place in True's house. We watched a father *murder* his kid and an *entire* party of people, then try to hang his *grieving* wife. He even attacked us! So, *yeah*. No, that's *gotta* be the most ***positive*** experience of my life. Not counting the thing that followed me home and tried to ***possess*** me, of course."

Life chuckled. Which inadvertently gave Zane a minor sense of pride and annoyed him all at once. What was so funny anyway? Those things had really happened. They still haunted him. "What?"

"You have a strange way of seeing things." Life snickered.

"Okay, now I'm just offended. How's the truth strange?"

"How should I—ah, yes. The way you described what happened in The After Land was simply not all there was. Yes?" "You'll have to explain." Zane sighed. So, she wasn't mocking him?

"It was never so simple as just negative or positive experiences." Life said thoughtfully.

She seemed to search for words in a momentary silence before she continued on. "The thought had not occurred to you that you were brought to The After Land to break the cycle's hold on Chester and Jess? The Darkness has an interest in all worlds to a degree, perhaps you have even rescued them from ITs clutches."

He couldn't imagine it. "Is it not just as likely that your appearance was also a summoning? Needed given that someone you were connected to, this child Bailey, requires your help to return to your world? A soul's connection to the Living World does not last forever. In time, it will weaken and eventually cease to exist."

"What??" Zane exclaimed. "Are you saying the longer she's there the more likely it is that she never comes back?" He didn't like a word of it. Would Bailey really get stuck forever? How long would be too long? "Even if all of that were true, we don't know what we are doing. I don't even know how to help her."

"Is it not something to learn? In theory, would not the best solution be something *already* at your disposal?" Life smiled again.

"You mean this?" Zane asked. He held the crystal towards Life's blurring shape in the water, watched the sunlight hit its surface.

Life nodded. "Perhaps the crystal is the key to what you seek. Were it not the crystals that brought you to this world in the first place?"

Zane didn't like the idea of being so dependent on the crystals. Even if it was possible that they hadn't been misled, even if they weren't malevolent, they were still vexing. He wasn't sure he could trust it. Not to help him reach Bailey, and even less so for the power to protect his sister. He wasn't even sure the ritual had done anything for him. He was the same as yesterday and the day before.

As Zane looked back to the water, he realized Life's image was giving way to the movement of the waves. A sudden gust of wind tossed branches to the sea and a whirl of sand began to envelope him. He covered his eyes to shield them from any of the grains that rushed past his face. And when he opened his eyes again, he found himself standing in a crowd of white winged Faeries.

Confused, Zane scanned the area, almost immediately relieved to be taller than Fae. What was he doing back in FlareWing? As he watched the joyful movements of a couple twirling through the crowd, he made out Phelia and Grace in the distance. It wasn't just him? Just as Zane began to call out to them, his voice buried beneath cheers and music, Grace's eyes met his. He watched her point urgently in his direction and they sought out each other in the middle of the Fae.

"Zane!" Phelia and Grace shouted in sync.

He pressed a hand on their shoulders. “Hey. What’s going on? Why is everything so loud and shiny? What are we doing in FlareWing?”

“We don’t know!” Grace shouted, barely louder than the noise around them. “Phelia and I were just talking in a room a minute ago! About a dream she had when we suddenly ended up here—well, we aren’t sure if it was *exactly* a dream but...”

“I’ve got this bad feeling. We even got separated from Blitz and Fayth. Fayth was with father, and Blitz was in your room--” Phelia frowned.

“My room? Why was she in my--”

“Zane!” Victor called out from somewhere behind them. Zane turned around and watched him wend his way through the Faeries. “What happened?” He raised a brow. “What are we celebrating?”

“According to the Fae,” Twister chimed in, guiding True by the jacket, “the return of *Father Princess*—or at least, that’s what they’re calling him. Fae are celebrating in every world right about now. It seemed the crystals nabbed me too. I wonder, should I consider it a curtesy?”

“Who is Father Princess?” Grace asked. “Why not Prince or...?”

“They think it’s cute. Calling him Father is a tribute. To his role in Father Wing’s life and FlareWing--”

“Why would anyone be entitled to that?” Victor asked.

“—Because,” Twister said, as he pointed towards two figures emerging from The Grand Tree, “that man next to Father Wing is Morgan. **Lady Lily’s human lover.**”

Forty-Four

Eustis...

WAR.

Eustis didn't like that Kennet had been right. His parents had blamed him. They wrote him a check and he left without being able to say goodbye. Eustis did his best to put on a brave face as he saw him off and took comfort in the fact that his cellphone number was safely tucked away in his pocket. He'd no longer have the number his family paid for.

Everywhere he went, even in his house, the new bodyguards were within eyeshot. He buried his annoyance with amusement. The men had, in fact, taken an earful from his parents after he and Kennet beat them home. The men had been almost convinced that they'd run off and left town. Now that he thought about it, the bodyguards weren't the only ones he'd noticed following him.

He was sure, almost certain, that there had been someone else following him around the grounds as well. Every time he thought he'd seen them whether it was during a conversation with his parents, or a shadow ducking out of sight at the last moment while he strode through the halls, it put him on edge. After the family doctor made an unwelcomed house visit to check Eustis' wounds given his 'stunt' with Kennet and his mother's absurd insistence that he could cripple himself if he didn't relent, he slowly ascended the staircase towards his bedroom.

The sound of shuffling as Eustis shut the door behind him gave him pause. He slowly turned around to see a woman standing a foot away. "So, you're the one stalking me." He sighed with a frown. He debated calling to the guards outside the door. The woman jumped towards him, and for a moment almost appeared frightened, then cupped his mouth.

"I'm not stalking you!" She said defensively. She'd recovered quickly from her scare. "If you don't shout, I'll release you. Nod if you understand." She demanded. Eustis obliged, submissively bobbing his head. Though he had half a mind to tell her that she'd been the only one raising her voice. As she dropped her palm and stepped slightly away from him and the door, Eustis crossed his arms.

"Of course, you are. I've seen you just about everywhere I've gone. And now you've made your way into the house. You aren't the best at stealth, I'll have you know, but the bodyguards my parents hired aren't exceptional at their jobs either. I'll commend you at least for making your way into the house." Eustis said, as he made his way to his bed. He was careful not to wince as he took a seat, not willing to show weakness in front of her. "If you're here to kidnap me, I suggest you just name your price for my freedom."

"Ugh." The woman recoiled. "What kind of *creepy* kid are you? You're just going to *pay* your kidnapper?"

"So, you admit that you are trying to take me. Either that, or you are going to bully me somehow. Even though I'm pretty sure we've never met. Which would mean that it is related to some grudge with my parents. Either way, it is better than ending up who knows where."

"I am not here to kidnap you!" She fumed. "*Ugh!* Of all the—listen here you **little**!" She stammered, taking a breath. "As if the likes of *you* can call *me* a bully. Torturing little red headed girls is your agenda. I've bullied no one." She retorted, her tone diminishing the appearance of calm on her face.

"How *long* have you been stalking me, exactly?" Eustis asked, shooting the woman an incredulous look. "Just who are you?" Déjà vu. Why did this conversation sound so familiar...?

"Oh, for crying out loud. It isn't like you would've been my *first* choice. This is what I get for trying to get involved. Fine!" She huffed, turning around to face the door of his balcony "I tried. Don't blame me if you can't help that loud, bushy-haired girlfriend of yours then." Before she could make her way out the door, Eustis crossed the floor and grabbed hold of her arm. What was she talking about?

"Are you talking about Grace? W-what's wrong with Grace?? Is she in danger?" The woman faced him again, a slow sneer spreading across her face. In an uncomfortable way, the expression seemed to suit her well.

"Ah. So, you do like her after all. What kind of *idiot* bullies the girl he likes? Boys are so dumb." She said, rolling her eyes.

"I-it's not like that! Grace, she's a friend. Or at least, I hope." Eustis tried to explain, for no good reason considering this woman was a stranger. He could feel the creep of a slow burn all the way to his ears.

Eustis had no clue what was going on or who this woman was. He didn't know why she followed him or how she knew Grace, but he figured at least, if nothing else, he didn't have to trust her to listen. If Grace was in trouble, if he could help her, he wouldn't hesitate.

"Ha! I like that look on your face." She laughed, obviously amused. "You're going to need every *shred* of that determination for what I'm about to tell you. You might not even be able to stand afterwards. I, for one, did everything I could to run in the opposite direction when I found out what those stupid crystals got us into."

"You don't make any sense," Eustis frowned. "Who are you and what's happened to Grace? What Crystal?" Eustis asked impatiently. He wanted to dismiss what the woman was saying, but the look on her face and the twisting of his insides told him not to be so quick to turn her away.

Perhaps he wanted to be needed by Grace and fearful that this was all a trick. Logic said not to listen to people that sounded out of their minds, let alone ones that were bold enough to sneak into your bedroom in broad daylight. But on the off chance that it wasn't some sick joke, he was not going to leave Grace stranded when she needed his help.

"I'm Brilla," the woman said as she peered down at him. She reached into her pocket and withdrew a bright, rounded crystal. He watched in awe as it sent pulsing purple light around his room. A light, to Eustis' disbelief, that far exceeded the rays of sunlight from his windows. "And this is the *crystal* that is going to send you to war. If you're lucky, you might get there in time to save your little friend."

Forty-Five

Twister...

SKY ROOM.

Twister led the others to The Grand Tree, where his parents met them at the door. For the first time, he introduced his parents to his friends. Surely, none of them could have guessed that he would feel such an attachment to humans more than his own kind. When he really began to think about it in depth, he realized that he had sought out their friendship of his own volition from the moment he saw them in FlareWing. Or at least some part of him had.

It was a remarkable thought. He, who had distanced himself from all the Fae in their world. The one who never thought he'd make friends because he'd only be reminded of his size with every interaction. Things couldn't have been more different.

They never wasted a single breath to mock or insult him. Each of them, in their own right, had been very genuine in their interactions with him. Twister had never once taken offense to Grace's questioning, nor her comments about his size. Zane had been protective of his feelings, Phelia had not hesitated to treat him like everyone else she'd came across—or at least, that was the impression he'd gotten.

True had given him the room to express things he never thought he could say aloud, all the while being more than considerate. And Victor —though not much could be said for their day-to-day interactions— had given his trust. If nothing else, with his friends. And contrary to his indifferent air, he was attentive.

Now, he was more than a glad to consider them friends. They seemed to go together well, even with their new additions like Blitz and Fayth. *A glorious band of misfits, I suppose,* Twister thought in amusement. *If only the current circumstances allowed us to continue improving our friendship without all this looming overhead.*

"You know, Twister, seeing it up close you *really* look like your parents. They're so beautiful!" Grace said cheerfully. He blushed, embarrassed and at a loss for words. He meekly made eye contact with his father as his mother thanked Grace for the compliment, all too aware of the others' nods of agreement.

"Inside." Thorne directed as he cleared his throat. "Let us not keep Father Wing waiting on your presence." Twister followed close behind, a small sense of pride welling up inside him as he heard the whispered exclaims as they entered The Grand Tree. The dark textured wooden walls extended above them, eventually giving way to red moss and flower buds that extended far beyond their vantage point.

White, gold, red, and green ribbons draped in no particular pattern from over their heads, which could have very well been the sky itself since there wasn't a top to be seen from where they stood. They removed their shoes and Twister smiled as he watched the others' playful movements as they walked through the greenery. The familiar sweet smell of FlareWing's flowers kissed their noses.

"This is amazing!" Grace grinned, holding out her arms as she wiggled her toes. Victor walked up beside her and placed a hand on her head, forcing her to turn around and rejoin the others as his Twister's parents led them up the wide, winding staircase. "Oh. Thanks." She laughed before excitedly running her palms over the woven golden rail.

Each floor only became visible as you climbed the stairway, likely the result of protection magic. On most, Twister could make out a large door, which always looked in some way like the last, each decorated with an intricate design. Though similar, he'd found not a single one to be less beautiful than the one that came before. Wherever they were headed, Twister had never been. Soon enough, he recognized the familiar arch of a window as they reached the end of the stairs. "Are we going to the Sky Room?" Twister asked at his father's back.

His mother answered from somewhere ahead of him instead. "Yes, we are. You'll likely not remember it. Seeing as you were only just born when we brought you here to receive Father Wing's blessing." Father Wing's blessing? Did Father Wing ever personally bless a Faerie before that wasn't a Princess? He'd never heard of it. His brain could hardly process the casual way his mother spoke, as if she hadn't said something unbelievable. What did a blessing from Father Wing entail? Why had he blessed him in the first place??

"What's the sky room?" Phelia asked from Twister's side, without a moment's hesitation. He recognized that look in her eyes. The thing that seemed akin to magic. That level of curiosity that was somehow, though he'd have struggled to ever explain it aloud, beyond the bounds of normalcy. *Perhaps,* Twister thought, *it is not the curiosity itself that seems to differ but something else altogether.*

"The sky room is the upper most floor of The Grand Tree. A large sitting room with a caged balcony overlooking FlareWing. Father Wing apparently prefers to spend most of his time there." Twister answered politely.

Upon entrance, Twister did not, in fact, recognize the room. He could still hear the celebrations of Fae from somewhere beyond. The playful laughter of children not far behind. Before Twister could study the images of royalty lining the walls of the room, he watched an unexpected scene play out in front of them. Morgan, dressed in lavish blue and golden robes accented by a locus pattern dropped weakly to his knees, gently supported by the hand of Father Wing.

Twister watched as the man began to sob uncontrollably, cradling Princess Aurelia in his arms. In almost a manner too incoherent to understand, he paid the child compliments of varying degree. Not too unlike a grandmother reunited with her family after years of a deathly illness. Or so, that had been the impression that stained his thoughts.

Twister paused; the scene almost seemed to impose itself upon him. The matter private. He was not sure it was for them to see. The moment he began to gather the others, having opted to come back later, Father Wing's voice stopped them. "Sit." He commanded, and the sound of locks latching on the other side of the large doors implied they had very little choice in the matter.

"What are those dark whisps wafting off of him?" True asked in Father Wing's direction. Twister glanced her way, to Morgan, Father Wing and his parents, then back again. What whisps?

"I don't see anything." Phelia frowned.

"Me neither." Grace tiled her head. "Did I miss it?"

"Same here." Zane chimed in, shooting Victor a silent glance.

"Don't look at me. I don't see anything right now but the last time she said she saw something we all ended up seeing it. And chasing Chester Einrich through the streets of Snowville." Victor shrugged, sliding his hands into his pockets. "I'm inclined to believe it."

Father Wing's eyes flickered with a hint of mirth and a smile that Twister was becoming all too quick at perceiving. "Ah. You are witness to rarity." He said, and guided Morgan to a chair. What was True able to see that the rest of them didn't?

"These 'whisps' are faint residue of The Darkness." He gestured to an open area above Morgan's dark hair. The man's blue eyes still focused on The Princess. "There are few beings privy to their existence. Most, only feel their presence. Even the likes of man are capable of that much."

Twister suddenly felt the pressure of his father's hand on the back of his head, forcing him forward. *Ouch.* "Greet *properly*, boy." Thorne demanded. "Both Father Wing and Sir Morgan." Twister watched his father bow. "Please forgive his rudeness. It seems he is lacking in manners."

If Twister hadn't been sure of it before, he was now. The human ahead of them had to be Lady Lily's lover. But he was human. How was he still alive? He would be older than Father Wing himself. Still, his father was right. He'd forgotten himself.

"I apologize. Both for my rude behavior and interruption. Thank you for seeing us, Father Wing. And you, Sir Morgan, for giving life to The Princess. There is not a single Faerie alive who does not appreciate your sacrifice." Twister bowed.

"I'm sorry that you've had to see me this way." Words etched in flame danced into being in the air beside him. Twister had never seen such magic, but it was surely the result of Father Wing. His eyes followed a hint of red thread down the length of Morgan's throat. He realized that as the words came into being, Father Wing remained still and silent. Likely, his own words would cancel the spell.

"I know that the Fae are celebrating. Yet, it feels strange." He offered a painful smile in their direction and bundled Princess Aurelia back in the cloth. "To be celebrated for something unintended. Not long before you arrived, by way of some astounding magic, Father Wing shared with me the memories of his parents' lives, which included much of Lily. Just as well, what she'd done in my absence, and the birth of the first Princess—my *beautiful* daughter. He raised in her my stead." Morgan shook his head.

Twister recognized all too well the look of disappointment. "I'm not sure that I have anything to celebrate. Nor much reason for you to be thankful. At least, not gratitude where I am concerned. Though I am glad to see this world again, *thriving*. It was my wife—it was *Lily* that sacrificed most."

At some point during the conversation Grace had begun to cry. Twister wanted to argue that Morgan himself, regardless of what ever kept him away from FlareWing, had indeed sacrificed a lot. That perhaps, he would be better celebrating on Lady Lily's behalf, but he was sure his father would have his wings for it.

"But if he's Morgan then wouldn't that make him Father Wing's uncle?" Grace asked as Rune passed her a cloth to blow her nose. *Well, she isn't wrong,* Twister thought. *He* **is** *his uncle. Imagine that. Being a* *human and yet an uncle to one of the most powerful Fae in existence. Usually, it is the nephew that hopes to fill the shoes.*

"She's right." Phelia nodded. "Which would make you older than Father Wing? And yet..."

"Yeah." Zane agreed. "No offense but what are you, *immortal* or something? What, you drink from the fountain of youth?"

"I am human. Surely, I would have known if I was immortal by now. Or so I hope." Morgan responded. A silent chuckle beneath his smile. Twister thought then that there was something absolutely, unmistakably, amazing about his friends. They'd managed to make Sir Morgan laugh in the midst of so much pain and suffering.

"Father Wing mentioned The Darkness." True reminded them. "Is it possible that there's some relation...?"

Father Wing gave a curt nod. "I suspect Morgan was held captive somewhere out of reach. Some memories are whole, else in pieces. 'Tis likely—" His words suddenly came to a stop. A deep frown painted his features and a shadow cast over his red eyes. These small changes immediately shifted the air in the room. Twister's parents' movements became rigid and eventually stilled.

As Father Wing made his way to the balcony, Twister followed him, the others close behind. Father Wing bent the space ahead of him, effectively reaching in the air and pinching something Twister did not see. An area on the outskirts of FlareWing enlarged ahead of them. Like a magnifying glass hazily coming into focus, they watched the image form, encircled in a border of flames.

"A Faerie...?" Twister thought aloud. To his surprise, he was unable to place her features. Were there ever a group of Fae with brown skin, dark blue hair and... layered black wings? He watched as she mouthed frantic words. When the bottom of her fists struck the veil, she was hurled backwards through the air. Only to slowly make her way back again to repeat the same process. Each appeared more painful than the last.

"What's happening to her?" Victor asked, with a displeased look on his face. "Why can't she get in?"

"It appears that she is part Cursed." Father Wing stated plainly. Part Cursed Fae? Morgan made his way to Father Wing's side. The Princess shifted noisily in his arms. He abruptly took hold of Father Wing's arm with a bewildered look on his face.

Twister was shocked by the man's boldness. Even if Sir Morgan was his uncle, they'd only just met. Not even his parents touched Father Wing without a moment of hesitation. Twister looked over his shoulder towards his mother and father. They stood silently alert, but their deep-set frowns showcased their disapproval. Still, they made no move to attack him. *Well, I suppose that makes sense.*

"You are acquainted with her?" Father Wing asked as they watched the girl's panic-stricken expression. Morgan nodded his head, so hard that Twister almost had the thought to rub his own neck. Why did Sir Morgan know a Cursed Fae? He hated the thought, but he was beginning to wonder if his appearance was a trap. Feeling Father Wing's ancient eyes, he slowly returned his gaze.

Alright, that was it. Between the show of some of his abilities that Twister had never seen before, True's explanation, his last talk with the bathing Father Wing, and that exact moment, he was relatively certain he was capable of reading minds. Twister supposed that it was a bit insulting. To assume Father Wing's uncle would be a trap for FlareWing. Maybe more, even, that it would happen without Father Wing being suspicious of the possibility himself.

"Something's coming." True spoke, her voice shrouded in unease. Something like what, exactly?

Forty-Six

Quill...

ALMOST.

Quill was in immense pain. Echoes of laughter shook the space inside her head. Her limbs felt like lead. She could hardly force them forward. ***HE*** didn't tell her how badly it would hurt.

In the distance she could just make out the shimmering dome. Almost. Just a little further. There was nothing left. She'd done everything. The pain would not stop her. She would destroy it all...

Forty-Seven

Opal...

GIVE.

Opal flopped down in the grass. Her body was burning. It hurt even to cross her arms. It felt like every touch of the veil was mincing her to pieces. She didn't think she could take anymore. But what else was she to do? It was there ahead of her. That place from her parents' memories. And it hadn't occurred to her until Morgan mentioned the name Lily. The place that she saw in Quill's mind that day all that time ago, the place *IT* wanted destroyed, was her father's home.

She could see the Fae on the other side, happily moving about. They had no idea how much danger awaited them now. She wanted to warn them, but the moment she'd felt that pain coursing through her body, she knew. It was the curse *IT* bestowed upon her mother, the dark magic inside her, that made her efforts impossible to achieve.

It had taken her too long. She knew by now Quill could not be all that far behind. She should have found a way to stop her. Opal became quickly overwhelmed with fear and sadness. So much so that she began to cry. They were tears for Quill, for her mother and father, all the Faeries who were the current target of *IT*s hatred. They were even tears for herself.

"Chin up, little one." A voice called. Opal sniffed, and quickly wiped her eyes, surprised by the sudden realization that she was no longer sitting on the other side of the veil. In fact, she was floating in a magic space encased in flames. When she blinked, she almost couldn't believe her eyes.

Morgan?! What was he doing there? She immediately tried to press a hand to the border as a young boy with flowing red hair and burning eyes stepped into her view. When he spoke, she quickly realized he was responsible for moving her.

"You are not to attempt escape. I am keeping you there as a precaution. Not for our safety but your own. Considering your... *unique* disposition, if you were to escape inside of the veil, you will cease to exist. Given your attempt to cross into FlareWing with such urgency, you must pardon my impatience. I will ask questions, on behalf of myself and Morgan, who you seem to be acquainted with, and you shall answer. Do you understand?"

Opal nodded. She couldn't imagine what would happen to her but judging by the pain she'd felt just attempting to get inside, she had no reason to doubt the boy's words. She felt that he was being kind in a way, but the red-haired boy with the long lashes and gigantic wings, whoever he was, intimidated her.

"Why have you, come here and from where have you come?"

"I came from far away, I suppose. From inside ***IT***. Some people call ***IT*** a Shell, The Black Place, The Void. You, I believe, call ***IT*** The Darkness. I prefer not to give the thing a name. Thus, the term, ***IT***. I wanted to warn you. You are all in danger."

"Of what danger?" He asked. Opal did not know what to make of him. His demeanor was so calm, his eyes so serious and unyielding as they met her own that it sent shivers down her spine. How much was she supposed to say? Was there a such thing as too much, too little?"

As she opened her mouth to speak, a shockwave of magic thrummed around them. One after the other. It was then that Opal noticed the humans grabbing hold of the branches beside them to steady themselves. Could it be? Were these the humans Quill had been interested in?

"What's happening, Father Wing? What in the world could shake The Grand Tree?" A Faerie asked, no larger than her current form. Wait. Father Wing? He looked nothing like the images in her parents' memory. Well, almost nothing. Perhaps the bright red hair and those eyes. If the boy was Father Wing, then that meant he was the leader of the Fae. Maybe they stood a chance.

She watched him place a palm in the air and a swirl of magic whistled past her. Moments later followed by the belching of a horn. He pinched the open space to her right and Opal quickly made out Quill's form. She watched as she placed both of her palms to the veil and a black shadow slowly engulfed her. One palm strike after the other, a ripple of spiked black magic shot up the length of the veil.

"Tis unfortunate but I have readied your army, Thorne, Rune. Little one, it seems you shall not be needing this space much longer. The veil is going to give." Father Wing spoke with an air of distaste.

Without any hesitation, a flash of light hurtled towards them, which Opal quickly realized were the two Fae in question. Father Wing did not move to the side, but rather, parted the twined branches ahead of them and let them pass. Then, he walked over to Morgan and grabbed a bundle from his arms, placing it in a structure not quite unlike the one she was in now. It was only then, as she registered a faint cry, that she realized the bundle was a baby.

"We are going as well." Father Wing frowned. Morgan grabbed ahold of his robe, and to Opal's surprise, he seemed to understand his intentions. "This is the safest place for her to be. You may stay with her if you'd like. Below is no place for you."

Morgan quickly shook his head. Really, the man could never sit still. Just what was he going to do? Get stuck in that place again?

Father Wing did not attempt to persuade him. Instead, the space around them shrank away and they found themselves watching Quill from a distance as the veil began to crack. He couldn't be serious. Why would he bring the humans too??!

The dome began to fall away. The humans watched in horror. Flocks of Faeries brushed past them in the other direction while the sound of fluttering wings echoed inside what was left of the dome.

"It can't be." The voice of a small girl spoke unevenly, grabbing hold of another one's hand.

"What's wrong, Phelia? I mean, aside from the obviously *terrifying* situation. I'm terrified. Isn't anyone else terrified??"

"Grace, this is it. My *dream*. I dreamed that the *veil* shattered."

"Yeah, pretty sure that's not a dream then." The girl, Grace, slowly shook her head. Could that have been the reason for Quill's interest? Or more likely, for ***IT***s? Was it possible? Had a human child truly been capable of seeing this before it ever came to pass?

Forty-Eight

Morgan...

LILY'S EYE.

Morgan was equally in awe and terrified of the events unfolding ahead of him. He'd never seen a swarm of Fae with such serious looks on their faces, shrouded in an unwavering air to face death. He'd never had the chance to meet a Faerie general before now either, but he noticed the change in both Rune and Throne compared to their polite bows and light, respectful tones.

Saw immediately that the two of them were married. He'd known it in the way the they glanced at each other. By the small smile on Rune's lips when she spoke to him. Since, any hint of her smile had faded and her gentleness along with it.

Now, Rune seemed a formidable woman dressed in her army garb. The same shadow of a tree and the budding of a locus flower shined brightly on her chest, catching the light. Her long hair had been tied behind her head, revealing a scar across her eye and the bridge of her nose. He wondered then which one of her battles had left her with such a mark.

Not much could be said for Thorne's previous demeanor, but he too was surrounded by an uncomfortable sense of dourness. One that would have filled Morgan with fear had his unpleasant gaze been directed his way.

His heart was racing as Faeries scurried past them, being led away from danger by a portion of the army. Morgan looked to the children he'd briefly met earlier. Save for the one in the mask, he could see their uncertainty. What were such young children doing on the battlefield in the first place? Why had Father Wing brought them along?

It was then, as he watched them huddled close together at Father Wing's side, that Morgan became aware of the presence of five gems in their possession. In a pocket, in a bag, around the neck. It didn't matter where they were. He saw them clearly, faintly glowing, as the symbol on them caught his attention. He was certain he'd seen it before, but where? And just what were they? It was unmistakable that they were magical. Why did the children have them?

Morgan's attention was quickly directed back towards the veil when another succession of booms echoed. His eyes shifted to Father Wing for a moment, seeing him completely still. He seemed unfazed by the panic around him, his eyes trained ahead. For a moment he thought he heard him say something under his breath. Hadn't he said that the veil would break? So why didn't he attack? *What are you thinking?* Morgan thought to himself in disbelief. After all, from the looks of it even from their distance, the one attacking the barrier was only a child.

As they stood in silence, awaiting something worse, Morgan nervously focused his eyes on the small frame that looked to be constantly swaying in and out of a thick dark mass. Red smoke sprouted up around her and faded away again.

He couldn't quite make out more features, but he could recognize a young girl when he saw one. Walking menacingly with shadows sprouting like weeds behind her, was a Faerie. Or at least, she had wings of a Faerie. As the black spiked appendages began to point in their direction, almost a silent threat, she placed her palms against the glistening veil again. Morgan felt the hairs on his neck stand on end. All too quickly, the rest of the veil crumbled away to nothing.

Confusion and dread washed over him as he watched the shadows expand and shift into all matter of smokey, black beings. Littered among these creatures stood many Fae, all of which appeared a gray hue. Whatever many of the others were could hardly be put into words, let alone compared. Aside from the splashes of what Morgan could only think to call a sticky, thick, ink substance dotting their skin, each were unnaturally devoid of color. As the sludge dripped from their forms to the ground, it bubbled like a pot boiling over. He'd never seen anything like it.

With no word of warning, the ink-blotched creatures rushed forward in a kind of organized chaos. Thorne and Rune's voices roared ahead of the Fae Army. Lacking any hint of hesitance or fear they lead the army forward. A simultaneous "CHARGE" resounded over the sounds of quickly fluttering wings.

In mere moments, steel slid crossed steel and the sound of lumber cracking noisily filled the air. Merely a moment behind, a loud boom sounded, causing them to be forced backwards by a haphazard wave of pressure. So much so that, save for Father Wing, they almost found themselves knocked off their feet.

He could hear wild screeching between wails of agony. Puffs of smoke rose from sporadic dips in the ground and if Morgan took his eyes away from that direction, he could see just how far the damage had already spread beyond them. Had this been what Lily witnessed all that time ago? *Lily*. And it was then as he was thinking of her, when the army of creatures continued to grow in number, that he saw it. For just an instant, as the young girl led the enemies further into FlareWing, he was sure.

Morgan had been completely unable to stop himself from rushing forward. Even as he heard Father Wing's few words of warning. Even when he was vaguely aware of one of the children grabbing hold of his arm and inadvertently dragged them along.

"True!!" A voice called from his back. But he couldn't stop. Not even when he glanced back to see a pale green mask fumbling slightly behind him, and a large white beast cut off the space between them and the others. He'd never seen a furred beast with multiple tails before. Still, his body raced ahead of its own accord. Never mind the dusty, rocky debris cascading down around them, threatening to hit them with every step.

Subconsciously he noticed; with every strike of dark magic the land lost some of its luster, sprouting flowers burned, iced, flushed or withered away to nothing at all. None of it mattered. He had to reach the girl. "What are you doing?!" A voice shouted near to his right, breaking his concentration for a moment. "And dragging True along with you heading straight towards an enemy strong enough to break the veil!" He wanted to scream. He opened his mouth to shout, even knowing that no sound would come. Only, *it did.*

A sudden surge of pain attacked him. Screamed in agony as he doubled over, instinctively pressing a hand over his burning throat. Like swallowing fire. He became immediately aware of something entering his body from the distance.

"Twister," True called from beside him. She kneeled down and pressed a hand to Morgan's shoulder, seemingly to comfort him. How could a child stop in the middle of a battlefield to check on a stranger who had dragged her along without her consent? Of course, he hadn't been meaning to do so. "Something went into him just now, I think."

"What do you mean, *something*? We have to get back."

"No!" Morgan shouted, swiping an arm stubbornly in his direction as he felt his small arms pull the fabric of his shirt. "Her eyes." He croaked, tears welling up inside him. ***Lily's eye!***"

Forty-Nine

Grace…

UNBELIEVABLE.

Grace knew that in that field of horrors, she'd witnessed something unbelievably cool. Even though she had been terrified seeing True attempt to stop Mr. Morgan just to be yanked along with him. Terrified to race after her and then, to make matters worse, get split up from Victor.

She was terrified now, as she willed herself not to look around them. She knew she would only see worse things. She'd witnessed the Faeries full of joy during every visit. Even earlier that day they'd been celebrating. And yet, none of the Fae were smiling now. In fact, many cried when the veil was breaking, which only heighted her fear.

Unfortunately, it hadn't diminished. Not after Blitz and Fayth suddenly appeared when they'd been left at Dr. Brand's house as they were thrust into FlareWing. And definitely not when she and Phelia found themselves rushing towards a small Faerie child who'd been sobbing loudly, running through the field with a swarm of those creepy looking, drippy creatures racing towards them. Still, she'd somehow had the room to be in awe of the sudden appearance of a barrier forming around them when Zane leapt ahead to protect them. Even if it was short-lived.

"Ugh!—I can't! This thing isn't going to hold much longer!"

"How are you doing that?" Phelia asked suddenly. Her curiosity clearly getting the best of her as she went to take a closer look.

"How should I know?! Phelia, get away! Don't you *dare* touch it! It might break even faster!"

The young Faerie began to cry. Grace couldn't tell if it was a girl or a boy. She did her best to ignore her own fear. "It's alright. Don't worry. We'll find your family. Somehow. W-we won't die here or anything. Right guys...?"

"A-as if!" Zane groaned. "Fayth, how do I..I don't know? *Fix* the shield thingy?" Grace turned to look Fayth's way, but he only shrugged his shoulders.

"I haven't the faintest."

"You stupid cat! Aren't you practically *ancient* or something?!"

"I believe I've told you not to call me that. *Now* I won't help you."

"Fayth!" Phelia frowned. "We're in danger! Now is not the time for your pride. Zane, apologize to Fayth."

"If you haven't noticed, Phelia, I'm a bit busy trying not to let like a *hundred* monsters kill us."

"*Zane*!" Phelia shouted.

"*Fine!* I'm sorry, Fayth. Now can you tell us what we can do?" Zane groaned. Whether from effort or annoyance, Grace didn't know.

Fayth licked his paw and cleared his throat. "Apology accepted. The solution is quite simple, really. We *run*."

"***Seriously?!*** If we live, I'm *so* gonna kill—" Zane dropped to a knee, breathing more heavily than before. Grace wondered if it hurt. "I think we should get ready to run now!"

"Quickly, grab hold of me, each of you!" Fayth demanded, jumping towards Zane as a large glowing silhouette surrounded him. Grace squealed as she pulled the young Faerie closer and grabbed a fist full of Fayth's black fur as Zane's protection disappeared. At some point she had closed her eyes. A harsh gust of wind and the shrill cries of creatures forced her to open them again.

"We're saved." Zane sighed, and dropped to his back. "Lucky us. Wait—Fayth!" He shouted. "You're huge!"

"This is my normal size." Fayth retorted. He almost sounded proud.

"What happened?" Grace asked, as Fayth sprinted through the battlefield, dodging groups of monsters. Blitz, to her surprise, angled her wings back in the sky beside them, following Fayth's movement. She was fast, *really* fast. Momentarily distracted, she placed a hand over her heart. Her chest was on fire. *Again?*

"I don't know. Some guy just came out of nowhere, right when we were grabbing Fayth. He caused some sort of cyclone and blasted most of the monsters in front of us to bits. I'd never seen anything like it. He wasn't a Faerie. Looked human. Meanwhile, we've been going so fast I haven't been able to get a good look at the rest of the battlefield. Who knows what's happening to the others."

"Fayth says the Fae were evacuated to the crater." Phelia nodded towards the Faerie in Grace's arms. "A portion of the army are protecting citizens, so chances are we can find their parents there. Then we can hurry and find Twister, Victor and True."

Another human in FlareWing? One with powers, at that? Just when she thought to ask another question, a man leapt over Fayth's side and landed beside her. Startled, Grace ducked back, instinctively pressing the young Faerie to her chest. His long ropes of black hair swayed behind him as he gently laid a hand atop Blitz's head. "Thank you for working hard, kiddo."

"Hey, that's the guy." Zane said, sitting up.

Grace was overcome with another warm tingling sensation in her chest, only more intense than before. He had touched Blitz without hesitation. Spoke to her like he knew her. "W-who...are you?" She couldn't put her finger on it, but she could almost swear that she'd seen him before. Just recently, in fact. The man turned to her, tears brimming his brown eyes.

"Your ***father***." He smiled, wiping a tear from his eye, "It's been a *very* long time, Gracelyn. I'm sorry I made you wait."

What did he just say? Was it possible that this man was her father??

Fifty

True...

POINT OF THE BLADE.

True wasn't sure when they'd lost sight of Twister. He'd been there a moment before, she thought. Just before True tried to stop Morgan from going to the Faerie girl and inadvertently touched one of the black antennae that was speeding towards him.

The moment that her hand touched it, a ball appeared and encased it in light, then the antennae broke apart. She didn't have the time to question what had happened. What had Morgan meant when he said she had Lady Lily's eye? As the girl screamed out in pain, a flicker of a flame swirled into a large pair of fluttering wings and the rest of a silhouette quickly followed.

Before them was a much older Father Wing than the young boy they'd spoke to mere minutes ago, although he was not quite as old as the first time True had met him. His bright hair and silken robes bobbed in the wind as light sputtered from his palm. As he pulled his hand backwards, he wrapped his palm around an intricately designed sword.

True could only admire the shimmering spiral to wings decorating the grip and pommel, and the vines and budding locus flower dancing up the length of the blade before he used it to pierce a black shell that was quickly enclosing the girl.

Morgan seized the opportunity and grabbed hold of her shoulders, forcing her to the ground. Narrowly missing a swipe of Father Wing's sword. "What did you do to her?!" Morgan cried. "That peach eye...belonged to Lily!"

Father Wing tsked, and for the first time, True registered some hint of annoyance and disappointment in his features. When the girl's wings fluttered weakly against the ground and amidst her struggle to be free of Morgan's grip several more serrated black extremities threatened to strike him, Father Wing swiftly pressed the point of the blade against her neck.

Fifty-One

Victor...

DEVOUR.

Victor slid across the grass, escaping a swipe of one of the fox's burly tails. Which, Victor now knew from personal experience to be much harder than it looked. If he wasn't mistaken, it had the ability to harden them at will.

Every scathe felt like a boulder crashing into him. He did not want to experience a direct hit. If not for whatever the crystal was doing to his body, he wasn't sure he'd have been able to take it. His felt more nimble, lighter, faster even, than he'd ever been.

This wasn't the first time he found himself grateful for those self-defense lessons he'd taken after the ordeal with his father. He'd been drowning in a sense of helplessness back then. Terrified that he could find himself face to face with his father or anyone else again, unable to protect his mother, and it had been a great motivator for his learning.

Lately, he'd been finding more use for it, even if he hadn't initially meant to utilize that skillset to help True. Not that he regretted it. But, being on a battlefield, hearing the cries of Faeries and other beings alike, witnessing the horrors of lives being torn apart, blood staining the dying grass of FlareWing, and protecting himself from some huge nine-tailed fox had never been within the scope of his expectations.

As blurred shapes and lines of color whizzed past him, Victor made note of the large chunks of tree bark being blasted away from their proper place, almost as dangerous as the rest of the beast's attacks. The way this was going, how would he ever catch up to True and Morgan? Let alone, find the others?

"What's with this thing, anyway? What even is it?" Victor complained, as Opal blasted a dark purple and black wave of magic past him. The fox's large golden beads swung to the side as it dodged her attack. Victor hadn't managed to find out much about her, but he was glad for her assistance. She could have left him the moment they'd been cut off from Morgan and True.

"It's a Kumiho. An ancient fox-beast that was trapped in parchment. Quill set it free, and it feasted on livers to gain its power back and satisfy its hunger." Was Quill the Faerie—or whatever she was—that had broken the veil? Considering what Opal had been saying in The Grand Tree, they were at least acquainted with one another. Quill came to FlareWing and began to destroy everything.

He still recalled seeing her walking forward and shadows sprouting like weeds behind her. The weird charges of energy that struck the veil and the feeling of despair when the shards that once were whole and offered the Faerie world protection fell down around them. But if they were together, why was Opal helping them? Why try to warn Father Wing? Wasn't this a betrayal?

"As for what it wants from you, well...it wants to eat you."

"What? Didn't you just say it satisfied its hunger?" Victor frowned, rolling out the way of another attack. What's with animals? Mirror wanted them as pets, and this one wanted to have him for dinner. He was officially put off of getting a pet for the rest of his life.

"Yes, I did say that. But it keeps saying it wants to devour you." Opal shrugged.

"You understand it—the Kumiho?"

"Of course. I was born of a Cursed Fae," Opal said, unhappily.

When Twister told them the story Lady Lily, Lady Reva, and Sir Locus saving FlareWing, he never specifically mentioned Cursed Fae having offspring. But he had said that Lady Reva had been used by The Darkness. She gave birth to Father Wing or something.

As Cursed Fae, it would explain Opal's her looks and dark colored magic. Let alone her problems entering FlareWing upon arrival. Now that the veil was gone, she was free to roam across the fields. Only, so too were the rest of the things attacking them now.

"Yeah. This is a total drag. Sorry foxy. There's no *way* that's happening." Victor scoffed, "My mom would ***kill*** *me* if I let you eat me." He directed at the Kumiho.

Fifty-Two

Phelia...

STRANGER.

"You're Grace's father?" Phelia asked skeptically. "As far as we were aware, she's an orphan." What would be his response?

"That was the result of unfortunate circumstance," he replied, a frown wiping away the smile he'd had on his face a moment before. "It was my fault. She was never supposed to be in the Human World."

As he spoke, Phelia's mind fluttered back to the conversation they'd had with Uriel and the others. They'd said that she was from somewhere else. They'd even said she had a family. This man admits to being from some other world, and he did have powers. But wasn't this too much of a coincidence? "If she's not from our world, then where?" Phelia asked.

"Grail. Same as I, of course. As is her mother." He answered matter-of-factly. Grail? Phelia wasn't sure what to make of it.

"My mother?" Grace asked, meeting Phelia's gaze with wide eyes. "*I* have a *mother*?" Was it really okay for her to be hopeful already?

He smiled, "Oh yes. The most *beautiful* mother. She's waited so long to see you again. As have Blitz and I. Now I will finally be able to fulfill my promise."

"Blitz too...? You know her name?" Grace asked, looking the winged creature over, gently pressing a hand to her white horns. "You're saying Blitz and I have met before too...? She seems so young. Even though I don't know much about dragons or anything."

"Her kind are called Lyves, not dragon. But yes, of course. You named her after all. That's why you remember her name."

"Okay, okay. That's enough of that, Mr. *whatever* your name is. You say you're Grace's long-lost father, but just because you say it doesn't mean we'd just believe you." Zane chimed in, putting words to some of Phelia's unease. "You're a total stranger!"

"That man is undoubtedly her father." Fayth sighed, swatting an unnatural looking creature with a swirled head and drooping eyes. How did Fayth know that?

"As if we can believe a talking cat! Besides, just a little bit ago you set us up. Acting all knowledgeable just to tell us to run away!" He shouted.

"How prejudice. Singling out cats as untrustworthy. Besides, I've informed you on more than one occasion that I am not a 'cat.' I am under no obligation to know everything. More than that, Phelia," Fayth called, immediately dismissing Zane's complaints, "you should know it yourself. They feel very similar to one another. Those powers as well. If you were whole, you would have known well before me." If she were whole?

Was he referring to the memories she supposedly had locked away again? Just what was supposed to be locked away in her head that made any difference? Still, she supposed they *did* favor each other. Grace didn't have a rainbow hoop in her nose or matching rings in her ears, nor did she have his skin tone or hair color, but there were other things. Their smiles, that frown. Their noses...and surely those eyes.

Zane scoffed saying something under his breath she couldn't hear. The man clicked his tongue and turned around to watch Blitz blow a swirl of magic at a howling beast before it plunged towards the ground. He'd said she was something called a Lyve. Then, without missing a beat, he turned back towards them and directed his attention at Zane.

"My name is Noir. And I have half a mind to blow you off of this beast! *Listen* to me. Yes, she has my features, my eyes. Yes, she feels similar to me, because she is ***my daughter!*** And she has her mother's hair and cute little ears. Because we created her together. How else would I be here, or know her name?"

"You called her Gracelyn. We know her by Grace. We are literally in the middle of a war that let a bunch of evil things in when it is usually protected, they're killing Faeries and breaking everything. As far as I'm concerned, even if you did help us out back there, or know that little dragon—I mean Lyve, or whatever—you could be part of this. A ploy. From The Darkness, maybe." Zane huffed.

"You imbecile!" Fayth hissed. "I'll throw you off myself! As *if* I'd let some dark being touch my fur! Least of all, ride near Phelia!"

Fifty-Three

Zane...

PROTECT.

The cat must have had a death wish. Even if they were in the middle of a battlefield with a bunch of things murdering Faeries and trying to shred them apart, he was too comfortable talking to him like that. Zane resisted the urge to run up Fayth's back and take a fist full of his huge whiskers. How long could he yank them until he begged for mercy?

"Fayth," Phelia chided. "If you throw my brother off your back and into danger I'll simply jump after him. And Zane is just worried about Grace, he's no imbecile."

"Alright, alright." Zane scratched his cheek, closing his eyes. "Let's assume you're telling the truth. How are we to know?" It wasn't as if Zane was against Grace having a family that's been searching for her all her life. If anything, he relished the idea of someone as young as her obtaining that kind of happiness, but he struggled with the thought that they'd be so lucky after all their bad luck. They'd only just heard they weren't from the same world. Grace didn't have any siblings to question things like this, to protect her.

Zane found himself staring into his palms. Protect her. If Noir hadn't shown up when he did, would they have gotten out of that situation?

When he rushed ahead of Phelia and Grace, he hadn't even thought about what would happen afterwards. He never expected to feel that buzzing sensation and have a shield, barrier or whatever, keep dozens of monsters at bay. But what would have happened if it didn't? Would they have perished in FlareWing? Stuck in some world who knows how far from Snowville, while their father awaited them unknowingly at home?

He didn't know how to feel about the crystals. He almost wished he'd never found them. If he'd remembered his umbrella, or even kept running through the storm instead of stopping at *Snowville Temporary Infirmary* things might have been different now. Maybe he would never have been touched by The Darkness. Life had said that the crystals might lead him back to Bailey. What if Bailey was trapped there and he didn't have a crystal? Would she just waste away in *Snowville Medical* and never wake up again?

Just how thankful was he supposed to be with so many cons? Zane knew better than to think they'd ever have a normal life again after all of this. There would be no going back to before the crystals. But he also knew better than to think that they would ever be the same either. These experiences were changing them somehow. Even if he didn't feel very different right now.

If he could put a barrier between them all and the rest of the world and it would never falter, he'd do it in a heartbeat. Phelia, Grace, True, and Victor. So, nothing could touch them again. Maybe, if he could, he'd even shield their eyes.

He supposed, that wasn't really a good way to live. That was his own selfishness. Phelia at the very least, would hate it. Where was Victor now anyway? Was he safe? *I swear, he better not have found some place to fall asleep in this chaos. If he gets blasted away because he couldn't be bothered to run today, I swear I'm gonna...*

"I'll prove it," Noir nodded, taking Grace's hands in his. "I'll show you. I promise you. I only need *one* chance to prove it."

Fifty-Four

Eustis...

TAKING FLIGHT.

Eustis' legs wanted to give out on him, his lungs burned, and his broken rib screamed in complete agony as his raced across the field. He almost cried the moment he laid eyes on the two-headed boar with razors for teeth intent on taking a chunk out of him but focusing on getting away in the midst of pain rendered that a useless feat.

He clumsily jumped over branches and vines, sure that he narrowly escaped with his life a moment before when a dangerously large icicle sped past him. When he glanced over his shoulder, he saw the two-headed boar impaled by the frozen thorn.

Overcome with relief, Eustis slumped down to the ground, hoping to catch his breath if only for a moment. What in the world was going on? Brilla had said he would be able to save Grace, but he hadn't seen her anywhere. In fact, he hadn't seen a single thing that looked human since he got to the place. Unless he counted the occasional severed arm or leg scattered around in pools of blood. Panic started to set in as he worried that he was too late. Maybe Grace was somewhere in that field of terrors. Maybe she was already...

Just as Eustis began to lose himself in his concern, he was suddenly jerked from his spot on the ground. Wide-eyed, he watched as a monster's gaping mouth crashed down in the exact place he'd been occupying moments before. Just now, he'd almost died, right??

Before he could get a good look at the person who saved his life, he felt his body swing through the air and saw a spray of blood fall to the ground. A second later, a humanish head with black hair and eyes rolled across the grass. Eustis swallowed as he watched the head's right eye twitch slowly to a halt.

When he finally laid eyes on his savior, he saw a menacing looking man with long hair, glowing eyes, and shining armor. In his other arm, he held a gleaming spear. Eustis watched the blood trailing down his arm and black goo dripping from the tip of his weapon.

"*Another* human?" He groaned, seeming displeased.

Another implied that there was at least someone before him. *Grace!* "Does that mean you've seen Grace? She's got brown eyes and curly red hair."

The man shook his head with a lengthened sigh. "Of course. *Another* one of Twister's little friends. Running around the field like that...you humans are a troublesome lot."

"Twister?" Eustis asked, raising a brow. Who was Twister? Suddenly aware of the distance between him and the ground increasing even more than before, Eustis caught sight of wings flapping against the wind. No way. Were they...*flying*??

Fifty-Five

Twister...

MEMORIES.

Twister stumbled forward, unable to trust himself flying for the moment. After all, it had been because of those images flashing through his mind that he'd fallen out of the sky and found himself separated from True and Morgan. After he'd seen a most unfortunate scene: a Faerie child swallowed whole by one the dark, shadow turned solid enemies on the battlefield. Had some of them not been taken to safety? His heart pounded relentlessly, painfully on as he tried to make sense of what he was seeing in his mind. A circle of Fae around the fountain.

There were no flowers budding there...?

He fought to drag his feet forward, grabbing strands of grass by the handful, determined not to be completely blown away by the crashing pressures of magic around him. He recognized the green mixture in the bowls, could almost smell the citrus and mint scent mixing with wildflowers. He knew Blessing Salve when he saw it. But *why* was he seeing it? An uneasy feeling swam through him. He couldn't afford to be distracted by such things in the middle of war. Sharp pains attacked his head.

Wait...these images...just now, was that my father? He hadn't looked like that for a long time. Twister fumbled forward, his lingering doubts dispelled by a view of his mother smiling down at him, only the scar over her eye was nowhere to be found. A feeling of certain despair worked its way through him as he became certain that the images that blinded him were memories. Which meant, he was remembering his first time crossing the veil with his parents.

As if the realization had lowered a floodgate, images came in quick succession to each other, offering no moment of reprieve. That's right. Back then, they'd had no clue that by the time night fell in the Human Word, that they would face danger.

Had his father always smiled like that back then? It pained him to see a smile on his father's face that he no longer witnessed. Had his parents ever looked at each other with that much love in their eyes? Had they gazed upon him so gently, interacted with him so tenderly? Why hadn't he remembered such beautiful things before today?

But that warmth ended as abruptly as it began. A close friend of his father's? Had his father ever had friends in the first place? Shock gripped him as the man met his parents' friendly arms with a blade. His father had always been swift, he'd had no trouble moving his mother out of harm's way. And yet, it had left himself wide open, and the man's curved dagger pierced his abdomen. Twister couldn't understand what they were saying, but he felt his mother's fear as a whirling mass appeared in the sky and she outstretched her arms to shield him from some attack he couldn't see.

His lip quivered as he watched the moments play out before him. When she turned to face him, blood trailed down from an open wound. She couldn't open her eye. He must have cried then too. All the other children were crying. The other children, who were being rushed to the veil mere yards away. Only, many of them, and their parents alike, would never make it to the other side. A blast of magic crashed into the ground ahead of him, sending Twister flying backwards.

His head painfully struck the ground as he slid through the dirt. Still, the memories continued their assault. In the confusion, Twister had been separated from his parents. At one point, he'd turned to survey the waves of Faeries and search for his parents only to witness dark waves crashing down from the sky.

The shadowed currents engulfed them in varying number. Each time, the screams of the captured would cease as their bodies disappeared into the thickness. In several instances, even tearing them apart when their entire bodies weren't encased.

Against his will and logic considering his lack of attention to the bodies already strewed across the battlefield, Twister felt the burn of vomit at the back of his throat. Perhaps it was because he'd hit his head during his fall that he felt so dizzy.

By the time his parents found him hidden far away from their meeting point or the veil, tears clouded his mother's good eye, and his father bowed his head. His mother shielded his eyes until they found themselves back inside FlareWing. He witnessed a clear moment of shock and confusion from his parents' expressions as they looked down at him in his mother's arms. *Ah. I see. This must be the moment they realized I didn't return to my normal size. They hadn't known, none of us had, that I'd never be normal again.*

Twister didn't understand everything that his memory showed him. He didn't understand what transpired between his parents and the friend. Nor the man's betrayal and how it overlapped with The Darkness. It was no wonder he recognized that chill or saw the moment True was pulled under before. It had been a very similar tactic to the unexpected waves pulling Faeries in every direction, swallowing them up without discrimination. He'd seen this thing at work all that time ago, and yet, he'd forgotten it.

Twister sobbed, another thing he could never imagine doing amidst such dangers and found himself quite surprised that he hadn't already met his end there in the dirt. He cried for his younger self that hadn't remembered his parents' love and affection because he was lost in his own suffering.

He cried for his mother's beautiful face forever scarred by protecting him, the fading of his father's smile and loss of a man that had once been his friend but lead to a massacre of Fae. For all the lives lost that day and this one, and for himself now who still couldn't understand how to free himself of his magical affliction even with such memories revealed.

"We have to go that way! I just saw them going across the field. True, Morgan and even Father Wing!" Jumping to his feet at the sound of Victor's voice, Twister took to the air. He shook his head, trying to rid him of his thoughts and emotions and bring his focus back to the present. "If this stupid thing would just get out of the way! Opal, don't you know anything else about it?"

"Victor!" Twister called as he caught sight of him and a large white fox that lunged toward him. His reaction immediate, Twister barely managed to trap it in water as he sped towards them. Already feeling drained and out of breath, he awkwardly dropped onto Victor's shoulder.

"Twister. Thank you." Victor sighed, hunched forward with his hands pressed to his knees. "I didn't know you could pick up something that huge."

"Neither did I," Twister answered truthfully. "I didn't mean to pick it up really. Anyway, don't thank me yet. I can't hold this thing for long." He frowned. He was feeling weaker by the minute. The magic in FlareWing was diminishing quicker by the second, and the weight of the fox felt like it would crush him in an instant. He watched it struggle inside the water, thrashing around with a wild vigor. Twister hoped to drown it but knew it wouldn't hold long enough to accomplish it.

"We have to hurry and go after Quill." Opal cried. "Something's bad is happening!"

A harsh, ominous growl shook the air around them and the sudden distraction broke Twister's hold. He parted the wave that sprung towards them as the fox fell to the ground. It coughed and began to recover much too quickly for his comfort.

"Well, we've gone and done it now," Victor groaned, as it rose to its feet, its gaze intensely trained on them. Another growl sounded, buried beneath a string of distorted words. What a chilling sound.

"Go." A familiar voice cut in from behind them. Twister turned his head to see his mother's form stepping towards them as a hoard of spiked vines dragged the beast to the ground.

"Mother." Twister whispered. Many emotions wound around inside him. And even more words that he wanted voice. The battlefield was no place for it. "I'll stay and help you."

"Don't insult me, Twister." His mother frowned, watching the white fur fall away from the vines in batches. The beast ahead of them slowly morphed into the shape of a woman. The heavy golden beads still adorned her neck as she flashed her bloodied fangs, fighting to break free. "It is a mother's job to protect her son. As *if* this ***rabid dog*** could prove a match for me."

Fifty-Six

Quill...

WHAT IF.

"*You LIE!*" Quill shouted in agony. She no longer recognized her own voice.

DON'T LISTEN TO HIM!

The demand sprung from the back of her mind. Everything hurt. She could hardly make sense of what she'd heard.

Quill recoiled. ***"How does he know my mother's name? Why has your voice gone?? If that man has lied to me then why do we share the same eye?! SPEAK TO ME, FATHER!"***

Somehow, she had freed herself from her place on the ground. Sharp pains attacked her; she stumbled backwards. It burned. With each moment she could feel her grip loosen and her mind weaken. Is it possible that she'd been tricked?

An eye that mirrored one of her own looked back at her with tears sparkling across the lash line. Her very existence hung in the balance. This moment had been why she survived, why she went through this painful process and let ***HIM*** take parts of her flesh. Had all the stories that bred her hatred been falsehoods?

In the distance, Quill could make out the faint sound of Opal's voice calling out to her. Had this been why she had those looks on her face? She attempted to truly consider her words for the first time. "Why do you call ***IT*** your father?" "My loyalty lies with ***you***—no one else." "How can you know truth from lies if you never question it?" "What if you're ***wrong?***" How many of those questions and statements had she brushed off? Even considered to be treason?

HOW DARE YOU QUESTION ME?!!

The vibrations bounced around her skull and the pain spreading through her body intensified. It threatened to bury every morsel of consciousness she had left. But she knew what came after. They would become one; one mind, one soul, one body. She thought she wanted that. Or perhaps, she was feeling something altogether different that she didn't understand. Something that would make her wish for any excuse that meant this would not be her end. Even if that meant believing the words of someone she'd never known who might be saying something similar to someone she only sort of knew. Yet, she couldn't help but wonder...what *if?*

Fifty-Seven

Opal...

CRUEL.

Opal called out to Quill again as they made their way closer. She could see the constant black flickering of her mismatched eyes. Hear an almost deafening cry as hundreds of black liquid threads whipped around from the center of her chest. Dark energy expanded and contracted around her body, with each movement Opal's heart raced. She'd never seen anything like it. Quill was in so much pain.

"What's happening to her??" She sobbed. The moment she took another step forward with Victor and Twister close behind, Father Wing blocked their path with a wall of flames.

"It seems It is going to tear her apart." Twister frowned beside her. "From the inside..."

"True's in there," Victor hissed, clutching a fist to his side. "With some dark thing that looks like it is going to explode."

"But it wouldn't do that!" Opal whimpered. "I-It can't! ***IT*** kept her all this time. How could it get rid of her now??" She couldn't accept this. She *wouldn't* accept it.

Quill may not have been born of her mother, she may have succumbed to that stupid thing, but she was all she had. She turned to

Twister, taking hold of his hand. "Please! You know water magic! If you could just put out a few of the flames, we could go in and I-I could save—"

The pity in his expression hardened the lump in her throat. She furiously shook her head. She didn't want to hear anything but a yes. In a manner too cruel for the fragility of her hope, the boy gently kissed her hands in apology. She watched the light and shadow of the fire dance across his features.

"Even if I could conjure a river, I would be no match for a single spark that ignites them. The difference in our power is too great."

Fifty-Eight

Morgan…

BOLD.

A swift breeze stirred the flames and smoke around them as Morgan considered the expression and another bout of stillness from Father Wing. Only then did he realize in full what it was. Why there had been no hesitation before. Why he could, even if it would have protected Morgan himself, swung his blade at her. Even pressed the edge to her neck and showed no remorse when blood blotched the skin beneath it.

This was a matter of resolve. There was no way that he wasn't aware. In fact, Morgan was sure that he'd known it the moment she strode towards the veil, let alone made her way past it.

"You cannot do this." Morgan shook his head as he watched the beautifully menacing glow expand across the sword. "You cannot." He repeated, his voice more resolved to defy the maddening situation before them the second time. They'd heard her cries, and even now she was in pain. She was confused. She had not willingly chosen this path. "You hear her pain. I know you are not without sympathy."

"'Tis not a matter of my sympathy. Before she loses to The Darkness, before FlareWing falls to ruin and any more of this dark energy soaks into our soil, I will end her. And too, her suffering. Tis only a matter of timing. Else, The Darkness scrapes by unscathed."

"You mean...you'll kill her?" True turned, a hand over her heart. Even the child who knew nothing of her was not without pity. Surely under his intense, sharp red eyes Father Wing was hurting almost as much as he was. How could he not? After all, Quill, as Opal had called her, was also a Princess.

"You said before the children arrived in FlareWing that you knew who I was. And you know Lily. Her family, *your family*. Your mother and father are gone. Princess Mira is gone." Morgan pleaded, infinitely more aware that he was on borrowed time. "This is *my* child. My daughter. She is all I have left of Lily."

He dared to look away from Father Wing and at the excruciating expression on Quill's face. He hated that her features were becoming less and less like Lily's or his. He hated the possibility of losing all he had left in the world without a single chance to prevent their loss.

"I am doing all that I can to purify our land, else it crumbles away to nothing. 'Tis too much for Princess Aurelia to withstand. She is much too young. I shall not let you, the Fae nor that child die for this one. She is corrupted. Our veil in pieces by her hand." He slowly bowed his head. For the first time since their encounter, pain fully shrouding his character.

"'Tis only in my power to free her with a quick death. I *truly* apologize." The degree to which this man—unbelievably, his nephew—had to have control over his emotions almost frightened him. Still, he couldn't do nothing. He could not surrender to powerlessness again. Perhaps Father Wing could do nothing else, but Morgan could not lose her.

His father was gone. His wife. Their only child left, against all odds, squalled in pain before him. Deceived. Dying, somehow, by the very entity that tore his family apart. *No more,* Morgan thought in mantra the words etched into his heart. He had been in the clutches of this so-called Darkness. And yet, somehow, he'd been freed. Maybe it didn't need her. He was not half-Fae. He was just a human with little else to offer. But there was magic in his eyes. And it had used him for his voice once. Why not again?

He knew nothing about Quill aside from that she was a part of him, a part of Mira, and a part of Lily. He didn't need another reason to love her. As he stepped forward, he locked eyes with Father Wing, who he knew understood his intentions. *Please,* Morgan begged, *just let me try this once. And if it works,* ***kill*** *me.* Father Wing must have accepted his obscene bargain since he did not move to block his path. "You can't have her! Take *me!*" Morgan shouted as he continued onward. *This is probably the boldest thing you've done, Morgan,* he spoke to himself. *Save for that first kiss with Lily.* He never knew why he nor his father ever had the capability to witness magic at work and all it entailed. But it had led him to his greatest gains and most heartbreaking losses. Even if he were to die now, as long as Quill could survive with the chance to cherish this world rather than destroy it, he could accept this ending.

"Quill, your mother loved you. Even if she never got to hold you, I know she would have loved you more than anything. You and Mira both. She would ***never*** have let you go. She died protecting FlareWing from The Darkness." Morgan stopped; realization hit a little too late. A great number of the swirling threads shot towards him, forming large spikes as they sliced through him. In shock, he turned his head to look behind him. Even Father Wing had not escaped the assault. What about the girl? He couldn't catch sight of her.

"Hurry!" Father Wing demanded as his sword shook apart sending scattered whistling beams of light hurtling towards Quill's convulsing frame. Like metal pins, they struck the expanding blackness around her and forced sections into the ground below.

Quill screeched again, and a swell of black currents flowed in every direction, further darkening the sky. For a moment, the battlefield seemed eerily still. There were no more sounds of weapons crossing, the whimpers of Fae and creature alike faded away as he dragged himself painfully forward, still attached to the spikes.

His coughed and ignored the blood trickling down his mouth. His vision shook out of focus. He willed himself not to get distracted, not to stop dragging every perforated limb towards his daughter's body. By some miracle, he had not already lost consciousness from the pain.

One pull after the other, images raced through his mind. The day Lily decorated his hair with wildflowers and pastel stands of silk. "Lily..." He'd been more certain than ever that he couldn't let her go and impulsively proposed right then. To his surprise, she'd jumped into his arms and sent them rolling down the hillside.

There, tangled together by silk, and stunning rays of sunlight kissing the horizon, they'd decided the rest of their future. She shocked all of FlareWing just later that day when she brought him home and proudly declared her feelings despite protest. It was thanks to her brother's support that their relationship was slowly accepted by the Fae. He'd gone against even their parents' wishes in support of Lily's happiness. Locus had given them his blessing. Something that he felt both grateful and sorrowful to receive. His father hadn't had it quite so easy.

"Father..." He'd been overjoyed meeting Lily for the first time. She listened to all his tales with fascination, treated him as well as her own parents even when they refused to see him. And leaped for joy years after as they'd announced her pregnancy. *Who knew there were two?* He groaned in pain, still slogging ahead. The threads felt endless.

He recalled the day he was leaving home to meet Lily in FlareWing after getting the news that war was coming. A memory that resurfaced for the very first time. Morgan remembered the panic that coursed through his veins, his heart racing as he rushed out of the door, and the ground breaking away beneath his feet.

That's right. ***IT*** *took me away.* He recalled the moment he'd reached his hand towards the sky as his body continued to fall. The weight against his chest as a blistering cold swam through him. A moment entertaining the thought that he might have been having a nightmare: all he had to do was wake up from his dream and everything would be alright again.

Only, there was no dream. A jarring fear gripped him. He'd truly fallen into the depths of nothingness. The last remnants of fantasy vanished, time slowed almost to a halt, and the chill that had befallen his body quickly morphed into an unimaginable agony.

By the time the air left his lungs, and he teetered on the edge of consciousness, he could no longer remember his family. All that remained was a whisper of knowing somewhere in the back of his mind. A glint of living memory that would later both plague and allude him as he endured days, months, years of torment.

“Please, help me reach her.”

Fifty-Nine

Grace...

LOADED.

Grace stared with horror as they returned to the field from the crater. It had been bad enough to see the crying Fae, especially those who said some of their family members had not returned, let alone the solemn expressions mirrored by the army.

Lines of smoke rose from the damaged huts, Phelia commented on the remnants of wagons and broken trinkets that littered the ground—a long way, she'd said, from the awe they once inspired. Mutilated Fae whimpered nearby etched in thick red puddles; a sound she didn't think she'd ever be able to forget.

Even the trees shook and crumbled to the ground, in various stages of decay. It was a surprise that the fountain stood upright, though a series of feathered lines showed that its beautiful stone figures had not escaped damage. The creatures that had before been attacking in droves dwindled, though they had not seemed to grow any weaker. Nor suffer exhaustion.

What worried her most, however, was the massive fiery wall illuminating the darkness that had blotted out the sky. They'd crossed much of FlareWing to return the child with the others. There had been no sign of Victor or True.

Fayth mentioned that fire was started by Father Wing, which made plenty of sense considering that thing he'd done in The Grand Tree. Besides, if nothing else, the Faerie looked like a walking flame as far as she was concerned. A beautiful, confusing, and scary flame, but a flame, nonetheless. Chances were, Victor and True were somewhere near there.

"Grace!!"

She could have sworn she recognized that voice.

"Grace! I've been looking *everywhere* for you! Those monster things have practically been exploding or something. Does that mean we're *winning*? Whoa! That's a *big* cat."

She searched around her until a pair of blue eyes and short blonde hair leveled with her gaze. "Eustis??!"

"I am not a *cat*." Fayth growled.

"WHOA! It talks!" He said in awe, his mouth agape. What was he doing in FlareWing??? She watched as he swayed slightly left to right, in an almost uncomfortable rhythm, dangled from Thorne's hand. War had done nothing for his expressions. She couldn't tell if the man even cared to see them. Twister's dad and Eustis? What in the world was going on?

"Don't tell me *that's* Elephant Spit?" Phelia asked, peering over her shoulder. "How could he have possibly followed you here?"

"Hmm. Where have I heard that before...?" Zane wondered aloud.

"Have we met?" Eustis directed at Phelia.

"Who is this boy?" Noir leaned forward, eyeing him with suspicion.

"Who are you?" Eustis asked, looking nearly as confused as Grace was feeling.

"Gracelyn's father, of course." Noir retorted quickly.

Eustis shot a look of surprise in her direction as if waiting for an explanation she couldn't begin to give. This entire situation was making her head hurt. She understood pretty much nothing.

"What are you doing here anyway?" Grace more demanded than asked.

"Some woman with anger issues showed up at my place, stalking me. Then she started talking nonsense about some crystal and war. I was pretty sure she was there to kidnap me or something." A woman with anger issues that knew about the crystals. *Don't tell me he means Brilla? Why would she have been stalking Eustis? Kidnap him? Well, I suppose people might take him for money or something. Eustis is loaded. Wait...what about a crystal? Did she bring him or...?*

"Do you have a crystal??" Grace startled.

"You mean this thing?" Eustis asked, pulling a purple crystal from his pocket, cupping it in his hands. "She said that this thing would help me save you." Save her? Did she need saving? Well, she supposed earlier they did need some kind of help but from *him*? Besides, Noir had helped them and even defeated a number of those things while they'd been riding on Fayth's back.

Without a moment of warning, Thorne tossed Eustis to the side, sending him crashing clumsily beside her. Fayth voiced some unintelligible cry of displeasure as Eustis shakily caught the crystal between his hands. It almost dropped to the ground below them. "Whew." He breathed, before letting out a loud yelp when Phelia peeked around his side.

"It's even got the same symbol etched onto the surface. Just like what happened to the rest at the ritual." Phelia leaned back, but not before she shot Eustis a particularly unfriendly look. "I suppose we are to assume it is legitimate." She added.

"Oh, *great*. ***Another*** one." Zane stressed in a grim tone. "And the problems just keep coming."

"TRUE!" Victor's voice rang out ahead of them. They rushed towards the base of Fayth's neck, searching the ground. Zane pointed him out below. Grace followed Victor's wide-eyed stare, his attention turned towards the sky on the other side of the flames. Her heart skipped painfully in her chest as she realized what they were seeing.

True's body was suspended in air, well above the flame line. Something black and not altogether solid, pierced her stomach.

Sixty

True...

WIN.

True could hear a voice whispering softly in her ear. Such a beautiful sound that she could nearly forget the painful, jagged cold thorn transfixing her abdomen. Sweet like a mother's voice. Perhaps her own. But she quickly realized that the voice she'd heard and the image before her were not of her mother. If nothing else, her Faerie wings dispelled her wish entirely. Somehow, she knew. Lady Lily.

Twister couldn't save her this time. Neither could a dead Faerie. Was she losing her grip on reality? She was saying something about power. *Her* power? What power? That ball of light from before? She'd reached out to Morgan and touched that dark thing. But her so-called power had not made a reappearance since. In fact, she'd hoped otherwise when she touched the spikes in an effort to free him. Instead, she'd been impaled herself. Not even Father Wing had totally avoided them.

It was so cold. It was as if the thing was sucking the warmth from her body. She pressed her palms against her stomach, shakily staring down at the blood falling from her fingers to some area below. She'd wanted to help Father Wing, the Faeries, Twister, Morgan and Quill and the others. No one deserved this ending. They'd won before, hadn't they? The Fae defeated The Darkness. Or at least, drove it from FlareWing. But she'd felt it the moment the veil shattered, and those things invaded. Every moment the magic was fading away. Father Wing had said it too, that the world would collapse. That Princess Aurelia was too young to take it. Uriel and the others had been fighting this too. They'd been winning.

Fae died. Countless other beings. She felt some shimmer of resolve rising within her. She wanted to win. For an instant she'd thought it clearly. *If you need Quill to win, to destroy FlareWing, then that's just not acceptable.*

After all, if she wasn't totally losing her mind then that meant Lily was watching too. She and the Fae had already sacrificed everything for their land, for their people, and for their families. "You can't...have her." True wrapped her hands around the thorn. The Darkness, there had to be a way to rid them of it. A way for it to... "Wash away."

A sudden blinding light glided across her vision and a warmth filled her. Moments later, she grasped the sensation of falling. Faster and faster. Until she recognized the cold creeping its way beneath her skin and her mind began to haze over.

In a moment of clarity and dread, True understood that she'd felt this before. The last time she'd been in FlareWing and left out the door. Or rather, was pulled in. She could feel the air leave her lungs. She was filled with an overwhelming awareness that Twister couldn't save her this time either. Who knew where he was? Or Victor and the others. Somewhere on the battlefield. Hopefully safe. What would happen when she reached the bottom? Did a bottom exist?

She thought she'd opened her eyes, but she couldn't be sure. Either way, she knew that a blackness surrounded her. She tried to fight away the dizziness in her head, the moments of pain forcing her on the edge of consciousness.

The next time you find yourself in FlareWing or lost within reach, seek me. Could she possibly...?

"Father Wing."

Sixty-One

Victor...

A FAVOR.

Victor paced the floor, with half the mind to take his frustrations out on the boxes stacked in the corner. He hadn't been able to do enough. If Twister hadn't stopped him, he would have run through the fire to get her. He paused, furiously stuffed his hands in his pockets. He attempted to will away his anxiety and cease his shaking. He failed. He paced again.

"Victor, will you *sit* down? You're freaking us out even more." Zane called, looking over his shoulder from his spot on the floor. Victor bit his lip. He fought the extremes of his unrelenting emotions inside of him, sadness, impatience, disappointment, shock, anger, and even more anxiety.

Crap, crap, crap. How pathetic. Getting separated by Morgan, then the Kumiho. I couldn't protect her. If I'd had been paying attention, if I'd been quick enough the moment she was dragged off, this wouldn't have happened. Some ***friend****.* He'd talked so big before, reassuring her that he would protect her and yet, all he could do was watch.

"Uh...Twister said she should be fine. So, that means she should be fine, right guys?" Grace asked, hesitant. "*Right...?*"

"Father Wing healed her," Fayth sighed, curling up into Phelia's lap, "and he said to wait until she woke." Victor thought back to how large he'd been in FlareWing. For only a moment, he welcomed the distraction. Fayth had been massive. He would have given the animals in Mirror a run for their money.

If True had died, what would he have told her aunts? It was like the past was repeating itself. Victor felt more than a little unnerved by this pattern. They'd been in this situation before. Well, not *exactly* the same one, but much too close for comfort.

"Twister was the Faerie with the mixed color eyes, right?" Eustis questioned. "He looked like he wanted to come with, but he stayed behind. Should we take her to *Snowville Medical* or something? Not that I have any clue what was going on." Victor surmised that was because Twister had an obligation to FlareWing. Especially given his parents' positions. He'd seemed torn. He was definitely worried, even though he attempted to reassure them that there was no way she wouldn't make it with Father Wing helping her. It had been Victor himself, who encouraged Twister to stay home. He'd told him that they could meet up again later, but he wasn't particularly confident in anything he'd said back then. He only hoped to cure him of his guilt. It seemed like what he needed.

"I have a feeling that not even dad would be equipped to deal with this. I mean, we are talking about injuries sustained by The Darkness. Magic or something. I can't imagine anything they do is gonna work if Father Wing couldn't heal it." Zane wrung his hands, casting a nervous glance in Victor's direction. "I mean—*obviously* True's gonna be okay. As far as we know it was just the one wound. Plus, we all saw some of the crazy stuff Father Wing could do."

"Yeah, but that was a pretty *big*—ouch!" Eustis exclaimed, rubbing his side where Grace had elbowed him. To Victor's surprise, Phelia didn't chide her.

Noir—the tall, long-haired, swarthy man dressed in an intricate patterned tunic, a cloth belt and loose dark bottoms bare from the shin down—grabbed him by the shoulders to stop him. Victor watched the shells adorning the two loose strands of his interwoven hair sway with his movement. He looked him over a little more closely; various golden necklaces hung from his neck, and with even the smallest action on his part, one could clearly hear a light clinking of the bangles adorning his wrists and ankles. There was a light and calming air about him, though Victor felt inclined to think the man was also dangerous. He couldn't be sure if the warning sprang from a feeling of paranoia given recent events, or if he was simply beginning to distrust adult men in general. And yet, in further confliction to those feelings, his firm hold on his shoulders somehow grounded him. Just enough that the trembling of his extremities finally came to an end.

"Your friend, True, is it?" Noir asked, slightly tipping his neck in her direction.

"Yeah. Her name's True." Victor nodded, not exactly sure what he was getting at. He turned his head to look at her as she laid motionless against the wall, his and Zane's jacket's propping her neck up from the floor. He was all too aware that the hole in her fabrics remained hidden underneath one of Father Wing's robes: an ugly reminder that she'd been impaled just a few hours before.

"She is stronger than she looks, yes? She will be fine. Women often put us men to shame." He smiled with a firm nod. Victor nodded meekly, wishing for the man's certainty. It wasn't that he didn't know that True was strong. At least, he'd thought she was strong.

He knew that she must have endured a lot in silence, just like Sydney and her group, considering her words to him before. Even if she didn't *exactly* confirm his suspicions. And he knew that it required a certain kind of strength to live behind a mask everyone could see, to be herself, in a place like Snowville. Not to mention the effort she put into interacting with him and the rest of the group.

But the kind of strength he was unsure of had nothing to do with her mental or emotional headspace—not that Victor exactly knew what the reality of those were either—but a physical one. When he thought back to their time in Principle Mann's office or carrying her through the snow on her back with her busted ankle, Victor could also see her fragility.

More than that, considering what happened before their return to *Snowville Temporary Infirmary*, Victor was even more conflicted. They'd all been shocked when that light blasted across FlareWing. And a million times more when they'd opened their eyes and found themselves back in the abandoned building with Father Wing standing behind them. He held True in his arms, wrapped in a twirling white-orange glow. They instantly suspected the worst, the moment they realized he'd stepped foot into their world with Noir close behind.

...

"Wait, where are we?" Eustis had asked, turning around to survey the room.

"What's happened to FlareWing??" Phelia fussed.

"No, no, no." Grace shook her head, tears immediately filling her eyes. "Don't tell me all the Faeries and even Twister and the Princess are..."

"Did you get us out of there?" Zane asked, shocked. "I thought you couldn't leave."

"Is she alright?" Victor asked, reaching a hand towards them. Father Wing put a palm in the air, stopping them. A well of pressure pressed them to the opposite wall.

"Quiet." Father Wing instructed. Victor watched a swirl of air flow from his nose as he sighed and looked him over. He hadn't gotten a close look at him beyond his flames. Blood now stained his shredded robes. He was older. His usual size. Aside from a short, straight beard and his vibrant red hair still flowing to the floor behind him, he looked very similar to the former adult version they'd seen of him.

As the light surrounding him and True faded, he slowly took a step towards them and the force holding them against the wall eased. He waved a hand and the cold chill inside the building faded away. Then, without a word, Father Wing glanced at Victor and carefully placed True in his arms.

Victor's eyes quickly traced over her until he made out a hint of her pale skin peeking through the fabric of her clothes. Whatever had attacked her had gone clean through, out her back and out the other side. He worried at the thought of what else it had done to her besides ripping her clothes on the way out. How painful had it been for her? It had been larger than it looked. He could even see her belly button.

When the realization hit that this too, was something he shouldn't see, he cleared his throat and placed his hand there. It felt even more inappropriate, so he snatched his hand away and groaned in frustration. "What's the matter, Victor?" Grace asked worried. His fumble had gained unneeded attention. "Your face is all—"

"Nothing." Victor sighed, clearing his throat again.

He wasn't sure why, but Father Wing offered one of the robes from his back. Victor took it, thanking him, and placed her down on the ground. "Sorry, True." He whispered, sliding the robe over her stomach. Then, he unzipped his own coat and tucked it under her head.

"Mine too." Zane said, dangling his coat near his face in offering. "Yours is thinner."

"Thanks." Victor did his best to make it even on both sides. His attention slowly fading away to their last conversation before he, her and Twister found themselves suddenly in FlareWing.

"What happened to her?" Phelia asked, crouching down beside her, nudged away from touching her clothes by Zane. "Ah. My apologies, True. Although I'm not quite sure you can hear me."

"FlareWing," Father Wing interrupted, "survived. So too, have the remaining Fae."

"So, then Twister, and even Mr. Morgan?" Grace asked, clearly wanting conformation before relief. Not that Victor blamed her there. Father Wing gave a curt nod in her direction.

"They live. The veil is no more. We have lost civilians and members of the army. The number of which we will know with certainty come dawn. The enemies have been defeated." He looked about as he spoke, looking for something. When he did not seem to find it, he walked a few steps and paused as a chair, not unlike the one he rested in during the celebration of Princess Aurelia's birth, formed beside him. Was it alright for him to waste time sitting down with them in some neglected, dusty building in Snowville?

While the others slowly picked a place on the floor and looked in Father Wing's direction, Victor couldn't bring himself to sit. "But if the veil is gone then won't FlareWing be unprotected?"

"What's the veil?" Eustis asked.

Victor had questions. He didn't know anything about the blonde-haired boy that suddenly showed up with Zane and the others. The familiarity but awkwardness with Grace, the tension with Phelia, and that deep purple crystal had not escaped his notice. However, he hardly felt equipped to handle the emotions and uncertainties already inside his head. As far as he was concerned, questions about him and his sudden appearance could wait a little longer. At least until after their conversation with Father Wing and an update on True.

"It's like a magic bubble that keeps all the bad stuff out and good things in." Grace explained, folding her hands over in a rounded shape as she spoke. "But some kind of evil Faerie showed up with a bunch of shadow monsters and popped it so all the bad things could get in and start war. You must've seen them. There were Cursed Fae and mixed-up droopy thingies."

"Oh. Well, I missed the veil popping." Eustis said. "But I was chased by a two-headed pig thing and something with weird eyes tried to eat me so I'm quite clear on the *thingies*."

"Well, I don't think they're *actually* called thingies, but I don't know what they were." Grace shook her head. "Some of them looked only like one thing, some of them didn't. A lot of them weren't even Cursed Fae—those are the evil Faeries."

"Are Cursed Fae evil per se? They were all originally Light Fae influenced by The Darkness. Anyway, I don't know for sure, but they reminded me of that thing that dragged Fredric away." Zane said thoughtfully. Victor thought there was some truth to that. The creatures weren't dragging anyone away by chains, but it seemed similar. He'd brought up another interesting point as well. Were Cursed Fae truly evil? Moments of recognition and probably aspects of their former selves must be a possibility. After all, Sir Locus had been able to reach Lady Reva one way or another. And a half-Cursed Fae like Opal existed.

If The Darkness had been trying to take over his best friend but Zane had been resisting, then wasn't it possible that even Cursed Fae were just being used as tools? Opal had been so worried about Quill, enough to suggest that she was her own person and not just a pawn of The Darkness.

Victor sighed. *Why is every part of this so complicated? Figure out one thing and there goes a hundred more questions that could upend the rest of your deductions. What a drag. Now probably isn't the time for this kind of thing anyway. Right now, there are some possible answers at our disposal. And of course, there's the matter with True...*

"They were peculiar." Father Wing countered. "They were no longer whole. No singular species. A result of The Darkness' tampering. There exists a great number of mixed-race in other worlds. The 'creatures' you reference, those beings that crossed the boundary of FlareWing, do not exist."

"So, you're saying The Darkness has been playing surgeon? That's freaky." Zane shivered.

"FlareWing is not without protection." Father Wing continued. "The Fae army is well-equipped. Princess Aurelia and I are comparatively without harm. Quill, Morgan's daughter and the sister of late Princess Mira have been released from The Darkness."

Victor considered his conversations with Opal, the half-Cursed Fae. "Quill is the one who broke the veil. If she's Morgan's daughter, then that means she's also Lily's."

"That makes her a Faerie Princess too!" Grace exclaimed. "FlareWing got attacked by an evil Princess!"

"Two Princesses can exist at the same time?" Phelia squinted. "And you hadn't known?"

"She was taken before her own mother knew of her existence. 'Twas likely before Lily's fall. 'Tis not without reason I've known naught. Least all, after The Darkness' possession of her." Father Wing said, quickly dismissing any possibility of fault or accusation. "We do not consider Cursed Fae to be inherently vile. 'Tis an unfortunate consequence of their ailment. However, this does not change the dangers they impose on Fae nor other worlds and beings. In such a state, they are merely an instrument— extensions of The Darkness."

"The Fae honored Morgan's return. With the knowledge that Quill is the offspring of Lady Lily, will she also be offered the title of Princess?" Phelia asked.

"Quill is a Princess. The Fae's acceptance of that fact is obligatory. Fae are a caring kind. Her survival, given aforementioned circumstance, will likely inspire pity and sympathy. As it should." Father Wing shifted, leaning his head onto his hand. It seemed to Victor to have been done in an astonishingly graceful way, for something that in general completely lacked it.

"Twister mentioned before that all Fae originally come from Flare-Wing." Grace peered up at him, "So why didn't they come to help during the battle? There's lots and lots of Fae, aren't there?"

"They were instructed otherwise." Father Wing said placidly."When Quill first appeared near the veil, those beings had been situated inside her." Inside her? Victor didn't even want to know how.

"As of the beginning," Father Wing continued, "she strode forth a bomb awaiting implode. Not knowing the consequences of such with certainty, I instructed other Fae to standby. It seems Quill resisted The Darkness, which began an internal struggle for control of her body. During which, The Darkness attempted to consume the Cursed beings on the battleground."

"Ohhh. That explains why they started coming apart or exploding altogether." Eustis nodded in understanding. Victor didn't recall any of that happening, but he was willing to admit that his attention had been away from the rest of FlareWing. Something that he was now realizing with an unwelcomed amount of certainty, could have gotten him killed.

He'd trusted, perhaps too naively, that Opal, Twister and the rest of the Fae would help keep him safe. More than that, he couldn't handle the thought of looking elsewhere knowing True was on the other side. Part of it felt justified, knowing what happened to True even with Father Wing by her side.

He was aware that he was being unfair in his thoughts. Father Wing wasn't omnipresent. And he understood enough to know that dealing with The Darkness, no matter who it involved, was difficult and never without casualty. They were lucky enough as it was, that those casualties hadn't included any of them.

From the looks of him, Father Wing had been harmed too. Likely, he'd healed himself. And he knew he'd saved True, one way or the other. Something he'd failed to do altogether. So, Victor tried to focus on being grateful to him instead, as he continued to speak.

"The issue regarding Quill leaves much to debate. A willing participant or else, the damage incurred from her actions were extensive. Magical ability among the Fae has declined. Time will heal our lands and recover our magic. Healing the wounded will require heavy burden."

And yet, Victor thought somberly, *you used your power to heal True. Even though there's probably countless Fae who...*

"Recovery magic," Noir smiled, "is something with which we can offer assistance."

"Yes." Father Wing agreed. "Recovery magic is rare among all worlds. As it will benefit you and the Fae both, I have come with request. For you, friends of Twister, ally of Fae, to accompany Noir." When had the two of them even had the time to talk in the first place? Hadn't they arrived in FlareWing practically seconds after that glaring light? Accompany him to where, exactly?

"How quaint." Fayth purred. "To see the day that the Father of Fae himself asks a favor from humans."

"You're risking FlareWing falling apart to ask us to go with him? Why us? Why not send Faeries?" Zane asked, confusion painting every corner of his face.

"You already have ties to both Noir and his birthplace, do you not?" Father Wing questioned, turning his gaze in Grace's direction.

"Moreover, there is no current risk of FlareWing's destruction. Least, not from my travels here."

"I don't understand. Was Twister ill-informed then? When he said that both you and The Princess could not leave FlareWing?" Phelia asked.

"He was not. 'Tis simply not of consequence at present. Nor in the future." Father Wing said. After a prolonged moment of silence, he continued, offering an explanation. "'Tis as the Fae suspected, in part. Our—each Princess and I respectively—inability to leave the bounds of FlareWing were a kind of curse. Morgan's identity and return, the truth of Quill's existence, and a kind of magic rarer than healing sorts freed us of it. Thus, I am able to cross without difficulty."

"There's a magic rarer than healing?" Phelia asked, obviously not willing to let the opportunity escape her.

"Several." Father Wing corrected. "An exceptionally powerful sort being purification. The very magic utilized by that girl there."

"True? You're saying she purified something...?" Victor asked, for some reason disturbed by the pounding in his chest. Father Wing's serious eyes resolutely meeting his worsened it.

"She cured Quill of The Darkness' traces, and several of the Cursed in an immediate radius. Just as well, the soil beneath them."

"Woah! True can do that?" Grace squealed, suddenly waking Blitz who was curled up beside her. "That's soooo cool!"

"But healing magic and purifying magic aren't the same. She helped them, but it wouldn't fix her wound...?" Victor thought aloud.

"That is correct." Father Wing confirmed. "For that feat alone, FlareWing owes an immeasurable amount of gratitude."

"The Faeries she healed will be able to return home. Man...she showed us up but isn't even awake to hear about it." Zane groaned.

"She will wake. The body takes time to heed the instructions of magic." Father Wing stood and the chair he'd created slowly became one with the floor again. "I must return."

Sparks flitted up the length of his robes, slowly giving way to flames. Victor unintentionally reached out and grabbed a handful of the silk. Questions burned a hole through his brain, begged for release. *At least these,* Victor thought sheepishly. *I have to ask.* Luckily, he hadn't been burned. *And I'll apologize for my disrespect afterwards.* Father Wing's flames did not die. Instead, whatever magical process that had been started simply came to a pause.

"Father Wing, do you know about these crystals? About World Knights?" Victor whispered, unable to keep his multitude of emotions from seeping their way into his voice.

"I know of them." He answered simply. "More of crystals than World Knights, given their connection with Light."

"So, you knew that we were..?" Victor mumbled.

"I did," Father Wing nodded, matching his hushed tone. "With confidence, once you returned to FlareWing."

"And True's wound...was it...?" Victor swallowed. He wasn't sure he could to ask. Even if he did know the answer, what would he do?

"Her wound was fatal, yes." Father Wing responded. He'd seemed all too aware of what he wanted to know. And to Victor's dismay, equally ready to inform him regardless of his apparent indecisiveness. "'Tis not so now. For what good does it do you to know it? Appears to be very little. You blame yourself as if 'Twas *you* that impaled her." Suddenly frightened by Father Wing's ease at reading him, Victor quickly dropped his arm to his side. He glanced around at the others, who all seemed to be watching them closely but, thankfully, unable to hear their conversation.

"Y-your request," Victor stuttered, "I will discuss it with the others."

...

That conversation had happened a little over three hours ago. And since then, they'd already traded stories. He'd heard an explanation of Eustis' sudden appearance in FlareWing and a somewhat suspicious 'we know each other from school.' What each of them experienced on the battleground, Noir claiming Grace as his daughter and Victor described the events with Opal, Twister and the Kumiho to the best of his ability.

Eventually, his impatience and other conflicting emotions sent him pacing around the room. They'd long ago agreed to follow Noir. If not for any other reason, Father Wing had saved True. Twister and the rest of the Fae trusted him with their lives, and they'd inadvertently done the same. Besides that, Victor couldn't exactly imagine Father Wing purposely putting them into danger.

Not able to handle another moment idle, Victor delicately handled True, slid on his coat, tossed Zane's back to him, and placed her onto his back. The others followed close behind as he made his way down the staircase.

"What time is it...?" Grace asked. "Aww beans. My phone's dead. Shouldn't we go home first?"

"You have a cellphone?" Phelia asked with a hint of surprise. Did she not have one before?

"Oh. This? I-It's new." Grace shrugged, quickly tucking it away into her pocket. "I don't know the number, so I'll be sure to give it to you later."

"Mine's dead too." Zane frowned as he tried the power button a few times. "That's weird. I definitely charged it up last night."

"I didn't expect a cellphone." Phelia said, zipping up her coat and patting Fayth's head. Victor wasn't sure he would get used to that. He wasn't sure he could ignore his colossal form with the smoking eyes.

"Yeah. Same here." Grace shrugged.

"Everyone is free to go afterwards." Noir spoke, taking the lead.

Victor fell behind motioning for them to continue walking as he adjusted True on his back. He took care to pull Father Wing's robe tighter around her. What a strange thing, to know so personally how he smelled.

Whether it be the way he looked or some other reason, Victor half expected the man to smell like wood burning. Instead, every inhale of breath sent a whiff of cinnamon sugar up his nose. Somehow even more noticeable in the freezing air. The thought of Snowville's winter air sent Victor's attention to Noir. Wasn't he cold? The man wasn't exactly dressed for the weather.

"Well, don't you look happy taking the lead? Just because Father Wing asked us to go with you doesn't mean we trust you!" Zane spat. "Whatever this evidence is better be convincing."

"Could it be you're simply a naturally suspicious person?" Noir directed at him with a laugh.

"If any consolation, Noir, he's not yet trusted me either." Fayth sighed, muffled by Phelia's thick coat.

"Trusting a talking cat—whatever you are—personally, would prove difficult for just about anyone. Besides, we are being led off by an adult no one has ever met. Going somewhere we've probably never been. Anyway, don't worry Grace. I won't let anything bad happen to you." Eustis boasted.

"Aren't you afraid? I was terrified my first time. It's still scary. I mean, we did just leave a war and somehow none of us are dead. If it were a movie we'd probably have died for plot." Grace frowned.

"No." Eustis said quickly, puffing out his chest. He wasn't telling the truth. Victor could see his knees knocking from there.

"Don't touch her so freely, as if you're so close." Phelia scowled. "At what point exactly did you start to offer Grace any *protection* rather than *torment*?" What was that about? He'd never seen Phelia be so unfriendly. He did seem particularly interested in Grace. Was it jealousy or something else?

Distracted, Victor nearly bumped into a passerby. He apologized and took another step forward as they silently passed. Suddenly struck with a vague sense of familiarity, Victor stopped and turned around. The individual in question was nowhere to be seen. *What...was that?* He thought, keenly aware of the sweat forming on his palms, and a painful clenching in his stomach. A wave of dizziness struck him.

"Victor...?"

The sound of True's drowsy voice evaporated his unease and carried the rest of his symptoms along with it. He wasn't sure he'd ever felt so relieved in his life. "You're awake."

"What's wrong...?" She asked in a tone softer than normal. He ignored the pounding in his chest.

"For a moment I thought—never mind. It's nothing." Victor cleared his throat. "Are you alright? Do you remember anything? Are you in pain anywhere?"

He felt her movement against his back as she shook her head. "We were in FlareWing. Nothing hurts. Just...tired, I think."

"Do you think you can hold on to me?" Victor asked, wrapping his arms through her legs with an apology and tucking his shaking hands into his pockets. This was different than when it happened in the building. This was...

"Mm-Hmm." Her breath on his neck sent shivers down his spine but Victor willed himself to ignore it. "Think so."

"Alright, then you hold still and try to rest. We'll talk when we get the chance. Right now, we are doing a favor for Father Wing."

"A favor for Father Wing...?"

"Yeah." Victor nodded, quickening his steps to catch up with the others.

"So where are we going anyway?" Zane directed at Noir who turned his attention to Grace. "Assuming it's not to our *doom*."

"We have to go to the outskirts of Grail—our home is also your birthplace, of course."

"Outskirts? My birthplace? Why?" Grace asked, eyes wide.

"Because Gracelyn," Noir smiled, looking especially pleased, "we're going to get your mother."

AN INTERVIEW WITH THE AUTHOR:

1. Why was book 2 delayed?

I knew this question would come about. Haha. Book 2 was delayed for several reasons. One of which being that I lost all the work on my SD card, including book covers and the book 2 manuscript (it was 1/3 of the way finished without edits at the time and unbeknownst to me, my automatic doc save was not on). So, I unfortunately had to start the book over. It took a while to get back to writing after that. Luckily, a small portion of the book had been written in my notebooks as well. Ironically, my initial draft of book one was written entirely by hand. It saved my skin, even if it left me with a lot of emotions to deal with.

Beyond this, I had a lot of personal things happening at home. Aside from dealing with my usual issues, I had half of my things ruined in an apartment flood, moved from my hometown (STL) to Oklahoma, got sick, and then had an episode where I thought I might quit writing and drawing altogether. Aside from that, I have a comic that demanded attention. **Chaotic**, *I know.*

So, thank you all for your patience! It means the world to me. In the meantime, I am working really hard to give my comic one last go. If it becomes too overwhelming, I will settle for drawing only for fun. And I am not quitting writing for the foreseeable future regardless. I don't even know who I'd be without it.

2. Why are there more characters in book 2 than there were in book 1?

To clue readers in on more background and move the story forward, I included the point of view of several other characters. This will be the case with any other story in The Crystal Key Book Series (CKBS). While the number of characters with their own chapter and the length of said chapters will differ from book to book, the central characters stay the same. If they *are* given their own POV then you, as the reader, can assume there is something crucial about the role they play in that particular book.

I tend to categorize characters based on their roles in regard to my "Central/Main" characters. In this case, Phelia, Grace, Zane, Eustis (who did not have chapters in book 1), Victor, and True. Whomever else has chapters in a following book I refer to as "Supporting-Main" characters. For example, Twister in book 2. This does *not* guarantee them their own chapters in the rest of the series.

Aside from this, I think it is pretty refreshing to add perspectives of other characters to the story in general. We get to see the inner workings of their minds. Like Twister's anxiety, for example. Or Opal's doubts and Morgan's past, which are connected to FlareWing. I hope that you all can enjoy this feature as the story continues on.

3. Why didn't Mrs. Burroughs tell True's aunts about the bullying or her skipping classes?

Mrs. Burroughs is a character that has had her own run-ins with bullies in the past, which we know from her brief conversation with True. She can be stern. However, she seems to be pretty empathetic to True's situation. It is no secret that many students say bad things about True as is. And Mrs. Burroughs failed to get a direct confession. We can likely guess she's caught words being exchanged and glimpsed more questionable situations.

She could, as a teacher, report that the girls (bullies) were using hurtful language and running in the halls. But if you have dealt with bullies, you likely understand that this doesn't always do much good. And we already know that there are some students that will get away with nearly anything in Snowville. If Sydney—or rather, her parents—have enough influence in Snowville to bend rules in a hospital she might only get a slap on the wrist.

Rather than stirring up conflict, she offers True a much-needed break. Then again, she could simply have a soft spot for outcasts. I believe the truth of her actions lie within a gray area.

4. What gets you excited continuing the CKBS?

I kind of find myself more excited for each novel in the series. Not just in terms of a myriad of different characters making their appearances, but also the sheer amount of character development that is unfolding amid everyone's struggles. Which doesn't even account for the worlds they travel to, how their parents find their place(s) in the children's new lives, or how relentless The Darkness can be. In my opinion, it takes a lot on either side to wage this kind of war. Not only in terms of actual strength but being daring and creative. Unfortunately for those on the side of good, these words can, in a way, also describe The Darkness.

Moreover, I think that I am always really pleased to add elements of real life. Not just feelings, but hardships, life lessons...I like being able to get people thinking about themselves and others. There's something insanely powerful about self-reflection as you read a book or listen to a story. I am excited by the fact that this kind of reflection happens just as much within myself as I write their story as it does for those who read the series.

Best of all, I think I am most excited by just knowing that people are **enjoying** my writing. I'm so **incredibly** *lucky* that some readers reached out to me to tell me that they are falling in love with these characters.

Just the fact that they tell me things like "I see a little bit of myself in True," "I think Victor is my favorite character," "I like too many of them to pick a favorite," or even "I'm so glad to have found a good fiction book that doesn't have any cursing..."

I get emotional, really. Because no one has to do that, you know? Sometimes when someone hadn't been comfortable enough to leave a review, there are still a good number of them who ***want*** to tell me that they loved it. As a writer, you **need** that. You *need* to know that someone cares. That you are making an impact or accomplishing a single goal with even one person out there, at least. All of it rejuvenates me.

5. How will The Darkness affect the citizens of Snowville?

This is a neat question, although a bit hard to answer. Unfortunately, answering it would lead to spoilers. Sorry!

6. Why didn't the previous key holders/ World Knights go to the battle in FlareWing?

Considering they have quite a bit of experience facing The Darkness and putting themselves in harm's way, I'm certain that none of them would have left the children to go alone if there were any other choice. Since their Master of the Keys passed over 7 human years prior (this distinction must be made since the amount of time in one world to the next is not always constant or equal), it is a wonder that they were able to wait as long as they did. They cannot control how fast they lose their powers nor the time frame that the others receive their crystals.

There would have been no point in going to Phelia and the others before they discovered the crystals since they had yet to experience this magic—and probably would have had trouble convincing them. Just as them going into battle in FlareWing would have been pointless. At least in respect to them staying alive. Since they weren't apt at fighting before magical intervention, they wouldn't exactly be capable afterwards because of it. Not only would they have had no magic at their disposal in FlareWing, but they also needed to recuperate after the ritual.

Besides that, once their crystals run out of power, there's little else they can do. They lose the ability to travel the same way, to use magic to the same extent and more. They'd be lucky to find another catalyst. There are some exceptions to be made, of course, for those already born with magic and a select few instances otherwise, but none of their predecessors fit this criterion.

7. Why didn't they save Bailey in this book?

Considering how hectic things are in book 2, especially with the introduction of Fayth, meeting their predecessors, and being involved in a battle in FlareWing with no experience using magic for this purpose, there was little time for them to focus on Bailey. Of course, we know that several of our characters are struggling with the thought of her. Most notably, Zane. They must also figure out where to begin and follow through on some plan they don't currently have to free her from current circumstances. Not to worry. The resolution to this issue is covered in the next book!

8. During one of Eustsis' chapters, he mentions looking up the word Black in the dictionary but this isn't the definition I find on the internet. Can you explain?

Absolutely! I was planning on it! I have a habit of taking bits and pieces of my life, experiences, etc. and shaping characters around those, or in this case, using them to shape valuable, life-altering moments...

When Grace asks Eustis if he has ever looked the word black up in the dictionary, he also makes the decision to look up the word white. The difference in the description of these words surprises him given that these are the terms we associate with particular races. This was based off my own experience in middle school (in the early 2000s). These were literally words that were present in my Webster's dictionary. It also stated, sadly, that this was another term for "African American."

Please be advised that **nowadays, these definitions have been *updated* and *changed.*

Unfortunately, that doesn't make it any less jarring for my younger self.
I didn't have my own books back then, so I used to read the dictionary, copy the definitions in a little notepad, and practice using them for the day. Haha. So, it didn't take as long as I expected to make it to the B's. Telling all of you like this now it sounds a bit pitiful, but that was my life back then. I have come a long way since those days.

Similarly, these definitions have changed for the better and I am more than glad for it. In any case, using the previous definition better drives home the point that Grace is trying to make and it gave me a "safe" place to get that out of my head. Not to mention, of course, that it is also roughly this period with a modern spin in which the story is set. Of course, this is not meant to be quite as literal as it sounds. This *is* a work of fiction after all.

9. When did you first begin writing?

What a nice question. I started writing at a very young age. My late grandmother Linda said I had been doing so since I was about five years old. Not many years after that, I found myself using her computer (she had an old, bulky computer as they all were at the time) to write on Microsoft Word. Other times, I'd sit for hours trying to make landscapes on Microsoft Paint. She never had internet, as I recall, but I found plenty of ways to occupy myself. Haha. I've used notebooks and Word ever since.

I do ***not*** recommend letting children do this without learning how to type properly first, but that was no one's fault. I didn't begin learning to type until high school and no one I knew could do so at the time. Still, I look back on those days with a lot of love in my heart. Although my grandmother was convinced that I would be a nurse since I was "always taking care of people," as she put it, I think she would be happy that I continued writing. Not to mention, got over my nerves enough to put my stories out there in the world. I truly hope I am making her proud.

Personally, I think my earliest writings were some of the cringiest things on the planet; my sentences were short or stopped abruptly, I was missing a lot of plot (which is ironically one of my favorite parts now), and my stories fell short in plenty of other areas. Including length. As a child I don't think I realized it at all, because why would I? You know? But I started to get serious with my writing by the time 8th grade ended. The rest, as they say, is history.

10. What made you realize that your story was a series?

In my last Author's Interview, I recall mentioning that this series was not going to be my first published work, that it felt like this book forced me to work on it, and the answer to this question is similar. When I started on the first book, I had planned out characters and plot, but I was thinking small. So, I initially thought that at best, this would be two books or so.

I couldn't have been more wrong! Haha. I should have known from the beginning that this series would be my longest. I have other stories that I am positive would be a stand-alone book, and even a few that would be duologies, but before Crystal Key, I didn't have a single story that would span three or more novels. This series defied the neat little box I had. I only realized the exact number when I first finished the entirety of book one and planned out the characters and plot outline for the rest. I would tell you the number, but I'd rather keep it a surprise for now.

11. Why does Father Wing talk like that?

Ah. What a nice catch! I'll try to explain it as simply as I can. So, Fae age/time is unique. They live longer lifespans than humans and physically mature at a slower rate even though their days are shorter than a great number of other worlds. Father Wing is obviously a special case since he can age up or down at will. That said, we are all aware that Father Wing is remarkably...*aged*.

More specifically, we know that he's several thousand years old (in Fae years, which also spans a great deal of time in the Human World). We will get a bit more information on some of this in the next book! In any case, Fae lifespans average a couple hundred years or so. Which would mean that the period where Lady Reva, Sir Locus, and Lady Lily were all alive and living in FlareWing is even further in the past.

That said, it should come as no surprise that Father Wing is multi-lingual. It kind of comes with the territory. Haha. But his experience with some languages, like that of the Human World, has been limited compared to the rest of the Fae.

He speaks an old tongue in most of these, including early Faelin—the original language of Fae. During conversations with each other, they always speak Faelin, albeit a modern dialect. Since crossing the veil into the Human World has been a rite of passage and generally an often occurrence, Faeries naturally picked up English. As Father Wing is exposed to present day English language by Phelia and the others, he tries to slowly adjust his speech patterns and vocabulary to match them (this is not an uncommon occurrence with other ancient beings). I doubt he'll ever be rid of the "'Twas" or "'Tis" though, since he has yet to be successful dropping them in any other language either.

> ****Semi-related Bonus:** The words Fae and Faerie, which you have heard quite a bit, are totally synonymous with each other. They both can mean one or a group. Some Faeries have the habit of attaching "Fae" after a given name or characteristic of said person to differentiate between them when talking to someone who may be unfamiliar with their customs. We saw a great example of this when Twister mentioned "Aqua-Fae" in book one.
>
> It is surprisingly rare for Fae to have the same first name (especially any that look alike or inhabit the same world), and when

they do, it is because they are passing down a name to offspring. It is not as common as it used to be, but it served as a reminder of a certain person's legacy, and by extension the rest of those who carried the name.

12. What Is Book Three About?

Book Three is called Crystal Fragment and there's so much more happening from this point on in the series. Aside from new characters, there's saving Bailey at the top of the list, weighing options about outing themselves to their parents/guardians, and **unicorns**!! Who doesn't enjoy a good unicorn now and again?

Don't be afraid to go back and reread previous books in as we move forward in the CKBS. Trust me, the details matter. I love to bring parts back into play in another book. So much so that at this point it even happens subconsciously. Might just be one of the things I actually like about my brain. Anyway, I can't wait for everyone to get into it.

There's so much more than this, but I don't want to give spoilers! I had ***so*** much fun answering these! Thank you for those of you who got in contact. I look forward to your reviews (feel free to put your next interview questions on Google Play Books, Amazon, Goodreads etc.).

(∩^o^)⊃━☆ ☆

Please keep a look out for the next book in the series soon!!

Email:
ADMAUTHORCREATIONS@GMAIL.COM
Website:
WWW.ADMCREATIONS.COM

You'll find a QR code that leads you right to my website below.
THANK YOU SO MUCH!!

www.ingramcontent.com/pod-product-compliance
Lightning Source LLC
Chambersburg PA
CBHW070638310726
48982CB00001B/319
9781736996515